A CHRISTMAS ABDUCTION by Madeline Hunter

Caroline Dunham has a bone to pick with notorious rake Baron Thornhill—and a creative plan to insure his undivided attention. Yet once in close quarters, she finds herself beholden to their smoldering connection . . .

A PERFECT MATCH by Sabrina Jeffries

Whisked away from a wintry ball by the officer she knew only through letters, Cassandra Isles struggles with her feelings for the commanding Colonel Lord Heywood. For he, secretly a fortune hunter, must marry for money to save his estate—and Cass, secretly an heiress, will accept nothing less than love . . .

ONE WICKED WINTER NIGHT by Mary Jo Putney

Dressed as a veiled princess, Lady Diana Lawrence is shocked to discover that the mysterious corsair who tempts her away from the costume ball is the duke she once loved and lost. Now snowed in with Castleton at a remote lodge, will she surrender to the passion still burning hotly between them?

Books by Madeline Hunter

THE MOST DANGEROUS DUKE IN LONDON
A DEVIL OF A DUKE
NEVER DENY A DUKE

Books by Sabrina Jeffries

PROJECT DUCHESS
THE BACHELOR

Books by Mary Jo Putney

The Rogues Redeemed series
ONCE A SOLDIER
ONCE A REBEL
ONCE A SCOUNDREL
ONCE A SPY

Seduction on a Snowy Night

MADELINE HUNTER
SABRINA JEFFRIES
MARY JO PUTNEY

KENSINGTON BOOKS
www.kensingtonbooks.com

KENSINGTON BOOKS are published by

Kensington Publishing Corp.
119 West 40th Street
New York, NY 10018

All Kensington titles, imprints, and distributed lines are available at special quantity discounts for bulk purchases for sales promotion, premiums, fund-raising, educational, or institutional use.

Special book excerpts or customized printings can also be created to fit specific needs. For details, write or phone the office of the Kensington Sales Manager: Kensington Publishing Corp., 119 West 40th Street, New York, NY 10018. Attn. Sales Department. Phone: 1-800-221-2647.

Kensington and the K logo Reg. U.S. Pat. & TM Off.

ISBN-13: 978-1-4967-2029-0
ISBN-10: 1-4967-2029-6
Kensington Electronic Edition: October 2019

ISBN-13: 978-1-4967-2028-3
ISBN-10: 1-4967-2028-8
First Kensington Trade Paperback Printing: October 2019

10 9 8 7 6 5 4 3 2 1

Printed in the United States of America

Contents

A Christmas Abduction

Madeline Hunter

Chapter 1

Thirty miles out of Carlisle, the light snow turned to rain. For Adam Prescott, Baron Thornhill, it was a fitting end to a miserable journey.

By the time the mail coach careened around a bend and slowed to a stop in the coaching inn's yard, his greatcoat hung heavy with damp and a steady stream dribbled off his hat's brim onto his nose. He told himself that even this was better than being inside the coach with Mr. Liddle, an odiferous gentleman whose fashionable garments did not mask a lack of washing. Adam felt bad for the two elderly ladies inside who could not take refuge in the open air on the top of the coach. One had gazed longingly when he did so himself at the first stop outside London.

Now he climbed down to stretch his legs while the coach changed horses for the final stage of the journey. The other passengers hurried inside to warm themselves, but his mood did not beg for company. Rather he paced the yard for a few minutes, then took refuge under the inn's eaves and watched the steady drizzle make tiny ponds in the dirt.

Thirty miles more and he would be in another coach, this time with a warming pan and a fur rug, and with a velvet cushion under his ass instead of a board. No one would crowd him and no one would, heaven forbid, smell. After a pleasant afternoon ride through the country he would be welcomed into his cousin's family for a week of unfettered luxury at someone else's expense.

And after that, an entire lifetime of comfort, if Nigel's plan worked.

With such promise awaiting him at the end of this journey, he shouldn't even notice the rain or smells or his sore hindquarters. He should be dreaming about the fortune within reach.

So why wasn't he?

He had begun turning his mind to the unfortunate answer to that question when a disturbance distracted him. Scuffles sounded around the corner of the inn. Ruffians were engaged in a fight from the sounds of it. He took a step in the opposite direction; then a voice caught him up short. "Unhand me, you rogue," a woman hissed lowly before she gave a short cry.

Any inclination to retreat disappeared. He pivoted and marched to the end of the inn, then turned the corner.

And found himself facing the end of a pistol barrel. He stared, frozen in place.

A young blond-haired man in a broad, rustic hat held the gun high, peering down its sights. Not that Adam noticed him much, due to that pistol being so close to his face. Nor did he much note the bit of skirt disappearing around the back of the inn, although he absorbed he had been the victim of a ruse.

"You come this way now," the man said, stepping back. "I said this way. Are you looking to see me fire?"

Adam took a slow step forward. "I was merely distracted by how very large and black this end of a pistol appears when it is all but up your nose."

"A bit more now." The man took another two steps back.

Adam paced forward, wondering if this man really would shoot, or was any good at shooting if he would. He could perhaps simply turn and run back around the building. The close proximity of that barrel to his head made him reject that rash idea. Even the worst aim would probably find its mark this close.

"I must tell you that I have very little money on me."

The blue eyes taking aim wandered a moment, up and down. "A gentleman like you should have enough."

"You would think so, eh? Although, really, what is enough? I ask you, is there ever enough? Well, never mind. My situation is such that right now, on this day, I do not have enough, whatever your enough is. You chose the wrong gentleman. Now, Mr. Liddle, when he comes out, is probably flush with blunt. He is the sort who always would be. I should warn you that he smells, so you won't want to insist he follow you this closely. However—"

Just then the horn sounded, as the coachman warned the passengers of an imminent departure.

Adam cocked his head to see past the pistol. "I need to go now. What do you say we just forget about this? You go rob someone else, and I'll be on my way."

"You aren't going anywhere."

Sounds of feet and voices moving to the coach came around the corner. Adam patted his coat, opened a button, and reached toward his purse. In doing so his hand hit the folded vellum tucked into his frock coat. "I'll give you what I have, but I truly must return to the coach immediately."

"I don't want your money."

"What then? My hat? It is a very good one. It is yours." He removed it and handed it forward.

"I've no use for it."

Probably not. And yet, perhaps once he did. This criminal's speech lacked the tone and syntax one would expect of a pistol-toting thief. At some point this man had been educated.

"If not my hat and not my purse, then what do you want?"

No reply came to that. They stood there not speaking while the feet around the corner stopped landing and the voices muted. They were still facing each other in silence when horse hooves began pounding the ground and the mail coach rolled away.

With Adam's baggage still tied to its back.

Other wheels rolled, this time from behind the inn. A wagon came into view, with a woman wearing a large, deep-rimmed bonnet and heavy garnet mantle holding the reins. She let the ribbons drop, then climbed into the back.

"Get in." The man waved the pistol in her direction.

"Are you abducting me?"

"I said get in."

Adam walked around the wagon and climbed in. The horse stood at attention. A very nice horse, from the looks of it. Deep chestnut, with good lines. Maybe six years old. Too fine to be dragging this wagon.

Some bales of hay lined the edges of the open space of the wagon. The woman gestured for him to sit. Then she accepted the pistol from the man, who climbed to the seat and took up the reins. She sat on another bale, facing Adam, the pistol firmly grasped in her hands.

"I know how to use it," she said.

Her voice riveted his attention. Low, throaty, melodious, it was the voice of a mature woman but one still young. He peered at her through the drips of rain separating them, those coming off his hat and her bonnet, and all the ones between. He saw a face as young as her voice sounded. Not a girl, but not middle years yet either. Maybe twenty-five or thereabouts, he guessed.

Her hair, barely visible deep inside that bonnet, looked to be dark, and her eyes showed an arresting deep brown color. Her complexion appeared fresh and lovely and exceedingly pale in a good way, not pallid and unhealthy.

The wagon began moving. He waited to see if anyone was out in the yard. If so, he intended to call out for help and risk that pistol going off. She said she knew how to use it, but very few women really did.

Unfortunately, the rain had sent everyone to shelter, even the grooms and inn's servants. He could see some faces at the inn's windows as they rolled onto the road.

"I don't know what this is about," he said, loudly enough for the man to hear, too. "However, you are committing a serious crime."

No reply came.

"If you hope to ransom me, it won't work. No one will pay. You will be stuck with my keep to no purpose."

Nothing.

"I will be missed. My baggage is still on that coach. When it arrives and my property is there, but I am not, a search will be made."

That at least caused the woman to blink. "They will decide you slipped and fell into the stream behind the inn and the rain washed your body down a ways."

"You have a spirited imagination. They will think nothing of the sort. "

"It is the most logical explanation, and being lazy they will accept it. It will be weeks before they suspect something else might have happened. In the meantime, with Christmas soon, no one is going to spend much time looking for a stranger."

"I am not entirely a stranger to these parts."

"We know who you are."

Did they now? "If you know who I am, then you know that you risk your necks with this rash act. I am a peer and the Home Office will involve itself if I disappear. My cousin is also a peer and he will not look well on you once you are discovered."

"We know the power of the Marquess of Haverdale. His view of us will not matter by the time he learns of this."

So he would learn of it, eventually. At least they didn't intend to shoot him and bury him in a shallow grave. He had not led the best of lives, but even he did not deserve that.

The rain fell harder. Adam gave up trying to fight the results. He relaxed on the bales and let the weather do its worst. He speculated on what addlebrained scheme these two had concocted.

"Keep it dry, Caro," the young man said over his shoulder.

The woman draped her mantle over the pistol and tucked her bared hands underneath. Adam noticed how red and raw they appeared.

"You are both going to hang. How sad. It is a disgusting way to die. Have you ever seen it? I'll beg them to transport you instead, but my cousin will insist you hang and a marquess normally gets what he wants."

The man looked over his shoulder. "You talk too much. Watch him closely. He is trying to distract you."

"I won't be distracted. You watch the road. The rain is making parts barely passable."

"I am not trying to distract her. I am just passing the time with conversation."

"Too much conversation," the man muttered. "It's a wonder all those ladies can abide your company."

So they did know something about him. "Where I come from, conversation is expected. I am considered clever, even witty."

"Part of your charm, is it?" The woman offered a thin smile with the question. "In these parts we save talking for when we have something to say."

If there was to be no conversation it could be a long journey. They turned off the main road and jostled down a much poorer one. The wagon bounced in and out of ruts.

He began to stretch out on the bales, thinking a nap might spare him an hour of wet silence. As he did he noticed that the pistol no longer aimed right at him but rather down at the wagon's floor. The fingers holding it became visible as the mantle edged back.

"Have you no gloves?" he asked.

"Not ones fit for this."

Not leather then. Knit. He sat upright and peeled off his gloves. Recently purchased but not yet paid for, the gloves with their softness had seduced him as surely as a woman's velvet skin. He handed them toward her.

The woman hesitated. She glanced at the man's back, then took the gloves.

She had to set the pistol on her lap in order to pull a glove on her left hand. It was too big, but the fine lambskin meant it would not be too clumsy. Still, it interfered with getting the other glove on her right hand.

Adam leaned forward, took her hand in his, and pulled the glove on for her. He took the opportunity to push the leather lower on the fingers so it fit fairly well.

She watched with wide eyes. She glanced once at her companion in crime, then down again at what he did.

He picked up the pistol and put it back in her hand. She flushed at the evidence that he had indeed distracted her, but not with words. She grasped the pistol with determination while he set about making the glove fit better on her left hand

He looked into her dark eyes, so in contrast with her white skin. She was a handsome woman, with a face that would still be attractive thirty years hence, when the fashionable beauties of the day had long lost their prettiness. When she smiled a severity in her expression disappeared. He peered into the bonnet's shadow while something nudged at his memory.

"What is your name?" he asked.

"Caroline."

"I should not address you with such familiarity."

"I would prefer that you do not address me at all."

"Then I will pose a question while I have your attention. Have we met before?"

She just looked at him.

The wagon suddenly halted. "What are you doing? Caro, are you mad? We know he is a rogue and a rake."

She and Adam both turned their heads to where their driver glared over his shoulder. Not at their faces. His scowling gaze rested lower, where Adam still held a gloved hand in his own.

Caroline snatched her hand away. Adam lounged back on the bales and smiled apologetically. The wagon moved again.

And just then, at that moment, the rain turned to snow.

Chapter 2

Caroline regretted that she had scolded her sister, Amelia. Of course the girl's head had been turned by this man. Between his face and his charm, a female would have to be dead not to be affected.

That Caroline herself had briefly succumbed could be blamed on nature, not her character. She had assumed he would not dare anything with Jason two feet away. She had also assumed he would not find her worth daring anything for. She had not counted on his being a man who flirted and dared for amusement, and perhaps to advantage himself in a situation like this.

That was the problem with carefully laid plans. They were based on assumptions. They had to be. She had convinced herself that this would unfold how she needed it to unfold, and already it wasn't working out quite that way.

She really wished she had taken the reins instead of Jason. She could manage this wagon just as well. Then she would not have to look at their captive. Now she could not avoid it, since she needed to keep this pistol on him so he did not jump off the wagon and run into the trees.

He had lain down now, to take a nap it appeared, with his hat cocked over his brow, but she could still see his beauty. His limpid dark blue eyes alone would command attention. They had humor in them, even when facing a pistol. The result was the finest of lines on the side of the eye she could now see. As for the rest of his face, his regular features and rather perfect skin made him appear to have stepped out of a painting, where the artist embellished reality by removing the flaws nature inevitably provided.

And yet, now, with his eyes closed and his face in repose, he appeared harder than he did when he looked at her and smiled. Older. Perhaps even a little weary.

Of course he was a rake. With that face, what else could be expected? Women probably lined up when he entered a drawing room, all but begging to be seduced.

She realized that she had just found a way to excuse him for his horrible behavior. All because of one brief touch through a glove. A fine caretaker of the family honor she was! She would have to be on her guard not to let his manner and appearance lead her to question her plan on how to save Amelia.

He opened his eyes, looked to the sky, then sat up. He removed his hat and shook off the snow, then brushed his coat. "Will we go much farther?"

She shook her head.

"That weapon must be getting heavy. You can put it down for a while. I am not going to jump on you and take it."

So he said.

"I give my word as a gentleman. See? I'll keep my hands above my head like this." He waved his hands, then clasped them behind his head. "And I'll cross my legs so any move will take time." He entwined his legs together, hooking one boot around the other.

He appeared so comical that she smiled despite herself. "I never thanked you for the use of the gloves. It was not in your interest to do that. If my hands went numb, I could hardly shoot you."

"I would not know they were numb enough, however. With my luck today, I would take my chance only to have you shoot me dead in the road."

"Shooting you dead would not be necessary. An arm or leg would suffice to stop you."

He peered at the pistol, then into her eyes. "Are you that good an aim, that I might not end up dead by mistake?"

"I am that good."

"I will take your word on that." He looked at Jason's back, then leaned in to speak quietly. "Would you tell me why he decided to abduct me? Was it just my misfortune to take shelter under those eaves, or is there a reason?"

Goodness, his face was close now. Luminous in the overcast day. Her tongue felt thick, but she managed to speak. "He did not decide to abduct you. I did."

"Truly? You seem fairly sensible, but the situation is ludicrous. What if I had not stayed outside in the rain under those eaves?"

"If you had not taken shelter, we would have found another way to do it. I had several plans." One had been for her to enter the inn, flirt with him, and beckon him outside for a quick—whatever it was people did when beckoned outside. She had even worn a dress that might aid in that, hidden now beneath her pelisse and cape.

Just as well he had gone to the eaves. She had not had much faith in that particular alternative. She had little experience in flirting, and no evidence it worked when she tried it.

"Why? As I said, no one will ransom me."

"The marquess would not want to be known as a man who left his cousin to his fate because he was too miserly to pay a ransom."

There would be no ransom, but for now let him think there would be.

Jason turned the wagon off the road and onto the lane leading to Crestview Park. Lord Thornhill turned to watch the new direction. "Are we going to that house up there?"

"We are."

"What is it called?"

She didn't answer. The less he knew, the better.

"I'll dry these out for you, and give the hat a good brushing." The elderly, thickly built red-haired man took the garments as if he were a valet. Only he wasn't a valet, but half of a pair of servants who greeted Adam when he entered the low-slung stone house, with its two levels of windows and rambling wings. He did not miss that lacking a coat meant escape would become a good deal less comfortable.

The man left, limping to favor his right leg.

The young man did not follow Adam in. Caroline did, still holding the pistol.

"Warm yourself here," said the other half of the pair, a short, round old woman in a big white cap and apron. She led him into a good-sized sitting room and toward a roaring hearth fire. Solid, serviceable wood furniture filled the room, with two high-backed upholstered red chairs facing the fireplace. A simple writing table in one corner held a thick ledger on its surface. The space appeared comfortable but far from luxurious, as if nothing new had been put in it for many years.

At least they did not stint on the fuel. He positioned himself to both dry and warm. The old woman smiled with satisfaction at his expression of bliss in experiencing the heat.

"May I know your name so I can thank you properly for building up the fire in preparation?"

The woman's face fell. She glanced at Caroline, then said, "Smith. Mrs. Smith. He that took your hat is Mr. Smith."

"I want you to know that Mr. and Mrs. Smith are not in any way involved in your being here," Caroline said while she shrugged off her cape onto one of the red chairs. "They work here, and will help see to your comfort, but they are not part of it."

"That is good to know, but of little use to them. When my cousin starts looking for necks to stretch, he won't care about nuances."

Mrs. Smith blanched. She grabbed the cape and hurried out.

"That was unnecessary," Caroline said.

"She should know the truth. She is here. I am here. I am a prisoner. She is helping imprison me. That is all that will matter."

She untied her bonnet and cast it aside. Fire burned in her dark eyes. "You can frighten her as best you can and she will not be disloyal. She and her husband have been here for years, and are as good— Are you even listening to me?"

"Of course." Hardly. With that bonnet gone and the fire blazing, he could see her distinctly. His initial perceptions of dark eyes and hair and white skin, of a handsome face that would be more notable as she aged, held. Only now those eyes were ablaze with annoyance and her head balanced just so on exact posture and her presence warmed him as much as the flames at his back.

"Then hear me when I say do not try that again. If you do, you will not eat well here."

"Surely you are not threatening me with bread and water?"

"It won't kill you. In fact, it might do you some good to lose a few pounds."

"Excuse me?"

"I am not saying you are fat, only that you have thickened a bit, as men do when they leave youth behind and start softening in their middle years."

"*Excuse me?*" Thickened? Middle years? Softening? He was barely twenty-seven and at most weighed five pounds more than when in university.

"Have I insulted you? Oh, dear. I do apologize." She did not sound the least sorry. "Now you must come with me so I can show you your chamber."

She strode to the entry and called for Mr. Smith. The man showed up a few minutes later. With a flourishing gesture, Caroline bid Adam follow Mr. Smith up the stairs. She followed behind them both.

They trudged up to the attic level, and to a chamber intended for a servant. Rough plank boards and a slanted timbered ceiling contrasted with simple whitewashed walls. A low window broke through the eaves to provide a view of the countryside.

"You will stay here," Caroline said. "Your meals will be brought to you, as will water for washing and such. There is plenty of fuel for the fireplace, as you can see." On her mention of it, Mr. Smith knelt to build the fire.

Adam paced around the Spartan chamber. "What am I to do here? My baggage is gone. I have no clothing, no razor, no books, no anything."

She turned to leave with Mr. Smith. "I will find garments and books and send them up to you. As for how you spend your time, perhaps some reflection and penance would be good for the soul."

The door closed. A sound scraped against it. He waited a few minutes, then tried the door. It budged only an inch, enough for him to see that it had been barred. They had planned this for some time if they had constructed that to ensure he could not leave.

He paced around the small chamber one more time. It had so

little space that moving in it could not satisfy his restlessness. It was a damned prison. He tried the bed. At least the mattress had enough stuffing to cushion the ropes. He rose and checked a little wardrobe. It held nothing except a chamber pot.

He disliked confinement of any kind. This would become annoying quickly. Already anger nibbled the edges of his mood.

He bent to look out the small window. No tree outside, not that he could fit out the window easily. Down below, a stone wall held back the land from the foundations of the house and some steps that he guessed went down to the kitchen. If he jumped or tried to lower himself, he would drop four levels, not three. Only an idiot would risk it.

He threw himself on the bed. Penance, she suggested. She must know more than a little about him. As for her recommendation, plenty of penance awaited him if he found a way out of this cell.

That alone was enough to dampen his rising indignation. In a manner of speaking, this ridiculous adventure was a reprieve, brief though he expected it to be. A small delay before he chained himself to a woman whom he in no way suited or even much liked. Even her fortune might not repay him for the life she would subject him to.

He went to gaze out the window again. The rolling land said they were still in Cumberland and probably still north of the lakes. If he could escape he could probably find his way to Nigel without undue time or trouble. He still had some coin on him, and his boots and greatcoat should keep him warm enough. He rather regretted not retrieving his gloves now.

Then again, he could stay here and reflect, as Caroline put it. Review his carefree life before he sold himself in marriage to that woman. He could reminisce about lovers recent and old, about big wins at the tables, and ignore the bigger losses, about indulgences enjoyed despite no money to pay for them. He could revel in the infamy that meant even rustics like the ones in this house knew who he was.

Why not? And if he could get out of this chamber, the hills out there and the sitting room below offered some unexpected diversion. He did not know why he was here, and that alone was an interesting little mystery to be solved.

The scraping said the bar had risen. He sat up as the door opened. Caroline marched in and dropped a bundle on the bed. "Not the finery you are used to, but they should do and no one in society is going to see you. There's a Bible there, and one of Mrs. Smith's novels, and a journal or two. I added some newspapers. They are old, but not of London, so you may find them new enough. There are also a few necessities."

He eyed the stack of garments and publications. "How long do you intend to imprison me?"

"Five days if the weather holds. Longer if the snow keeps falling."

"Until Christmas then."

"Yes."

He would regret missing the festivities. A marquess knew how to do up Christmas smartly. Watching his nieces' and nephews' excitement always provoked a pleasant nostalgia.

"You do not have to bar the door and lock me in. If I did not try to escape off the wagon, I won't now. Nor would it do me much good if I managed it. I don't even know where I am." He smiled his best smile, to cajole her to reconsider.

For an instant her mouth softened at the edges and her eyes shone with new lights. Then her brow puckered while she glanced around the chamber to avert her gaze. She turned on her heel and left.

He returned to the window. Fifteen minutes later two figures came up the steps down below. At the same time, the wagon rolled into view.

The two figures, all bundled and hatted against the cold, climbed on the wagon; then it aimed toward the rolling landscape.

Mr. Smith had been driving the horse at the wagon. It had appeared that the young man who abducted Adam had climbed into the wagon. A third man worked here, too, however.

The three of them flowed away, getting smaller. As they did, spots appeared on the crest of the nearest hill. The spots trickled down the land toward the wagon.

Adam squinted at the overcast, snow-filtered distance. Horses. A small herd of them galloped toward the wagon and its hay. The two men began throwing bales onto the ground while the wagon slowly moved.

He gazed at those horses. He recalled how Caroline had looked familiar in some way. In a blink it lined up in his memory.

He knew where he was and probably why he was here. The goal might be a ransom, but the motivation was revenge.

Heavens, but she was being a fool. That was what happened when a woman lived in isolation with no society and precious few friends. She turned into a puddle when a beautiful man gave her any attention, even if he did so for dishonorable purposes. She was supposed to be filling her father's empty place, being clever and strong like him—not melting like hot beeswax when a bit of warmth entered Lord Thornhill's eyes.

Caroline threw another bale, harder than she needed, so hard that it made her arms ache from the effort. Old Tom noticed.

"Don't you go hurting yourself," he scolded. He set down the reins and began to rise.

"You stay there. You are the one who has been hurt."

"Should have stayed with Mum," Jason muttered beside her while he bent to lift a bale himself. "Don't know why you think you have to do a man's work when there are two real men here."

Had Jason not been a childhood friend and if she did not depend on him so much, she might have put him in his place for that. Not that his place would be clear to either of them anymore. The very notion of places rang hollow these days.

"You are not my brother, Jason, so don't you dare scold me. I will do as I see fit and there was no reason for you and your father to stay out in this cold twice as long while you fed them yourself."

"If the snow keeps on, we'll be doing this every day for a long time," Tom said. "Maybe Jason should stay here until it passes and not go off."

"While Jason is gone, I will come out with you," Caroline replied. "He has to go. We can't keep Lord Thornhill in that chamber forever."

"Why not?" Jason muttered. "It's more than he deserves. I'd have let him sleep in the barn."

"There was no way to bar him into the barn."

"You know what I mean. No need to give him all that fuel and a fresh mattress. A bit of discomfort is due him. And you told Mum to cook enough for him, which seems too generous to me."

"He will hardly be amenable to our demands if he has been freezing, eating gruel, and sleeping on a bad mattress."

"She has a point, Son," Tom said over his shoulder while he maneuvered the wagon among the herd that now crowded them.

Jason bent to his bales. "Don't be asking me to serve him, that's all. I'll not be bringing him meals, or playing his valet. You cater to his needs, Caro, since you think it so wise." His expression told Caroline that he still didn't like giving Lord Thornhill comforts of any kind.

She could expect nothing less, she supposed. Jason had taken the situation with Amelia very hard. He refused to blame her, which meant he had to blame someone else. Himself in part, for not watching over her better. Lord Thornhill mostly, since a gentleman should behave better. Jason and Caroline had been equals in play when they were children, but Amelia had been the younger sister who needed protection.

"That's enough," Tom said, turning to eye how many bales were left. All around them the horses ate, necks bent low. "If it turns colder the pond over the hill will ice and we'll have to break it up. Looks to be a bad few days ahead. They should be fine until tomorrow, though."

Caro's gaze surveyed the little herd through the steady fall of snow. She lingered on an especially fine mare of dappled pale gray whose coloring blended with the landscape. Three years old now, Guinevere had the blood of champions in her and should be bred with a stallion of equal lineage come spring. The one that qualified in these parts was not available, however. At least not at a fee they could afford.

One more reason to dislike Thornhill and his family. She would think about every item on that list the next time he turned that disarming smile on her.

Chapter 3

With dusk came cold. Adam built up the fire. Enough snow had fallen that the hills shone white, reflecting the failing light.

Nigel would know he was missing by now. Would he raise the hue and cry or tell himself something very ordinary had happened? *He probably nipped up to a chamber at the inn with some woman, and missed the coach's leaving while taking his pleasure.* If so, it would be another day at least before the full significance of that un-accompanied baggage was acknowledged. Even then he would never guess who had his cousin.

If he was right about where he was, he could walk to his cousin's estate cross county in a day if the sun showed long enough to give him some sense of direction.

He had made the best of a bad situation all day, but as the light dimmed outside he began to consider that had been a mistake. These might not be typical criminals, but that did not mean he should make this crime easier on them.

He allowed his anger to rise. His food would come soon. One of the men would bring it up, he guessed. When that door opened and that fellow appeared, his hands occupied with the tray he carried, one push should send him sprawling. Once at a disadvantage, he would be easy to overcome.

Then, door open, stairs clear, a quick bolt to freedom. He'd take a horse from the stable and find a village, at least.

He hoped his coat hung on a peg along the way, of course.

Footsteps on boards outside the chamber. The scraping of that bar. He pressed the far wall and faced the door, ready to lunge when it opened.

Only a man did not kick it back. Caroline maneuvered the door while she balanced a tray. She noticed him at the wall.

"What are you doing? Preparing to overpower me?" She set the tray down on the bed. "Let us have it then. Do your worst."

"My, you are suspicious."

"You are coiled like a cat preparing to pounce."

He shrugged off his intentions. "I was not expecting *you*."

"Obviously not. This is your dinner. It is quite good. I will tell the cook you send your appreciation of her efforts."

He went over and peered beneath the white cloths. "That would be Mrs. Smith. Only that is not her real name. You might have chosen something more original."

"Her name is indeed Mrs. Smith. She told you as much, after all. It is astonishing you think it isn't, despite the evidence of your own ears."

"She could not remember it at first when you introduced us. With a name a common as Smith, I think it would be hard to forget if it really were hers."

"*Any* name would be hard to forget if it were hers, don't you think? Nor did she forget it. You flustered her, that is all."

"So you say. I say you gave her a different name in an attempt to obscure her identity. If I am to play a role in this farce you are writing, at least show some creativity. Mrs. Pepperstone, for example. That would be a fine name."

"You are all nonsense and that is a stupid name."

"And you are half-mad, at the least."

She laughed. "I am not the least mad. Do I look it?"

"*You abducted a lord.* Only someone addlepated or half-mad would do such a thing. As for Mrs. Smith, a new name will not help her, as I said. She is in the thick of it, same as you, and will swing beside you." He angled his head so as to gaze below her chin. "Such a lovely neck. How sad it will be."

"You do not frighten me."

"I should." He moved the tray to the little table near the window and set the one chair beside it. "Do you provide conversation as well as food, or am I to live in silence, too?"

"There is nothing to talk about." Yet she didn't leave.

"I think there is a good deal to discuss. Why I am here, what you hope to gain, what will satisfy you so I can depart—" He set aside the white cloth. "Whether this is not about me at all, but other members of my family. Many things."

He glanced over at the last. She reacted, much as she tried not to.

He proceeded to cut the fowl on the plate. It smelled delicious, but then he was very hungry.

Caroline stood there for a ten count before speaking again. "Why would you think this was about your family?"

He casually chewed some pheasant. Mrs. Smith was an excellent cook. "I saw the horses the men were feeding."

"If that held significance to you, maybe you are the one half-mad. Many farms in these parts have horses."

"I expect some have several and I know some have whole herds. Twenty, thirty, even more. I thought it odd that you have seven out there in addition to the ones in the stable. More than you would need for farming and a household." He looked over at her. "Too few for a farm that breeds them."

Those dark eyes just watched him.

"Unless—" He helped himself to another forkful of food while he let the word dangle.

"Unless what?"

"Unless there was once a much bigger herd, but it had decreased unexpectedly. Been sold off, for example." Another bite. "Or suffered from a disease."

He heard a sharp intake of breath, like a backward hiss. He looked over. Flames in those eyes now. Her expression had tightened.

"I knew I had seen you before," he said. "You are Miss Dunham. This is Crestview Park."

"You no doubt think you are very clever."

He set down his fork and turned to her. "He had no choice. My cousin only sought to protect the other farms in the county."

"We could have separated the ones that were sick. We could have kept them all here and let it run its course and kept others away. He did have a choice. He *wanted* to have them all killed."

"That is too harsh."

"He had bought Galahad and didn't want another born who might challenge his champion. So he tried to obliterate the bloodline."

He wished he could insist Nigel would never do such a thing, but Adam had seen his cousin's ruthlessness on more occasions than he wanted to remember. He had also seen Nigel's delight in possessing Galahad. In winning with him and in being the envy of the Jockey Club. Crestview Park had a long history of producing some of the best racing horses in England, slowly and carefully, until the strangling disease had taken hold here.

"That was over two years ago. You are rebuilding quickly." His memory reexamined those dots on the hillside and their sizes. "Ah. He didn't get them all, did he?"

"It doesn't matter. Even if we rebuild, it will never be the same. It broke my father. Not only financially, but in his spirit. He died last year."

"I didn't know that."

"No one in your circles would know, since we don't sell prize thoroughbreds anymore."

"And now I am to pay for that? Is that why I am here?" If this woman schemed for revenge, this might be more dangerous than he had thought.

She gestured to his table. "Finish that up. I'll be back soon to take the tray away. Please have your boots off by then, so I can take them, too."

"My boots?"

"You know who I am. You know where you are. You probably think you can walk to your cousin's home. But I don't think you will go out in that weather without boots."

"He knows." Caroline informed the others of Lord Thornhill's clever musings while they all ate dinner. The meal was always late, due to the work the farm needed and the few hands to do it. "He saw the herd, and guessed the rest. Not why he is here. He has that wrong. But where he is and the family who live here."

"Thank goodness," Mrs. Hoover said. "I'll not have to pretend I have a different name at least."

"You will. And you, Jason—he's barely seen you, so I don't want him seeing you again until it can't be helped."

"I won't even be here."

"You still think to go?" Mrs. Hoover said. "Surely not, Caro. There's snow and—"

"No more than four inches, Mum," Jason said. "Of course I'm still going. I'll ride a horse and bring another with me."

"A horse! Amelia can't come back on a horse!"

"Don't see why not," Old Tom said. "Safer than a wagon. Less bumpy, too. She won't be jostled nearly as much. You take the chestnut mare, Jason. She's mild enough and sure-footed."

Mrs. Hoover turned to Caro, exasperated. "We must wait for the weather to clear."

"Then we contend with either frozen or muddy roads and lanes," Caro said. "Listen to your husband. He is right. The horse will be safer even then."

"I don't like it." Mrs. Hoover passed around the platter of pheasant again.

"We could just leave her where she is," Caroline said. "Do you think we should? Let her stay with Aunt Elizabeth and let Lord Thornhill go?"

Mrs. Hoover shook her head. "You be careful with her, Jason. You hear me?"

"I'll be careful. If she is not doing well on the horse, I'll hire a carriage. I've some coin."

"Where'd you get coin?" Old Tom asked.

"Never you mind."

Caroline finished her meal. She drank the rest of her beer, then rose to help Mrs. Hoover clear the table.

"You are not to worry," Caroline said when they were alone in the kitchen. "Once Amelia is here, it will all settle into place. He's a gentleman, and there are rules about these things for them. Remember how my father would do things he'd rather not because he was a gentleman, too, and honor counted for more than money?"

"It's not money we expect from him," Mrs. Hoover said. "He may be a gentleman by birth, even a lord, but there's been talk about him in the county since he was a boy and would visit his uncle. Wild doings. He never outgrew that either." She shook her head and turned to the washbasin. "I hope you are right about all of this."

"I am doing what my father would have done. Papa isn't here, so it is left to me. I can't call him out like a man would, but I can make sure he faces her, and accepts his duty. He will not be able to avoid her this way. He will not be able to put us off, or refuse to receive us, the way he could in London or at his cousin's house."

Mrs. Hoover sighed heavily while she lifted a hot kettle from the hearth.

"Say, let me do the washing today," Caroline said, grabbing an apron off a peg.

"You need to go up and get that tray."

"I'll wash and you can get it. You will be getting the better half of the bargain. Bring some water, so we don't have to take that later. And remove his boots from his chamber."

Mrs. Hoover gave her a long look, lifted a pail of water, then headed to the stairs.

"Just take the tray and boots and leave," Caroline said. "Don't let him draw you into a conversation. He will try to frighten you then. So don't dawdle."

"Is that what he tried with you? Made you linger so he could frighten you?"

"Something like that. It didn't work, though." The last was a lie. She did not want to talk about what had frightened her and how she had lingered in part to watch how the dusky light made him even more handsome, casting his face in silvery tones so he looked like a beautiful statue come to life.

She plunged her hands into the water. She could be such an idiot at times.

Chapter 4

Adam woke with the dawn. He lay abed a good while, not wanting to relinquish the warmth of the coverlet. For a prison, the room had a comfortable bed.

He finally cast the bedclothes aside, strode to the fireplace, and threw on some fuel. A blaze roared. He stayed there while it heated the small chamber and the pail of water, then went to the window and bent to look out. Already he could tell that the sun would shine today, but the frost on the window's glass indicated it would not help much with the temperature.

He judged there to be a good four or five inches of snow. While he took its measure on the wall below, two figures emerged from the house and climbed the stairs, bundled and anonymous. One hat looked like the same as that worn by his male abductor, though. That figure walked away, and the other returned to the kitchen door.

He washed, shaved, and dressed, deciding that his own garments would survive one more day. Those brought to him yesterday looked to almost fit, although whoever owned them was a bit stouter. Not as stout as the old man, but more so than the young abductor. While he would not buy the coats himself, they were of better quality than he expected, and the shirt had been ironed. The cravats had no starch and would only be acceptable in the most informal of ties. Still, no one intended to make him look like a rustic.

Having finished his day's preparation, he pulled the chair to the door, sat, and examined the latch and closure. Last night, lacking anything to occupy him, he had begun testing the bar on the other side. First he tried the razor but quickly nicked himself. One of the journals brought by Miss Dunham had firm binding and was thin enough to press through the small crack, however. It seemed to him that when he slid it up, the bar had initially resisted but then risen a bit. Could he raise it enough that it slid down one of the makeshift ledges holding it on either side of the door?

He slid that journal through again. The bar rose an inch or so, but then he felt its weight defeating the journal. He pulled the journal out, lest it crumble and get caught, bearing evidence of his activities.

Being right at the door, he heard footsteps coming up the stairs. He swung the chair away to the table, and threw himself in it just as the bar scraped. The door opened.

Miss Dunham carried in breakfast. That brought a smile to his spirit. Her absence last night when the tray was taken had disappointed him.

She appeared fresh and bright and all business. The morning light cast her pale complexion in the coolest whites. Her dark eyes and hair made a stark, memorable contrast. She wore the simplest of dresses in brown, plain wool with a white knit shawl tied around her shoulders.

She strode across the chamber and all but dropped the tray on the little table. "We all have things we must do today. It may be hours before anyone comes for this."

He lifted the cloth and noted the food but also the implements. "If you leave the door open, I would be glad to bring it down myself."

She folded her arms over her chest and lowered her gaze on him. "You must think I am very stupid."

"Not at all. I give my word as a gentleman not to escape."

"Would that I could trust that word."

"I have given you no reason to think you cannot."

"Your whole life is a reason I cannot. Do you think we are so isolated we don't hear about the gossip and scandals in London and elsewhere? Such stories are prized in these parts since they give people something to talk about."

"What ones have you heard about me?"

She shrugged. "I can't remember the recent ones."

He laughed. "Are my scandals so bad that it embarrasses you to mention them?"

She flushed. "Fine. There was that problem you had with that actress you threw over who was going to kill herself, for one thing."

"She had no intention of killing herself. She dined for a month over the threat of it, though."

"And that family who accused you of breach of contract, and intended to see you in court."

"Which they never did, because I had contracted nothing and promised even less. When I said sue or be damned, they went away."

She set her hands on her hips and lowered her lids. "In the last eight months your name has been linked to three women at least, who were described as your mistresses."

She had him there. "Such friendships are apart from matters of honor, such as keeping my word."

"Three. In eight months," she reiterated bluntly. "Such inconstancy does not speak well of your character."

"I can explain that, but the truth does not speak well of me either. Each of those ladies chose to end an alliance when she learned that I made a decision last year to no longer go into debt over women. With the lack of jewels and other expensive gifts I became far less charming to their eyes."

She seemed to find that interesting. "So you have begun to reform?"

He laughed. "I wouldn't go as far as saying *that*. I merely decided not to owe every good tradesman in London."

"Which has led to changes in your habits."

"Of a sort." He still owed money everywhere. Just not as much.

She smiled. "An important sort. You cannot be a rake anymore. Becoming domesticated probably has much more appeal now."

That smile softened her whole expression. She might have just heard long-awaited happy news. "*Domesticated?* I don't think—"

She was already at the door. "You should eat that before it gets cold."

No one came for the tray. Morning stretched into midday. He read one of the journals, then looked out his window, left to his thoughts. He pictured the Christmas preparations taking place at Nigel's estate.

It would be the first time in years that Adam had not attended those festivities. His father had brought the family each time, often braving worse weather than what lay outside this day. It had been a way to have good food and entertainment that their own family could not afford. If Adam's father had resented the better fortune of his older brother, he never showed it. Why should he? Having been named a baron in his own right, Adam's father had done better than most younger sons.

Of course, this year others would be at Nigel's besides family. Mr. Millerson had been invited along with his daughter Margaret. Pretty Margaret. Lovely, vivacious, spoiled, cruel Margaret. She thought herself fit for a duke no doubt. Adam wondered what her father had promised her to get her to agree to marry a lowly baron.

Jewels, probably. A house in London for certain. A percentage of the profits of that canal partnership that her marriage would allow him to buy into with Nigel? It was a massive endeavor, with canals large and small all over northern Cumberland. If she received any of that, it probably would go into trust so her wastrel of a husband did not gamble away the money and stocks.

He had overheard her berating her maid once. Margaret's words had sliced the poor woman's emotions to shreds. The maid's transgression had been minor but Margaret's criticism ruthless and hard. He had walked away, imagining that tongue turned on him every day, and not for his pleasure.

Movement outside. The wagon came into view, beginning its little journey toward that hill. Only one figure on it today. Adam wondered where the other two were.

The wagon stopped not far from the house. The driver stood

and turned around. Adam realized that someone had come out of the house down below him. Mrs. Smith's white cap identified her. The two exchanged some words; then Mrs. Smith walked away, down the length of the house.

Right before the driver turned to sit again, he turned his face upward, as if looking at the window from which Adam watched. White skin and dark eyes showed beneath the brim of the man's hat before the figure turned. The driver was none other than Miss Dunham.

Why would she be going to feed the horses alone? The men must be occupied elsewhere. If Mrs. Smith had not returned to the kitchen door, the house might well be empty now.

He grabbed the fork off his tray and headed for the door.

Ten minutes later he walked through an empty house, in search of his boots.

The horses galloped down the hill. Caroline stopped the wagon. Guinevere, never one to hold back her speed, led them.

Caroline climbed into the back of the wagon. She ached from yesterday's chores and adventures, but this had to be done. She paused a moment and pictured her father and how being a gentleman never stopped him from lending a hand in the work if it was needed. Holding his memory in her heart, she lifted a bale and rolled it off the side of the wagon.

She had managed two more of them when she sensed movement on the snow behind her a split second before a horse and rider charged across the white expanse. Not Jason, who had left early this morning. Not Mr. Hoover, whose bad leg had acted up last night and who rested now in the cottage he shared with his family. She knew how they both rode and would have recognized either one from a distance, even if she already knew neither would be riding here today.

This rider sat on the horse differently. Expertly. She knew who he was.

How had he escaped that barred room? Her heart sank at the evidence that he had managed it despite her precautions. Now he would ride to his cousin's house, swear down information with a magistrate, and send them all to gaol. She wondered if she really would hang after all. The notion left a sick foreboding in the pit of her stomach.

The horse and rider aimed for the trees to the right of the pasture. In a few moments they would be gone.

Suddenly they pivoted, turned, thundered right toward her, and stopped twenty feet away.

Lord Thornhill looked down on the wagon and her. One of his disarming smiles broke. "If you are the one man today, you must have been the third man yesterday."

She turned to address one of the bales. "How did you get out of that chamber?" Her mind spoke the same question but added a few curses.

He dismounted and walked his horse to the wagon. He proceeded to tie it to the back. "If I tell you, you'll make sure I can't do it again."

She noticed he had found his boots, coat, and gloves. What a disaster. Not only had he escaped; he'd also proven she was hopelessly inept at executing her own scheme.

"Where is the old man?" he asked.

"He hurt his leg a week ago and it has taken a turn. He needs to rest it more." Old Tom had returned to helping her before he should have and now paid the price.

"And the young man?"

"On errands."

Adam climbed onto the wagon. "Then it is just you and me. You take the reins and I'll take care of the hay."

She swung one leg over the bench seat's back, then paused. "Why didn't you keep riding? You could be well away by now."

He lifted a bale and threw it out toward some horses. "I recalled that I gave you my word not to escape." He turned that smile on her again. "I also wanted to see you in pantaloons."

Her position, straddling the back of the seat, showed how she looked in pantaloons rather too well, she realized. She tugged down on her coat and finished her move so those pantaloons would be hidden while she sat. She heard a soft laugh behind her.

She moved the wagon and bales flew. "That should be enough," he finally said.

To her surprise, he climbed over and sat beside her.

"How do you know what is enough?" she asked. "Have you taken care of horses?"

"As a youth I dawdled around my uncle's stables. Now I make good use of my cousin's when I visit. I find horses excellent society, often better than that in the drawing room."

How well he put it. Few people understood what he meant, but Caroline did. She had always had an affinity with her father's horses and had learned to care for them while still a girl. That had made that horrible day when the men came with muskets all the worse and a tragedy from which she had never really recovered.

She turned the wagon and headed back to the house and out-buildings. Lord Thornhill did not try to take the reins from her, even though he wore his good gloves now. He must have found them where she set them near the door. There really wasn't enough room for both her and Adam on the seat, which meant that they were pressed against each other. She inhaled the scent of the soap she had left him and noticed how those gloves fit his hands perfectly, as if molded to their strength with liquid leather.

"I suggest we come to an understanding about my stay with you, Miss Dunham."

"I am listening."

"You now know I can get out. I propose you simply allow that and spare me the effort of getting that bar up again."

"Next time perhaps you will not stop before you disappear into the trees."

"I will swear my parole. In olden times, when a knight was taken in battle, and was being held for ransom, he was not imprisoned. If he swore his parole he had free movement in the house and grounds. He might join the household knights on hunts, and would eat at the high table."

"We don't have a high table. Just one. If you dine at it, you will dine with servants."

"Which will save you and those servants the trouble of feeding me up in an attic."

Considering most of the servants, if she could even call her faithful retainers that, could not serve anyone at the moment, his proposal had some appeal.

"What happened if one of those knights broke his parole?"

"That rarely happened, because if it did the world would know that man had no honor." To her shock, leather-encased fingers lightly touched her chin and turned her head until she was looking into the bluest eyes she had ever seen. "Whatever you have heard, whatever you think, I am a gentleman, Miss Dunham. When I say I will not escape, on my honor I will not."

Her chin and neck quivered under that touch. She could not pull her gaze away from his. Confusion swirled in her mind, and shock at her lack of will. She remained enthralled for a half minute until he released her, but that release was all his doing, not a matter of her demanding it.

She snapped the reins to get the horse moving faster. She needed to get back so she would not feel his warmth against her side like this, and so she would stop stealing glances at that face of his. As stupid as she felt for again succumbing, she grasped the one good thing to come out of the encounter. She counted on his being a gentleman once he saw Amelia. If he kept insisting like this that he was one, it would be impossible for him to refuse to do the right thing when that happened.

Miss Dunham brought the wagon right to the stable yard. She hopped out with a quickness a dress would have denied her. The coat she wore had little length. It looked to be a boy's coat, chosen so it would not drown her in fabric. That meant, however, that he had a fine view of how those pantaloons encased her legs and hips while she unhitched the horse.

He climbed down himself and looked around. On the other side of the house, past the gardens, a cottage showed smoke rising from a chimney. Beyond that some livestock dotted two pens. He followed her into the stable, leading the horse he had ridden.

A large structure, it had stalls for at least a dozen horses, all empty. The horse she now guided into one of those stalls was not the chestnut from yesterday. That horse was nowhere to be seen.

Caroline came out to retrieve grooming supplies.

"I will do it. Some activity will be welcomed," he said.

She stood speechless while he pried the pail's handle from her grip and removed the brush from her other hand. He took them into the stall. After a hesitation, she followed him.

"It is a fine little herd you have there," he said while he worked. "That bay mare is magnificent."

"You know horses well."

"I would not be a Prescott if I did not."

"I suppose not."

He glanced over at her. She still wore the man's hat that had obscured her identity when he watched the wagon yesterday. Low-crowned and wide-brimmed, it cast her lovely face in a shadow, but her eyes' brightness would not be defeated.

"Even so, I perhaps know them better than most Prescotts," he added. "I advise my cousin sometimes. He would not request that if he did not think my judgment better than his. Which he does, grudgingly."

"Did you advise him to buy Galahad?"

"He did not need me to tell him that Galahad was one of the finest horses England had seen in years. Your father's eye was unsurpassed, and his patience finally rewarded."

Adam thought it a compliment. She did not react that way. "Galahad has been put out to stud now," she said. "The fee is enormous."

"That is the true value of a champion."

"The bay you admired is from the same stock, only a different line."

"Is she fast?"

"Not only fast, she has the heart for it."

He might be discussing a horse with a member of the Jockey Club, so easily did they fall into the language of racing. She was saying that the mare had speed, and also the desire to win and the strength to stay the race.

"I asked your cousin to allow us to breed them. The mare and Galahad. I asked him to give us a lower fee, or to allow us to pay over several years."

He kept the brush moving over the horse's flank, but he knew what Nigel had said to that. Nigel was not famous for his generosity. "He refused?"

She nodded. "After what had happened, I thought—"

She thought there should be enough guilt, or enough justice, that the owner of Galahad would help the farm that bred him rebuild.

Adam picked up the pail and moved to the next stall and the other horse. He was pleased to see her follow him. "That was wrong of him," he said while he used the brush. "However, if you think taking me will force him to change his mind, if you expect to see Galahad coming home over that hill, you will be disappointed."

She turned up her face to him. A playful belligerence showed in her eyes and half smile. "I do not think I will be disappointed at all in abducting you."

He regarded her while his mind tried to tease the meaning of her confident statement. It didn't get far in such considerations because she appeared so lovely there in the most unconventional way. Those pantaloons, probably a youth's, fit her nicely and showed the shape of her legs and most of her hips. The coat nipped at her waist and bulged higher where it buttoned over her breasts. His mind started removing that coat, then more.

Her expression changed. Softened. She knew what he was thinking, and she was not running away.

He needed no more encouragement than that. He followed his inclinations, as was the habit of his life. He strode across the space separating them, pulled her into his arms, and kissed her.

Chapter 5

She should have turned and run, but she didn't. Watching him groom the horses had mesmerized her. His hand, unsheathed from that glove, looked so masculine while it held the brush. The horse appeared in a state of bliss, as if she knew that a seductive man handled her.

Even so, when he came toward Caroline with his face firm and his eyes determined, she should have known what would happen and run. He was not for her, and she was not for him, and the last thing anyone needed was for this kiss to happen.

Yet it did happen, and she found herself breathless with astonishment, shock, and delight. The last was very bad of her. She had no business enjoying that kiss. None at all, for many reasons. Yet she did, too much, and his embrace warmed her inside and outside. His arms became a shelter, an enclave of comfort, intimacy, and excitement.

The kiss itself seared her heart. It had been years. Forever. Her memories of girlhood kisses had grown so dusty from age that she might have been untouched. Nor had the mouth that claimed her then belonged to a man. Certainly not this man who had kissed too often and knew too well how to do it.

She had no defenses. She had not even realized she needed any.

So she permitted it too long, submerged in happy confusion that blocked any intrusion from her conscience.

He pulled her closer yet. His hand fussed at a button on her coat. Her better sense reasserted itself and saw what she was doing. Indignation met a wall of sadness, but she still pushed away from him and staggered back.

Nothing about him apologized. Not words from that mouth or regret in those eyes. If anything, he appeared as if he would follow her steps and embrace her again.

She backed up more, lest he try. "You should not have done that. You know it, too."

"I am not well schooled in self-denial, especially when it comes to an intriguing, lovely woman like you."

"I am not a woman to be a plaything to a rake. I am insulted you thought I might be."

"It was an honest expression of honest desire, Caroline, not a search for a plaything."

"I think it was a calculated strategy to have me drop my guard in other ways, and to petition for release. A man like you does not have any need of a woman like me." She strode away. "Do not do it again," she said furiously over her shoulder. "Good heavens, wasn't one Dunham daughter enough for you?"

Since Caroline did not march him back to his attic chamber at the point of a gun, Adam decided that meant she had agreed to the terms of his parole. Since her departure indicated she would not want company he chose to remain outside and investigate the property further.

He walked closer to the cottage beyond the garden. Smoke still rose in a ribbon from the chimney. He thought he saw Mrs. Smith's face peer out a window at him. Perhaps the old couple lived here, rather than in the big house. It was the kind of privilege only afforded the married servants, and valued ones at that.

He retraced his steps and walked around the stable. Beyond there lay a large paddock surrounded by sturdy fences. Fifty horses would fit in it easily, perhaps as many as seventy.

This was where it must have happened. He pictured the space teeming with horses, all pacing and noisy because they sensed the danger. Within a half hour all of them were dead, shot by men at close range from behind the fence. Unable to defend themselves, they had stampeded around the paddock in a frenzy.

He had been invited to participate in that carnage. As if anyone would want to shoot thoroughbreds like that, as sport. Too many had volunteered. Nigel had joined in. To add to the injury, they had left the remains for the Dunham family to deal with.

He had assumed Caroline had abducted him as part of a plan of revenge for that day. From her parting words in the stable, however, it seemed he may have been wrong.

Wasn't one Dunham daughter enough for you? He propped his boot on the bottom rung of the paddock's fence and looked into the enclosure while he considered the accusation embedded in her words. She believed that he had kissed her sister and perhaps done more than kiss.

Hell, he didn't even remember she had a sister.

All the same he searched his memory for another Dunham. Calling up every female met at parties and assemblies would take too long, so he took the opposite approach and tried to remember all the women he had at least kissed in the last few years.

That alone meant reviewing a good number of faces. Try as he might, he could not picture anyone with the last name of Dunham.

It was possible she had used a different name. It was also possible that his memory failed him due to his being foxed when the meeting occurred. He often claimed that never happened, but the problem with drinking to the point of obliterated memories was that one did not remember what had and had not happened, including one's state of inebriation.

The wind had risen by the time he concluded he could not prove he had never kissed another Dunham sister. He made his way back to the house and entered through the kitchen door, where he shook the snow off his boots and hung his greatcoat on a peg next to the coat Caroline had donned earlier.

He wandered into the kitchen. Mrs. Smith could not be found there, but something delicious smelling cooked in the hearth in a cauldron. He found the stairs and went above.

His departure had been hasty. Now he took his time. Besides the large sitting room he visited a small library and a chamber that served as a study or office. A morning room, long and narrow, stretched across the back of the house. A dining room could hold a decent party.

It was an old house, and handsome in its way. More dark wood panels than was fashionable now. Dark papers on the walls, too, and a few floors paved in tiles instead of boards. He judged it to be a couple hundred years old at least.

He settled into a stuffed chair in the library with a book on thoroughbred breeding. Since it was a topic of interest, he soon became engrossed. So it was that Miss Dunham arrived without his awareness. He only realized her presence when the scent of the household soap reached him.

She had changed into a blue dress with little adornment.

"I hope you did not give up the pantaloons on my account. There's no reason to stand on ceremony with a prisoner."

"It had nothing to do with you."

"For whom then? From what I can tell no one else is here."

"Of course others are here. Mrs. Smith—"

"Some food awaits in the kitchen, but she does not. I think she went home to her little cottage."

She made no retort to that. So they were alone here, as he thought.

"You should be up in your chamber," she said imperiously.

Perhaps so, if they were alone. "This suits me better."

"It is not for you to say."

"I swore my parole and will do so again if you want. If you insist I live all day in that attic, go get your pistol, because I will not return there until I retire otherwise."

"If you give me cause, I will indeed get that pistol. Just so you know."

"It was one kiss, Caroline. I am not going to assault you. However, since you mention it, I apologize for succumbing to the impulse, small though the transgression was."

"Small? It was very, very wrong of you, and you know it."

"I know it was wrong. Not very wrong, let alone very, very wrong."

"I can't believe you insist on that. Considering my sister—"

"Ah yes, your sister. What is her name again?"

She gasped. "You are a terrible, incorrigible, conceited man." She gathered her composure. "I am having dinner at six o'clock. If you go down to the kitchen at seven o'clock, there will be a meal waiting for you. After you eat your meal, return to your chamber. You can carry your own water up. Since you have sworn your parole and have free movement, you don't need us to serve you."

Then she was gone in a flourish of plain blue wool and flaring brown eyes.

Caroline left the study at six o'clock and walked down to the kitchen. This was where the household had taken their meals ever since her father died. Carrying food up to the dining room seemed an unnecessary elaboration. It had been much easier to join the Hoovers below.

Redolent now with the smell of rabbit stew, the kitchen had been improved so Mrs. Hoover could cook for everyone at Crestview Park. The table had space for fifteen to sit and during the good times the servants from the stable and fields would come in, washed and tired, to take their meals there. Some remained long after they could be paid, mostly for the cooking. Eventually, however, financial realities had seen even those loyal retainers find other situations.

Only the Hoovers remained now. *We know nothing else*, Mr. Hoover had said. *You can't do it all yourself anyway.* So it was that she found a new family in them and they all shared the same impoverishment.

At least Amelia had been spared the worst of the deprivations. Caroline always found a way to buy her new dresses and for six months kept a carriage just so Amelia could visit friends without arriving on the wagon. Their aunt and uncle had joined in the plan and invited Amelia to spend time with them in Carlisle while they doted on her and gave her something of the life she was supposed to have had.

Caroline peered into the cauldron that Mrs. Hoover had left simmering. She ladled out some stew, then carried her plate to the table. She found the bread baked in early morning and set it on a board near her plate. She drew some beer from the keg, then sat to eat.

She wondered if Mrs. Hoover had made any plans for their

Christmas meals. Last Christmas had been barely celebrated, coming so close after her father's passing. They should do more this time, lest they all lose the ability to experience the joy of the season. Of course, the amount of joy would depend on how things were settled with Lord Thornhill and Amelia. At the moment Caroline's optimism on that had dimmed considerably.

No sooner than she had eaten two bites than she heard boot steps on the stairs. She swallowed a curse, gritting her teeth instead. She had clearly told him seven o'clock and it was only ten minutes past six.

Lord Thornhill strolled into the kitchen as if it were a drawing room, looking ravishingly handsome and ever so charming. If she were a man she would find a way to wipe that vague amusement off his beautiful face.

"I said seven o'clock."

"I was hungry and the smell of that food permeates the house." He went over and stuck his nose to it. "Rabbit?"

She sighed. "The plates are in the cupboard over there. You may serve yourself."

She ignored him as best she could while plates clanked and the ladle dipped. He carried over his plate and placed it right next to hers. While he went looking for a fork, she shoved his plate across the table.

Boot steps behind her paused, then reoriented themselves around the table's head. He settled down at his new place.

"Where did you get the ale?"

"It is beer." She pointed over her shoulder toward the keg, then thought better of it and stood. "Don't move. I will get you some." She did just that, making sure it was not too much. She did not need this man imbibing more than a half pint at most. Left to help himself, who knew how much he would enjoy?

She brought the crockery cup back and set it before him. If he thought it too little he said not a word.

She returned to her meal and he turned to his. She had wanted to dine separately so she would not have to talk to him. She would be damned before she entertained him now.

"This is very good," he said. "You have a prize in Mrs. Smith."

"Enjoy it while you can. Her husband normally hunts for us and this is the result of his last venture out. He will not be able to do so for at least a week because he hurt his leg. He rose to help me too soon, but I have told him he must rest it for an entire week now."

"What about the other one? The young man who helped abduct me? Can't he hunt for you?"

She poked at her food, wishing she had refused to talk. "Not right now. He has other duties to which he attends." It sounded like she was hiding something, even to her.

He was good enough not to press the matter. Silence fell again.

"About your sister," he said after another five minutes. "When am I supposed to have kissed her?"

Caroline set her fork down hard enough that its contact with her plate rang through the kitchen. "*You don't remember?*"

"I don't think I do, no." He cleared his throat. "I have been combing through my memories, and there is no Dunham female among them." He had the decency to at least look chagrined. "Perhaps her face— Does she look like you?"

"Enough that you thought you had seen me before. Her hair is not as dark and her eyes are blue, however."

"I thought I had seen you before because I *had* seen you before. I am sure of it. At the country fetes my uncle and now my cousin holds. I come up for those, and you were at some of them."

"I am well aware that you attend the fetes." Bold of him to even mention it. "I was not at the last one, to my regret. You did not remember me from a country fete years ago."

"I did. One year you wore a yellow dress and were present when your father handed Galahad over to my cousin."

She *had* worn yellow that day. "My sister wore blue and was right next to me. Did you lure her with a memory of her garments, too? Tell her how memorable she had been? Flatter her into trusting you?"

"I am sure I did not. I regret to say, as I have already said, that I have no memory of her at all. Even her name."

"Amelia, you rogue. Her name is *Amelia*."

He pondered that name as if she had spoken Egyptian. "Amelia. Amelia. Amelia Dunham. No, nothing." He flashed that damnable smile of his. "There has been a mistake. I never kissed her."

She came close to throwing her dinner plate against the wall. Instead she held on to the thread of temper that remained and stood, took her plate and cup to the sink, and left them there.

"Please put your things in the sink before leaving," she said as she passed him.

"You are angry because I don't remember. Consider this, however. Perhaps it did not happen."

His words caught her at the bottom of the stairs. That last thread snapped. She turned to him. "Oh, it happened. Nor was it only a kiss, you scoundrel. You seduced her. You got her with child, and you *don't even remember her name.*"

She turned on her heel and marched up the stairs, taking small satisfaction at the look of shock on his face.

Chapter 6

A child. Was it possible?

Adam finished his meal not even noticing that he fed himself. All of his thoughts were on Caroline's accusation.

He needed more information. He put his plate and cup in the sink and went in search of her.

He saw that the study door was closed and assumed she had taken refuge there. He tried the door and found it locked. "Caroline, open the door, please."

No sound or movement came from within.

"Miss Dunham, we need to talk. You cannot say such a thing and walk away."

Still no sound. *Damnation.*

"See here, if I can break out of a locked chamber, I can break into one. Either that or I will wait until you retire and see you then and there."

"You wouldn't dare." Her voice sounded muffled but close, as if she was right on the other side of the door.

"Wait and see what I would dare. I'll not let you sleep until you have answered my questions. I deserve that much."

"You deserve nothing except a horsewhipping. Would that my

father were alive. He would have called you out. I wish I could in his stead."

"Open the door, damn it."

Nothing. He eyed the door, to see how firmly its hinges were embedded.

"Wait for me in the library," she said. "We will talk there."

He strode off to the library and cooled his heels half an hour before she arrived.

"Forgive me," she said. "There was a letter I had to finish."

The hell there was. She had made him wait just to prove she did not have to come at all.

She sat on a small wooden chair. "You have questions?" she asked primly.

"Many. First of them is what makes you believe I seduced your sister?"

"She told me you did."

"She named me?"

"When the evidence of her condition could not be ignored, she admitted to me that she had succumbed to the blandishments of the infamous rake Lord Thornhill. It was devastating news, but I don't blame her. I blame you. She was an innocent and inexperienced. She would not know that your words were lies and your intentions nefarious."

"I am not nefarious and I don't seduce innocents."

"Are you so sure? After an afternoon of drinking and whatever, have you never broken what remains of the few rules you claim to follow? Can you swear this?"

It was a hell of a question and raised once more the problem of remembering that which cannot be remembered. "It has never happened before. Not those rules."

"Oh, not *those rules*. Because you are a gentleman, you mean. Even foxed, you would restrain yourself if *those rules* raised their flags. Of course you did not really know her, however. You could have convinced yourself she was not forbidden to you, especially if your judgment was impaired by drink."

She was proving adept at cornering him. "I am very sure that a mistake has been made. Perhaps another used my name."

"Do you expect me to believe something so unlikely? That another scoundrel and rake was there and chose to behave abominably using your name? I am not stupid, sir."

"Where was this seduction supposed to have taken place? When?"

"At last year's fete, as if you don't know."

"Since I was not involved, I don't know."

She stood abruptly. "Lord Thornhill, my sister is not a liar. Given a choice of her memory and yours, I think it safe to say hers is more reliable. She has been seduced but once, and would remember the man. You have seduced so often that I doubt you can name even half of your conquests."

"Other than youthful adventures at brothels, I can name every woman I have ever—um, all of my conquests, as you put it, although in truth in some cases I was the one conquered." This was an odd conversation to have with a woman, but he saw no way to avoid it if she kept accusing him like she did.

"Then it appears either you are the liar, or you had a new experience yourself late last summer. Now, the evening wears on and I have work to do tomorrow. You will have to excuse me." She swept out of the chamber, leaving him far from satisfied with what he had learned.

He followed her. "Do you have an image of her? A miniature, for example?"

"I do not. Nor would any image do her justice. She is very beautiful, however. I can see why you might have lost your head on seeing her." She began mounting the stairs. "It doesn't excuse you, of course, but it is understandable."

The stairway's shadows swallowed her. He watched until her footsteps disappeared when a door closed.

She had tried and convicted him on her sister's testimony. Nor could he swear he was innocent.

There was some humor in being taken to task for a pleasure he did not even remember. It was the kind of devilish development that made the angels laugh. Less humorous was the way this revelation interfered with knowing Caroline better. He stood by the stairs, imagining her in her chamber. Nefarious scoundrel that he was, he pictured her removing her dress and stays and finally her hose and chemise, revealing layer by layer the body he had surmised while she wore pantaloons. The mental pictures made him hard and half-convinced him to go up to her, stupid mistake though that would clearly be.

He went in search of some spirits in the library, thinking that if he was guilty of sinning with Amelia, he had definitely seduced the wrong Dunham sister.

"He claims to have no memory of it." Caroline spoke after eating her breakfast. Mrs. Hoover stood at the hearth, starting the day's dinner. With no one hunting, the good woman had sacrificed one of her chickens to the pot today.

"Not something she would get wrong, it seems to me," Mrs. Hoover said. "A woman remembers the first time at least."

Caroline thought anyone would remember every time. Except a rake. She imagined all those names and faces melted quickly from such a man's memory. Lord Thornhill's claims to the contrary did not hold much credence with her.

"He may refuse," Mrs. Hoover said. "What then?"

"I don't know. I'm counting on him accepting responsibility when facing the truth of it here, where he can't avoid Amelia. Perhaps I am too optimistic." If she was, this entire plan could end very badly for all of them. The logic of it had seemed unassailable when she started down the path, but the pitfalls seemed to grow with each day. Increasingly Lord Thornhill's assessment that she was half-mad to even attempt this looked correct.

"He seems a gentleman, for all his sins. A bit weak when it comes to women, is all. That is common enough. I'd not give up hope yet."

"How is Tom faring?" Caroline wanted to change the topic. She had spent much of the night debating the character of Lord Thornhill and Amelia's fate.

"He's saying he can get up and help you, but I told him he must rest that leg another few days."

"I said a week. I want him well healed, not having it give him trouble for years on end. Don't let him leave the cottage. If matters become dire about the food, I will go hunt." She knew how. She just disliked it enough that she avoided it if she could.

"I'll keep close watch." She wiped her hands on her apron. "This will just cook away like yesterday's stew. It will be ready when you want dinner. Until then there is cheese and fresh bread and eggs if you want them. You can cook that much."

Caroline's lack of cooking skills had achieved infamy in the house. "Yes, I can do eggs."

"I'll leave the porridge warming here on the hearthstone for His Lordship. I cooked some salt pork, too, so he keeps up his strength."

"He will find it, I am sure. I need to go out soon. It became very cold last night and I have to check the pond to make sure it didn't ice over."

Mrs. Hoover swung her cape around her shoulders and picked up a pail with some of the porridge and pork. "You be careful. Don't forget how Tom says to do it if you need to break the ice."

"Don't tell him I might be doing it. He'll only worry."

With a nod, Mrs. Hoover left.

Amelia returned to her chamber and changed into the pantaloons and shirt. She pulled on half boots, wishing she had nice high ones like men wore. The snow would come over the tops of these, and her feet would be wet soon.

She grabbed her coat off the peg below and let herself outside. The feeding could wait for afternoon. Right now she just wanted to make sure the horses had water. They could eat snow, but it wasn't the same.

She saddled a horse and rode across the pasture to the hill. She crested it and looked down. The pond of several acres lay at the base on the other side, fed in part by drainage and also a small spring.

As soon as she saw the pond she knew she would be there for a while. Despite the overcast sky, light sparkled on its gray surface. She rode closer to confirm that it had indeed iced up.

She dismounted and took down the pick that she had tied to her saddle. She approached the edge, set her legs apart for balance, then swung the pick and brought it down on the ice with all her strength.

The metal bounced off the surface. The ice did not even show cracks.

She swung again. And again. She stopped to catch her breath. While she did Guinevere broke away from the distant herd and came galloping toward her.

She petted the horse's neck and gave her nose a kiss. "Don't worry, girl. If this doesn't work I'll bring water out to you in pails on the wagon when I bring you dinner." The time and work involved in doing that made her lift the pick again.

She eyed the pond. It seemed to her the ice was not as thick farther in. Five feet away from the edge water could be seen beneath the solid surface.

She set her boots gingerly on the ice in front of her. It held solidly. She took another step. Then another. Not daring to risk more, she raised the pick and stretched forward while she brought it down with a satisfying thump.

The tip penetrated the ice. Small cracks formed and water flowed through. She was congratulating herself when a larger crack appeared, aiming right for her.

She turned even as she felt the ice on which she stood moving. All of a sudden it sank in one large mass, and her body followed. Bitter cold shocked her and the water dragged her down and back. She found some sense within her panic and fought to get her head above water. Relief flooded her when her face broke above the surface. Desperate, she grabbed at a big ice slab behind her that had not given way.

Shivering and exhausted, she clung with all her strength, inching her body out a bit. Then she screamed, even though she knew no one would hear her.

Adam finished his breakfast and returned upstairs. Silence greeted him with each step. No one was here, not even Miss Dunham.

It was early to bring out the hay, but perhaps she had done so. He dressed warmly in the garments she had loaned him and went to saddle a horse. Perhaps she could manage on her own, but another pair of arms would make it easier and he had nothing else to do. Nor would he mind a good ride.

He paced toward the hill, looking for evidence of the wagon. It had not been in the stable yard, but perhaps it was stored elsewhere and she was not using it after all. He was about to aim for the trees, to explore the little woods there, when a horse appeared on the top of the hill. Pale and perfect, she was the bay Caroline had called Guinevere.

The horse rose up on her hind legs and pawed at the air. Then she turned and charged down the hill, right toward him, full speed. He had seen many horses race in his day, even the champion Galahad, but he did not think he had often seen a horse run this fast.

She swooped around him twice in a large circle, then charged back up the hill, as if daring him to race. Even though the horse he rode was no match, he took off after her.

She did not stop at the top of the hill but headed down the other side. He reined in his horse to see where Guinevere aimed. A large pond of several acres lay there, and beside it stood another horse.

Once more Guinevere rose up and pawed the air. He looked at that pond, searching for a young woman in pantaloons along its edge.

Then he saw her. Not on the edge. Inside the pond itself. Only her head showed, and the arms of that boy's coat. His heart rose to his throat and he kicked his horse.

He was out of the saddle in a shot, running to the pond's edge. "Caroline!"

"Oh, thank God," she cried.

His breath returned when he saw she was conscious, and alive.

"Don't move. Stay right where you are," he called.

"I fear the ice I am holding will give way if I do anything at all." Her voice broke while she spoke, and the rest came haltingly, while she cried. "It is very cold. Like being buried in a frozen world."

He stood on the pond's edge and examined the surface while blood hammered in his head. His mind raced for a plan to get her out.

"Don't tell Tom," she said, then swallowed a little sob. "He will be furious I fell in and blame himself."

"I'm going to blame *you*. What were you thinking?"

She muttered something about the ice not breaking and trying it a bit farther in. "I was never more than a step or two away from the ground."

"You should have come and gotten me before you even came here," he said, furious that their argument was probably why she had not. "You should have asked for my help."

"If you could wait until I am out of this cold water before scolding me I would appreciate it." She sniffed, then added in a miserable little voice, "I really would."

The defeat and worry in her voice broke his heart. He tried his weight on the ice. It gave just enough for him to not risk it. Perhaps if he lay down . . .

"Are you standing on the bottom?" he asked.

She shook her head. "Do not come out here or we may drown together."

It wasn't drowning he worried about. "How long—"

She swallowed another sob. "I don't know. It seems forever."

He shrugged off his greatcoat. He lay down on the ground with half his body over the ice. "I am going to throw the end of this to you. Grab hold when you can."

It took three throws before she grasped the bottom edge of the coat. "I have it now."

"Can you hold tightly? I am going to pull you in."

She cast off her wet knit gloves one by one, then twisted her hands into the coat's fabric. "My fingers are cold and stiff, but I think I can hold it."

"You must. Do not let go whatever happens. Even if the ice breaks in front of you, hold on."

He began pulling the coat toward him, bit by bit. Ice fractured around her and she moved closer through the shards. He could plainly see the fear in her eyes. He kept pulling more of the coat. Finally her body popped out of the water and slid toward him.

He grabbed her arms, then the rest of her, and pushed himself back onto the ground, dragging her with him. Finally he had her soaked body in his arms. The tears had their way then, and she shook while she cried from relief and cold.

He took a moment to catch his breath, then stood and picked her up. Guinevere looked on.

"She saved your life," he said. He threw his coat around Caroline, then lifted her into his arms. "Now we have to get you to a fire and warmth."

He set her in the saddle of his horse, then swung up behind her. He grabbed the reins of her horse and began the way back, embracing her shaking body close to his.

Chapter 7

He all but carried her up the stairs, and lifted her completely once they made the top. "Which door?" he asked.

She pointed to her chamber door. She would have answered with words, but her teeth would not allow it, they gritted so hard in order not to shake her whole head. She had never before been so glad to see this house, or so grateful to be alive. But she still felt as if she were submerged in that water.

Cold. So very cold. She wondered if she would ever be warm again.

He carried her in, kicked a chair near the fireplace, and set her down. He bent and built up the fire, adding fuel until the flames reached high.

He rose and turned to her. "Can you stand?"

She shook her head. She did not want to stand. She wanted to huddle here in his greatcoat because if she removed it she would freeze.

He set her on her feet. "You have to get out of those garments. They only hold the cold close to your body." He peeled away the greatcoat.

She tried to unbutton the coat she wore, but her fingers would not cooperate. He took her hands in his, holding them in a little shelter of warmth that felt wonderful. Then he went to work on the buttons himself.

"I should... You should not..." she murmured while she watched his fine hands do their work.

"Hush now. I do not importune women close to freezing to death. As it happens, my skill at undressing women is vast, and my innumerable views of feminine bodies have jaded me. You are safer with me than with a physician."

The cold seemed to be worse and deeper, down to her bones. She would do anything to stop it. She allowed him to strip away the coat, then the shirt and pantaloons. Somehow her nakedness became clothed in her nightdress. He wrapped her in a blanket he stripped off her bed.

Removing the wet clothes helped, but not enough. She still shook. And she was still so tired and cold. She started to weep.

He moved the chair closer to the fire. "Come here." He sat in it and reached for her. "It will help, I promise you." He set her on his lap and wrapped his arms around the bundle she had become. He made sure her feet were swaddled, then reached within the blanket for her hands. He took them both in his right one so his own warmth would seep into her.

She cried hard then, out of fear for her close call and misery at her chills, out of relief that he had saved her and gratitude for the care he gave her now. He said not a word but let her weep until her emotions found some peace.

Then she just gazed at the flames as very slowly, bit by bit, the worst of the cold began to pass.

She fell asleep in his arms, her head resting on his shoulder and her breath teasing his ear. He could put her in her bed now and pile quilts on her. With luck she would feel no ill effects of this misadventure.

He kept her on his lap, suffering the heat from the fire and blanket, making sure she did not need more warmth and that her rest was a normal sort. The hands he cupped no longer had icy cold skin. He untucked the blanket a bit so he could see if any damage had occurred.

Nice fingers. Tapered and long. Not especially delicate. They showed the results of months of labor on this farm. Knit gloves would never spare her that. When he returned to London he would buy leather ones and send them to her. If he had the fortune for it, he would send the men to do the work instead of her.

Once she recovered he would scold her severely for venturing onto that ice. It was not something to try when alone, no matter what she might have seen her father or Tom do in the past. When Adam had not seen her at first, only her horse, when he had realized what Guinevere was trying to tell him, his blood had run as cold as the pond's water. It would be wrong for such a remarkable woman to meet such an ignoble end.

She stirred, and he thought she would waken. Instead she nestled closer. He held her closely while the flames subsided and both took and gave warmth with the body in his arms.

Caroline opened her eyes to streaks of rose and orange outside her window. The sun must have come out and now set with a splendid display. She watched the colors peak and dim, then turned her mind to why she was in bed at dusk.

It came back to her in a rush. The pond. The ice giving way and the cold water claiming her. Lord Thornhill finding her and bringing her back.

Other memories joined the worst ones. Being held on the saddle. Being undressed. Being held in front of the fire.

She sat up and looked around. He must have put her in bed once she fell asleep. She needed to thank him for all of it. After the way she had spoken to him while he was here, she wondered if she would find appropriate words.

She rose from bed and padded to her little dressing room. She checked herself in the looking glass. Lord, she looked a fright. She wrapped herself in a long and heavy woolen shawl, slipped on some shoes, and made her way down to the kitchen to find some food.

Mrs. Hoover bent over the cauldron. She looked over when Caroline entered.

"You are to stay in bed until tomorrow," she said crossly.

"No one told me that."

"I'm telling you now. And His Lordship told me, so he is telling you, too."

"Where is he?"

"Out with the wagon. Feeding the horses. He left almost an hour ago, so will be back soon. I'd be in my chamber by then if I was you."

"I am grateful to him, but please remember that while he is a lord, he is not our lord or lord of this manor."

Mrs. Hoover straightened and waved her ladle in Caroline's face. "You could have died. What then? What of this manor and of us and your sister? How often did Tom tell you never risk going on the ice, no matter what?"

"I have seen him do it."

"You are not him. He's had over sixty years to learn how to do it right. And if you saw him, he was not alone. If Lord Thornhill had not been here . . ." She turned away and lifted her apron to wipe her eyes.

Caroline embraced her. "How did you learn about all of this?"

"He came and got me, didn't he? Said you needed hot fluids, soup and such. Suggested tea, but we've none of that, of course. He asked Tom what needed to be done with the horses besides bringing them hay." She spoke between sniffs. "He may be terrible about women, but I'll not hear a word against him after this."

"Do you have any of that soup made yet? I could use something. I am hungry."

Mrs. Hoover pointed to the table and took a bowl off the shelf. "Chicken soup from the bones out of the stew. Should be hot enough."

Caroline spooned the rich liquid into her mouth. It warmed all the way down.

Mrs. Hoover sat beside her. "I was thinking just as you came in that he might be a good husband for Amelia after all."

Memories jumped into Caroline's mind, of a kiss that should never have happened. "He is a rake. He will break her heart."

"Yet he seems to know about horses. That would be a help here, it seems to me."

"He isn't a farmer or horse breeder. He is a gentleman by birth and a peer and more likely he will return to London with or without Amelia. I would not build a lot of hope about him." She spoke to her own heart more than to Mrs. Hoover's ears.

The temptation to become sentimental about Lord Thornhill was strong right now and Caroline knew she had to fight it. Yet he had saved her and taken care of her and perhaps even worried about her. Itemizing all the ways he really would not do under other than dire circumstances did not change the softness she felt toward him, much as she counted on it doing so.

"He chatted with Tom a bit when he came to get me. Seemed he knew at least some about horse breeding. Not as much as your father, of course."

Few men had known as much as her father. Even fewer had his natural talent for it, as if he could smell a future champion on first seeing it born. Caroline had learned a lot just by standing by his side, but she could never duplicate his skill and instincts.

She finished her soup and went above to return to bed. Perhaps Mrs. Hoover was right. Maybe Lord Thornhill would stay at Crestview Park and lend a hand to the horses. With time maybe he could even manage it all. He might even get his cousin to permit Galahad to breed with Guinevere.

The idea should please her and give her heart. Instead a heavy thickness lodged below her heart. She forced herself to acknowledge the sadness for what it was.

If Thornhill took an active part here, she would see that face and those eyes daily—while he built a life and a family with her younger sister.

The next morning Adam went down to the kitchen to see what Mrs. Smith had left for breakfast. He found porridge and crisped salt pork and coffee again. Hardly the variety or richness he would be enjoying at Nigel's house right now, but he found it more satisfying.

A step he now recognized came down the stairs. Caroline entered, dressed in gray pantaloons and a white shirt. The linen fell over breasts he doubted suffered the restriction of stays. She served herself some food and sat at the long table.

"What are you doing up and dressed? You should be resting today, Miss Dunham."

"Any more rest and I would go mad." She ate heartily, then gave him her attention. "I see they almost fit."

He looked down at his garments. He had used the ones she provided again. "Well enough. Thank goodness for the braces, though, or these trousers would be down at my ankles when I stood up."

She giggled. "That would give new meaning to your being an upstanding gentleman."

"I will picture that now whenever a man is called that."

"They were my father's. He was similar in height, and an active man his whole life. There is a shorter coat than yours that you can use if you want to ride with me. I am going out and you can come along if you want."

Eager now, he finished his coffee quickly. "Where are we going?"

"I thought I should see how the rest of the manor fares with this cold and snow."

They saddled the two horses in the stable, mounted, and rode toward the hill. She pointed to her right. "Those woods are ours and are good for hunting. Fowl and rabbits mostly, but on occasion deer. We will go around to the other side this way so we stay in the sun."

That sun shone brightly, making the land glisten with sparkles of rose and blue. The snow softened all sounds, even the crunch of their horses' hooves through the frosty surface. Little wind meant the cold was bearable, even invigorating.

They rode around the north end of the woods and onto a fairly flat plain. "It is an oddity," she said while her arm swept the view. "It is as if the land just rose in one big mass. When we had the large herd, they tended to summer here but did not care for it in winter. There is water, but it is over at the far side, near our border. It is down a little cliff, however, so not convenient to horses."

"It is a plateau then. Is it fertile?"

"Grasses grow on it, not much else. I doubt it could be farmed, but it might do for sheep if we wanted to build that kind of husbandry. Your cousin tried to buy it from my father, but I can't imagine why."

Nigel had tried to purchase part of the Dunham property? He

had enough already, nor did this look to be a profitable patch. "Perhaps he sought to make amends."

"My father would have none of it, no matter what the reasons. His solicitor offered again after my father's death, but I refused, too. That was probably rash and sentimental. The money would have been useful."

She turned her horse abruptly and used her heels. Adam followed and they flew over the land, around the hill, past the pond, and on. To the west he could see the horses.

"They appear well enough," he said when his and Caroline's horses slowed to a walk and plunged in among them. "Now this one here is handsome. I had not noticed him before." The young stallion was almost black and maybe two years old. "Are you going to race him?"

"One or two races would be good, to establish his speed and value. The fees, however..." She pointed to two other horses. "More important is to breed the mares. Guinevere, and those two. We need to bring in other blood."

"I disagree. If you race this one and he wins or places, Crestview's name will be reborn. If you race Guinevere you will be famous at once. Even breeding the others will become easier as other farms seek yours out."

"I know how it is done," she said mildly.

"Of course. My apologies."

She laughed. "You can't help it. You are a man. Even Jason tries to tell me my business at times, and he is no baron."

Adam fell in beside her as they moved out of the herd. "Jason? Who is he?"

She turned to look at him. "Ah, that is right. You never learned his name. Jason is the young man who helped me abduct you."

He lined up his impressions of this Jason in his mind. Blond hair, blue eyes, attractive enough, taller than average, and a bit lanky. Well spoken. All of that did not raise any jealousy. That he was a close friend, close enough to join her in a crime, did.

"Where is he now? I haven't seen him since that first day."

"He went to bring my sister home. You didn't think I had her locked up in the attic, too, did you?"

Chapter 8

"I assume you have a horse in London." Caroline had slowed her horse to a walk while they approached the house and stable. She spoke after he fell in beside her. She had risen in the morning none the worse for her plunge in the pond. No fever or malady had taken hold overnight, to his relief.

"I do."

"A good one?"

"He is a fine gelding. I have had him four years."

"With your eye, I would expect him to be better than fine."

"He is finer than I could hope to own. Fortunately, my cousin believes that it won't do to have a Prescott on anything except very fine indeed. There is the family reputation to uphold."

She looked over. "Has he been so generous that you are in his debt?"

"Not financially." There were other kinds of debts, however. Other ways to extract payment for generosity. Margaret Millerson, for example.

Nigel wanted Millerson's money in that canal project, but the two men did not really trust each other. They were too much alike. So a marriage between families would serve as it always served, as a blood tie that proved good intentions. With an allowance dependent on Nigel, and other debts like the horse and social connections, Adam was hard pressed to refuse.

He had not thought about Margaret for two days now and was surprised that the proposed match appealed far less now, when it had never appealed much at all.

"After you marry my sister, would you want to stay here and help rebuild Crestview Park? Would he object to any of that?"

She asked it ever so calmly, as if the first part were a given and the second parts the only unknowns.

"Marry your sister?"

"Of course. That is why you are here. I thought you knew that by now."

He had enjoyed this ride with her. He liked horses. He liked her. Now they were in a conversation about his future that ideally would be held elsewhere, if at all.

Caroline had brought him here, abducted him, to coerce a marriage with her sister. "Why didn't you just write to me in London, explaining the situation and learning my reaction?"

"Would you have responded? I could not count on it. Nor could I depend upon your seeing her if I brought her there, or to your cousin's house. More likely we would have been turned away. Now you will have no choice but to see her and hear her name you, and remind you of the truth of it. Then as a gentleman you will do the right thing."

"Only if I truly am the man who seduced your sister, something I have no recollection of."

"I think you will remember everything when you see her."

He considered the implications of that while they dismounted and led their horses into the stalls. He left his and came over to help her unsaddle hers. "When will Jason have her back here so I can meet her?"

"You have already met her. However, she will be here in a day or so. So you can marry her."

Caroline thought he had figured all this out. He should have. He would have if his thoughts had not become increasingly preoccupied with Caroline herself.

"And if I refuse?" He set the saddle on the beam where it lived.

He turned to face her and saw her expression set in one much like that while she held him at pistol point in that wagon the first day.

"You will marry her," she said. "I'll not have my sister live her life in shame because you lacked courage. The border is less than a day's ride away and we will go to Scotland and you will wed there."

"And if I refuse?" he repeated with irritation.

"I promise that you will agree."

"Or what? Am I to marry at the point of a sword? Or the end of a pistol? Who will hold either? You?"

"There will be no shortage of volunteers. I may now lack the courage, but others will not. You may think I am beholden to you, and might take your chances with me, but you would be mistaken to do so with the men."

She meant Tom and that other one, this Jason. The one who had not been here since the first day. Of the two, the young one would be the danger, not Tom.

"If you force this it will not hold. It will not be legal, Caroline. Contracts made under coercion are not legitimate."

"There will be witnesses that say you were willing. You can go to the courts and claim you were forced, but it will be a very long time before you are heard and I don't think any judge will believe you. I expect men say that all the time to get out of marriages."

She began walking to the stall's entry. He blocked her path. "Why might you lack the courage? You had more than enough four days ago."

"Because you have helped me. I think of you as a friend. It was probably a mistake to allow that, but after yesterday—it would be difficult to shoot you now."

"I should hope so."

"Now, I should go. You still need to unsaddle your horse."

"Not yet." He did not move. "Caroline, do you want me to marry your sister? Truly? Because doing so would be—"

"Be what?"

"Unnatural. She is not the sister I want."

Her expression fell. She looked away and visibly struggled with her composure. "She carries your child. You don't get to choose."

"Don't I?" He lowered his head. "Don't I, Caroline?"

"N-no." Her voice broke on the word. She turned away.

He reached for her and turned her back. He lifted her chin so he could see her face beneath that broad brim of the man's hat. He swept the hat away and looked into moist brown eyes that carried too much sadness. God help him—he bent and kissed her lips carefully. "She is not here yet, darling. At least let me kiss you while I can."

"You should not." She barely breathed the denial.

"No. But—" He brushed her lips with his again. She did not resist. She did not pull away. He kissed her again, fully. He took her in his arms.

Sweet kisses, touched by salty tears. She embraced him awkwardly and kissed him back, but he felt the sorrow in her, the awareness that this could never be. She believed that and it kept his impulses in check. He did not want her doing more than this, which she had agreed to with that kiss, even if he wanted much more.

The potential hopelessness of their passion affected the kisses and embraces and even the air around them. He made each kiss count because it might be one of a handful he would ever have. He lifted her closer so their bodies pressed together and he could feel her breasts and hips against him. He cajoled her mouth open so they might join more closely.

"You will not—" She breathed out the command that was half a question, too.

"No. I promise."

She believed him although she had no real cause to. And yet perhaps here, these last days, he had been a man she could trust. He only knew he had not been the man who left London, nor the one expected at his cousin's house. He kissed her like he was going to stay here forever, riding the hills with her, grooming Guinevere for her first race, watching the seasons change on that hill.

The images added a poignancy to the pleasure the closeness brought him because at the heart of them was the promise of an emotion he would probably never have, at least not with this woman. He realized with both amazement and certainty that he would not want it with anyone else.

He caressed her, down the wool of the coat and over the fabric of the pantaloons. She rose against him when he smoothed the roundness of her bottom with both hands, holding her close so he pressed against her. The sensation sent him careening into a drive for more. Despite his promise, he began calculating if one of the stalls had clean straw to serve as a bed.

The familiar ruthlessness of his hunger caught him up short. He had made a promise, and if ever he kept one now was the time. He gentled his kisses again, calming them both while he did so. Yet the last one begat another, and another yet, because he feared there would be no more, ever.

Somehow, with a final caress, he summoned the strength to step back and release her. She released him, too. They looked at each other briefly, deeply. Then he stood aside and she walked to the house.

Caroline tried not to look at Thornhill all through dinner. At least they were not alone. Tom hobbled over from the cottage so Mrs. Hoover could feed them all properly in one sitting. The men kept up a lively conversation about the horses while Mrs. Hoover served her stew and dumplings and some boiled carrots dug up from the kitchen garden last month. Caroline wondered if Thornhill spoke so much in order to disguise how she did not talk at all.

Her head was too busy for dinner conversation. In it she relived what happened in the stable and tried to reconcile herself to the odd reality that she did not feel nearly as guilty as she should. He had asked to kiss her while he still could, and she had allowed it. They had done nothing wrong. Yet.

Could she live here after that wedding took place? Watch him and Amelia together? Be the strange older sister who donned pantaloons to help with the animals? Thornhill would never tell anyone that for a day or so, before he married, he had kissed a different Dunham woman. She would never tell anyone either. It would remain a fond memory of grabbing a little joy before it became wrong to do so.

It all sounded so reasonable when she lined it up that way. So honest. Only in her heart she knew it had been wrong. She also knew that she would not be able to be the old friend of the husband, and sister to the wife. Her heart would break every time she saw them together.

She might have to leave, if her heart did not take the next few days in stride. Leave this land and the horses. She could go to Aunt Elizabeth in Carlisle, she supposed, just as Amelia had visited so often. Only Amelia had been a marriageable young woman whose beauty compensated for her lack of fortune. Caroline would be the spinster relative with no prospects and no money.

It did not sound like an appealing life, but she would accept it if it meant Amelia could be happy in her marriage. It would be wrong, so very wrong, to in any way interfere with that, even through old memories.

"You must admit he is a fine-looking man." Mrs. Hoover leaned over to murmur into Caroline's ear while the men talked on.

Caroline looked at the fine-looking man in question. "Yes, I suppose so."

"Suppose so, do you? As if any woman would not notice. Of course he knows it. Men that look like that always do."

"Yes, he does." And yet she did not think him especially vain. He knew his advantages but also his own flaws from what she had seen of him so far. He was no saint, but at least he did not pretend his weaknesses were virtues.

"I don't think Jason will come around to liking him much for a long time. He may even leave here once we are done. He said as much to me last week. Said he didn't want to serve a lying scoundrel who took advantage of innocent girls. I'm hoping you will talk some sense into him."

Thornhill kept glancing at their whispered exchange, even while he still regaled Old Tom with stories of races he had witnessed. He probably guessed they discussed him. She didn't think she could convince Jason that this was not a lying scoundrel, much as she now disagreed with that description.

Perhaps she would leave with Jason. She would take a few of the horses as her birthright and find a small plot of land to rent and start over with Jason's help. She would not have to give up all she knew then or be a dependent relative.

Old Tom began struggling to stand. Thornhill rose to help him.

"I should walk him back," Mrs. Hoover said. "I'll come back and clean up."

"I can clean up. You take care of Tom."

"I will walk with you," Thornhill said. "You can lean on me, Mr. Smith."

Mr. Hoover drew himself straight. He gave Caroline a long look, then faced the baron. "My name is Tom Hoover, not Mr. Smith. My wife there is not a Smith either, nor is my son, Jason. We have been here since before horses roamed this land and if you marry Miss Amelia you are stuck with us, too."

"Tom—" Caroline began.

"Na, don't, Caro. I'll have my say. There's things I want to know from this man before I accept his shoulder for support."

"What do you need to know, Mr. Hoover?" Thornhill asked.

"Caro here has run this place for over a year now, and done a fine job of it. She ran it the year before when her father was not himself. After you marry into the family, what are your intentions here? Do you intend to displace us all?"

"He can't do that, Tom," Caroline said. "There won't be enough money to displace anyone for a number of years still."

"And what of her?" Tom angled his head toward her without acknowledging her comment. "Will you be expecting her to leave and you run the place?"

"A lot would depend on Mr. Dunham's will," Thornhill said. "However, it would be my intention that Miss Dunham never leave this land, and have a hand in its management as long as she chooses."

Caroline was astonished by the ease with which he said that, as if he had thought it out already and decided her hand in the continued management was important.

A big smile broke on Tom's face. He beamed a grin at his wife. "I told you I should come tonight. Share a pint with a man and it clears the air. You can stop worrying now, see?"

Shaking her head, Mrs. Hoover threw on her cape and tucked a basket over one arm. "Share a pint with a man and there's a lot of fool talk, seems to me. Come on now, and watch your way so you don't break something with a fall."

Thornhill pulled his greatcoat off its peg, slid it on, then walked beside Tom. As they left the kitchen and began up the stone stairs, Caroline saw Thornhill's arm go around the older man to ensure he did not fall on the steps.

She closed the door behind them, then turned to the sink.

Water already warmed on the hearthstone, and she poured it into two basins. She made quick work of the dishes and cups, then began scouring the cauldron.

She was drying it over the fire when the door opened and Thornhill returned. He hung his coat and paced through the kitchen while she finished. The house all but quaked with its emptiness. The air grew heavy with their mutual awareness that they were alone here now and would be until early morning.

"Am I going to have to bar you into that chamber again?" she asked while she straightened the crockery.

"I don't think so."

But he didn't know for sure, from the sounds of it. It would help if excitement did not keep sparkling in her blood. It would be hell to deny herself, and yet she must.

"They are good people," he said. "I am glad you had them with you these last years."

"For what little they received in the bargain they were saints to stay. You must promise to take care of them."

He neither responded nor left. She felt him still behind her. Felt his desire reaching for her.

What he contemplated could not happen.

"You should go above now. You really should," she said, keeping her back to him.

No sound. Then slow boot steps, coming closer. She closed her eyes and tried to contain what that did to her. She imagined caresses like she had experienced in the stable, and hot kisses on her nape, and arms surrounding her. Then more. Much more.

The steps stopped. Then they sounded again, firmer now, walking away.

Chapter 9

Lord Thornhill was gone.

Caroline accepted the truth after breakfast. He had not been down to eat while she was in the kitchen. She went looking for him afterward and finally ventured up to the attic chambers. The garments she had brought him and that he had worn yesterday waited on the bed, folded neatly. All of his own things had been removed.

She ran out to the stable. Only one horse greeted her. Thornhill had taken the other and broken his parole.

She had been a fool after all, to believe him and trust him. He had lured her and charmed her and taken advantage, just like he had with Amelia. Nor had she proven stronger than her sister. She had softened and melted and surrendered her good sense. He had not even had to try very hard.

It would be a miserable Christmas now, not one with some joy. They would all spend the day waiting for the county magistrate to come and take them all to gaol.

She went about her day, doing the chores. Tom insisted on driving the wagon when they brought hay to the horses. She should have refused, but she needed the help. Neither he nor Mrs. Hoover even asked where His Lordship was. Everyone agreed without words not to speak of the failure of the plan.

In the afternoon, Caroline took one of the muskets from the gun rack near the kitchen, mounted her horse, and headed toward the woods. Tom couldn't hunt, so someone had to and it would have to be her. She had a good aim and brought down two pheasants before long. She tied them to her saddle and headed home.

Just then the crack of another shot broke the snow-packed silence. She followed the sound to see a poacher lifting his prize off the ground. She trotted closer to warn him off. As she neared she recognized the greatcoat.

Thornhill held up a large hare. "Mrs. Hoover should be able to do something with this, I think."

"Where have you been? I thought—"

He came over to her horse. "You won't mind if I tie these here, will you? I don't want the blood to get on my coat." He looked up at her. "You thought what? That I had run off? Tom knew I would be gone today. He is the one who gave me the musket."

"I hope you got more than one hare if you have been hunting all this time."

He swung up on his horse. "I only now started hunting. Since you did so well, I can skip the rest and go get warm."

"Then where were you?"

He smiled. "Does it matter? I am back, true to my word."

They turned and aimed back to the house. Her mood lightened with his return. She couldn't stop smiling, her heart felt so bright. She had been imagining Amelia giving birth to a child with no father while her sister faced a merciless judge. Also she had been picturing her never seeing Thornhill again.

"It is a fine day again," she said.

"I would prefer it were summer."

"You seem to do well enough in the cold."

"I enjoy all seasons. But right now, if it were summer, you would not be wearing that coat that hides your breasts."

She glanced down and blushed.

"And if it were summer the grass would be high and the air warm." He stopped his horse and hers stopped, too. "I could take you to the other side of that hill and lay you down and find the buttons on your shirt and remove your pantaloons and see you, as I have often imagined, but not chilled from a freezing pond."

She dared not look at him. His voice, rich, clear, and quiet, entered her blood. The place where she pressed the saddle prickled until she wanted to squirm against the hard leather. It was wrong for him to speak like this to her. Scandalous. Yet she did not want him to stop.

"I could kiss every inch of you, Caroline. Your mouth and neck, your breasts and stomach. Your thighs, high and pale. Everywhere. I could be with you the way I imagined all last night. In you."

She stared straight ahead, barely breathing. He might actually be doing those things now, from the way she felt.

"Do not tell me it would be wrong, darling. It would be right in every way. If ever in our lives it would be right, it is—"

His voice stopped abruptly. She glanced over to see him squinting into the distance. She set her attention there, too, and saw what he saw. Two horses came from the northwest, off the road that wound toward Carlisle.

"Who is that?" he asked.

"Jason." She swallowed hard. "And Amelia."

He took a deep breath, as if the longest sigh in history wanted to emerge from him. Instead he moved his horse forward.

"Does she know I am here?" he asked.

"She thinks she is coming home for Christmas. I asked Jason not to give her the particulars about your visit."

Visit, hell.

They drew near the house. The other riders had gone around to the front. He stopped the horses and reached over to untie the pheasants and hare from her saddle. "I am going to bring these to Tom so he can clean them for dinner. I will join you shortly. Don't tell her I am here. Let it be a surprise."

He rode off while she continued to the house. She would enter through the kitchen, he assumed. Amelia might use the main doors, but Caroline would be practical.

He dropped the animals outside Tom's door. The old man must have heard, because he came out. "Hunting, I see. Should last us a few days."

"Perhaps not. Miss Amelia has just returned. I expect Caroline will want to feed her well on her first day back."

Tom made a face. "Gave the girl airs, she did. That aunt of theirs made it worse, dressing the girl up like a doll. Nothing that can't be changed, though. You go and see her and I'll take care of these here and tell my wife the news." He offered a man-to-man smile. "Been a while, eh? Eager to see her, no doubt."

"You have no idea."

He took his time making his way to the house. He went around to the front. He dismounted and tied his horse. He took a bundle from the saddle, then dawdled a few more minutes while he admired the snow-covered landscape. Finally he let himself in the big door and removed his greatcoat.

Voices came from the sitting room. Caroline's low, melodious one and another higher, younger one. He tucked the bundle behind a bench in the reception hall and approached the door.

Caroline still wore her pantaloons. Beside her on a divan sat a younger, softer, less starkly contrasted version of herself. He judged Amelia to be nineteen at most. She wore a richly colored sapphire dress of high quality and recent fashion. On a chair nearby rested a deep scarlet mantle and elaborate bonnet.

His gaze stopped for a five count on her hands. She wore scarlet gloves. Lambskin gloves that fit her delicate hands to perfection.

She appeared the grand lady of the house and Caroline the faithful retainer. He resented that far more than he should.

Caroline noticed him in the doorway. She touched her sister's arm. "Look who is here, Amelia. See who has come to visit."

Amelia looked over at him. Her brow puckered in confusion. Then her expression fell and her eyes widened. "Oh. Oh, my."

Oh, my, indeed.

He advanced on them. He bowed. He even smiled. She just stared at him.

Up close he could see the bulge that revealed her pregnancy, even though the style of dress disguised it well. He made a point of noticing it in a way she could not ignore.

Caroline began offering a story about his arrival that made it appear he had come of his own accord. He would have none of it.

"Your sister is dissembling. In truth she and Jason abducted me, so you and I could marry. That is why I am here."

Amelia looked ready to faint. She even swooned a bit. A figure rushed out from a corner. Jason. Adam had not even seen him there, sitting to the side. Now Jason hovered over Amelia, worried. He glared back at Adam. "She's a delicate sort and the journey was long. You should be more careful with her and not give her shocks like that."

"She is fine. Aren't you, Amelia? Thank you for bringing her home, Jason. Miss Dunham, perhaps I could have a little time alone with my intended? She and I have much to discuss."

Caroline rose. "Of course. Come with me, Jason. Give them some privacy. Perhaps you would take care of the horses we were riding, while you deal with your own."

Jason left grudgingly, with many dark looks over his shoulder. The door closed on them both.

Adam gazed down on Amelia. She in turn gazed down at her gloves.

"Look at me, please."

She slowly raised her head.

"There was always the slightest chance that your accusation against me was true. Now that I see you, I know it is not. You and I have never spoken before, nor even been in this close proximity. While we may have attended the same fete, we had nothing to do with each other. I know it, and you know it. So please explain to me why you told your sister that I am the father of your child."

She finally blinked. Long dark lashes fluttered over her robin's-egg blue eyes. "Well, you are the sort to do such a thing, aren't you? And as you are a peer, and usually in London, and not known for constancy, no one would expect you to do the right thing by me."

"You lied so that you would have a story regarding a man whom no one would openly accuse. Why not just name the real father?"

"I couldn't do that. No one would believe me, and even if they did nothing would be done about it. He is married, you see."

Ah. Caroline demanded a name, and the real name not only was of no use but also compounded the sin. So "Lord Thornhill" was a convenient lie with, to Amelia's mind, no consequences. Amelia did not know her sister nearly well enough.

"Give me his name now and I will see what I can do to make sure there is at least a settlement to care for the child."

She cocked her head. "I don't think that will happen. He is not the sort to be impressed by such as you. Your being a baron would be of no consequence."

This man had truly turned her head if he had her believing that. There were few men who were not impressed by a lord.

"His name, Amelia. I must insist that you share it, for the good of you, your child, and your family."

Caroline kept her ear to the keyhole, for all the good it did. A muffled conversation reached her, but not the words. At least they both were talking, and she could not hear Amelia crying, so it must be going well.

Thornhill had appeared more lordly than normal when he entered that room. His frock coat and waistcoat had been brushed at some point, by himself she assumed. She had no idea where he procured the clean and starched cravat. She had noticed none of this while they rode back.

His manner had been less than gentle with Amelia, but then he would not be happy under the circumstances. Still, with time, they might make a good marriage. If that notion left her hollow, that was her own fault for allowing herself to think of him as something other than her own sister's intended.

The door abruptly opened. She almost fell forward. She looked up to see Thornhill gazing down.

"Did you hear?"

"I tried but could not make out the words. You should have spoken louder."

He smiled vaguely and stood aside. "Your sister has something to say to you."

She did not have to enter the room far to encounter Amelia. Subdued and docile, she met her sister a few feet from the door. "I made a mistake," Amelia murmured. "It is not Lord Thornhill. I am going up to my chamber to rest now."

With that Amelia rushed past her.

Caroline stood where she was, stunned. Thornhill closed the door again.

"How . . . ?"

"She made an error. Leave it at that. Come sit with me while we decide what to do next."

Caroline wandered around the chamber, her mind all mixed up. She sank back into the divan. "So who is it? That child is not a miracle. Some man—"

"Do not press her for a name. I know who it is, and there will be no marriage. Her seducer already has a wife and family."

Caroline's heart sank. "I have been most kind about this, but now I will scold her severely. Even a girl knows not to allow a married man to—"

"She will need even more kindness now, Caroline."

She sighed heavily. "What is to be done? I suppose, if her condition was not noticed in Carlisle, that after the child is born she can return there and try to make a life for herself."

"It is unlikely her condition was not noticed. I saw it at once."

"Then what?"

He shrugged. "She lives here, at her home, I suppose. She is not as delicate as you have led her to believe."

"*I* have led her to believe?"

"You indulged her, then sent her to your aunt, who did so even more. Put her in some pantaloons and let her groom horses with you. If it is good enough for you, it is good enough for her."

"You are angry that you were abducted and accused in error, and to no purpose. I understand that. We will give you one of the horses and you can go. You will be at your cousin's by Christmas, easily."

He turned his body so he faced her. "I think I would like to spend Christmas here. I went to the village this morning and sent a letter to my cousin explaining I would not be attending his celebrations. He will not miss me."

So that was where he had gone. Yet he could still go to his cousin's now if he wanted to. Only he didn't. The implications of that teased at her. She dared not hope he dallied for her sake, and yet . . . "If you had told me you were going to the village I would have asked you to bring back a few things."

It was a stupid thing to say but all she could summon short of spilling out her relief and gratitude that she would see him for a few more days at least.

"Like salt and flour? Mrs. Hoover requested it. I also brought back sugar and a few other provisions."

The last of the sugar cone had been used months ago. Mrs. Hoover would be elated.

It gave Caroline joy that he would remain with them a few more days. But Amelia . . . "I wish we had family down in the Midlands or somewhere else far away and Amelia could go there until the child is born. She might still have a reputation left afterward, and a life."

"That is one way such things are handled. Another is the girl marries a man who accepts he will raise another man's child."

"That would take a handsome settlement, I assume."

"Very handsome."

"So that is not a choice either. Not that there is a convenient man about. I don't think you are offering yourself."

"No."

She began to stand, but he pulled her back down and leaned toward her. "There will be no privacy on the floor with your chamber now. I assume Amelia will sleep up there. The attic, however, is still my kingdom. Come visit me tonight and we will find a solution to the problem that is Amelia."

She looked into his eyes and knew they would not only talk through her family's problem if she went to him. He might not have seduced Amelia, but he had every intention of seducing the other Dunham sister.

She could not agree. She did not disagree. She stood; then on impulse she bent down and kissed his lips. An inner debate waited in the hours ahead, but she already suspected how it would end.

Adam knew that kiss had not been a promise. It did give cause for optimism, so he spent the next hours in good humor.

He set the sugar cone in the kitchen as a present for Mrs. Hoover. Then he wandered out to the stable. Jason was finishing up with the horses. "Do you need help bringing out the hay?"

"It's warmed up a bit and some snow has melted. They will find the grass now on the southern slope of the hill. No need to bring the hay."

Adam watched him move. The horses liked his handling, and one kept nibbling at his hair. "It was not me. She just told her sister."

Jason paused. Then he lifted a hoof and inspected it. "Who then?"

"A married man. There will be no more abductions."

Jason cursed. "Not much life for her now. I was at that fete. I should have watched her better."

"Don't blame yourself. She could have a good life if another man marries her. One who cares for her, and would not hold one mistake against her."

"If you find that man, you send him to me."

Adam strolled over to the horse while Jason went around the other side to inspect another hoof. "Why not you?"

Silence. No sound. No movement. Then a blond head rose and looked over the horse. "She is a gentleman's daughter. I am a servant. That is all we are in truth. We may all eat at that table together, but we are not of the same place in life."

"No one knows all the places better than I do. However, you are well spoken and hardly a typical servant. As this farm rebuilds you will have more responsibilities. I expect in five years you will be a steward. That is a servant, too, but of a different sort entirely. More like a solicitor is a servant."

He laughed, shook his head, and moved back to the horse's rear hooves.

"How did you come to be educated?" Adam asked.

"Mr. Dunham had me take lessons with Caro—with Miss Dunham. We're about the same age. He told my parents to send me over in the mornings when the tutor held lessons. I wasn't the best student."

"Neither was I."

His head popped up again. "No? Well, we've something in common."

"Several things. That and horses. I have wondered about something. Would you have shot me that first day?"

"I am sorry to say I probably would have. I was wanting to, so if you had given me the excuse—" He looked up again. "My apologies for all of that, seeing as how you were innocent."

"Jason, is there any other woman you have ever met for whom you would shoot a peer? Would you have done that for Caroline? For the girl you first kissed?"

Jason smiled roguishly. "One and the same, ain't they? Don't tell her I told you. We were fifteen and curious. Wasn't much to it. I couldn't figure out what all the fuss was, but she is like my sister, ain't she? Now Amelia—never kissed her. Wouldn't dare even when she was old enough. I just knew it would have been different, though."

"If you are in love with her, perhaps you should consider what I said about a marriage. If you do not see her as a sister, she may not see you as a brother. Raise the possibility with her, and give her time to think about it."

Adam waited for Jason to deny being in love. When it did not come he patted the horse's flank and left the stable.

Chapter 10

They had a feast that night with the hare and pheasant and even used the real dining room. Mrs. Hoover made a honey cake now that she had enough flour. Amelia ate sparingly. Most of the time she kept her gaze on her plate, although on occasion Caroline saw her send resentful glares at Thornhill. He noticed, too, but his spirits were so high he didn't seem to care. He showed the humor of a man just spared from the gallows.

"A gentleman would have married me anyway," Amelia said that night while Caroline brushed out her hair. "Then I'd be a lady and live in London and go to grand balls. Now I'll just be a fallen woman with a baby who has no father."

"Of course he has a father. You named the wrong man, but you know the right one. If you tell me—"

"I can't. Thornhill made me promise not to tell you."

"He did, did he? I'm your sister. If you can't tell me, whom can you tell?"

Amelia sealed her lips closed hard. Caroline guessed the answer. She could tell Thornhill, which she had. So he knew, but her own sister did not. That would never do.

After tucking Amelia into bed, Caroline marched to the stairway and went above to the attic chambers. Thornhill's door stood open. She peered around the threshold to see him sliding something under the bed. His coats were off and his shirt sleeves rolled up. A pail of water warmed on the small fireplace hearthstone.

He looked over and saw her. "Why do I think you did not come up here to give me a kiss?"

She stayed at the threshold and crossed her arms. "I want to know his name."

He shook his head. "I will talk to him, but you will only get trouble for your time if you do."

"You know him, then."

"I probably know most of the men who were at that fete who might impress Amelia."

"It is your goal to vex me."

He walked right up to her. "Caroline, my only goal today, the single one that occupied my thoughts, was getting you to come up here tonight." He reached around and closed the door behind her. "It appears vexing you was the path to success."

The sails of indignation deflated at once. She looked around his cell, thinking it had been unnecessary to force him to live like this, especially after he gave his parole. She could hardly have him in the chamber next to hers, however. Who knew what ideas he might get?

He took her hand and stepped back, leading her farther into the chamber. The tiny creases at his eyes' edges subtly deepened.

"I amuse you," she said.

"No. You charm me. You are adorable and precious."

"I think, my lord, that your eloquence is the result of dishonorable intentions."

He sat in that one chair, still holding her hand. "Not too dishonorable. Sit here with me so I can hold you again." He drew her closer, then down so she sat on his lap. "We have many things to talk about, Caroline."

"What things?"

"My next few days here, mostly."

His last days here, he meant. She kept her expression steady, but that arm embracing her and that face so close to hers almost defeated her. The truth about Amelia had cut two ways. On one edge was relief that Caroline would not have to see the man she loved marry her sister. On the other edge was sadness that he had no reason to remain here now.

"I have them all planned if you are agreeable to my thinking," he said. "Tomorrow is Christmas Eve. Mrs. Hoover can start her cake. Jason and I will go hunting for Christmas dinner. You and Tom and Amelia can take the wagon to the woods and bring back some boughs of greenery."

She had to smile at the thoroughness of his plan. "It will be a wonderfully festive celebration."

"I think so. That will be the next day when we will all eat, drink, and be merry. The day after is the servants' day off. Unless the household is to lack washing water and fuel and warm food, those who are not servants will have to serve. That means Amelia and I will be servants to the rest of you."

"Amelia won't like that. She will think I should be a servant, too."

"You have served her and this legacy plenty. She will do it. Trust me."

He seemed very sure about that. She wondered what had been said while she listened at the keyhole.

"Then the next day," he began, then paused.

She waited for the rest. *Then the next day I will have to leave.*

"The next day, it is my turn to abduct you. We will make a little journey to Scotland, as you always intended. Only you and I will wed, not Amelia."

She gazed down at him in the stillness. He gazed back, right into her eyes. Waiting. Searching.

"I am no great prize, I know," he said. "Other than my title I have little to offer except a reputation that will embarrass you and more debts than are decent. However, you have stolen my heart, Caroline, and given me more happiness and purpose these last days than I ever thought to know. I must at least try to convince you to be mine." He slid his hand behind her neck and pressed just enough to bring her lips to his. He showed the kind of convincing he had in mind.

She could have answered his proposal right then. The words were in her head. The warmth of that kiss undid her, however. Words became unnecessary. Intrusive. She accepted how the sweetness turned passionate, then almost desperate. She welcomed the way her blood sizzled and coursed down her center.

He nuzzled at her ear while he caressed down her side. "We will wait if you want, but I—"

"I don't want to wait."

Was that a thank-you she heard before his kisses pressed her neck in a dozen thrilling ways? Her mind narrowed to nothing except the sensations he created in her body, and to the building desire filling her body.

His caress smoothed over her breast so naturally that she almost nodded, it felt so right and good. He tantalized her with new pleasures so intense that impatience entered her joyous abandon. The arm embracing her shifted and she felt her dress's tapes loosen.

"Stand here." He set her on her feet in front of him. The fire warmed one side of her and the cool of the chamber touched the other side, but the heat inside her came only from him and her and what he was doing.

He slid the dress down until it pooled at her feet. He turned her to work the laces of her stays and removed them before he turned her back again. She stood there in nothing more than stockings and a chemise. The cloth of the chemise hung loosely off her breasts. She looked down at how they had grown heavy and full and how the tips had tightened against the fabric.

He pulled her closer, between his thighs, and eased the chemise down until her breasts were naked. To her astonishment he leaned forward and licked at one tip and the sensation sent her reeling. He kept torturing her with his tongue while he pushed the chemise farther down until she was completely naked.

She could barely stand now. She could hardly see. He tongued at the other breast. A pulse throbbed low, between her legs, demanding more pleasure, beating a little drum of desire.

He took her breast into his mouth, but his tongue still flicked and aroused. His embrace lowered to her hips and caressed, then held, her bottom. His other hand slid between her legs and touched that throbbing pulse.

Shocking pleasure overwhelmed her. She gripped his shoulders so she would not die from it all. Her mind cried whimpers of need and maybe her mouth did, too. She heard nothing except his voice while he moved her toward the bed. He laid her down and covered her, then undressed.

With only a shirt and trousers to remove, it did not take long. She caught a glimpse of him limned by the light of the fire, all lean strength like the thoroughbred he was, good lines, his chest and arms as arresting of attention as his face.

He joined her in the bed and gathered her into his arms. "Does something amuse you?" he asked while he covered them both. "You have an impish smile."

"I am thinking it was wise of me to demand Jason stuff the mattress. He thought you should sleep on the ropes alone. Or the floor."

"It is not a bad bed. Small, but enough space for the two of us."

Considering how they lay, it was enough space. His body lined hers and his chest hovered over her. His head dipped to kiss her and lead her back into passion.

Slowly, carefully, he aroused her. His kisses drew her toward abandon. He teased at her breasts with his tongue and teeth and caressed her body with confident, knowing hands. Her shyness fell away, and then her dignity, and finally her hold on herself. She moaned from the pleasure and it seemed that only made him find ways to make it better. When caresses on her thighs rose higher, he touched and toyed at her private flesh until impatient desire had her grasping him with fevered need.

He mounted her, finding ways not to crush her with his weight. He bent her knees, then rose high on tight, taut arms and began to press into her. He filled her slowly, but it still left her breathless. Even as it pained her she did not emerge from the stupor of intimacy that filled her consciousness.

He withdrew just as carefully, then filled her again. And again. Pleasure teased at her even within the soreness. She could tell he restrained himself for her sake, could feel the power building in him that he held in check. Maddening sensations started to overwhelm the pain and she moved, rocking up to accept him, joining him in the hard, consuming kisses he dipped his head to give her.

His thrusts came harder then. She did not find that unpleasant and even urged him on with caresses and kisses because it brought them closer and banished the rest of the world. Their hard passion might have lasted a few minutes or many; she could not tell. There was no time, only emotion-drenched intimacy.

Finally he was on her, his deep breaths in her ear as he collapsed after his finish. She wrapped her legs around him, and her arms, too, and held him close. She turned her head so her lips touched his cheek.

"Yes, I will marry you."

Chapter 11

"Where did you get that, Adam?" Caroline watched while Thornhill stood on a chair and tacked a ribbon to the top of the sitting room door's threshold. An apple hung within it and a mistletoe bough dangled at its end. It added a bright note to a chamber already decorated with green boughs on the windowsills and five thick candles awaiting dusk and lighting.

"A woman in the village had the ball and mistletoe. I added the other greens. I thought to catch you under it and steal a kiss."

"I think you have had enough the last two nights."

He checked the ribbon. "There will never be enough, darling."

Perhaps not. One kiss became more with them. She had surprised him by arriving at his door last night. Still sore from her first time, she had not been able to stay away. He had been unable to deny them both, although he displayed heroic restraint and care again.

He hopped off the chair and pulled her into yet another deep kiss. "I think we should tell them today at dinner. Then we can do this whenever and wherever we want."

She laid her head against his chest. She enjoyed a few moments in his arms before the day's Yuletide festivities began.

Boughs of evergreens decorated the house. Down below Mrs.

Hoover finished her dinner and cake with Amelia at her side. Amelia had complained about the chores she was expected to do now, so Caroline gave her a choice in them. To Caroline's surprise, the choice had been learning to cook.

She looked through the frosted windows. Fresh snow had fallen last night but not too much, and now the sun shone on an unblemished blanket of white.

"Jason is coming with a big log," she said.

"Tell him to bring it in here to dry," Thornhill said.

She went to open the front door and call Jason in. He set the log on its end near the fire. "Should be fine in a few hours."

He paused to look around the room, at the greenery and berries and candles. His gaze settled on the mistletoe bough for a long moment.

"Stay and get warm," Thornhill said. "I'll see if there is some hot coffee below."

A little confused, Jason took position in front of the fire and pulled off his work gloves. Thornhill left and shortly returned. "It will be up soon."

"I'll get some later. I still need to get the wagon and hay going, what with the snow again."

"No, no, stay. You should take a few minutes on this day."

Jason shrugged and turned back to the fire.

Five minutes later, Amelia arrived with a tray. She stopped right inside the door. "Has the king called on us? If not, I don't see why I am carrying refreshments up those stairs."

"Stay there. I will take it," Thornhill said. Yet he did not move.

Over at the fire, Jason watched Amelia.

Caroline watched them all.

Jason looked above Amelia's head. With an expression of resolve, he made the few strides that brought him under the bough, too. He took the tray and set it down on a table. Then he did not steal a kiss. Instead he took Amelia's face in his hands and kissed her fully.

Caroline could not ignore the kind of kiss it was. Shocked, she took a step forward to stop him. A hand on her shoulder pulled her back.

She looked up at Thornhill.

Jason picked up the tray again. "I think I'll drink this in the morning room. Why don't you sit and have some, too, Amelia? You have been working as hard as I have."

Wide-eyed and perplexed by that kiss, Amelia followed him out of the room.

Thornhill smiled.

"Are you matchmaking?" Caroline asked.

"I appear to have a talent for it."

"Jason?"

"He is clearly in love with her. He probably has been for years. I am surprised you did not see it."

"She will never marry a servant."

"He is not a common servant here. She knows his interest now. She has already begun reconsidering him, and how she views him. That will take some time, but— Who knows what she will do?"

Caroline stretched up and kissed him. "I will pray that the love she already has for him becomes that kind of love. It would be a wonderful conclusion of her misadventure. Is this a Christmas gift to me?"

"I thought of it as a gift to Jason and Amelia."

"The mere chance of this match lightens my heart, so it is my gift, too. Thank you, for this and everything else you have done for me."

"I think that went well, don't you?" Caroline asked. Her question broke the silence that fell after an energetic passion left her screaming into the night on her release. Adam hoped no one went running to her chamber to see what accident had overtaken her.

He doubted she knew she had done that. Nor did he think that she now congratulated them both on the artful sensuality of the last half hour.

They had announced their forthcoming wedding before dinner, and it made for a very merry feast. Afterward, in the sitting room while the Yule log crackled, there had been games and songs, then more of the Christmas cake.

"No one seemed too shocked," she added. "Except perhaps my sister. She does not resent it, though. She only asked me later why I would marry such a demanding man."

"She is unhappy that I said tomorrow she and I would be the

servants to the rest of you. She thinks you should join us because officially you are half owner of the manor."

"She is correct in that. My father's testament left it equally to us both. I should play the servant with you."

"I have decided you will not. Not another word will be spoken on this matter."

"My, you *are* demanding. And commanding." She nuzzled his neck.

Both when necessary. He wanted Amelia to serve Caroline, for once, even if it was in this mock fashion. Amelia did not comprehend how her sister had lived and worked while Amelia played the gentleman's daughter. He doubted Amelia had noticed the toll it had taken on Caroline's hands.

That thought had him feeling down beside the bed until his hand hit a bundle propped against the wall. He grasped it and pulled it up. "I have something for you." He set the bundle on his chest right in front of her nose.

She sat up. "What is it?"

"Gifts. Small and hardly good enough for you. Useful at least, perhaps." It had probably been a blessing to only have the village shops available. If in London he would have been tempted to spend hundreds for jewels and luxuries. Hundreds he did not have. For these small gifts he had enough, though. In time, with Caroline at his side and his one talent put to use with the horses, perhaps there would be more than enough.

She took the bundle and felt through the muslin wrap. She petted the red silk ribbon that bound it together. "This alone would be enough."

It had been a day of laughter and joy and a night of unbearable pleasure and powerful emotions. A dark anger now threatened to ruin that, and he swallowed the reaction. He pictured his cousin and Margaret Millerson today, living as if the luxuries they enjoyed were their due.

Later, he thought. Not too much later, but not now.

Caroline pulled at the ribbon and unfolded the muslin. She lifted a fur muff. "Oh, my." She rubbed the fur against her face. "It is beautiful and I will treasure it. Not very practical for riding a horse, of course, but—"

"It is to keep your hands warm when you ride in a carriage."

She was good enough not to say she had no carriage.

"As for riding, keep looking," he said.

She peeled back more muslin and squealed with delight. She lifted lambskin gloves and immediately pulled them on. "They fit perfectly. Like another skin."

"You can pick up a farthing while wearing them."

"I can also hold and shoot a gun."

"That too."

"There is something else—" More muslin and another squeal. "Good solid work gloves! You have given me a whole wardrobe for my hands." She fell back into his arms and kissed him.

He held her against his body. "I never want to see you with red, raw hands again, Caroline."

"I am surprised you found all of this in the village."

"Most shopkeepers have a special drawer that rarely opens. Small luxuries await the right patron. I would have bought a wardrobe for your body as well, but that will have to wait for town."

"I have nothing for you," she whispered.

"You gave me yourself, Caroline. There is no gift more precious."

She rose on her arm and looked down at him. "Perhaps I do have something else." She caressed down until she reached his cock. "You may have to tell me how to wrap it, though."

He told her just how to do it.

Two mornings later, Caroline slipped out of Adam's bed while he slept. The announcement of their marriage had been met with shock, happiness, and good cheer, but that did not mean they could openly share a bed.

He had not been in his chamber when she arrived the night before. He still had duties as a servant down below. A day of that, with only Amelia to aid him, had left him working long into the night. Food from Christmas meant no one had to cook much, but the dishes still needed washing and the pots scrubbing.

Amelia had complained about having to help when Caroline did not. It seemed unfair to her. To Caroline, too, who again petitioned Thornhill for her to be made a servant. He would have none of it.

He meant to humble Amelia, she knew, perhaps so she would be amenable to Jason's eventual proposal. Mostly, however, he knew that Amelia would live at Crestview now, and if a peer of the realm could help groom horses Amelia could help groom chambers.

Caroline was in the kitchen with Mrs. Hoover when Tom hobbled down the stairs outside and opened the door. "Riders coming up the lane. A carriage, too."

They all looked at one another and shrugged. "I can't imagine who it could be," Caroline said. All the same she went up to greet whoever was coming to their door.

A coach and two riders on horseback drew closer. The riders wore livery. The huge carriage sported an abundance of brass and two liveried footmen. As it rolled to a stop in front of her house she saw the escutcheon on its door.

Jason came up behind her in the hall. "Go above and wake Lord Thornhill," she said. "Tell him his cousin is here."

A footman hopped off the back of the carriage, opened the door, and set down steps. A man emerged. The face beneath his hat's brim was a fuller, older, coarser version of Thornhill's. His shorter body showed more weight. Caroline gritted her teeth. This man would soon be family to her, but she still hated the sight of him.

One of the footmen came to her at the door. "The Marquess of Haverdale has called for Lord Thornhill."

"Please ask him to come in and wait by the fire."

"He intends to remain outside."

"If he chooses to remain in the cold, so be it. He is welcome here. No one is going to assault him."

The servant looked shocked by the very notion of an assault on his lord. He returned to the marquess and delivered her message.

The marquess appeared indecisive. The damp and cold won out over any inclination to stand his ground. He approached, bowed, and followed her into the house.

"Lord Thornhill will be with you soon." She ushered him into the study. "Will this do? The blue chair is very comfortable."

He gave the chair's seat a little brush with his gloves. "This will do."

"I will leave you then. I have preparations to make for the day." She closed the door upon leaving, hoping her father was not turning in his grave.

* * *

Adam took his time dressing and going below. He had expected the carriage. He had not expected Nigel to be inside it.

Caroline sat in the reception hall. "I put him in the study."

"I did not expect him, if you are wondering about that."

"I was wondering."

"I would not invite him here, knowing how you feel. Now, keep the family in the kitchen. My cousin can be dramatic in his anger and I do not want witnesses to his histrionics."

"Will he be as angry as that? He has no reason to hate us."

Someday he would tell her just why Nigel would be angry. Not all of it, though. It would take a while to decide what she needed to know.

He entered the study and closed the door. Nigel glared at him from where he sat on a blue chair. A folded paper rested on the desktop within his reach. He tapped his finger on it.

"Hell of a thing to receive that. Good of you to let me know you were alive, at least."

"I sent word as soon as I could. Did you have a good Christmas, secure in knowing I was safe?"

"Good enough, although Miss Millerson was distraught with worry even with the news."

"The hell she was. She was indignant that I did not crawl if necessary to have the privilege of her company."

"Now, we talked about that, and about the benefits of that match to you. Come back with me. All is not lost on that account."

Adam rested his hips against the desk's edge. He removed a folded vellum document from his frock coat and set it down. "There will be no match. Here is the special license. You paid for it, so you may as well have it."

Nigel fingered the vellum, then tossed it in the fire. Once more he tapped the letter Adam had sent. "What did you mean by the threat in it?" He picked it up and read: " 'If you do not want your family, the peerage, and all the realm to know about Amelia Dunham, send your coach to her home two days after Christmas. I will explain all later.' " He threw it down. "Who in hell is Amelia Dunham?"

Adam tossed the letter into the fire to join the license. "I had intended to have this out with you after I returned from Scotland, but we may as well do it now since you are here."

"Of course I am here, when my own cousin threatens me." His voice boomed in the little space they shared.

"Swallow your anger until you hear something insulting and wrong. You seduced Amelia at your county fete last summer. She will name you publicly if necessary. She was an innocent, and my guess is she hardly comprehended what you were about until it was too late." He paused. "I will accept it was a seduction, and not something worse."

"Are you judging me? *You?* That is a fine joke."

"For all my sins, I never ruined an innocent. It isn't done, and you know it. Worse, you did it as an act of revenge. Her father would not sell you some land you wanted. Her sister had just refused again. How much will it cost you to change the route of the canal you wanted to build there, with that land not open to you?"

Nigel's face reddened. "Thousands. Fool man. Stupid woman. Stubborn, the two of them. I offered more than it was worth, too."

"I doubt that."

"So you know of my little indiscretion. I don't care."

"I don't think the gentlemen in your clubs will think it so little. I am sure your wife will not. She tolerates your mistresses. A bastard born of an innocent you ruined is another matter."

Nigel's face fell. "The girl is with child?"

"She is at that."

His cousin recovered. "And the price of your silence is a carriage to take you to Scotland?"

Adam sat in the other chair and stretched out his legs. "I am not so good as to stop there. I want much more than that. A settlement for the girl, for one thing. That is the only proper thing to do. Shall we say enough in trust to provide an income of five hundred a year?"

Nigel chewed his lower lip. "Only if she keeps the child. And if it is a boy, I want to see him from time to time."

"I think that can be arranged. You will see him, but he will not see you. There is one other thing you must do."

"There isn't anything I must do, damn it. But let us have it."

"Galahad."

"I'll not be selling you Galahad. Or giving him to you, or anyone else."

"Not sell. This spring, however, you will send him here to be bred with some mares, so Crestview can rebuild its bloodlines and expand again. Two months of his services are all that is needed." He averted his gaze. "I have chosen to believe you did not play a long game, and deliberately ruin Dunham with that massacre of his horses so he would be amenable to a land sale."

Silence fell beside him. Nigel might have ceased breathing, it grew so quiet. He glanced over to see his cousin looking down at the carpet. And in that instant those blue eyes glanced up and their gazes met. Nigel might appear cowed, but a ruthless star sparkled in his eye.

He had indeed played that long game. Adam's chest thickened. In that moment he knew that his dealings with Nigel would only be the most formal sort in the future. He would never be friends with this man again.

"What did you want that damned carriage for? Damned inconvenient to bring it. Scotland, you said."

"In an hour or so I will depart, along with Miss Dunham. Caroline Dunham. We are getting married."

Nigel was on his feet in a snap. "The hell you say. I'll not have it. It will be the end of the allowance you get. This family is a thorn in my side and if you marry into it I am done with you." He paced and ranted for several minutes.

Adam just waited.

He saw the exact moment when Nigel's good sense broke through the cloud of bluster in his head and he realized what this marriage meant. No more cursing then. Only quiet contemplation. That star began sparkling again. "If you are married to her, you control her land."

"Not to sell. I won't have that right, of course. But the use of it, yes, as her husband that will be mine, assuming her sister is agreeable to my intentions."

"So for a price you could allow a canal to go through that parcel in question."

"Damnation, I suppose we could." He feigned shock, then grinned. "Come to me in a month with your proposal. It might be better received if in addition to a payment, you gave us a share of that company."

"I already have five partners."

"So now you will have six." He stood. "I must prepare for this journey. I trust you have a horse for your return, or another carriage down the lane."

Nigel did not care for being thrown out. He rose in a huff and marched to the reception hall. At the door he paused. "The girl—"

"She will be well cared for. And I will see that your child is educated and raised properly, whether Amelia marries or not."

Chapter 12

Gretna Green was not the closest Scottish town to Crestview Park, but the roads meant it was the easiest and fastest to access. Two mornings later Nigel's best coach rolled into the center of the little town and its passengers stepped out.

Old Tom needed help from Thornhill, but Mrs. Hoover, excited by the day's event and by her first real journey in years, simply jumped down. She tugged Caroline aside. "I'm still thinking we shouldn't have left them alone together. Jason has been giving her some long looks. I am afraid he is smitten."

"I am sure they will be fine. We couldn't all come, and Jason is of more use there than Tom would be." Caroline had not said one word to Amelia to insinuate she had any concerns about Jason, but she had asked Thornhill to speak to Jason himself. He had refused and insisted that Jason would know what to do. Considering Thornhill's history, she wondered what *know what to do* meant.

The man in question came toward them with Tom.

"So do we find the anvil?" Tom asked with a big grin.

"I think we can do better than that," Thornhill said. "Every village has a church. We will find it."

That did not take long, since it was a small town. Thornhill returned with the vicar in tow, after finding him in a nearby tavern.

"We don't get many this time of year," the vicar said. "I'm happy to witness your vows if you want, though."

They entered the little church, cold and damp and dark on this overcast day. Evergreen boughs rested at the base of each window and around the sanctuary. Caroline removed her muff and handed it to Mrs. Hoover. Hand in hand, skin on skin, Caroline and Lord Thornhill faced the vicar to say the vows.

When it was done, Tom and his wife clapped while Caroline and Thornhill kissed. Then all of them filed back out to the open air.

"Did I hear tell there's a tavern around the corner?" Tom asked. "Seems to me this calls for a drink of good whiskey to celebrate."

"You two go," Thornhill said. "We will be there soon."

The Hoovers ambled off, arm in arm. Two snowflakes drifted down in front of Caroline's eyes. Then several more. "Snow," she said.

Thornhill took both her hands in his and faced her in the church-yard. "I hope it snows every year at this time, to remind us of taking hay in the wagon and the views from the house."

"I look forward to any future we have together. At Crestview I hope, but wherever you go I will go."

"Of course we will stay at Crestview. And I can predict the future for you. Crestview will soon be as great as it ever was, and once more that kitchen table will feed fifteen hands and servants. You will have at least two children, a boy and a girl. Amelia will have a son; then she and Jason will have five more. As steward he will live in that cottage, and our children will play together. When the Hoovers pass, we will bury them near your father."

He believed every optimistic word. Her throat burned on mention of her father. "Won't you miss London? Your life was there."

He kissed her. "London is in our future, too." More snow fell now, dusting their garments. He took her hand and they followed the Hoovers' path. "We will make long visits, so I can attend Parliament and you can enjoy the theater and parties and have time to order new wardrobes."

He continued describing a life very different from what she had known, especially the last few years. An impossible life. She allowed his fantasy to sweep her up, however, and she laughed over the details as he continued giving them.

They found the tavern and heard the sounds of cheer within. He reached for the latch, then paused. "I forgot! How careless of me. I meant to tell you that my cousin gave us a wedding gift."

"He did? What is it?"

"Galahad for two months in the spring." He opened the door as if he had spoken nothing of consequence.

She could not move. *Galahad.* Suddenly all the predictions about Crestview and London and new wardrobes became real possibilities.

He smiled at her. "Come inside and get warm, darling, and I will tell you the rest."

Don't miss the Madeline Hunter's passionate new romance . . .

HEIRESS FOR HIRE

on sale Spring 2020

Read on for a preview . . .

Chapter 1

Did you kill him?

The voice spoke in his head vaguely, as if traveling through distance and fog. Not as the voice of his conscience, the way he had heard the question in the past. A different voice now. A female one.

I doubt it. Help me here.

He looks dead to me.

I promise that he isn't dead. Now, take this and hold it while I . . .

A bit clearer now. Closer. So close it made his head bang with pain, like each word was a hammer blow. The more words, the more blows, and the closer they sounded. That made the blows harder.

Maybe I should call Jason to come here.

We do not need Jason. See?

Bam. Bam.

Bad enough already, without that.

*We are not the ones at fault here. Hold the lamp closer, so I can make sure it is safe. Wait, give the lamp to me. I think he is— He is! Now I wish I **had** killed him.*

You should never say such things. Even here you should not. What are you doing with that?

Bam, bam, bam.

Bringing him around so I can find out why he is here.

Bam—

The fog disappeared, washed away by an onslaught of liquid that brought him back to full consciousness. He tipped his tongue out to lick some drips on his lips. Not water. Wine.

He did not open his eyes right away. He spent a few moments accommodating the pain screaming on his scalp. His legs felt strange and his arms hurt. He tried to move both and could not. He realized they were both tied behind him, and together, bowing his body. Someone had trussed him like a sheep, only backwards.

He sorted through his aching head for where he was, so he might determine if he was in danger.

Then he remembered. Hell, yes, he was in danger.

He opened his eyes to see the end of a pistol mere inches from his head. His gaze traveled up the arm that held it, until he looked into the furious dark eyes of the murderess, Margaret Finley.

Hell.

Minerva added a few more curses under her breath while she held the lamp close to the intruder's face. She had not expected to find Chase Radnor skulking around her home. Had she known it was he, she might have hit him even harder with that bed warmer.

"He looks to be coming to," Beth said. She raised the warmer as if to give another blow.

"Put it down, he is tied now and I have my pistol."

"He looks big. The ropes may not hold him. He may overpower you. I should be ready just in case."

"He will not attack me." More's the pity. She would have justification to shoot him then.

Mr. Radnor had indeed come to. He just did not know it quite yet. His long lashes moved. After a moment he strained against the bonds. Minerva waited for him to accommodate his situation.

Why was he here? For that matter, how had he even found her? London was a big city, and she made it a point to never associate with the kind of people who would be in his circles. Yet here he was, and suddenly her future had become precarious again.

Various reactions assaulted her while she trained her pistol on his harshly handsome face. Fear. Anger. Mostly, however, a surge of the unsettled spirit that had plagued her for over a year once, and that she thought she had banished forever.

Finally those lashes rose. Sapphire eyes focused on her pistol, then his gaze moved up until he looked right into her eyes. He again strained at the ties that bound him. Then the scoundrel smiled.

"Mrs. Finley. How nice to see you again."

Beth sucked in her breath. Her thick body bent so she could dip her capped head closer to the lamp and face. She frowned. "Is that—"

Minerva nodded. Only two people in London knew Minerva Hepplewhite had once been Mrs. Finley. Well, three, counting the man trussed on the floor of her study. That name, and the life that went with it, had been abandoned almost five years ago, when she, Beth, and Beth's son, Jason, had come to London.

"You can untie me," Radnor said. "I never take chances with pistols, and I am not a danger in any case."

"You are an intruder. I think I'll leave you like that while I swear down information against you," Minerva said.

"We both know you will not do that. It would spawn too many questions about you."

"I am not afraid of questions."

"Aren't you? You changed your name, after all."

"Only to keep people from prying."

"Because you wanted to escape what prying would reveal. Now, untie me. I have something important to tell you that will explain why I am here."

She hated how that provoked her curiosity, and also her trepidation. He might tell her that the investigation had been revived. Then again he might reveal that at long last the poacher involved in that accident had been found.

Or he might tell her that he had come to take her to gaol.

"Explain yourself first." She leveled the pistol firmly. "I am not inclined to trust a housebreaker."

He gave one furious tug on the ties behind his back. He narrowed his eyes. "I have come to inform you of something that benefits you significantly."

"What is that?"

"Margaret Finley has inherited some money. A great deal of it."

A Perfect Match

Sabrina Jeffries

*To my parents, who both love the Christmas season so much,
and always made sure we had a good one, even in Thailand.
I hope we have many more Christmases together.*

Chapter 1

Yorkshire
December 1808

The ballroom at Welbourne Place was so crowded that despite the winter weather, ladies' fans were flapping as vigorously as wings of doves in flight. Miss Cassandra Isles sympathized. Even the scent of evergreens in the festive decorations—kissing boughs of mistletoe, rosemary, laurel, and holly—didn't help. If she didn't escape the stuffy room soon, she might scream! But she didn't dare leave until Captain Lionel Malet stopped prowling about in search of her eighteen-year-old cousin, Katherine "Kitty" Nickman.

Cass sighed. On the surface, the captain possessed everything a woman would want in a husband. As the youngest son of a viscount, he had rank and connections. And he certainly was good-looking for his age, with his casually disordered black curls, his blue eyes, and his manly demeanor.

But he still repulsed Cass. Was it his calculating mannerisms? His brittle smiles? The way he admonished Kitty at every turn?

Perhaps it was just *him*, period.

Unfortunately, with Kitty lingering in the retiring room, he was now heading for Cass, probably to probe her for any information he'd been unable to pry out of her and Kitty and Aunt Virginia when he'd brought them here in his carriage.

Once he reached Cass, he barely bowed, as if recognizing her lack of approval. "I see you've already lost your pretty companion."

"I'm sure she'll return shortly. You *were* speaking of Kitty, weren't you?"

"Who else?"

"I have no idea, sir. How many rich women are you courting at present?"

His icy gaze sharpened. "I'm interested in your cousin for herself."

She stared at him. "If you say so."

Ignoring her barbed comment, he glanced about the room. "I hope Miss Nickman hasn't wandered onto the terrace. There are men at this affair who roam the dark, hoping to force a kiss on an unsuspecting maiden."

Men like you? Cass nearly said. His possessiveness worried her. It wasn't as if he and Kitty were betrothed.

"I hope you're not describing yourself," she said. "If you think to gain my cousin by compromising her, that would be foolish."

He stiffened. "You misunderstand the situation, madam. I love Miss Nickman."

Love? She doubted the man even knew the meaning of the word.

Not that Kitty couldn't make men fall in love with her. She was gorgeous, with wheat-blond hair, clear green eyes, and a perfect figure. Indeed, every woman in the room would hate her if she didn't also have an amiable temperament, a big heart, and a winning way with everyone she met.

Then there was her petite figure that made her look like a fragile flower in need of a big strong man to guide her, which, unfortunately, she was. Because she was also a naïve heiress to an enormous fortune. That complicated every courtship.

"If you love her," Cass told the captain, "you can have no objection to waiting a few months before making an offer."

When annoyance flashed in his expression, it reconfirmed her conviction that he merely wanted to get his hands on Kitty's dowry.

But he masked his reaction swiftly enough. "Doesn't every young lady aim to find a husband with all due haste?"

"Not before having her London season. Given the size of Kitty's inheritance, I think—"

"Forgive me, Miss Isles, but what you think doesn't matter as long as her mother approves of me. And I happen to know that she does."

"I beg to differ." When her words seemed to surprise him, she added, "I know my aunt very well—she will never agree to a suitor with nothing to commend him but his connections." Cass *hoped* that was the case, anyway. "She's determined to give her daughter a proper season in London, and you must surely be aware that once she does, Kitty will easily snag a wealthy and titled husband."

Cass wasn't about to tell him that Aunt Virginia was actually dazzled by Captain Malet's rank, his silver tongue, and his dashing uniform. No amount of cautioning her would get her to listen to Cass's opinion of him.

It would be one thing if the captain truly did love Kitty, but Cass didn't believe he did, and she was equally uncertain about Kitty, who'd been secretive about her interest in the man. One moment Kitty was flirting with him, and the next she was disappearing to go Lord knows where.

Until Kitty said unreservedly that she was in love with the captain, Cass had to keep the two apart as much as possible. Cass refused to see her beloved cousin suffer the same heartache Cass had once endured over a gentleman in Bath.

She crossed her fingers behind her back. "My aunt will also bow to my opinion in the matter, as will my cousin. They trust me to look after them."

The captain leaned close. "Ah, but neither will trust you when I mention your spinsterish jealousy over Miss Nickman's success in attracting a potential husband."

A laugh erupted from her. Spinsterish jealousy? Was "spinsterish" even a word?

She ought to reveal her age. Or inform him of her own sizable inheritance. But she meant to make sure that any suitor showing an interest in *her* wanted her only for herself. That was why she was keeping quiet about her dowry for the present and why she'd demanded that her aunt and cousins do the same.

After all, she had plenty of time to marry, and for now she didn't care one jot if everyone in society assumed she was the poor relation. Her late parents had married for love, and so would she. She meant to get Kitty settled in a love match before concentrating on her own happiness. There were to be no fortune hunters for her *or* Kitty.

"Well, sir," she said, "it seems we're at an impasse. So I shall search for my cousin, and you may do whatever you please."

"I'll go with you," he said.

"Into the ladies' retiring room? I think not."

She marched off, annoyed when the man followed her at a discreet distance. Why *was* Kitty taking so long? She'd never been the sort to primp and preen. And when Cass entered the enormous parlor fitted out with comfortable furniture, a mirror, a washstand, and a screen behind which sat a chamber pot, she could find no trace of her.

Cass hadn't seen her in the ballroom either. The captain's comment about the terrace leapt to mind. Lately, Kitty did have a tendency to wander off.

So Cass headed out herself, relieved to find that the captain had disappeared. But once through the French doors, Cass realized that the terrace encircled the house, and sets of stone steps led down to the garden itself. Kitty could be anywhere.

Cass rubbed her arms. She should have brought her shawl. Her aunt had predicted it would snow before the night was out, and Cass began to believe it. The air felt frozen, and it smelled like . . .

Burning tobacco. The scent of a cheroot hit her from somewhere close by. She whirled to see a man leaning against a pillar, watching her from the shadows.

There are men at this affair who roam the dark, hoping to force a kiss on an unsuspecting maiden.

How ridiculous. She would *not* let Captain Malet's remarks strike fear in her. "You might announce yourself, sir, before frightening a lady half to death."

The stranger chuckled. "Do forgive me, madam. That wasn't my intent." He pushed away from the pillar and came into the light from the ballroom. "But I admit to being curious about the lucky fellow you were hoping to meet out here."

He lifted an eyebrow rakishly, rattling her generally impenetrable armor. She couldn't imagine why. Just because he was handsome—with brownish hair, a charmingly crooked smile, and a muscular build—was no reason to let him beneath her defenses. After all, he smoked cheroots, which only proved he wasn't her sort.

Then he dropped his cheroot and stubbed it out with his booted foot, bringing her attention to his attire. He was decidedly *not* dressed for a ball. He wore a many-caped greatcoat over what appeared to be trousers rather than breeches. If she had to guess, she'd say he was dressed for travel. He still had his hat on, for goodness' sake.

Alarm bells rang in her head, and she crossed her arms over her chest. "I'm looking for a lady, actually. She's blond and fair, shorter than I, and is wearing a coquelicot gown with primrose accents. Have you seen her?"

"A coque-what? You might as well tell me the gown is made of cheese. But other than you, no one has come through that door since I arrived."

That explained his travel clothes, although it did *not* explain why he was lurking about out here instead of entering through the front door to be announced. She should probably go back inside. "I see. Then you're of no help to me."

When she placed her hand on the door handle, he put his against the door to keep it shut. "Perhaps you could be of help to *me*. I'm looking for Miss Katherine Nickman."

"Kitty? That's who *I'm* looking for! Do you know her?"

A veil descended over his features. "Not by sight. Might you be willing to introduce us?"

Good Lord. The fortune hunters were coming out of the stonework now. "And who will introduce you to me?" she asked tartly. "That should come first, don't you think?"

His gaze skimmed her form with decided interest. "Since we're already acquainted by virtue of sharing this stretch of terrace, I was hoping we could dispense with formalities."

The droll remark made her smile in spite of herself. "You're very cavalier about introductions, sir."

His eyes gleamed at her. "So are you. If you'll recall, you spoke to me first."

He was flirting with her, of all things. In her role of poor relation, she rarely found herself the object of interest from such a good-looking fellow. "And I begin to think that was a mistake." She cast a critical glance over his attire. "You are obviously not dressed for the occasion."

"Something I'm already regretting." His rumbling voice sent a jolt to her senses, which was utterly unwise.

"Were you even invited to the ball?" she pressed him.

He crossed his impressive arms over his equally impressive chest. "That's a rude question. Were you?"

She laughed outright. "I don't generally push my way into social affairs."

"Why not? You fit in beautifully. Much better than I."

"We've already established that," she said dryly. "Although it hasn't stopped you from lurking about out here like a thief."

He drew himself up with mock pride. "I'll have you know, madam, that I'm only a thief where lovely ladies are concerned." He leaned just close enough to give her a whiff of his bay rum scent. "I do steal the occasional kiss."

A thrill shot down her spine before she squelched it. "Then you should go inside. You'll find plenty of kissing boughs to serve your purpose. Of course, if you were not invited—"

"Can't you vouch for me?" he teased.

She eyed him askance. This mad flirtation had gone on long enough. "Not I. I must find my cousin."

His amusement vanished. "Miss Nickman is your *cousin*?"

"She is. And what is it to you, sir?"

He seemed all business now. "I have an important message for her from her brother."

Cass started. "Douglas?"

"Unless she has another brother," he said sarcastically. "Of course Douglas."

Any friend of Douglas's was a friend of hers and Kitty's, assuming that this man wasn't feigning the connection. A few gentlemen eager to marry a fortune *had* misrepresented themselves to Kitty in the past. "How do you know Douglas?"

"I'm a colonel in his regiment, the Twenty-Fifth Hussars, here on leave of absence." He bowed. "Colonel Lord Heywood Wolfe, at your service."

The floor melted away beneath her feet. This handsome fellow was Douglas's boon companion? Who'd joined him in any foolish escapade, whose witty remarks Douglas had often repeated for effect in his letters, keeping her and Kitty vastly entertained?

If so, then heaven help her. The colonel was even more intriguing in person than on paper. Aside from his droll manner, he towered over her like a hawk over a swallow, though she wasn't short for a woman. And his eyes assessed her with far too much interest. Good Lord.

But what if he was lying? After all, Douglas would surely have written to tell them that his friend was on his way to England. This man could claim to be anyone he wanted. She was alone out here with him, and she'd be wise to proceed with caution.

"Now," he went on, "will you please do me the honor of telling me your name?"

Chapter 2

Heywood had clearly gone about this all wrong. That's what he got for rushing over from the Nickman estate once he'd heard about Malet accompanying the women to Welbourne Place.

Not that Heywood could have entered the ball anyway. Aside from the issue of his travel attire, Malet would immediately know why Heywood was there: to prevent the man from marrying Miss Nickman. Heywood had made a promise to Douglas on that score.

And if, in the process of rescuing Miss Nickman, Heywood ingratiated himself with the young heiress? That wouldn't be bad either. Douglas had already given his blessing to such a marriage, provided that Miss Nickman found Heywood appealing.

Unfortunately, all he'd done so far was put Miss Nickman's cousin on her guard, which he regretted. He would need the cousin in his camp to gain Miss Nickman's approval of the courtship.

Besides that, he liked the cousin. A friendly sort, she had a keen sense of humor and wasn't bad looking either. Although he generally preferred blond women, her light brown hair suited her coloring and she had a peculiar attraction all her own.

She stared back into the ballroom, a frown forming on her smooth brow. He followed her gaze. The crowd seemed to be thinning out, possibly going off to supper. Any minute now the lady would realize the impropriety of their private encounter. Then she would hasten inside and he would lose his opportunity to speak with Miss Nickman.

"Madam—" he began.

"I'll tell you my name if you answer one question, sir." She stared him down. "Where were you and Douglas posted before Portugal?"

Ah. Not just pretty, but smart and cautious. "Hanover. Where we fought a battle at Munkaiser."

When relief showed on her face, he let out a breath. "Dare I hope the interrogation is over?"

"How did you find us?" She smiled thinly. "That's not part of any 'interrogation,' mind you. I'm just curious."

"I followed the directions Douglas gave me to his home, and when I found no one there, the servants told me where you'd all gone."

"Oh. That makes sense."

When she said nothing more, he quipped, "Should I keep calling you 'madam' or do you prefer to be addressed as 'Miss Nickman's cousin'?"

She chuckled. "Forgive me. I'm Miss Cassandra Isles."

Right. Miss Nickman had mentioned Cass Isles in her delightful letters to Douglas. Those letters had made him long to meet Douglas's sister.

"You know," he said mockingly, "I have only your word for it that you're Miss Isles. You *could* be leading me on. So now you must answer a question for me."

She uttered an exasperated laugh. "Of course. Ask me whatever you like. I have no secrets. Indeed, I'm probably the dullest female you'll ever meet."

"Somehow I doubt that." He sifted through the little he remembered about her. "Since Christmas is nearly here, tell me, what's your favorite Christmas dessert?"

"That's easy. Syllabub."

Not the answer he was expecting. "Syllabub is a drink, not a dessert."

She tipped up her chin. "Anything with cream and sugar in it is a dessert."

"Even coffee?"

"Well, not coffee. Unless the coffee is in ice cream."

He couldn't resist teasing her again. "You have a complicated definition of dessert."

"At least I don't call mincemeat pie a dessert." She made a face. "Beef suet, ugh."

"But Christmas isn't Christmas without mincemeat pie."

"Then you're out of luck by coming to our neck of the woods at Christmastide. Everyone around here serves only plum pudding. Which you hate."

He burst into laughter. "And you love. Only two people in England, other than my family, know I hate plum pudding—Miss Nickman and you." He thrust out his hand. "You've met my challenge admirably. It's a pleasure to meet you, Miss Isles."

"Likewise, I'm sure," she said, sounding breathless as she took his proffered hand.

The contact caught him off guard, making him wish she wasn't wearing gloves. That he wasn't either.

God, what was wrong with him? He was a practical man. Fetching as this chit might be, he couldn't allow her to distract him from his purpose. He reluctantly released her hand. "You are not at all how I pictured you. The few times Miss Nickman wrote about her 'older' cousin, I imagined someone . . ."

"Spinsterish?" she asked with a decided edge to her voice.

"That isn't a word."

"Exactly! It's not a word in the least. I'm so pleased that you agree."

"Good," he said, her reaction bewildering him. If he'd learned anything from his own sister, it was that women did *not* like to be considered "spinsterish." "I didn't realize your cousin was describing a woman of your age. Which is . . ."

"I'm twenty-two, sir, and not on the shelf yet."

Younger than he'd thought, given her poise. "You're just old enough to know your own mind and clever enough to question the claims of shabbily dressed strangers who accost you on terraces."

That made her laugh, thank God. "You were privy to those letters?"

"Of course. Douglas is my friend as well as compatriot. We often read our correspondence from home to each other. Surely you and

Miss Nickman did the same. If I remember correctly, you live in the same household."

"Yes, and we're as close as sisters."

"Well, Douglas and I are as close as brothers. Kitty's letters and those of my own family were all that kept us sane during the long weeks between battles."

With a secretive smile, she stared back into the emptying ballroom. "You enjoyed Kitty's letters, did you?"

"Indeed we did. Sometimes laughter is difficult to come by in an armed camp."

"I'm sure that's true, Colonel," she said in a melodious voice.

God help him. That voice would charm thieves.

Remember why you're here.

Right. He should press her again on the subject of her cousin. "Now that we've dispensed with the formalities, would you be so kind as to introduce me to Douglas's sister so that I may pass on her brother's message in person?"

She blinked, as if startled out of some reverie. "Of course. If you'll just follow me inside, we'll go look for her."

"I'd rather not."

"Why?"

Because he didn't want to encounter Malet before he could warn Miss Nickman of the man's true intentions.

Not that he could tell *Miss Isles* that. He wasn't sure where her loyalties lay. "I'm in mourning." For emphasis, he tugged on his black armband. "Joining the ball would be grossly inappropriate."

"Do forgive me, sir. I forgot . . . That is, I temporarily didn't remember . . ." She dragged in a steadying breath. "Please accept my condolences on the recent death of your father."

"Thank you," Heywood said, not sure what more to say. Though he hadn't lived at home in years—hadn't even been able to visit his family for more than brief stretches—he nonetheless felt the loss of his father like the ache of a phantom limb. The idea that Father was beyond his reach plagued him.

Still, he'd seen a great deal of death since Father had bought him a commission in the Hussars at sixteen, so he'd learned how to shove his pain inside his box of memories so he could continue his missions.

"In any case, if you wouldn't mind finding your cousin—" he began.

She colored. "Of course. She can't have gone far. Shall I fetch my aunt as well?"

"If you wish. But the message is primarily for your cousin."

"I see. Well then, I'll just bring Kitty." She cast him a rueful smile. "Aunt Virginia doesn't like being pulled away from the whist table. She gets to play in company so rarely." Miss Isles opened the French doors. "I'll return shortly."

He peered inside, watching as the lady passed the massive hearth with its merrily burning Yule log and then disappeared through a door. Now he could only wait.

There were no stars, and the air felt thick with the promise of snow. He hoped it held off until he spoke with Kitty Nickman and possibly her mother. He very much feared that the women might already have fallen prey to Malet's sly flatteries.

If that was the case, Heywood would lay out what he knew of the man and pray that they trusted his and Douglas's judgment. He felt fairly certain he could at least convince Miss Isles. She seemed sensible enough to recognize, once the facts were presented to her, that Malet was the worst sort of scoundrel.

A murmur of voices below the terrace caught his attention. "When you bring my rig around," a man said, "park it here, below the terrace. The moment I come down these steps with Miss Nickman, you must be ready to leave."

Heywood scowled. Speak of the devil. That was Malet's voice.

"Yes, Captain," said his coachman. "What about her mother and Miss Isles?"

"Don't worry about them. Just make sure you do your part. There's some fellow sniffing around her here, and I'm not taking any chances. I've worked too hard and spent too much blunt trying to gain the chit's affections, only to have some stranger whisk her away."

That confused Heywood. Had Malet seen him somehow? But then why talk as if he didn't know who the "fellow" was?

"Shall I assume we're not returning to the Nickman estate, master?"

"You're correct," Malet said. "But don't worry. You'll be paid amply for transporting me and my fiancée to Gretna Green in record time."

"Thank you, sir."

Fiancée? Gretna Green? Had it progressed as far as that?

Heywood peered over the railing in time to see Malet stalk back into the house and a coachman hurry along the line of carriages parked along the drive until he came to the one that must be Malet's.

Damn it all to hell. Malet and Miss Nickman were eloping. Heywood may have arrived too late. Either that or he was arriving just in time.

Regardless, Douglas would never forgive him if he did not find a way to keep Miss Nickman from marrying this blackguard. So that's what Heywood must do.

It took Cass longer than she'd expected to find Kitty. First she looked for her in the card room. There Aunt Virginia was so intent on winning at whist that she merely waved her hand in a shooing motion when Cass approached her.

Next Cass passed through the supper room, but neither Captain Malet nor Kitty was there, which alarmed her. If that dratted fellow had coaxed Kitty into being alone with him, Cass would have his head! The longer Cass peeked into the other rooms without finding Kitty, the more worried she got.

Then she glimpsed the young woman marching down a hallway and muttering to herself, obviously in a temper—Kitty, who so rarely got angry at anything.

"Are you all right?" Cass asked.

Kitty blinked. "I'm fine. I was just . . . having an argument with a friend."

"Is it anyone I know?"

A panicked expression crossed Kitty's face. "Certainly not. Why *would* you? Know them, I mean."

Kitty was behaving oddly, to be sure. "Where did this argument take place?" Cass demanded.

"In . . . um . . . the retiring room."

"I was just in the retiring room," Cass said. "You weren't there."

Wrapping her arms about her waist, Kitty murmured, "I left

there, and I . . . decided to see what the rest of the manor looked like."

When she followed that outrageous remark with a weak smile, Cass rolled her eyes heavenward. Kitty had always been terrible at lying. Normally, Cass would wait her cousin out until she admitted the truth, but after traipsing up and down Welbourne Place, Cass didn't have the patience for that. And did it really matter who the friend was? Kitty had a number of casual female friends.

"Well," Cass said, "right now I need you to come with me." Taking Kitty by the arm, Cass stalked toward the ballroom. "Colonel Lord Heywood Wolfe is here with an important message from Douglas, so I told him I'd bring you onto the terrace to talk to him."

"Why in heaven's name is he outside?"

While they headed for the terrace doors, Cass explained. But as they neared them, she pulled Kitty to a halt. "Promise me you won't tell him that I too am an heiress."

"Why would that come up in a conversation about a message from Douglas? I mean, it's not as if—" Kitty halted as the significance of Cass's words apparently hit her. "Wait. I thought you *liked* the colonel! You've said it many times—that you think he's as clever as a bear."

"Not a bear, dearest. A fox. Clever as a fox."

Kitty had a tendency to mangle well-known phrases. But she never took offense when anyone corrected her. It was one of her most endearing qualities. Because Kitty was corrected a *lot.*

" 'Bear,' 'fox,' " Kitty said with a wave of her hand. "What difference does it make?"

"Well, foxes are known for being crafty whereas bears—" Cass shook her head. "It doesn't matter. The point is, it's precisely *because* I like him that I don't want you to tell him I'm an heiress."

"Ohhh. Because you want him to marry you for love."

"Exactly." She colored when she realized what she'd said. "Not that he's interested in marrying me. I mean, he barely knows me. I suppose you could say he knows me from the letters, but—"

"Cass!" her cousin said. "I get the point."

"Right. Sorry." Even she acknowledged she had a tendency to go on and on sometimes.

"And you are far too prickly about your inheritance." When

Cass started to protest, Kitty held up her hand. "Not everyone is after you for your fortune, despite what that fellow you fancied in Bath told his friends."

"It's not about him. I'm just not ready to marry yet."

"Hmm," Kitty said, clearly not believing her protest.

Time to change the subject. "By the way, Colonel Lord Heywood mentioned how much your letters entertained him. Apparently Douglas always read them to his friend."

"Of course he did. You write very amusing letters."

"You told me what to say," Cass said. "They're still *your* letters."

Kitty snorted. "You chose all the words and put them into sentences. My telling you to describe our visit to some assembly hardly makes what's written in them mine. All the droll remarks and lovely turns of phrase are yours." Kitty's shoulders drooped. "I suppose we ought to tell the colonel the truth. That I'm stupid."

"Don't say that. You aren't stupid."

"If I weren't, you wouldn't be writing my letters. I get words mixed up all the time, I *hate* reading, Captain Malet chides me for telling stories wrong, and—"

"Don't you *dare* listen to that scoundrel!" Cass looped an arm around her cousin's waist. "He doesn't know anything. You merely have different abilities."

"That's what Mr. Adams always says."

Mr. Adams? Cass examined Kitty's face. How odd that she would mention her mother's solicitor. As a widower with two small children, he seemed like someone beneath Kitty's notice. But he did have a kind heart, and his earnest features were quite handsome.

Still, Kitty had to know that her mother would never countenance such a marriage to a man of trade.

Cass smiled. "Mr. Adams is quite right. You draw well, you sing like an angel, and your needlework is exquisite. You have plenty of qualities men prize in a wife."

Looking glum, Kitty pulled away from her. "Like my fortune."

"And your beauty and kindness and sweet temper. Any man would want to marry you. So I doubt your future husband will be disappointed that you can't pen entertaining missives or tell a good tale."

"But I do so wish I was clever like you." A heavy sigh escaped Kitty. "That's why I'd prefer that Douglas not find out I can't even write him a decent letter." She lifted her gaze to Cass. "Do you think you might promise not to tell the colonel about that? Because he'll surely tell Douglas."

How could Cass resist that sweet, anxious face? "I promise. You keep my secret and I'll keep yours."

It wasn't as if she was likely to see the colonel after tonight, anyway. His family lived all the way over in Lincolnshire, almost forty miles off, and she lived here. Besides, he was only on a leave of absence. He'd be gone back to Portugal by the time she and Kitty even had their season. Then it wouldn't matter what he thought of her letters.

"Now, dearest," Cass told Kitty, "let's go find out what message was so important that Douglas sent his friend to deliver it personally."

But when they went out to the terrace, it was to see the first snowflakes drifting down . . . and no sign of Colonel Lord Heywood.

"Oh, no!" Cass cried. "It's snowing!" And apparently he was gone.

Then his voice came out of the gloom. "It's about time you two showed up. You can both shelter under this." He stripped off his greatcoat, which he handed to Cass, and she draped it over the two of them. "But we can't stay out here," he went on, "or you'll be wet through. My coachman is bringing my carriage around now. We can traverse the drive while we talk."

He led them down the steps and around to where a carriage with a ducal crest pulled up in front of them. The crest reassured Cass that they were safe with him. He would hardly be riding in a ducal carriage, probably his brother's, if he were some fortune-hunting scoundrel.

After they got in, Kitty handed him his greatcoat. "Your equipage is lovely," she said, as soon as they were headed off down the drive. "Ours isn't nearly so roomy." She pointed to the carriage lamps shining through the windows. "And we don't have bright lanterns like these, to be sure."

"I can't take credit for it, I'm afraid. The rig belongs to my brother Sheridan." He uttered a self-deprecating chuckle. "I mean,

His Grace, the newly minted Duke of Armitage. I can't get used to Sheridan's being a duke. I don't think he can either."

"Well, tell your brother that I think it's very fine," Kitty said. "I wouldn't mind traveling anywhere in a coach like this."

"Forgive me, sir," Cass interrupted, "but we must discuss—"

"Right." He pulled a letter out of his pocket. "This is from Douglas."

Cass lifted an eyebrow. "You couldn't just have given it to me to give Kitty?"

"No," he said flatly. "Douglas wanted me to put it into her hands personally so I could explain the contents in more detail as well as answer any questions. Since I was returning to England anyway, I was happy to undertake that mission."

"How intriguing," Cass said as Kitty took it from him. "I'm dying to know what's so important that it constitutes a 'mission.'"

She and Cass read the letter together by the light of the carriage lamps:

Dearest Sister,
My sincerest hope is that this finds you well, and that
you have not yet met Mr. Lionel Malet—or succumbed to
his false blandishments. He is—

"I thought it was *Captain* Malet," Kitty whispered to Cass. "And what does 'blandishments' mean?"

Cass said, "It means 'flatteries' or 'smooth talk.'" Cass shot His Lordship a furtive glance. "And there's no point to whispering. I'm sure Colonel Lord Heywood can hear you perfectly well."

The man smiled faintly. "Please call me Heywood. I feel as if I know you both already through Douglas. And through Miss Nickman's entertaining letters, of course."

Cass winced. It was harder than she'd expected not to be able to acknowledge her authorship of the letters.

"Then you must call us Kitty and Cass," Kitty said with a knowing smile for Cass.

"Kitty!" Cass protested.

"Why not? We know *him* already through letters, too."

Heywood tipped his hat to Kitty. "To answer your question,

Malet was indeed a captain until he was cashiered for 'conduct unbecoming the character of an officer and a gentleman.' "

Kitty leaned up to whisper in Cass's ear, "Even *I* know that's very bad."

Cass nodded. If she remembered correctly, cashiering was when a soldier or officer was stripped of his rank so that he couldn't sell his commission and then was discharged from the army or navy. Thank heaven for Douglas and his sense of responsibility. Kitty might actually heed her brother's warnings about Mr. Malet.

Kitty and Cass continued reading, but the rest merely confirmed what the colonel—Heywood—had said:

> *I am sworn to secrecy on the matter that has destroyed Malet's reputation among those who know him, but I assure you it is a serious charge. He is not the gentleman he appears to be. So avoid him or you may find your own reputation ruined. At the very least, you may be forced to marry a man who will treat you ill.*
>
> *My friend Heywood will answer your questions and make sure that Malet does you no harm. Please show Heywood the utmost courtesy as my emissary.*
>
> *With much affection,*
> *Douglas*

"Well!" Cass sat back. "That is quite a letter. Not that it surprises me one whit. I didn't like Mr. Malet from the first moment I met him."

Kitty gazed out the window. "It seems to me that Douglas is being overly cautious. I mean, why would Mr. Malet fix on *me* to ruin? Or to marry, for that matter? Why not Cass, for example?"

"He's a fortune hunter, Kitty." Cass suppressed a sigh. She should have known Kitty would have trouble keeping her secret. "He doesn't fix on ladies like me, *who have no dowries.* Just ladies like you who do."

Heywood frowned. "It's more than that. Douglas and I are the ones who discovered his perfidy and brought charges against him. In return, he threatened to get back at us by stealing away one of our sisters, both of whom are heiresses."

Cass's stomach sank. How horrible!

"Mr. Malet really said such a thing?" Kitty said, clearly as shocked as Cass.

"He did." Heywood rubbed his jaw. "I'm not worried about my sister, Gwyn—she and my brothers can hold their own against a regiment of Malets. But Douglas feared that you weren't so well protected."

Kitty was no longer paying attention to him. "Where are we going?"

When she leaned forward to gaze out the window, Cass did the same. She saw nothing but dustings of white over dark shapes of bushes and trees—no lights from the house, no flat contours of the lawn.

They were decidedly not making the circuit of the drive at Welbourne Place. What was more, the coach had picked up speed now that it had reached the main road.

Cass stared hard at Heywood. "What are you about, sir? We are leaving Welbourne Place entirely!"

He crossed his arms over his chest. "Forgive me, ladies, but I felt it best to whisk Miss Nickman away from Lionel Malet as quickly as possible and by any means at hand. The man is dangerous."

Kitty just sat there incredulous, but Cass couldn't stay silent in the face of such blatant male arrogance. "You're *abducting* us? *Now?* In the middle of a ball?"

"Not 'abducting.' Rescuing. Malet was planning to carry Kitty off to Gretna Green just as soon as he could get her into his waiting carriage. Tell me, Cass—under the circumstances, what would *you* have done?"

Chapter 3

Heywood figured he was about to get an earful, judging from how Cass was curling her hands into fists in her lap.

"I wouldn't have abducted a couple of ladies, to be sure," Cass bit out.

"I'm not abducting you!" he practically shouted. "I am intervening. Malet gave me no other choice. The conversation I overheard between him and his coachman made it clear that Malet planned on leaving with Kitty as soon as he found her inside and could lure her into his coach. Indeed, Malet's plan was only foiled because I got my equipage into position sooner than he did."

That seemed to stun both ladies into silence. The fact that Kitty in particular said nothing made Heywood even more cautious. Kitty might actually fancy herself in love with Malet. And though the woman might not know much about Malet's true character, it had not escaped Heywood's notice that she hadn't sensed the man's perfidy the way Cass seemed to have.

Then again, Kitty seemed nothing like Cass. Hard to believe they were cousins. In appearance, Kitty reminded Heywood of every debutante he'd ever met—cut from the same cloth as their mothers. With her honey hair and perfect posture, she had that porcelain-doll fragility that most men wanted...as if she might shatter if someone so much as touched her. In his youth, he'd been certain he wanted that sort of woman: the kind he could protect, the kind that made him feel like a man.

But years on the battlefield had taught him to appreciate a woman who could stand at his side and hold her own with the enemy, who had some flesh on her bones and some fire in her eyes. Like Cass, actually.

Except that Kitty had been the one who'd written the letters he had so enjoyed. That was the main reason he was interested in her. Besides, Cass had just made it clear she wasn't an heiress. And he had to marry one if he was to stay in England and nurture the small, run-down estate Grandmother had bequeathed to Father and which he had left to *him*.

Heywood was eager to give it all the work it needed. He was ready to leave the Hussars, to marry and start a family. Despite his success at soldiering, he didn't actually *like* it. The pain and death seemed endless—Britain had been fighting the French for as long as he'd been in the army, which was going on eleven years now.

Besides, it had been Father's wish, not his, that he advance in the Hussars. Now that Father was gone . . . He shook off the pain of that.

Cass released a heavy breath. "So your plan was to abduct Kitty yourself in order to avoid having Mr. Malet abduct Kitty? And I'm merely along for the ride?"

When she put it like that, it did not sound like the best plan he had ever come up with. "Can we please stop calling it an abduction? It's a rescue, an *intervention*. You were with her, so I had to take you both. Besides, I couldn't travel with her alone without ruining her reputation. With two of you, the matter is less critical."

"You think so, do you?" Cass said, clearly irate. "Once my aunt realizes we're gone, she'll enlist people to find us, which in itself will ruin us."

"Yes, exactly!" Kitty cried. "I can't be ruined . . . I just *can't* be! What will Mama say? What will our *friends* say?"

Great. Now Cass was stirring up her cousin's ire. "Your mother won't say anything to anyone until she knows for certain what happened. And I made sure Malet's coachman knew my name, so she'll hear the truth before anyone can alert the other guests."

"And what truth is that?" Cass asked.

"That the two of you are with me. That Douglas sanctioned my intervention. That she has nothing to worry about. I'm sure she'll recognize my name the moment the coachman tells her of it."

Cass rolled her eyes. "Then what's to keep Malet from riding after us once he realizes that you're behind this so-called intervention?"

He ignored her obvious skepticism. "First of all, he won't realize it right away. I gagged his coachman and tied him up. Then I found an unattended carriage near the end of the line and deposited the coachman inside. I figured the last to arrive at the ball would also be the last to leave."

"How quick-thinking of you," Cass said with an arch smile. "Clearly you have experience at kidnapping women."

"Beginner's luck." He refused to correct her yet again on the subject of his *rescuing* Kitty. "My point is it could be hours before the coachman is found. By then we'll be safe at Armitage Hall."

Kitty sat up straight. "You're not taking us to Gretna Green?"

"Of course not. I'm trying to prevent an elopement, not perform one."

"Oh, thank heaven!" the young heiress exclaimed. "Then that's no skin off my back."

Cass murmured, " 'Off my nose,' dearest."

" 'Nose,' 'back,' " Kitty said. "What difference does it make?"

"It makes a big difference, especially when you're using it incorr . . ." Cass paused when she spotted his raised eyebrow. "You're right. It makes no difference."

"No, indeed," Kitty said. "As long as the colonel isn't carrying us off to Gretna Green, I don't care."

Hmm. He was having a hard time reconciling this Kitty Nickman with the writer of all those entertaining letters. But perhaps she required a pen to be witty.

"Glad you approve," he said.

"Well, *I* don't approve, Colonel," Cass put in. "Why didn't you just give us Douglas's letter and then threaten to trounce Mr. Malet if he came near us again?"

"Because I know how seductive Malet can be. And I assumed

Malet was having his carriage brought around because he'd already gained her cooperation."

Kitty huffed out a breath. "He had *not*, I assure you. I wasn't party to any elopement plans he spun on his own."

"He called you his fiancée," Heywood pointed out.

"Fiancée!" Cass glanced at her cousin. "You agreed to marry him?"

"Of course not. Mr. Malet is quite mistaken." Kitty fiddled with her skirts. "I don't know why he would say such a thing."

When Heywood snorted, Cass tipped up her chin. "If Kitty says Mr. Malet mistook her interest, then he did. That wouldn't surprise me. The man is a snake in the grass."

"I thought it was 'snake in the woods,'" Kitty said.

"No, dearest," Cass said, avoiding his gaze.

"But snakes are bad no matter where they are," Kitty persisted.

"Excellent point," Cass said with a thin smile.

Something was odd here. The woman who'd written the letters he'd admired should have known such common turns of phrase.

"Anyway," Heywood said, "whether in woods or in grass, his snakelike nature is precisely why I had to act quickly. And it sounded as if Kitty had given him reason to believe she would welcome the abduction—"

"Don't be ridiculous," Kitty said warily. "No one *wants* to be abducted."

"Well, something must have encouraged him to act," Heywood said.

Silence fell on the carriage. Then he heard a distinctly unladylike oath. It must be coming from Cass. Kitty didn't seem the sort to make oaths.

"I know what encouraged him," Cass said. "Just this evening, I told him I'd oppose any attempt he made to marry Kitty, and that Aunt Virginia and Kitty would heed me. Perhaps that pushed him into taking reckless action."

Heywood crossed his arms over his chest. "Or perhaps Kitty had already agreed to run away with him."

"I told you, that's absurd!" Kitty cried.

"Sadly, I don't believe you." He fixed her with a hard look. "I know how convincing Malet can be with a lady."

"Oh?" Cass said. "Do you often come behind him to clean up his messes?"

"Often enough to recognize when he's about to create another one," he snapped. "With your cousin, who is clearly hiding something."

"You are a very rude fellow," Kitty said stoutly.

"And to think that I liked you." Cass sniffed. "You're not the man I thought you were."

"A man of action? A soldier always prepared to battle the enemy?"

"An arrogant lord."

He cast her a dry smile. "I *am* a duke's son and a colonel. I'm entitled to a certain degree of arrogance, don't you think?"

"And how does that characteristic separate you from Malet?" Cass asked.

The accusation grated on him. "My intentions are good. His are not."

"How can you be sure?" Kitty asked.

"I know him and his antics," Heywood said. "Trust me."

Cass shot him a long look. "All right, I'll concede that, but still you could have consulted us or at least shown Douglas's letter to my aunt."

He raised an eyebrow. "You said yourself that she 'doesn't like being pulled away from the whist table.' The matter was urgent. I couldn't wait for her cooperation."

"He has a point, Cass," Kitty said. "Mama likes Mr. Malet. She would probably have ignored your warnings."

"I realize that!" Cass retorted. "Why do you think I felt the need to frighten the man off? I had no idea his response would be to attempt a kidnapping."

Heywood kept his gaze on Kitty. While protesting the idea that she'd encouraged Malet she acted as if she wished to give the man the benefit of a doubt. Something wasn't right in her reactions, if only he could put his finger on it.

Cass, however, was perfectly straightforward—she detested Malet. Heywood felt an odd relief that Cass wasn't the kind of woman to fall for that arse.

Not that it mattered, since Malet wouldn't dare to treat her as he had Valeria in Portugal, anyway. He'd only preyed on Valeria because she'd had no family to defend her. But Kitty had Douglas and her aunt and probably innumerable other relations.

They rode a long while in silence . . . until the sound of snoring filled the carriage. It came from Kitty, the delicate debutante.

"My cousin is quite tired," Cass said, her tone apologetic.

"I can tell."

That made Cass bristle. "You have the audacity to be snide that Kitty is exhausted when you're whisking us off against our will?"

Heywood wished he could see her better. Because he suspected that Cass in a temper would be quite a sight to behold—all passion and storm and biting wit. No doubt she was fighting to keep that storm at bay, to be a lady.

What was she like when she was *not* being a lady?

He shook off that line of thought, or tried to. What the devil was wrong with him? Given his circumstances, his attraction to Cass didn't matter. He must concentrate his efforts on Kitty. Yet he couldn't keep from asking, "Why did you say earlier, 'And to think that I liked you'? You hardly know me."

Rubbing condensation from a portion of the window, she stared out. "I-I knew you from your letters."

"The ones Kitty read to you."

"We share everything," she said warily.

"Then tell me, how does Kitty really feel about Malet?"

For a moment, Kitty's snoring seemed to diminish, but perhaps he only imagined it.

"I wish I knew," Cass said. "But she doesn't confide in me about him. Or about any man, really."

"So why did you say you never liked him? Did he ever try to court you?"

"Don't be ridiculous. I'm not the sort of woman Mr. Malet notices."

"Then he's a fool."

Damn. He hadn't meant to say that. He wished they could escape the stagnant air of the carriage, to where the frosty temperatures could clear his mind.

A long silence ensued. She gazed out the window, and the glow of moonlight on snow turned her profile into a study in alabaster and ivory.

Alabaster and ivory . . . what maudlin nonsense. What was next, the sun turning her profile into fire opals and rubies? It was Kitty he should be gazing at, if he meant to live up to his responsibilities. But his eyes stayed on Cass's silhouette.

"Anyway," she said after a moment, "it wouldn't matter if he *was* interested in me. I'd never choose him."

"I'm glad to hear it. A woman of your caliber would be wasted on Malet."

Judging from her sharp intake of breath, that was another remark he should not have made. But he wouldn't take it back.

She cleared her throat. "Is your family at Armitage Hall?"

"My mother, brother, and sister are, at the very least. So you needn't worry about you and Kitty not being properly chaperoned."

"Thank you. I wouldn't want to see Kitty ruined."

He stared hard at Cass. "You're not worried about your own ruin?"

"I learned long ago how to keep myself out of the line of fire."

Her uneasy laugh gave him pause. "Interesting choice of words."

She shrugged. "I'm a soldier's cousin. Besides, no one cares enough about a poor relation to attempt her ruin." Her eyes glimmered in the dark. "Even you, sir."

That told him all he needed to know. Cass wasn't nearly as immune to him as she pretended. It shouldn't affect him, but it did. Because he wasn't remotely immune to *her*.

Damnation. She was a complication he did not need.

She folded her hands at her waist. "At least we don't have to worry about Mr. Malet for the moment," she said in a throaty voice.

"What do you mean?"

She nodded toward the window. "The weather outside is frightful. If he doesn't depart until later, he'll have trouble following us."

Heywood frowned as he looked out. "Or even leaving Welbourne Place at all. It's a good thing we're headed south."

"Indeed it is," she said. "Though if we don't reach Armitage Hall before long, we may yet find ourselves stranded on the road."

"I doubt it. Let it snow. The horses are equipped with frost nails, and the estate isn't far. Besides, Malet thinks I headed north to Gretna Green, so he'll go in that direction first."

"Why on earth would he think that?"

"Because that's what I told his coachman I was doing. I figured it would buy us some time before we have to deal with the man again. The weather will be far worse up north. And when he finally does show up at my brother's estate, we'll be ready for him."

"That's assuming your mother will give refuge to two unannounced and unmarried ladies in our situation."

He'd already considered that. "You can trust me to handle my mother's questions to our mutual satisfaction."

Cass tipped up her chin. "In other words, you intend to lie."

"Would you rather I reveal all to Mother and risk being overheard by our servants? I've already had to buy our coachman's silence—the fewer people who know the truth, the better. Once the gossip gets out, you'll never repair the damage to your reputations."

A heavy sigh escaped her. "In any case, I'm more worried about my aunt. I hate to think of her frantic over not knowing why Kitty and I have disappeared."

"That will teach her to pay her daughter more mind. If I had not stepped in when I did, Malet would be off with Kitty and *you* and your aunt both would be frantic to know what had happened to her."

"I realize that." She yawned, quickly covering it with her hand. "Still, I don't approve of your high-handed methods for forcing the issue. Nor, I suspect, would your mother if she knew of them."

"Feel free to tell her. There's no going back for us now. The road to your home will already be impassable. We have no choice but to take shelter at Armitage Hall until the snow melts. Look, why don't you stop worrying and try to sleep a little?" He grinned at her. "I swear I won't ravish you or Kitty until we reach Armitage Hall."

She glared at him. "That isn't remotely amusing."

"I suppose not, under the circumstances," he drawled.

A big yawn escaped her. "My goodness. Clearly I shouldn't have had that last glass of negus at the ball."

If he remembered correctly, negus was made of watered-down

port with lemon juice and sugar. Who in God's creation got drunk on that?

Apparently Cass did.

He chuckled. "No matter." Covering her and Kitty with his greatcoat, he murmured, "Just sleep. It will be a few hours before we arrive."

She laid her head against the squabs. It wasn't long before he could hear her even breaths between Kitty's snores.

He shook his head. The two women were so different. Kitty, on the one hand, was as insubstantial as champagne. Hard to believe she could have written all those clever and witty letters.

Cass, on the other hand, was as bracing as brandy, an interesting woman he couldn't help liking.

He sighed. A pity she had no money. If he couldn't marry an heiress whose dowry would help him save the estate his father had left him, he'd have to sell it for a song, then continue in the army for however long it took him to make enough to support a family.

Those were the simple facts. He could not afford to marry for love.

Chapter 4

When the carriage turned onto the gravel drive, Cass awoke. Her foggy brain struggled to take in where she was and why she and Kitty were covered with a voluminous greatcoat that smelled of cheroots and bay rum.

Then Heywood said, "We're here," and everything came flooding back. They'd been abducted by the only man who'd ever really interested Cass, at least on paper.

And apparently he'd carried them off to fairyland, because the snow-dusted mansion at the end of the drive bore all the marks of an enchanted castle. Twice as large as Welbourne Place and probably four times as large as Aunt Virginia's manor, it had turrets and towers crowned with cupolas and windows that reflected the waning moon in ever-changing slices of light. Good heavens.

As soon as the coach halted in front of a massive ornamental door, Kitty jolted up in her seat. "Where are we? What are we doing? What's wrong?"

When Heywood chuckled, Cass rolled her eyes at him and took Kitty's hand. "Nothing's wrong, dearest. We've merely arrived at Armitage Hall."

Kitty blinked twice, then looked out. "Oh. I see."

A footman had already come running out to put the step down

and open the carriage door. Heywood reached under his seat and handed them pattens to buckle around their ballroom slippers, thus protecting them from the snow.

"How considerate!" Kitty exclaimed.

"And fortuitous," Cass added, eyeing Heywood closely.

"My sister and mother use them regularly. That's why they're always in the coach." He climbed down and turned to help each of the ladies out in turn. "Truly, Cass, you seem to be suspicious by nature."

"She *is*," Kitty said. "Let's not beat around the brush—Cass always assumes the worst about gentlemen."

Cass threw her shoulders back. "Are we going to stand out here in the cold discussing my faults or are we heading inside where it's warm?"

With a laugh, he offered each lady an arm. "Shall we?"

The carriage pulled away, and Cass glanced back toward the drive. She caught her breath to see the snow already coming down in sheets of white. "It appears we made it here in the nick of time. It doesn't show signs of stopping."

"Yes." His rumbling voice resonated clear to her toes. "We should be cut off from Malet for a few days at least."

Thank goodness. Perhaps Mr. Malet would *finally* realize he'd picked the wrong heiress to intimidate.

They went inside. Despite the late hour, a woman in her fifties dressed in a nightgown and wrapper descended the stairs. Her graying red hair fell to her waist and she was closer to Kitty's height than Heywood's, but other than that, she and Heywood bore a decided resemblance. It was in the shape of her jaw, her high cheekbones, and her aquiline nose. So this pretty woman must be Heywood's mother.

"My goodness, what have we here?" she asked, taking in Cass and Kitty with a curious gaze as Heywood gave the footman his greatcoat and hat. "I heard the carriage drive up in front and couldn't believe you would return from your visit to Douglas's relations in such bad weather."

"I'm glad I did. These are two of the ladies I went to visit. On my way there I found their coach bogged down in the snow as they returned from a ball. The weather was already much worse there than it is here, so I dared not go farther north to take them home or else risk all of us becoming stranded."

Cass barely resisted the urge to roll her eyes at the outrageous untruths, but his mother merely murmured, "How very wise of you."

"I dropped their coachman off at the nearest inn and brought the ladies here. I didn't think they should be left alone at an inn, and it wasn't entirely proper for me to remain there with them. I hope you don't mind."

His mother raised an eyebrow at him. "You know I don't, though I suspect there's more to this story than you're saying."

"Would I lie to you, Mother?" he asked, cool as the snow they'd tracked in.

"If it kept you from getting into trouble? Absolutely." She swept a weary hand over her face. "But let's delay this discussion until tomorrow. I'm sure the ladies would like a hot cup of tea and a soft bed right now. So, be a dear and introduce me."

Cass tried not to laugh as Heywood, suitably admonished, did so.

When he was done, Cass said, "We're sorry to drag you from your bed so late, Your Grace."

"Nonsense. I love having guests, even when my son has come by them in a most unconventional fashion."

Cass had to bite her tongue to keep from informing his mother just *how* unconventional a fashion it had been. But Heywood was right—it would serve no purpose to let his mother in on the secret.

Just then the butler stumbled in, still wearing his nightcap. "There you are, Mr. Fox," the duchess said. She conferred with him a few moments in hushed tones.

As he hurried off, she faced them all with a smile. "It's settled. We're putting Kitty in my son Thornstock's bedchamber and Cass in my son Greycourt's old one. Neither Thorn nor Grey is returning from town until Christmas Eve, and I was planning to put Grey and his new wife in a bigger room upon their return, anyway. Thorn can take one of the other rooms. He's not picky about such things."

"If it helps matters," Cass said, "Kitty and I don't mind sharing a bedchamber or even a bed."

"Nonsense," the duchess said, most firmly. "We want you to be comfortable in case you have to stay through Christmas."

Kitty's face showed her chagrin. "Begging your pardon, Your Grace, but I hope we don't impose upon you as long as all *that*."

"It's no imposition, I assure you, though I do understand. There's no place like home for the holidays." The duchess patted Kitty's hand kindly before turning to Cass. "Fox is fetching the maids to make fires in your rooms and put fresh linens on the beds as well as help you change your clothes. I can loan both of you nightdresses and all the gowns, reticules, et cetera, that you might need. Since Gwyn and I are still in mourning, we aren't using much of our wardrobes at present."

"We'd be most grateful for anything you could provide, Your Grace," Cass said. "As you might imagine, we came here with only the gowns on our backs."

The duchess cast her son a look of pure mischief. "Yes, how odd that you ladies left a ball with no cloaks or capes or any sort of protection from the weather."

"That's my fault," Heywood said blandly. "We were in such a hurry to outrun the storm that the ladies forgot their cloaks in the stranded carriage."

Cass eyed him askance. The fellow lied with amazing aplomb.

But apparently he couldn't slide just any old tale past his mother, for she turned to stare at Cass. "Is that really what happened, my dear?"

"Oh, yes, Your Grace," she gushed, "we were *so* overcome with gratitude at the sight of your courageous son rushing to save us from certain death that we quite forgot our wits. We left everything behind in the coach—our reticules, our cloaks . . . our senses—in our eagerness to be rescued by our very own knight in shining armor."

To Cass's surprise, the duchess burst into laughter. "More like a knight in tarnished armor, knowing my son."

"Good God, Mother," Heywood grumbled.

"Oh, dear, am I embarrassing you?" his mother said with what sounded a great deal like glee. "I didn't think anything shamed you, Son. Before you became a colonel, you were, shall we say, as eager as your older brothers to sow your wild oats. Though it's been a few years since that was the case."

"At least you acknowledge that." Heywood arched an eyebrow. "And in my defense, Cass has a tendency to exaggerate."

"She does indeed, sir," Kitty said brightly. "How did you know?"

"I'm good at deducing things," he said, but he kept his gaze on Cass, as if trying to figure her out.

Which made her uncomfortable. Or perhaps it was just her inability to breathe around him that was making her uncomfortable.

"In any case," the duchess said, "please excuse our havey-cavey household. We've been short of staff for some time. So I'll have to take Kitty up to Thorn's room myself." She nodded to her son. "Would you mind showing Cass the way to Grey's bedchamber? The maid should already be there."

"Of course," Heywood said, with a furtive glance at Cass.

While Cass was still trying to read his look, the duchess said, "Thank you, Son. I'll have Fox send someone up with tea as soon as it's ready." She held out her hand to Kitty. "Now, come, my dear, let's go to your room before you fall asleep on your feet."

But Kitty was engrossed in observing Heywood and Cass. "You're standing under the kissing bough," she pointed out. "You know what *that* means."

Heywood looked up and smiled. "I do indeed." Then before Cass could so much as think, he bent to press a kiss to her lips.

It was perfunctory and chaste, meant to appease their audience. Yet it sent a frisson of excitement down her spine. And when she drew back to stare into his face, she realized he'd had a similar reaction to that brief contact, because his eyes glinted with something that looked like desire.

Nonsense. She must be imagining things. A duke's son could have his pick of the ladies in society; he'd hardly be interested in a gentlewoman of no rank like her.

The duchess was watching them now with interest. When Heywood cleared his throat, the woman quickly turned back to Kitty. "I'll see you in the morning," she said to Cass and Heywood as she ushered Kitty up the stairs.

Heywood bowed to Cass. "After you, madam. Grey's room is upstairs, too, but on the floor above Thorn's bedroom."

They followed the duchess and Kitty up.

Feeling the silence weigh on her, Cass said, "I notice that your mother takes seriously the custom of wrapping greens around the banister rails for Christmas."

"My mother takes seriously any sort of Christmas celebration. That comes from having lived for nearly thirty years in Prussia, where they decorate large fir trees for the holiday. Father was ambassador there, you see, so we've become accustomed to having a household full of greenery during the season."

"Including the fir trees?"

He nodded. "The British don't practice the custom, but I'm told that Queen Charlotte always has one in the palace."

"How very interesting."

"You have no idea. At some point, Mother will surely have us making the tiny gifts that go on the tree. Since none of us have children yet, Mother invited the servants to bring theirs for Boxing Day, and she's making sure there's a gift on the tree for each child."

"Oh, how kind of your mother. That sounds lovely."

As they ascended the next flight, Heywood said, "It's a great deal of work. This place is massive, with plenty of rooms. Mother keeps most of them closed up, but the ones that are open she decorates with sprays of holly at the very least." He looked at Cass. "Incidentally, Gwyn's room is up here, too, so you'll have female company."

"Gwyn is your sister, right?" she asked, hoping that idle conversation would keep her mind off their brief kiss.

"Half sister. She and Thorn are twins by Mother's previous husband, whose death enabled my father to court and marry our mother. Poor Gwyn and Thorn were left fatherless before they were even born. And Grey, whose father was married to Mother before the twins' father, was left fatherless at a year old. So my father was the only father any of us ever knew."

"And now he's gone, too. Your poor mother, to be widowed three times."

He slanted another glance at her. "Do I remember correctly that you lost both your father *and* your mother when you were young, which is how you ended up living with your aunt and cousin?"

"Yes. My parents died in a fire when I was nine. My aunt and uncle took me in without hesitation and looked after me from then on. So Kitty is more like a sister to me than a cousin."

"And you'd do anything to protect her," he said.

"Of course."

They'd reached the next floor. He led her down a dimly lit hallway, then paused outside a closed door. They could hear noise from inside.

"The maid is still setting your room to rights." He leaned against the wall. "We should let her finish."

"Finish what?" she said archly. "Unpacking my nonexistent trunk and setting out my nonexistent clothes for tomorrow? I can handle that myself—I'm quite accomplished at managing imaginary tasks."

Amusement glinted in his eyes. "But surely you wouldn't want to change your own linens or build your own fire if you didn't have to. And by the way, thank you for not telling my mother what was really going on."

"There was no point." She smirked at him. "Besides, I suspect she will get the truth out of Kitty before my cousin's head even hits the pillow. Kitty is the worst liar I know."

"I suppose that speaks well of her character."

"It does. Kitty also has the best *character* of anyone I know."

He searched her face. "Better than you?"

"Oh, yes. I'm much too cynical," she said lightly. "While Kitty thinks well of everybody until they prove themselves to be bad, I think well of nobody until they prove themselves to be good. It's my greatest fault."

"I knew it!" he said, startling her.

"That it's my greatest fault?"

"That you were the one who actually *wrote* all those letters to Douglas."

Oh, no. She scrambled to formulate an answer. "I-I have no idea what you mean." She stifled a groan. What a brilliant response. She would have to do better than *that*.

"Don't be coy," he said. "We both know your cousin could never manage such deft prose."

She wished she could revel in the compliment, but she still hoped to keep her promise to Kitty. "Why would you assume that?"

"Because in one of your missives to Douglas you used the same line about how you—or rather, you pretending to be Kitty—thought well of everybody until they proved themselves to be bad, et cetera, et cetera."

Oh, dear. He remembered that? She didn't know whether to be alarmed or flattered. "I was merely recalling what Kitty originally wrote."

"I doubt that. Between the two of you, you're the more clever by far. I daresay Kitty would never come up with such a bon mot, much less write it."

A pox on him. Why must he be so observant? Kitty was going to be *terribly* hurt that Cass hadn't kept their secret well enough to fool him. "How can you know that about my cousin? You just met her. You just met *me*, for that matter."

"True, but I've seen enough to notice the differences between you. So why don't you admit it? Kitty's letters to Douglas were really your words. Your tales. Your witticisms and observations." He loomed over her now, his face darkening. "And all the years I was imagining Douglas's sister, Kitty, as being so sharp and interesting, it was really *you* I was thinking of."

She swallowed hard. He sounded angry, though she couldn't think why he would be. "Does it matter?"

"Of course it matters! Until I met you, I had no interest in Miss Isles . . . only in Miss Nickman, the lady who wrote fascinating letters. And now you tell me that the woman who intrigued me was *you*?"

His words made her heart clamor in her chest, which was pure madness. "I . . . The writer of the letters intrigues you?"

"Can you really be that oblivious?" He caught her chin in his hand. "Of course she does. And now I know why."

"Why?"

His eyes shone, even in the dim light of the hallway. He kissed her then, not as he had under the mistletoe, but as she'd always imagined a husband kissing her . . . with a warmth that enveloped her and made her want more.

When he broke it off, his hungry expression made her shiver deliciously.

"That's why," he bit out. "Because of this . . . this *attraction* between us."

He kissed her again, hot and hard, and she discovered there was so much more to kissing than she'd *ever* imagined. His mouth not only covered hers but parted her lips so he could slip his tongue inside.

Oh. Good. Lord. The feeling was beyond *anything*. Especially when he began to court her mouth with his tongue, sliding it in and out in silken strokes that made desire pool in her belly.

Eager for more, she looped her arms about his neck and pressed into him. He took that for what it truly was, an invitation to insanity, and pushed her against the door so he could kiss her with abject abandon, his hands roaming the sides of her and his body flush against hers as if he wished to absorb her into him.

She understood, since she wished the same. No kisses she'd ever had were so all-consuming—the few pecks on her lips by suitors dulled in comparison. He managed to convey such exquisite intensity that it made her ache and want and need anything he would give her. *Everything* he would give her.

All too soon he dragged his mouth from hers to stare down into her eyes. "Admit it, you wrote those letters. I already know the answer, but I want to hear you say it."

Still trembling from the force of his kisses, she murmured, "Of course I wrote them."

"I knew it," he said, sounding fierce in his satisfaction.

She would have made some hot retort, but then he bent to kiss her again, blotting out her thoughts about anything but the taste of him and how masterfully he held her. He was conquering her like the bold officer he was, and she wasn't even trying to resist.

Lord save her.

Heywood realized what he was doing was wrong. Even knowing that Cass had written the letters didn't change that. Kitty was the one he needed to court, so the last thing he should be doing was kissing Cass.

Then why couldn't he stop?

Because her lips made him ache and burn. Because he'd spent years wondering about the woman who'd made him laugh countless times. The woman he had thought was Kitty. But it had been Cass all along. Now, despite the late hour, he wanted to keep on kissing her. He didn't care why. He just wanted to explore every inch of her luscious mouth, to revel in its sweet taste, to soak in her scent—something flowery that made him harden.

Or perhaps his reaction was fueled by the sensation of her soft body against his. . . . Damn, but it felt amazing.

He tugged on her lower lip with his teeth and relished the moan she uttered.

"We shouldn't be doing this," she whispered.

"You're right. And yet I don't want to stop. Do you?" He went back in for more, wishing he could kiss her for hours.

Suddenly, the door behind her was opening. She pushed him away, and he backed up to allow the door to open.

He was still fighting for control over his impulses when one of the maids peeked out. "Beg pardon, my lord," she mumbled, her face reddening. "I-I wasn't sure if the young miss was downstairs or—"

"I'm here." Cass smiled soothingly at the maid. "His Lordship was just telling me about the Christmas traditions of the household."

"Ohh!" The maid's face brightened. "It sounds as if it will be very lovely, Miss Isles. The family brought back some interesting Prussian customs. You will enjoy your holiday here, I'm sure."

"So our customs aren't too foreign for you?" Heywood asked curtly, frustrated at having his interlude with Cass interrupted.

"Oh, no, my lord. I mean, we haven't had a chance to do the Christmas part of it yet on account of your family not living here a year ago and being in mourning for your father this year, God rest his soul. But with your brother and mother in charge, it should still be very nice. Or so the duchess promised."

"Then I know it will be so." He smoothed his features into nonchalance. "Now, if you would give us a moment, I have a few more things I must tell Miss Isles."

"Of course, my lord." The maid retreated into the room, although he noticed she didn't close the door.

"In the morning," he told Cass, keeping his voice low, "I want to hear all about how you came to be writing letters to Douglas while pretending to be Kitty."

"You are very nosy," she said with a hint of rebellion. "And what business is it of yours, anyway?"

"As Douglas's closest friend, at the very least I should be looking out for his interests," he said. "Am I right that he had no idea?"

"Of course he didn't. Nor do I see why that requires you to be 'looking out for his interests.' "

"Because knowing how sisters behave with their brothers, I assume you two were pulling the wool over his eyes all these years as some grand joke."

"Don't be absurd. We would never play a 'grand joke' on Douglas when he's off fighting for his country." She crossed her arms over her bosom. Her very attractive bosom. "I suppose you're just angry that *you* were fooled, too. But we didn't know you had anything to do with it, or perhaps we wouldn't have continued it for so long. In fact, I'd greatly appreciate it if you would keep our subterfuge secret now, too. And not tell Kitty that I revealed it to you. I promised her I wouldn't."

"Why?"

"I can't discuss it tonight." She looked back at the maid and lowered her voice. "I'm exhausted, and thanks to a certain individual, I won't even get to sleep in my own bed. So I hope you'll forgive me, my lord, if I retire."

"Of course, my lady," he said, matching her tone as he made an exaggerated bow. "By all means."

A ghost of a smile crossed her lips before she squelched it. "Thank you." Then she curtseyed and went into the bedchamber, closing the door behind her.

He stood frozen a long moment, shaking his head. Never had he met a more infuriating female. Or a more fascinating one.

Cursing himself for that unwise thought, he marched downstairs to his own bedchamber. Bad enough that the woman he desired—the one with smoky gray eyes and golden-brown curls escaping her hairpins—was the one who wasn't an heiress. But now that he'd let himself get carried away kissing Cass, he would have a hard time settling for Kitty.

He would have to start to put some distance between himself and Cass. And start focusing on Kitty. He would do that tomorrow.

Too bad he couldn't stop thinking about those kisses.

Chapter 5

Cass awoke very late, no surprise there. With a certain gentleman's kisses filling one's head, it was hard to fall asleep. By the time she'd slipped into slumber, it had been near dawn. Now she felt like a slugabed.

All of a sudden, she sensed someone watching her. She turned her head to the door and saw Kitty peeking around the corner of it.

"Oh, thank heavens you're finally awake!" Kitty cried. "I thought you were going to sleep all day. I've looked in on you half a dozen times at least!"

Cass sighed. There were days when her cousin's boundless energy wore on her. This was one of those days.

She rolled over to put her back to the door. "Go away," she mumbled.

"Don't mind her," Kitty said. "She's always grumpy in the morning. She doesn't mean it. Come on in."

The realization that Kitty was talking to someone else made Cass bolt upright in the bed and catch the covers up to her neck. What the devil?

Then, with a mixture of disappointment and relief, she realized the person Kitty was ushering in wasn't Heywood but a young woman holding a breakfast tray. Of course it was—even Kitty wouldn't be so foolish as to usher a *man* into Cass's bedchamber. And Cass wasn't disappointed that the person wasn't Heywood. Not in the least.

Liar.

Kitty plopped down on the end of the bed. "Gwyn, this is Cass. Cass, this is Gwyn, Heywood's half sister."

She'd already guessed that. Gwyn was a younger version of her mother, only taller. And with green eyes instead of blue. But she had the same jaw as her mother and Heywood, the same crooked smile, and the same nose.

Gwyn was gazing on Cass with a bemused expression. "Lovely to meet you. I would apologize for having been party to your cousin's waking you from your slumber except that Kitty has spent the past two hours singing your praises and making me positively eager to meet you."

"Kitty has a tendency to gush about the people she loves," Cass said. "Don't get her started on her brother, Douglas."

"Too late," Gwyn said with a smile. "But we already knew about Douglas, since Heywood sings his praises, too."

Cass would have remarked on that if not for the welcome aroma that had captured her attention. "You wouldn't by any chance have coffee on that tray, would you?"

"I would, indeed," Gwyn said as she set the tray on the table next to the bed. "Kitty made it clear that you prefer coffee to tea. Just like Heywood, as a matter of fact, although he claims that his preference comes from serving in the army for so many years. You aren't by any chance a secret member of the Twenty-Fifth Hussars, are you?"

Cass laughed as she poured a cup and then added cream. "No." She could see she was going to like Gwyn. "And if I were, I wouldn't admit it. How could it remain secret otherwise?"

Gwyn chuckled, but Kitty was not amused. "Hurry up and eat your breakfast," she said. "Heywood has invited us to go dashing through the snow in a one-horse open sleigh!"

"Where on earth is Heywood getting a sleigh?" Cass asked.

"Papa brought ours from Prussia," Gwyn explained as Cass ate a slice of buttered toast and sipped coffee. "Sleighs are common there, so Mama tried to talk him out of bringing it here by pointing out that it never gets cold enough in England to use one. But he swore that Lincolnshire had plenty of winter weather." She gestured to the window. "Apparently he was right."

Cass took her coffee over to the window so she could look out. "Heavens," she whispered. "That's quite a wonderland of snow, isn't it? Almost as much as we get farther north."

"Yes," Kitty said, her voice trembling, "so we can't go home anytime soon. It's quite concerning." Then she brightened. "But it's lovely weather for a sleigh ride together with you. So get dressed."

"In what? My ball gown and dancing slippers?" Cass asked, though she too would love a ride in a sleigh.

"No need to worry about that," Gwyn said. "Mama and I have pulled together some clothes for you two, since we've pretty much got both heights covered. And if neither of you shares our shoe sizes, we'll borrow boots from a servant who does."

With that, Cass and Kitty had two maids trooping in and out, bringing riding habits and walking gowns and whatever the well-dressed lady might need for a jaunt outdoors.

Before long, Cass, Gwyn, and Kitty were dressed in riding habits as they headed downstairs to the coat closet to find warm outer garments. As soon as they'd chosen cloaks and scarves, they were joined by Heywood and his brother Sheridan, the Duke of Armitage. Cass would have known the duke anywhere since he was a thinner, more serious version of Heywood, with greener eyes and browner hair. Heywood performed the introductions, though it seemed to Cass that the duke was too distracted to pay them much mind.

Heywood, however, seemed cheerful, and he *looked* quite different in daylight. Now she could see that his brown hair was actually sun streaked and, like his tanned skin, spoke to his long sojourn in Portugal. Last night it had also been too dim, even in Armitage Hall, to see that his eyes were of a hazel so warm it mirrored his smile.

So warm that it made her heart race, which couldn't possibly be healthy.

"I trust that you ladies slept well?" Heywood asked, though he was staring right at *her*, turning her insides to mush.

Before she could answer, Sheridan snorted. "I'm not sure how *anyone* sleeps well during an abduction."

Her gaze narrowed in on Kitty, who blushed. "I-I know we weren't supposed to say anything, but I was tired and the duchess was so kind. . . ."

Heywood gave a rueful shake of his head. "Turns out you were right, Cass. Mother got the truth out of her. This morning the entire family threatened me with bodily harm if either of you finds yourself embroiled in scandal as a result of my actions."

"But they know the situation, right?" Cass asked, unaccountably disturbed at the idea of his family criticizing him.

"We do," Sheridan put in. "And we're more than happy to support the tale that you and your cousin were coming home from the ball when you were caught in the snowstorm." He stared at his brother. "Are you *certain* Malet won't ruin their reputations by revealing the truth?"

"Not until he's sure he's lost any chance with Kitty. And since he knows by now that I took them, he also knows that I will tear him apart publicly if he even attempts to smear them. I know *his* secrets, too, after all."

Kitty smiled weakly. "At least we'll get a sleigh ride out of this mad affair, right, Cass?"

"Indeed."

"The two of you are far too forgiving," Gwyn said. "If it had been me, I would have entered this house screeching bloody murder."

"We know, Sis," Heywood said dryly. "You screech bloody murder if Thorn cuts your allowance by a single guinea."

"Not true!" she said in mock protest. "It has to be two guineas at the very least."

Sheridan rolled his eyes. "On that note, I believe I will go."

"You're not joining us for the sleigh ride?" Gwyn asked.

"Afraid not. I have too much work to do. The sleigh only fits two, anyway, and Heywood is more than happy to carry each of you around one at a time."

Gwyn sniffed. "I don't need Heywood to drive a sleigh. I can drive one of our guests around myself."

"Ooh, take me!" Kitty cried. "You said you would show me the ruins."

Cass stifled a groan. That left *her* to ride with Heywood alone. What the devil was her cousin up to now?

"If we're going to the ruins," Gwyn told Kitty, "we'll need much warmer outer garments than we'd planned."

"In that case, while you and Kitty paw through the closet some more, Cass and I will take the first go-around." Heywood looked at Cass. "That's assuming you didn't have your heart set on touring the ruins, too."

"I merely want to see how the snow looks in sunlight. And to test your sleigh's mettle, of course. I don't care about the ruins."

He grinned. "That's good, since I have no clue how to find them. After all, I've only been at Armitage Hall a few days."

"Why, sir," Cass teased him, "I believe you're the first man in England to admit that he gets lost occasionally."

"Oh, don't let him fool you!" Gwyn called out from the coat closet. "He's as irritable as any other fellow when his navigational prowess is challenged. He used to drag us all over Berlin—on foot, mind you—while insisting he knew where he was going."

"I *did* know where I was going," Heywood said, sparing a wink for Cass. "You lot simply couldn't appreciate the value of taking the scenic route in order to tour the city."

Gwyn emerged from the closet with a fur muff in one hand and a wool scarf in the other, which she held out to Cass. "You'll probably need these, too, especially if Heywood decides to take any 'scenic routes' in the sleigh. It's cold outside."

As Cass wrapped the scarf about her neck and put her hands in the muff, Heywood snorted. "You're just jealous that I'm a better driver than you, Gwyn."

"In your dreams," she said gaily. "You're only saying that because we don't own a second sleigh. If we did, I'd race you and make you eat those words."

"Don't listen to her," he murmured to Cass as Gwyn returned to the closet. "She can't drive a gig, much less a sleigh."

"I heard that!" Gwyn called out.

He was still chuckling as he led Cass out the door. She was smiling herself. His banter with Gwyn made her wish she had an older brother. Her cousin Douglas wouldn't suffice—he was her age and hadn't been home in years. But she could tell from watching the duchess's children that they were comfortable with one another. *Loved* one another. It made her wish she'd had siblings of her own.

Then Heywood placed a hand in the small of her back to help her into the sleigh, and all thought vanished into the ether. Goodness. She was glad she'd chosen a very thick cloak for their jaunt. Otherwise, the warmth from his hand would melt her clear to her toes.

Her reaction to him was foolish, really. He couldn't possibly have any real interest in her, those kisses notwithstanding. Why, he probably kissed women like that all the time. But still, the thought of riding beside him left her breathless.

That would not do. The last time she gave her heart to a man, she'd had it badly battered. So this time she must take better care of it. Which was difficult when Heywood joined her in the sleigh, his hard body right up against hers. Had his brother said that the sleigh only fitted two? He'd lied. It only fitted one and a half, particularly when one of the people was a heavily muscled army officer. She and Heywood were squeezed so tightly together that she didn't know where he ended and she began.

Good Lord. Her blood was pumping just at the sensation of being pressed to him, no matter how chastely.

He must have felt it, too, for he refused to look at her as they glided down the drive between two snow-covered lawns toward a line of birches that separated the estate from the main road. The sleigh bells jingled merrily and the horse trotted sure-footedly along the drive.

"Where are we going?" Cass asked as they neared the main road.

Now that they were alone together, he looked somber. "You'll see. It's not far." He dragged in a heavy breath. "So why don't you tell me how you came to be writing the letters from Kitty to her brother?"

Devil take it. She'd hoped he'd forgotten. "It's . . . um . . . rather complicated."

"All the best deceptions are," he said coldly.

"It wasn't like that." Cass debated how much to reveal. But if she were to convince him to keep the secret on Kitty's behalf, she should probably tell him all of it. "Back when Douglas first left home, Kitty was only eight. She'd had trouble learning to read and write as it was, but she desperately wanted to correspond with her brother, to cheer him up."

Cass stared down at the muff encasing her hands. "She tried to do it herself, but her handwriting was illegible, her grammar was abominable, and she didn't know what to say."

"Douglas would have understood, I'm sure. She *was* still a child, after all."

"A child whose father had rigid standards for his children that she couldn't meet. Since I was four years older than she, I sort of took over the duties of a governess."

"At *twelve*?"

She shrugged. "I convinced him that I was perfectly capable of schooling Kitty. That way she and I could hide the fact that she... had problems with learning." Realizing she sounded disloyal, she added hastily, "Kitty is the sweetest, most generous woman you could ever meet, but I'm sure you've noticed that she's not, well—"

"Very bright."

Cass sighed. "The trouble was, she was still terrified of disappointing her father and mortified by her difficulties with writing. She always had to give the letters to him to be franked, and he always took the liberty of reading them."

"So you took over her correspondence to make sure she appeared to be clever."

"Exactly."

His face showed none of what he was thinking. "But Squire Nickman has been dead now for two years. Surely you could have explained all of this to Douglas."

"And have him know that it wasn't really his sister writing him so faithfully? Have her suffer the humiliation of having her flaws discovered? I couldn't do that to her. After her father died, she started to blossom. Where she would hardly speak in his presence, she now voices her opinions readily to anyone who will listen."

"Rather like you."

She eyed him balefully. "My point is, she has become a different woman since her father's death. She's not nearly as self-conscious. Besides, once we'd embarked on that scheme, it was difficult to go back. It didn't seem necessary to trouble Douglas with the depth of our deception while he was away fighting for our country." She shifted to look up at him. "Why does it matter to you? Why do you act as if *you* have somehow been betrayed?"

"You'll understand shortly," he said, though his expression gave away nothing.

They pulled onto the main road instead of touring the estate as she'd expected. Unencumbered by ruts or other carriages, the sleigh fairly flew along. A short while later, they turned down a different drive, headed for another house.

Heywood drew up in front of the smaller, run-down home as if he knew it well. Crumbling cornices, missing roof tiles, overgrown ivy tipped with snow, and front steps in disrepair were signs that its owner had deserted it.

"What is this place?" she asked. "It isn't the ruins Gwyn was referring to, is it?"

He gave a choked laugh. "No. Those are just manufactured to look that way. These ruins are real—the manor house of my estate, Hawkcrest."

"*Your* estate?" she said, hardly able to credit it.

He gazed upon the house as if torn between pride and despair. "My father left it to me after his mother, my grandmother, left it to *him*. It was always the property given to the second son, and as such was unentailed. I'm told it used to be quite fine." Drawing a folded paper out of his greatcoat pocket, he handed it to her. "You can get some sense of how it looked then from this."

Wary of his solemn mood, she opened the sheet of paper to find a sketch of a lovely Palladian home, with pretty gardens nearby and ivy growing up its walls of red brick. "How different it was!"

"Years of neglect have reduced it to a shambles. Uncle Armie was supposed to be taking care of it for my father while we were abroad, but clearly he chose to ignore it." He faced her, bitterness etched in his features. "Of course, he didn't mind pocketing the rents he was supposed to use in maintaining the house."

"Rents? It has tenants?"

Dragging in a heavy breath, he nodded. "He neglected to repair their homes as well. Bloody arse." He caught himself. "Excuse my language. It's just that each time I look on it, I'm hit by anger and despair all over again."

"I can understand that," she said. "It's unconscionable for anyone to neglect a pretty place like this."

He smiled at her. "Would you like to see the inside?"

"Oh, yes!" She paused. "As long as timbers won't rain down on me, that is."

"It's in a better shape inside, though not by much."

He helped her out of the sleigh and tied off the horse. As they climbed the steps, he pulled her here or there to keep her from treading on the crumbling bits.

Once they entered the house, she was struck dumb by the quality of the marble floors and the wood paneling on the walls.

Not to mention... "Look at that stunning staircase!" She stared up at the carved oak balusters and banister of the once-beautiful piece. The steps needed to be redone, to be sure, but the staircase still had an elegance all its own. She ran a hand over the intricately carved newel post. "Such craftsmanship should never be neglected."

"I agree," he said, his voice hoarsening. "It's my favorite part of the house. How did you guess?"

"Perhaps I can read your mind."

He stared at her hand, which was still stroking the newel post. "I doubt that. If you could, you would *not* approve."

His eyes glittered in the dim light, sending a sweet frisson of anticipation down her spine. "Oh?" she choked out. "And why is that?"

"Because my mind is wondering what it would feel like to have you touch *me* as tenderly as you're touching that post." After drawing off one of his gloves with his teeth, he took her hand in his and drew *her* glove off.

Oh, dear. She should make *some* protest to that, shouldn't she?

Instead, she stood there like a ninny, waiting to see what he would do next. And when he pressed her palm to his warm, whisker-rough jaw, a tremor of pleasure shook her.

"Are you cold?" he asked.

"Yes." It wasn't entirely a lie, was it?

Unbuttoning his greatcoat, he pulled her close so he could wrap it partly about her. When she raised an eyebrow at him, he said, "It works better than if I take the coat off and put it on you. This way we can share our bodies' heat."

"It will make it awfully hard to continue touring the house," she teased.

He tipped up her chin with one finger. "Is that what you want to do?"

The intensity in his gaze made it impossible for her to look away or even speak. She shook her head no, perfectly aware of what he was really asking.

He proved that by kissing her, gently at first, then with more fervor. Her response was to slide her hands inside his open morning coat and about his waist, a gesture that apparently encouraged him to deepen the kiss.

They stood there several moments while he plundered her mouth, softening her resistance with every plunge of his tongue. Then he kissed a path to her ear, where he rasped, "You are too damned tempting by half."

"I don't . . . mean to be."

"I know that." He tugged on her earlobe with his teeth, firing her blood. "I also know I have no business kissing you like this."

"That's true."

"Shall I stop?"

"No," she breathed. Oh, she *did* like to live dangerously.

With a growl, he unwrapped her scarf, then kissed down her cheek to the small amount of her neck showing between her cloak and the ribbons of her borrowed quilted bonnet. Then he kissed and tongued the hollow at her throat, turning her to mush.

"Is this why you brought me here?" She clung to his waist. "To have your wicked way with me?"

"Oh, trust me, if I'd intended that, I wouldn't have brought you to an ice-cold manor house with no furniture."

"Saved by the weather," she said lightly, then pulled his head back up so she could meet his gaze. "But just for the sake of argument, how *would* you . . . go about having your wicked way with me? Assuming we were somewhere warmer. And more comfortable. And *if* you were even to do such a roguish thing."

Fire sparked in his eyes, so hot that she wondered if she should have spoken those impulsive words aloud. Then he shifted her so her back was against the staircase balusters.

Oh, dear. Any other woman would panic. But she knew in her bones that he was a gentleman. That she could trust him.

"First," he said hoarsely, "I would strip all these layers of winter clothing from you . . . leaving you in your shift and naught else."

The image he conjured up set her heart pounding in her chest. "That sounds *quite* wicked."

"Oh, I'm just getting started." He pressing a lingering kiss against her temple, where her pulse beat madly. "Next, I would take down your mass of unruly curls and run them through my fingers."

"H-How did you know my curls were 'unruly'?"

"No matter how you pull them up and tuck them in with hairpins, they're still going to rebel." Lowering his voice to a bare whisper, he said, "And I *like* rebellious, unruly curls. They're particularly appropriate for rebellious, unruly ladies."

"I'm not rebellious and unruly," she said stoutly. But sometimes she was, and they both knew it.

"Once I had us both aroused and eager, I would slide your shift off over your head and stand back to get a good look at you in all your naked glory."

Her breath dried up in her throat. "Do I get to have a good look at *you* naked?"

He blinked. "Do you want one?"

"Of course."

"Yet you're not rebellious and unruly *at all*," he teased.

She thrust out her chin. "It's merely that I've never . . . seen a man undressed. It follows that I would be a little curious."

"Just a little, eh?" He bent close to her ear. "For you, sweetheart, I'd take off every stitch of my clothing until we were naked . . . together." His breath came fast and hot against her cheek, already warm from the blushes he was provoking. "Then I'd begin the touching."

"The touching?" she squeaked.

He took one finger and oh so lightly ran it down her neck and then over the curve of one breast. "I'd caress your breasts with my hands and mouth until I had you swooning in my arms."

His finger circled her nipple, making her breath come in quick gasps. She fancied she could actually feel his bare finger circling her bare nipple, though that was highly unlikely since she was fully clothed.

"And then..." he said, his thumb now rubbing her nipple, making her yearn for more.

When he paused, she prompted him with, "And then?" Good Lord, she was swooning in his arms already. How much more could there be?

He shoved away from her abruptly, his breath coming in hard gasps. "We should stop talking about this. Before I do something I regret."

The swift change caught her off guard. "But you wouldn't."

"I might. You have no idea how easy it would be for me to..." He huffed out a breath of frustration. "Unfortunately, that wouldn't be right. Not with you."

"I see." She did. He was being the sensible one. And somewhere deep inside she appreciated it.

Very deep inside. Because she still couldn't get past the idea of his caressing her breast with his mouth. She wanted to try that with him. Desperately.

Then the rest of his words hit her with brutal force. "What do you mean, 'Not with you'? Because I'm a maiden? Because you don't actually know me very well?" She swallowed hard. "Or because you want someone else?"

He raked his hair away from his forehead. "None of those. Though it *should* be all of those."

"I don't understand."

"I know." He released a heavy breath. "Earlier you asked why I act as if *I* had somehow been betrayed. So I'm going to tell you why."

He began pacing the foyer. "When I agreed to help save Kitty I had an ulterior motive. Until then I'd had an idea in my head of who she was, what she was like. Her letters—*your* letters—had sustained me through many a battle. Douglas knew that about me, and we'd discussed whether I would have his permission to marry Kitty if I liked her and she liked me."

Her stomach began to churn. "But Kitty wasn't who you thought she was, thanks to me."

He nodded. "Unfortunately, my reason for needing to marry her hasn't changed."

A chill swept through her. She could see where this was going. Especially since Heywood wouldn't look at her. "You need Kitty's fortune."

With a wave of his hand to indicate their surroundings, he said, "I want to do right by my inheritance. But the manor and the tenant farms are so run-down that repairs will cost more than I have, since the army doesn't allow the sale of a colonel's commission. And it will take a large sum indeed to set the estate to rights."

She resisted the temptation to tell him about her own fortune. It was too important to her to know whether he truly wanted her for herself and not for her money. If she told him now, she would never, ever be sure. She just couldn't take that risk.

"So you mean to court Kitty then?" she asked, fighting desperately to keep the jealousy out of her voice.

He rounded on her. "Don't be a fool. Of course I don't mean to court Kitty. Not now, not ever."

Oh, thank goodness. She wasn't sure she could bear that. "Why not? Because she isn't clever and witty?"

Stalking up to grab her by the arms as if he meant to shake her, he said, "Because I cannot wed one woman while I'm lusting after her cousin. If I were to marry Kitty, you would always be near. She's your closest relative. Anytime she and I went to visit her mother, we'd see you. *I'd* see you."

Fighting to hide how those words had wounded her, she pulled away from him. "Not if I marry, too. I could, you know. I'm not some pathetic woman who can't attract a man. When I have my season—"

"I've no doubt of your ability to find a husband, trust me," he said in a hollow voice. "But you'd still be in the same family. At least if I marry some other woman—one not related to you—I could arrange matters so I'd never see you again." He stiffened. "But not if you're still in Kitty's life, which, of course, you would be."

The truth suddenly dawned on her. "That's why you're so angry that the Kitty of the letters isn't Douglas's sister, the heiress."

"Not angry, exactly," he said. "Just . . . discouraged by my dearth of choices. I can either marry an heiress so I can retire and concentrate on setting my estate to rights. Or I can sell the estate at a substantial loss, continue to serve in the army, and try to support a family on an officer's pay, which isn't that much."

"But in the latter case, you would at least be happily married," she ventured.

"Ah, but I wouldn't have much opportunity to enjoy that, would I? I couldn't—*wouldn't*—take my wife with me to war. It's no place for a woman. Or children, for that matter. So I'd have to put up with seeing my family every few years, whenever I could get leave. What kind of life is that? Not one I relish, I confess."

"Perhaps you could get a better posting," she said. "One where you could take a wife with ease."

"I don't want a better posting. I want to begin my *real* life at Hawkcrest. It was my father's dream that I serve in the army, not mine. With Mother getting older and Sheridan needing help with the ducal estate, I want to be here. For them. For myself."

She forced a smile. "That's why you need to marry an heiress."

"Yes."

"Then you should marry one," she said, and headed for the door, now desperate to get back to Armitage Hall before she did something or told him something she would always regret.

Chapter 6

The snow didn't melt for a whole week, or rather it melted just enough to freeze into a sheet of ice at night, which still made the roads impassable. The day of Christmas Eve was the first time they saw any real thawing.

Heywood had never liked being cooped up inside for most of the day, but he hated it when it meant spending time with the one woman he couldn't have. Especially when Cass—and Kitty—had charmed his family so thoroughly, though in different ways. Kitty's sweet nature had won their hearts, while Cass's sensible ways and witty retorts had won their minds. Meanwhile, he'd spent the last week avoiding mistletoe, avoiding sleigh rides, and avoiding *her*.

But with the snow thawing, he'd come to the drawing room late in the day in search of her. He'd put it off as long as he could, but now they had to consult about how to handle Malet so as to do the least damage to the ladies' reputations. Still, he took a moment to stand in the doorway and watch as Gwyn, his mother, Cass, and Kitty debated the merits of various schemes for constructing a gingerbread house.

Cass looked like a bachelor's dream this morning. She wore another of Gwyn's gowns—some frothy chocolate-brown confection-looking thing—that was a bit tight on her, which meant it showed off her figure to great advantage. He imagined he could even see her cleavage beneath her lacy fichu. Her hair was messily put up into a loose knot he just wanted to undo, and her cheeks and lips were rosy as cherries from the fire.

He liked cherries. He liked to lick the juice as it ran down his fingers. He'd be happy to lick anything off of Cass, off her bosom or her plump lips or her—

Devil take it! How much longer must he endure this torture? That interlude at Hawkcrest had damned near killed him—her coyly encouraging him to describe what he wanted to do to her while he struggled to keep from letting her see how aroused he was. Many more encounters like that and he'd be begging her to marry him and to hell with the consequences.

Thank God that at that moment Gwyn spotted him, jumped up, and hurried over to pull him to the table. "You have to break the tie. Kitty and Mama want to make our gingerbread creation look like Armitage Hall. Cass and I think it should be a fairy-tale castle."

"I can easily resolve your problem." He picked up a slab of gingerbread and bit off the end.

The ladies gasped, and Gwyn swatted his hand when he reached for another piece.

"What?" he asked. "Once you don't have enough gingerbread, your dispute is settled."

"You are such a *man*, Heywood," Gwyn grumbled.

"If you're trying to insult me, Sis, you'll have to try harder." He grinned at her unrepentantly. "And to be fair, you ladies are such *women*, to be fussing over what kind of pretend gingerbread house to make."

"His Lordship is right," Kitty said. "We're making mountains out of molars."

"Molehills," Cass gently corrected her as she stirred a bowlful of a white substance.

"Now, see? That's what I mean." Kitty sniffed. "What does it matter if it's a molar or a molehill? It's all the same."

Stifling a laugh, Heywood picked up another piece of gingerbread, broke a piece off the edge, and popped it into his mouth while the ladies were distracted.

"Heywood Wolfe, stop that this minute!" his mother said. "So help me, if we have to get Cook to bake more gingerbread when she's already busy preparing tomorrow's feast I shall ban you from Christmas dinner!"

"No, you won't," he said. "You would never ban your favorite son from anything."

"You're not her favorite son," Gwyn said. "Thorn is."

"Don't be ridiculous," their mother snapped. "I don't play favorites."

Heywood grinned. "Pretend all you like, Mother. I'll keep your secret in front of the others." He lowered his voice to a stage whisper. "But you and I both know the truth."

"I dare you to repeat that in front of Thorn and Grey," Gwyn said. "They'll be here any minute, and I rather fancy the prospect of watching them beat you in a battle of wits."

"Beat me!" Heywood said. "Not a chance."

"There will be no beating and no battles this Christmas," his mother said firmly. "For the first time in years I'll have all my children together for Christmas, and I mean to enjoy it."

Though Kitty was giggling at the interplay, Cass was ignoring it.

Cass was ignoring *him*, which he found annoying. He walked over to stand beside her chair. "What's in the bowl?"

"Icing."

"Aren't you going to gild the gingerbread?" He remembered the gingerbread houses of his childhood, golden and shining and so enticing for a boy.

"No gilding," Gwyn said firmly. "It's dangerous for the children."

"How so?"

"Because we can't afford real gold leaf, only Dutch foil. And there are many reports that the copper in Dutch foil is bad for children."

"Ah." Money. It was always about the lack of filthy lucre. Even for him. He peered into Cass's bowl. "What flavor is the icing?" he asked, though he already knew from having helped Mother with countless gingerbread houses as a child.

"Vanilla, of course. But I'm not sure it's stiff enough to hold the pieces together. I may need more sugar."

Before she could stop him, he scooped up a dollop with his finger, then licked it off. "Hmm. I agree. Definitely needs sugar."

Cass's smile caught him off guard. Her smiles were like watching the sun peek from behind a cloud, giving him hope that the day might be fine after all. Why must she have such a lovely smile?

His mother snatched the bowl and put it out of his reach. "Will you stop that? If you keep eating all our hard work, we'll have nothing left. Go make yourself useful, and fetch your brother. The footmen are already setting up the tree in the ballroom. I was thinking of waiting to decorate it until Grey and Bea—and later, Thorn—arrive, but with the snow only partly melted, that might be quite late. So I suppose it's best that we at least get a start on it. Tomorrow, we won't have time, and I hate to disappoint the children on Boxing Day."

"Boxing Day. Right." He vaguely remembered his parents handing out boxes to the servants on the day after Christmas, adhering to the English custom, though the family was living in Prussia. But once he'd left home, he'd thought no more about it, and the practice had faded into the recesses of his memory. "Will these children be eating the Armitage Hall made of gingerbread?"

"They'll be eating a gingerbread *castle*," Cass chided him, though her eyes were dancing. "Assuming you don't eat all the parts of it first."

"Just one more . . ." he said, and reached for another piece of gingerbread.

His mother slapped his hand. Hard.

"Ow!" he said, rubbing his hand with a frown. "You'd think the stuff was actual gold from the way you ladies protect it."

"If it were gold, you wouldn't *have* to fetch Sheridan," Gwyn said mildly. "He'd already be in here calculating its worth and figuring out which bills to pay off with it. 'Tis a pity it's *not* gold."

Heywood's gaze shot to Cass. "If it were, Sheridan would have to fight *me* for it," he said.

A blush rose in Cass's cheeks that made him ache everywhere. Then she shifted her gaze from him, leaving him feeling bereft. God, but he hated this. It wasn't fair. He *knew* what he wanted. He just had no right to claim it.

Frustrated now, he left to find Sheridan. Any conversation with

Cass about Malet would have to wait. Because if Heywood got her alone, he couldn't be responsible for his actions. Then he'd have no choice but to marry her. Unlike Malet, he would never seduce and abandon a woman, no matter how much he desired her.

Shaking off the memory of poor Valeria's lifeless body, he went in search of his brother. It took him only a short while to unearth Sheridan from the stacks of papers upon the desk in the study, which had once been their uncle's and then their father's. How strange to be in a place that by rights was home, yet didn't feel remotely like home to Heywood.

"Mother wants you," he told Sheridan.

Looking haggard, Sheridan pushed his chair back from the desk. "For what?"

"The tree has been erected in the ballroom. Though if you need me to tell her I couldn't find you . . ."

"No, I'll go." Sheridan rose. "I need a break from poring over numbers that I can't make work to my satisfaction."

As they strode down the long hall with its picture windows, Sheridan paused to look out at the ice-crusted lawn and the melting icicles under the eaves. "You realize that Malet will be here as soon as the roads are passable. If his aim is revenging himself on you and Douglas, he will at least try to regain Kitty. Or have it out with you."

"True. But it should take him a bit longer to come here. He'll have headed north." He'd told Sheridan everything after his brother had badgered him for the truth. Almost everything, that is. Sheridan didn't know about his dilemma with Kitty and Cass.

"Have you a plan for dealing with him if he does show up here?" Sheridan asked.

"I do. When he comes to the door, my plan is to shoot him through the heart."

Sheridan eyed him askance. "And then you will hang."

"Ah, yes," he said dryly. "I still haven't worked out that tiny flaw."

"In other words, you have no plan."

Heywood shook his head no. "My original plan was to court Kitty myself, then marry her to keep her out of Malet's reach. But now that . . ."

"Now that you've discovered Kitty is . . . shall we say . . . a bit . . ."

"Dull witted?"

"I was going to say 'naïve,' " Sheridan said sternly.

"That, too," Heywood said. "And truly, I could accept a certain amount of naïveté in a wife." Though he liked Cass all the more because she wasn't one of those wide-eyed innocents who didn't know men even had urges. That was refreshing to a rough-and-tumble soldier who'd spent as much of his life in armed camps as in the rarefied atmosphere of society. "But I'm not sure I want to marry a woman lacking in the good sense to run a household."

"I didn't realize you were looking for a wife," Sheridan said.

"Aren't *you*? We both have estates in need of wives with sizable fortunes. Indeed, you ought to marry Kitty yourself. I'm told she has quite a large dowry."

Sheridan searched Heywood's face. "Perhaps I don't want to marry an heiress. Perhaps I find Kitty's cousin, Cass, more attractive."

A surge of jealous anger shattered Heywood's calm. "Do you?"

Sheridan burst into laughter. "I wish you could see your face right now. You look downright murderous."

Heywood turned to walk ahead of him down the hall. "That's ridiculous."

"You stare at Cass like a wolf eyeing a lamb. She stares at *you* like a—"

"Lamb fearing a wolf?" he bit out, disliking Sheridan's characterization entirely.

"More like a lamb eyeing a shepherd. She trusts you. I can't imagine why, considering how she ended up here, but she does. So if your intentions aren't honorable—"

"What are you, her guardian? Cass is none of your concern."

He said it so forcefully that Sheridan stiffened. "Forgive me. I meant no insult."

Damn. After years apart, he and his brother had begun to forge a new relationship this past couple of weeks. Heywood didn't want to damage that.

"I know." Heywood dragged his fingers through his hair. "You mean well. But I'd prefer you stayed out of it."

"All right. Just don't damage our family's reputation. It's hard enough for Mother to weather the gossip about her three dead husbands. If you do anything untoward, it will reflect badly on all of us."

Though Heywood bristled at the warning, he knew his brother was right. "I won't. I swear."

"One more thing. I know you're set on marrying an heiress and Cass isn't who you think you need. But happiness should be one of your criteria as well. If you wouldn't—*couldn't*—be happy with any other woman, you must take that into consideration. Because, to paraphrase a certain scripture in the Bible, what does it profit you if you save your estate but lose your soul?"

Heywood gritted his teeth. "I never took you for a religious man."

"I never took you for a fool. But you're making me re-examine that supposition."

Halting in his tracks, Heywood turned on his brother. "So you think I should shirk my responsibilities. That for the sake of my . . . urges, I should abandon the tenants and property that Grandmother entrusted to me."

"No, not if your 'urges' are all there is to it. But if you feel something more . . ."

"Like what? Love?" He snorted. "I'm not foolish enough to be a slave to that. And you shouldn't be either, given that Mother and Father were more friends than lovers."

"That was *their* marriage. You must forge your own."

Heywood didn't want to forge his own. Keeping his heart protected was safer. He remembered only too well how it had felt to be sent off to war as a lad. Yes, it was the way of the aristocracy, but he refused to take that path with his own children.

His own children? Now he was thinking ahead to having children? What kind of madness was that?

They'd reached the drawing room, but no one was there with the half-constructed gingerbread castle. "Damn. The ladies have gone," he told Sheridan.

"To the ballroom, probably."

"Right."

They both headed there.

But Heywood's mind teemed with scattered thoughts. What

was it about Cass's effect on him that made him take leave of his senses? And why couldn't he be lusting after Kitty instead of her fetching cousin?

Because, as usual, he wanted an illusion. Nothing was ever as it seemed. As a boy, he'd imagined that the army would be an exciting profession. But what he'd taken for excitement was really a morass of boredom and battle and long periods of yearning for family. He'd imagined Kitty as the perfect wife for him, capable of funding the revival of his estate. Instead, he'd discovered she was very different from the woman he'd imagined her to be.

He and Sheridan entered the ballroom to find three of the ladies already hanging presents on the tree set up in the corner. Kitty must have gone to fetch something, for she alone was absent.

Cass brightened as they walked in. "Oh, good, you're both here. I want to put this one on the very top." Gazing right at him, she held up an ornament made of tinsel wrapped around twigs that gave it the shape of a star. "I figure even tinsel stars belong somewhere they can shine above us."

"I agree." *And you belong in my arms.* A pity he had no right to say it.

"Would you mind putting it on top of the tree for me?" she asked, with a glow about her that made his heart clench.

"Better yet, I'll help you place it up there yourself." He dragged a chair over to the tree, then took her by the waist and lifted her up onto it.

"Oh!" she exclaimed, her eyes warming as she gazed down at him from the chair.

He couldn't seem to release her waist—her pleasingly shaped waist that made him think of taking her into a bedchamber somewhere and . . .

"Heywood," his mother chided in a low voice.

Right. Of course. Cass wasn't for him.

He released her and stepped back, hoping neither Cass nor his mother had seen the longing in his face. Still, what would he do when Cass was gone? After the past week, he couldn't imagine never seeing her again.

She stretched up to place her star at the top of the tree, and his blood heated. He could see her trim ankles and even a bit of shapely, stockinged calf. Good God, he had to get control over these obsessive—highly unwise—urges.

"So Cass," his mother said, "do you have some suitor at home whom you fancy? Who might be looking forward to your return?"

He tensed, waiting to see what she would say. It hadn't occurred to him that she might have suitors.

Cass avoided his gaze. "Not at present, no. But I'll be having a season in London alongside Kitty, so I'm hopeful I'll attract a suitor then."

"I daresay you'll attract more than one," Sheridan said, taunting Heywood with a smile.

Heywood ignored him. "I daresay you will."

"You're both too kind." Cass met his gaze with a heart-wrenching look of her own. "Would you mind helping me down, sir?"

"Of course not." He clasped her waist and lifted her off the chair and onto the floor. But once again, he couldn't seem to let go of her. Her waist seemed to fit perfectly in his hands, and her eyes were a fetching shade of smoky gray that—

"My lord," she murmured, "you can release me now."

"And if I don't wish to?" he asked gruffly, though in too low a tone to arouse the suspicions of the others, who were busy across the room, making more gifts to hang on the tree. "What will you do then?"

She regarded him with a clear-eyed gaze. "I'd wonder why you dally with a woman like me," she said, her voice as low as his, "when you need a woman like Kitty."

"Don't tell me what I need," he whispered. "I know that better than you."

And in that moment, he realized the truth. He had found the woman who suited him, his perfect match. So to hell with what he thought he needed for Hawkcrest. If Cass proved willing to follow the drum and live on his paltry income, he would take her as his wife, even if it meant giving up his own dream for the future.

Because the thought of living without her was simply more than he could bear.

Chapter 7

Something was different about Heywood today. Cass couldn't put her finger on it, but he seemed more...earnest. More intent on flirtation.

It intoxicated her, even though she knew that desiring him was foolish.

"How else can I help you ladies?" Heywood asked, his gaze fixed on her.

"I suppose someone should go fetch Kitty," Cass said, "or at least find out how far she's coming along on the gingerbread house."

Heywood narrowed his gaze on her. "You mean the one in the drawing room?"

Sheridan glanced from Cass to his mother. "We were just there. We saw no sign of Kitty."

How odd. Anxiety gripped Cass. Surely Malet could not have sneaked in and carried Kitty off? It seemed unlikely.

"She's probably just resting in her room," the duchess said.

Heywood looked at Cass, apparently understanding at once her concern. "Perhaps we should make sure of that."

Gwyn, being a very discerning soul, said, "I agree."

At that point they split up to search for Kitty. Cass went up to Kitty's bedchamber, only to find she wasn't there. The others scattered about the mansion, looking for her. When Cass was nearly at her wit's end and was staring out at the snow, wondering where else to look, Heywood came to her with an envelope in his hand.

"I found this behind the gingerbread house in the drawing room," he said.

The envelope bore Cass's name. With her stomach churning, she opened the letter. There were crossed-out words and plenty of mistakes, but she was used to that from Kitty:

> *Dearest Cass,*
>
> *I hope you can forgive me, Cuzin, but I have ~~run~~ ran away with the man I love. I've been in love with Mr. Adams For Ever. At least two years. He's very swete to me. So we're gone to ~~Grentuh~~ Grenta Green to be wed. Please tell Mama I'm happy and will write to her as soon as possbile. <u>And please don't follow us.</u> I am delited to be with my own dear Mr. Adams at last.*
>
> *With much ~~afee~~ affecshun,*
> *Kitty*
>
> *P.S. Tell his Grace that we borrowd his slay on account of all the snow. We'll bring it ~~write~~ rite back after we marry.*

Heywood had apparently been reading over her shoulder, for as soon as he was finished he murmured, "I can see why you needed to write letters for her."

"And we can be sure that her 'love' didn't write them for her since Mr. Adams is a well-educated solicitor." Despair gripped Cass. "Oh, Aunt Virginia will be furious with me!"

"Why? It's not your fault, and I shall make that clear to her. If anything, it's mine for getting her away from home where this Mr. Adams could prey on her more easily."

Just then the others came in. "We can't find her anywhere," the duchess said.

Wordlessly, Cass handed over the letter. They read it and were kind enough not to comment on Kitty's poor writing ability.

"Who is this fellow, anyway?" Sheridan looked at Cass. "Is he at least a decent chap?"

Cass explained who Mr. Adams was to her family. "Kitty actually mentioned him in passing the night of the ball. I should have realized she found him appealing. He always treated her kindly, and she always asked after his children. He's a widower." When Gwyn lifted her eyebrows, Cass added, "A young, handsome widower."

"Thank heaven," Gwyn said. "Otherwise, I'd drive the sleigh up to Scotland myself to save her."

"You couldn't," Heywood said. "They stole the sleigh, remember? And how did they manage that, anyway? You'd think a servant would have noticed."

The duchess wore a pained expression. "I sent a couple of the men out with it to cut down the fir tree and haul it in. Kitty and her beau must have seen it in the drive and taken it while the footmen were bringing in the tree."

"Then let's hope they don't run afoul of Malet on their way to Scotland," Sheridan said. "And how did this Adams chap know to look for her here?"

Heywood rubbed his jaw. "I imagine that after Malet's coachman told his master that the ladies had gone off with me, Malet took Mrs. Nickman home. Once there, he would have heard that I'd left my card, and he would have known I was in England, bent on protecting Kitty from him. This Mr. Adams could have insinuated himself into the search. Perhaps he offered to come down here while Malet took the road up to Gretna Green? Mind you, I'm just speculating."

"It doesn't really matter *how* he found out, just that he did," the duchess said. "Something must be done about the elopement."

"If we leave now, we might catch up with them," Sheridan said.

"I doubt it," Heywood said. "Besides, they might decide to travel by ship to Scotland. The coast isn't that far from here. I don't know if we could get there before they embarked. Or, once we did, find them in Grimsby or Boston or whatever port town they ended up in."

"No one is going after them," Cass said. "If they're in love, then that's enough."

The duchess looked shocked. "But my dear, if he's a fortune hunter—"

"He's not. I know Mr. Adams very well. His father was solicitor to my aunt and uncle before the young Mr. Adams took over. For the first two years he worked for the Nickmans, he stammered every time Kitty entered the room. Now that I think about it, he was clearly smitten even then. He's about ten years her senior, just enough to be a settled fellow who will give her a respectable life, but not so old that she won't find him appealing."

Gwyn stared at her. "You're sure he's not after her money."

"I'm not *sure,* but I don't think so. He has money of his own. His father's business is well established, and he has picked up the reins admirably."

Heywood glanced around at the group. "Then I suppose we must bow to Cass's greater knowledge of what Kitty might want." The others nodded in acknowledgment.

"Thank you," Cass said. "At least she'll be safe from Mr. Malet. Which, I suppose, means that it's time for me to go home."

"Nonsense," the duchess said. "It's very near dark and far too dangerous for you to travel, even if Heywood and Sheridan go with you. You might as well stay here tonight and tomorrow. You won't want to travel on Christmas. Every coaching inn will be closed."

"Yes, you should remain here," Heywood said in a low rumble that tugged at her heart.

"Very well." But there was a catch in her throat. She wasn't at all sure she was doing the right thing. She might just be setting herself up for more misery.

Still, it made her think. Perhaps she *should* tell Heywood about her fortune. Kitty had given up everything to be with the man she loved. There was no guarantee that Aunt Virginia would approve of her choice after the fact, and if she didn't the couple might not be given anything—no dowry, no inheritance. Yet Kitty had risked it.

Meanwhile, Cass was hedging her bets, asking Heywood to give up all his hopes in order to be with her. Was that fair? *She* wasn't giving up anything. Perhaps she should follow Kitty's lead and go after the man she loved.

Loved?

Yes, she loved Heywood. She loved his protectiveness and his many kindnesses. She loved that he appreciated her wit. She loved that he had first become attracted to her through her letters.

By expecting him to be willing to give up his future for her, was she being too exacting? Perhaps. It was probably as unfair as it was to expect Mr. Adams to wear sackcloth and ashes because he wanted a woman who happened to have a fortune.

Well, no more. She would do her best to gain Heywood. And if it meant telling him everything? Then she would do that, too. Because even if he did want her fortune, she would still rather be married to him than anyone else.

She wanted Heywood. And that was that.

It was nearly midnight when Heywood headed up the stairs, intending to go to bed. He'd hoped to find a moment alone with Cass, but that hadn't happened. First, there'd been the tree decorating. Cass had seemed very enamored of the custom and had thrown herself into it with great enthusiasm. Not wanting to lose a single minute with her, he'd stayed to watch, though he could have bowed out.

Normally they would have opened their presents next, but with half the family having still not arrived, Mother had commanded that the gift giving be done on Christmas morning. That suited him just fine. He still hadn't had the chance to talk to Cass alone, which dictated whether he gave her a ring or something less significant. He could almost believe that his mother, half sister, and brother had conspired to keep him and Cass apart, but that seemed very calculated, even for his family.

His other siblings, who were supposed to be traveling from London, had sent word by a footman that they would be at Armitage Hall in time for Christmas dinner tomorrow but couldn't promise better than that because the roads still made for slow going.

To his surprise, however, as he passed Thorn's room he spotted Cass standing in the middle of it, staring at nothing. The fire had been lit, probably by some servant who hadn't heard that Thorn had been delayed, but no candles were burning. Still, he could see that Cass wore only a nightdress and a wrapper.

God help him. How was he to endure *that* temptation? "What are you doing?" he asked from the doorway, not wanting to spook her.

She faced him with a dazed expression. "I don't know. I was trying to sleep, but I couldn't get Kitty out of my mind. So I came here, hoping to find another letter from her. Or something to explain why she would sneak out without even telling me."

Ah, yes, Heywood had forgotten that Kitty had been sleeping in Thorn's room. Mother had planned to move her today, but her elopement had put an end to that.

Cass flashed him a rueful smile. "I think it has just sunk in that she's gone off with Mr. Adams."

He walked into the room. Cass needed someone to listen. Surely he could be that person, no matter how flimsy her gown and wrapper. No matter how gorgeous her hair, now that it was tumbling from beneath her mobcap and down over her shoulders like froth in a bowl of syllabub. "I doubt she purposely left you out of the decision. Adams probably didn't give her much opportunity. They saw we were preoccupied and took their chance to elope."

She shook her head. "You don't understand. Kitty and I tell each other everything. Yet when she made the most important decision of her life, she didn't confide in me."

"Your cousin doesn't strike me as the sort to think through decisions. She just leaps."

"That does sound like her." Cass tucked an errant curl up under her mobcap. "But how is it I never even guessed that Mr. Adams was . . . in love with her? Or she was in love with him? Perhaps if I had—"

"You would have stopped her from eloping?"

"I suppose I might have, before. But if she loves him . . ."

"That's your only criterion, isn't it?"

Cass stared at him. "Yes. Though I know it isn't yours."

A harsh laugh escaped him. "Until I met you, I would have said that was true."

She blushed. "What do you mean?"

It was now or never. Kitty wasn't the only person who liked to leap sometimes.

Closing the door behind him, he headed for Cass. "I'm tired of fighting what I feel. Tired of pretending I could marry any heiress just to save Hawkcrest. I can't. I won't. I want *you* as my wife. No matter how that affects my future."

Her eyes widened. "First, there's something I must tell—"

"No. No more words." He slipped his arm about her waist and pulled her close. "I'm done with talking. I want to show you how I feel."

"But—"

He kissed her, probably harder than he should have, but he hoped not. The thought of losing her for any reason was too much. This, *this,* was what he needed. He would prove to her that he wanted her, poor relation or no, and then hope that any resistance she had would fade away.

When she kissed him back with great fervor, his satisfaction was so powerful he wanted to crow it aloud. But that would require tearing his lips from her, so instead he pulled off her wrapper and tossed it aside.

"What are you doing?" she whispered against his mouth.

"Making you mine, assuming that you want that, too." He drew back just enough to see her face shining in the firelight and her lush body nicely outlined by her linen nightdress. God help him if she said no. He might combust. "I may have abducted you, dearling, but I'm no scoundrel."

She looped her arms about his neck. "I know that. And I do wish to be yours."

"Now? Here? Because if you want to put it off—"

"Certainly not. I don't think I could wait even one more day."

"That's all I needed to hear," he growled.

Then he slid both hands up to cover her breasts, reveling in her gasp. And when her sweet nipples hardened as he swept his thumbs over them, he thought he would explode right then and there.

She was so lush, so eager. Her breasts fit his hands perfectly, which made him want to just toss her down on the bed and ravish her. But he wanted her first experience with lovemaking—their first time together—to be special. And that meant taking things slow.

He could manage that, right? Surely he wasn't so far gone, so smitten, that he couldn't keep control of his urges.

Perhaps what he should do was increase *her* urges. Dropping his hand to below her belly, he caressed her through her nightdress, exulting when her breathing quickened, and her nightdress dampened.

Ah, yes, she was his. She would *be* his. His heart soared at the thought.

Apparently he had a heart and it knew what it wanted. Her. Only her. And the money be damned.

Chapter 8

Cass knew she shouldn't be doing this, especially since she hadn't told him about her fortune yet. But now that he was here and wanting to marry her in spite of everything, she didn't wish to ruin this moment. Being in Heywood's arms made her happy, and having him say he wanted her for his wife made her even happier. So she would take her chances.

Now that she'd agreed to his madness, he turned thrillingly fierce, which should have alarmed her. Instead, it delighted her. Between rough and thorough kisses, he fondled her breasts through her nightdress so deliciously that she could hardly think.

"Heywood," she whispered.

"Yes, dearling."

The endearment thrilled her. "I want to see *you* undressed."

"Right." He grinned wickedly at her. "I remember."

Her cheeks flamed as she thought of all the naughty things she'd said the last time they were together, but it didn't stop her from wanting to act on them. She pulled at his coat, and he slid out of it. His waistcoat and cravat quickly followed, giving her a glimpse of his tanned throat before he tore off his shirt, revealing far more skin.

She gulped. *That* was interesting. His chest seemed sculpted from marble, with muscles that clearly came from his being a soldier. And he had dark blond curls on his chest! She hadn't expected hair in such a place, having never seen a man half-dressed, in art or otherwise.

She lifted her hand, then paused with it midair. "Can I touch you?"

"Oh, God, yes," Heywood rasped.

As she swept her hands over his chest, she felt his muscles clench. His jaw tautened, too, and the very thought that she could affect him so profoundly made a surge of wanton heat rise in her belly and lower.

But when she ran her thumbs over his nipples the way he'd done hers, he growled, "Enough, you teasing wench. It's *your* turn."

"That's hardly fair," she said lightly. "If I take off my nightdress, I'll be naked. And you're still partly clothed."

"I can easily remedy that." He unbuttoned and stripped off his breeches and stockings, then kicked off his shoes, leaving him in only his drawers.

His prominently bulging drawers. He reached for the buttons, then grinned at her. "Shall we disrobe together?"

The sight of his mostly naked legs, so sinewy and hairy and *male*, already overwhelmed her, but if she undressed and he backed away in disappointment, then having *his* body to look at might keep her from dwelling on that too much. "Yes," she breathed. "Together."

He unfastened his drawers; she unfastened the buttons on her nightdress. Then together they stripped their undergarments off.

Unfortunately, she didn't at first notice what *he* looked like down there because she was so focused on watching his reaction. It was most gratifying. He scoured her with a look that flamed every part it touched.

"God help me, Cass, you're a soldier's dream come true." With a purely wondering expression, he skimmed his hand from her shoulder to her breast to her belly and then to the curls between her legs. "So soft, so delicate . . . and all mine." When he cupped her, sending her heart into a pounding rhythm, she started.

"Wait!" she cried.

He groaned. "Dearling, please don't make me stop."

"That's not what I mean." She backed up a few steps. "I-I forgot to look at *you*! Let me see."

His frown cleared, and his smile turned cocky. "Ah, now that's different."

"Different" was the word, all right. He looked nothing like her down there. He had a reddened rod of flesh between his legs, a bold fellow that thrust itself out from its nest of curls with outrageous impudence.

Her mouth went dry. What was she supposed to do with that . . . that *thing*?

But he gave her no time to worry over it before he took her in his arms, kissing her deeply as he backed her toward the bed. Then he tumbled her down upon it before kneeling beside her. "I'll do my best to make this pleasant for you, Cass, but you'll have to tell me what you like."

"I don't know what I like."

He chuckled. "Not yet. But you will. Indeed, it might take a lifetime of practicing together to determine the many things you like. But we can start with this."

Lying down next to her, he leaned over to suck her breast.

"Ohhh, I like *that*," she said. "Very much."

"I like it, too." He sucked the other breast, and she thought she might die of pleasure.

Her breath seemed to have stuck down deep in her throat, and she couldn't help arching up for more of his attentions. He obligingly gave them to her, caressing both breasts in turn with mouth and tongue and teeth. Just as she wondered if she could take much more of the thrilling sensations coursing through her, he slipped his hand down between her thighs to stroke her where he'd briefly stroked before.

My oh my. That felt *magnificent.* The man was a magician at rousing her need and then satisfying it, in an ever-heightening circle. He slid one finger inside her, then another, while with his thumb he rubbed the spot that ached for him. A jolt of desire lofted her even higher. Who could have imagined that mere fingers could offer such delicious ecstasy?

"How about that?" he asked raggedly. "Does *that* feel good?"

"Ohhh, *yes*," she breathed. "So . . . very . . . good."

"Close your eyes. You'll like it even more."

When she did as he bade, she discovered he was right. She *did* like it even more. Until something larger than fingers edged up inside her.

Her eyes shot open. "Heywood?"

Then she realized what she was feeling. Heywood had moved to kneel between her legs and was putting his . . . disturbingly large member inside her.

"Is this really necessary?" She wanted to go back to the pleasurable part.

"To make you mine?" His eyes glazed over as he paused inside her so he could meet her gaze. "I'm afraid it is. But if you want me to stop—"

She stared up at his strained expression. "No, please don't."

He pressed a kiss to her forehead and then began to move again. At first it was uncomfortable and not at all what she'd expected. Their bodies were so entwined, so intimate, that she felt he could see to her very soul. But the deeper he thrust inside her, the more she adjusted to it, and soon she was undulating against him, trying to find . . . exactly what she needed.

As if he guessed what that was, he pulled her knees up, and she felt a stirring between her legs that had her nearly swooning. Then he reached down to finger her in the same place as before, and the caress catapulted her into a new realm of enjoyment.

"Heywood," she whispered. "Oh, goodness, *Heywood*."

"Do you like that, dearling?" he choked out.

"Very . . . much."

He did both for a while—stroking her while also driving into her with his rather large rod of flesh. Briefly she wished her aunt had prepared her for such an . . . unusual act, but she soon forgot about anything except the feel of him inside her, the sweet bliss of him touching her down there.

"Dearling," he said, "are you . . . all right?"

She choked out a laugh. "That's an . . . understatement for . . . how I'm . . . feeling."

Her response seemed to make him swell inside her. "Good," he bit out.

Then they were too caught up in pleasuring each other to say more. He fondled her in every part he could reach, and she clung to his shoulders as a butterfly clung to a flower. He made her *feel* like a flower—pretty and feminine and oh so worthy of his desires.

He drove into her over and over, rousing her blood, making her wish to climb ever higher. Then, as if a lightning bolt from the sky had hit them both, she felt a deep keening down there, which was answered by a coarse oath from him.

Soon they were sliding into oblivion, reaching a pinnacle of ecstasy. She cried out, which spurred him, too, somehow, and then they were vaulting into a world of glorious physical sensation.

"My love," he whispered as she went over the edge with him. "My dearest love."

It was the sweetest thing he'd said to her. "My love," she replied.

Then they fell into that place where only lovers go—that perfect happiness of needs fulfilled and love requited.

There was no going back now. She was his. And Lord save her if this proved to be the end of it. Because now that she'd put her trust in him, she could never return to the life she'd led before.

Heywood dozed off. When he awakened, he realized that Cass lay beside him, sleeping blissfully. He sighed. Their union had been everything he'd hoped for. He couldn't and wouldn't regret it. Still, having decided to marry, they must now deal with Hawkcrest. He was going to have to sell it.

She must have sensed his gaze on her, because she opened her eyes to stare at him with that sultry look that made him want to ravish her again and again.

"Merry Christmas," he said.

She snuggled against him. "Is it here already?"

"It is indeed. Christmas Day in the morning. The very early morning, that is." He brushed a kiss to her lips. "And apparently you're my present."

"As you are mine." She gazed up at him with a trembling smile. "Is what we just did . . . you know, before we fell asleep . . . always like that?"

"Not for me." He shifted to lie on his side, facing her. "But then I never felt anything for the women I was ... er ... with."

"I can't imagine doing something so intimate merely for pleasure."

"Nor can I ... *now*. It certainly pales in comparison to what you and I just shared."

Her eyes darkened. "But I suppose you were 'with' a great many women before we met."

He winced. "Not as many as you'd think."

"At the very least I assume one of them was involved with Mr. Malet and that's why you despise him so."

"Actually, that's not why." He supposed it was time he told her. Otherwise, she would assume all manner of incorrect possibilities. "I despise him—Douglas and I both despise him—because of what he did to a woman even younger than Kitty."

Her eyes went round. "What was her name?"

"Valeria. She was the orphan of one of the English soldiers and his Portuguese wife. Both Douglas and I missed our families, so we treated her like a little sister. She had no brothers and was a bit of a tomboy, so she would follow us around the camp as a little sister might."

Idly he twined one of Cass's curls about his finger. "At fifteen, she turned secretive. We assumed she was growing into a woman and tiring of our company." His voice hardened. "But that wasn't it at all."

"She was following Malet about," Cass said.

"Precisely. She'd fallen in love with him. And like the scoundrel he was, he took advantage. No one knew of their ... affair, if that's what you could call a union between a girl and a man twice her age. Apparently he'd insisted that she keep it quiet, and she did."

"So how did you learn of it?" Cass asked.

"After he'd had his fun, he discarded her, as was his wont. It broke her heart. She languished away, refusing to eat or drink, refusing to say what was wrong. By the time she finally told us about it, she was on her deathbed, and naught could be done for her. We confronted him, but he laughed at us. *Laughed.* Said we were just angry that we hadn't had her first."

"No wonder you hate him."

Heywood was glad she understood. "I thought Douglas was going to kill him then and there. But I stopped him, knowing it would ruin Douglas's life, too. There were better ways to avenge her. So I went to our commanding officer and told him the whole story. With Douglas and me as witnesses—and Malet's less-than-stellar reputation—the general was more than ready to have Malet cashiered."

"What a blackguard he is! Now I'm glad you had the good sense to carry me and Kitty off. I shudder to think what might have happened to Kitty if you hadn't been there."

"So do I." He brushed a kiss to her lips. "Besides, I wouldn't have met you."

She swallowed hard. "So you don't mind so much that you gave up a fortune for me?"

"You're the one who will suffer," he pointed out. "We'll have to sell Hawkcrest at a loss, then decide whether you wish to live on my—"

She stopped him with a finger to his lips. "No more." Oddly enough, she looked guilty. "You've been honest with me, and now there's something I must tell you. I wanted to tell you before, but you wouldn't let me, and I was enjoying what we were doing, so . . ." She dragged in a heavy breath. "Kitty isn't the only one with a fortune. I have one, too."

Heywood narrowed his gaze on her. "What do you mean?"

"I-I have an inheritance that's nearly equal to Kitty's. My father left me a large dowry."

"Douglas never said anything about it," he pointed out, unable to keep the suspicion from his voice.

"I asked him not to. I asked the same of Kitty and my aunt."

He rolled onto his back to stare up at the ceiling. He couldn't believe this! "So why couldn't you at least say something to *me* about it?"

She laid a hand on his chest. "Because I didn't want you—didn't want any man—choosing me for my fortune."

"Even though you knew it was important to me." Anger built in him, a nasty drug that poisoned his enjoyment. "Even though you realized that if I didn't marry a woman with money, I would lose my own inheritance."

"I would have told you eventually. I just . . . wanted to be sure that you cared for *me,* not my dowry. I don't think that's unreasonable."

"Of course you don't," he said bitterly. "You've been pulling the strings of all of us mere mortals."

The blood drained from her face. "What on earth do you mean?"

He faced her again, fighting to ignore her shocked and hurt expression. "For one thing, you kept Kitty's secret about her not writing the letters."

"What does that have to do with anything? I did that because she asked me to. Because her lack of writing ability embarrasses her."

He could understand that, although at the moment he didn't wish to. "You made sure I didn't know you could save my estate."

"I told you why. And there was another reason, too. I wanted Kitty to be settled before I let it be known that I had a substantial dowry. I knew she would require all my attention to make sure she didn't marry a fortune hunter herself."

"Like me," he growled.

"I didn't say that. But yes, when you told me that you needed a fortune, I did consider you might marry *her* for it. As you might realize, that made me rather reluctant to reveal my true situation. Then you said you couldn't marry her, wouldn't marry her as long as it meant being near me, and everything changed."

"Exactly. And at that moment, you should have told me the truth."

"Really? Why? Did you expect me to accept your attentions, fearing that they were only borne of your need for my money?"

The logic of her assertions perversely infuriated him. "I expected you to be honest with me. I expected that if you cared about me, you wouldn't have let me believe I was losing everything by marrying you."

"I tried! Last night, I said I wanted to tell you something, and you said it didn't matter."

He dragged in a breath. She was right. She *had* tried to tell him. So he shouldn't complain. But part of him was still furious. She'd known he was worried about their future. About their income. She could have relieved his fears at any time.

Yet she'd chosen not to. "It doesn't matter. None of it matters. I will act as I must, independent of what you believe or think about me."

"Heywood, please . . ."

"No, I won't listen." He slid from the bed, his face stormy. "You are not the woman I took you for. I don't want a wife who sees me as some . . . fortune-hunting scoundrel. Keep your dowry. I can go on perfectly well without it."

Heywood expected her to beg. To express a suitable remorse for having hidden the truth from him. Then he would take her into his arms, say that he loved her, and graciously accept her money. And all would be well.

But he hadn't reckoned on Cass's pride. She rose from the bed and said, as if she weren't standing there without a stitch on, "I understand. Thank you for setting me straight about what you feel for me." Then she drew on her nightdress and wrapper and left.

He stood there, not sure what had just happened. Cass had walked away from him, even though he'd taken her innocence.

Cass had refused him.

Very well. If she wanted things that way, it was fine by him. Let her put some other hapless fellow through her test or whatever it was she was up to. He would not have his strings pulled. No, indeed. Not *him*.

He left the room, intending to find his own room and sleep. But by some strange alignment in the stars, he ran into his mother. Damn.

"You're up very early," Mother said.

"I find it hard to sleep when my life is in turmoil."

"You mean, when the woman you love is bereft and confused."

He tensed. "What are you talking about?"

His mother stared at him. "You know perfectly well. I happened to glimpse Cass, that lovely young lady who adores you, going up the stairs to her room and looking quite upset. Can you truthfully say she was not with you?"

A pox on it. How was it that his mother always knew everything going on in their house? "It's none of your concern."

"Oh. So you mean to cut me out of the matter the same way you cut *her* out of it."

"I didn't . . . I wasn't . . ." Damn his mother for knowing how his mind worked. Feeling a need to defend himself, he said, "She has a fortune. Did you know that? All this time . . ."

"I see," his mother said. "You're angry because she didn't tell you."

"Yes! I have a right to be angry."

His mother regarded him steadily. "Why? Because if you marry her, you'll gain everything you wanted and needed? Which she took her time about revealing?"

The way she put it, he sounded selfish. "She should have told me sooner."

Mother nodded. "She should have, yes. But she wasn't sure of you. Kitty told me that Cass was courted by a fellow in Bath when she was younger, a gentleman she fancied . . . until she overheard him telling his friends he only wanted her for her fortune. So you can hardly blame her for being skittish. After all, when you first met her, you were bent on marrying Kitty."

Heywood stared at his mother, laid low by her revelation. Now every word he'd said to Cass seemed cruel. "That was only because . . . I mean, I truly thought . . ."

"I am not telling you what you should do, Son. But I think you should consider matters from *her* point of view. She is wary of fortune hunters, and rightfully so. How can you blame her for that?"

He hated it when his mother made sense. "I'm not a fortune hunter."

"I imagine you made that perfectly clear when you rejected the woman you love."

He winced. He had indeed. So he had a choice. Either he could set everything straight between them, or he could figure out what to do without her in his life.

The latter sounded very unappealing. So it was time for him to figure out how to make amends.

Chapter 9

Cass had barely kept from collapsing into tears as she'd fled Kitty's—no, Thorn's—bedchamber. Heywood had dealt her a terrible blow, and it had left her reeling.

She'd gambled at love and lost. She wanted to be angry at *him* for it, but how could she? The truth was, she hadn't trusted in his character. She hadn't believed in his affection for her. And now she'd spoiled everything.

Sick at heart, she went to her borrowed bedchamber, intending to try to sleep, but that was impossible. She lay there replaying their argument, wondering what else she could have said to prevent his manly pride from being damaged.

Normally, she would have confided in Kitty about these feelings. But Kitty was gone, and there was nothing she could do about it. Now the sun was coming up over the horizon, and it seemed pointless to lie in bed going over what she should have said or done.

So she got up, called for the maid, and then let the young woman help her get dressed in a lovely forest-green gown that she hoped made her look pretty. It was Christmas morn, after all. She should at least *pretend* to be joyful.

She headed downstairs, not surprised to find that no one else was awake. Peeking out the window, she noticed that a great deal of the snow had melted. There were only patches here and there now. She could do with a walk. So she found a cloak in the coat closet and headed out to the garden she'd seen from her window.

The weather wasn't as cold as it had been, and there were a few blooms that had survived the snow—Christmas roses, for one. As she wandered the garden, she heard a coach approaching. She ignored it. Doubtless it was some friend of the Wolfes' from town, come to make sure all was well with the duchess and her family after the snowstorm. So Cass continued to roam about, trying not to think about Heywood while taking note of what grew and what had perished in the snow.

After a while, a voice arrested her. "Well, well, I see you're not exactly suffering from being abducted by a scoundrel."

Mr. Malet? Her stomach roiled. Good Lord, he'd found them. Or rather, he'd found *her.*

Forcing herself to appear calm, she faced him. "Not suffering at all, to be honest. The Wolfe family has been very kind to us."

Standing at the entrance to the garden, Malet looked as polished and despicable as ever. "And where is your lovely cousin?"

"Out of your reach, sir. She's found herself a husband who actually wants her for herself and not her fortune."

He dropped all pretense of politeness. "I should have known that bloody arse would marry her to get back at me. But the colonel will come to regret that, I swear, because—"

"Not the colonel, actually. It was Mr. Adams." She smiled. "She eloped with him yesterday. I'm afraid you're too late."

That seemed to surprise him. "So *that* was who she was talking to at the ball. I didn't get a look at him, so I assumed it was the colonel once I heard he'd taken Miss Nickman. That Adams fellow told me he would come this way to find Miss Nickman for me while I headed to Gretna Green. Damned schemer. That's what I get for trusting a solicitor."

"A solicitor with more character in one finger than you have in your whole body."

That clearly angered him, for she could see him ball one hand into a fist. "You'll be wishing you'd gone off with that solicitor yourself when I'm done with you, Miss Isles. I know precisely who turned Miss Nickman against me."

Her heart stilled. "I can't imagine who you mean."

He came nearer. "Don't pretend to be stupid. You're a clever, conniving wench who knows how to turn matters to her advantage. Which is why I mean to make you my whore. It's the least you owe me for ruining my plans."

"*What?*" Her blood turned stone-cold. "You've lost your mind." She turned to go back to the house.

But he caught her arm in an iron grip. "When *you* go missing, everyone will assume you ran off with a man, too, though no one will guess that *I'm* the culprit." He started dragging her toward the entrance to the garden. "I'll place you in suitable London lodgings, where I can visit you at my whim . . . once I've taught you the appropriate respect, that is."

"That's ridiculous!" she hissed, struggling against him. Where *was* everyone?

She kicked at him, and he loosened his grip on her arm with a grunt of pain. Pivoting away from him, she ran for the door to the house.

"You *bitch!*" he cried. "I'll make you pay for that!"

Suddenly, Heywood loomed up in front of her. Pushing her behind him, he launched himself at Mr. Malet with a roar.

As the two men rolled around in the garden, she hesitated at the door, wondering if she should get help. But it rapidly became apparent that Heywood didn't need any.

He had Mr. Malet pinned to the ground and was pummeling him. "This is for Valeria," he growled as he punched him in the face. "This is for Kitty." He punched the man again.

Then he rose and dragged a staggering Mr. Malet up with him. "And this is for *daring* to touch my fiancée." He gave the scoundrel a third punishing blow, and Mr. Malet crumpled at his feet.

Fiancée? Did he mean it?

Heywood kicked Mr. Malet. "Get up, you coward. Next time you'll think twice about picking on my woman." He spat on the ground. "You come here again, you arse, and you'd better bring an army with you because I swear I'll kill you."

A new voice came from the entrance to the garden. "He did bring an army, Brother. Fortunately, they were no match for me and Joshua. I needed the exercise after being cooped up in a coach all morning, and Joshua needed someone upon whom to vent his spleen."

Cass looked over to find two of the handsomest fellows she'd ever seen—except for Heywood, of course. One had wavy black hair and eerie bluish-green eyes while the other had long and straight black hair and hazel eyes. It was only after the latter fellow moved closer that she realized he had something wrong with his leg and was using a cane.

But apparently that was his only deficit, for he shoved a rough-looking blackguard ahead of him, as did the first man. Both black-guards looked rather the worse for wear.

"Grab your master and get out," Heywood told Mr. Malet's henchmen.

Grumbling to themselves, they took one arm each and hauled Mr. Malet out of the garden.

Cass flew to Heywood's side. "Are you all right?" She took out her handkerchief and dabbed away blood from his split lip.

Heywood gazed down at her with his heart in his eyes. "I should be asking you that."

"No," drawled the fellow with the blue-green eyes. "You should be asking what has possessed her to agree to marry a rapscallion like you."

Looping an arm about her waist, Heywood pulled her close. "Cass, this is my older half brother, the Duke of Greycourt, and that fellow there is my cousin, Joshua Wolfe, who lives on the es-tate. Grey and Joshua, this is Miss Cassandra Isles, my fiancée. If she'll have me."

"You mean you haven't *asked* her yet?" Grey said.

"Not the way I should have," Heywood admitted.

"That doesn't surprise me," Joshua said. "Your family has a dis-turbing tendency to stumble into your proposals of marriage."

"Ah, but even stumbling proposals of marriage work in the end," Grey said. "Just ask my wife."

Heywood groaned. "I suppose you two are going to plague me about my marrying."

"Not me," Grey said. "Beatrice would have something to say about that if I did."

"I would indeed," a woman's voice answered him. "Fortunately, you know better."

The woman who came through the garden entrance was strikingly tall and brandished a pistol. "They're all gone."

Grey frowned. "I told you to stay in the coach."

"I did. Until I saw a fellow you two missed, who was trying to sneak into the woods." She shrugged. "So I told him to get into his master's coach. And apparently my pistol convinced him that he should."

"You gave Beatrice a loaded pistol?" Joshua snapped at Grey. "Are you mad?"

"Not that mad," Grey answered.

"But he didn't know it wasn't loaded," the woman interrupted. "Nor did the other three who came out looking decidedly disheveled." The woman smiled at Cass and held out the hand *not* gripping a pistol. "Good morning. I'm Grey's wife, Beatrice. I'm also Joshua's sister, and before you ask, Grey and I are not related in the least except by marriage."

Which made this pistol-wielding female the Duchess of Greycourt. Good Lord. "Lovely to meet you. I'm . . . um . . . Heywood's fiancée?"

"Miss Cassandra Isles," Grey said to his wife while also extricating the pistol from her. "Whom he hasn't yet asked to marry him."

"But whom he still wants us to consider as his fiancée," Joshua said. "Personally, I'm not convinced. For one thing, she's far too pretty for Heywood. And for another—"

"If you lot would just go inside," Heywood bit out, "I'm sure Mother has some task or another for you to perform, involving the tree and its many ornaments and baubles and whatever else she has in store for the day."

Beatrice brightened as she gazed up at her husband. "You were right! There *is* a decorated tree!"

"I told you. We had one every year when I was a boy."

"And you can see it right inside," Heywood said, making a shooing motion at his relations. "Move along now. That way to the tree."

"Not without you," Grey said, mischief in his eyes. "Why don't you come with us?"

"And look what your mother has done with the garden, Grey," Beatrice said. "She managed to get some winter roses going."

"I see that," Grey answered. "It's very—"

"Out of the garden, all of you!" Heywood shouted. "Now!"

Beatrice blinked. "Well! You don't have to be rude about it."

"Apparently, I do," Heywood grumbled under his breath.

His relations must have realized they'd overtaxed his patience, for with a laugh and a few backwards glances at her, they finally went inside.

"I thought they would never leave," Heywood said testily.

"You certainly have a much more colorful family than I do," Cass said.

He eyed her askance. "Really? Your cousin ran off with a solicitor, and your aunt can't leave the whist table. So I'd say your family would fit in with mine very well."

A lump stuck in her throat. "Is that . . . what you want? Because last night—"

"Last night I was a fool, dearling." He cupped her face in his hands. "I let my pride prevent me from recognizing the tremendous gift you were offering me. But when I saw Malet trying to steal you away, it solidified what I already knew—that I could never bear the absence of you."

"Oh, Heywood, neither could I."

"And once I heard about that fellow in Bath and how stupidly he behaved . . ."

Her cheeks flamed. "Who told you about that? No, wait, I know who. It was Kitty, wasn't it? I swear, my cousin is incapable of keeping a secret."

"Ah, but she knows when to keep one when it benefits the people she loves. After all, she kept the secret of who wrote all her letters. Of whom she *really* wanted to marry. Of the fact that you were an heiress. Without those machinations, you and I might never have met. I certainly would never have carried the two of you off, and you would never have accepted me as a suitor because I knew of your fortune."

"Without those machinations, you might be preparing to marry Kitty instead of me," she said archly.

"Doubtful." He chuckled. "I fell in love with you the moment I heard your letters read aloud. Every word made me burn to meet the woman who wrote them. I would never have settled for Kitty when I knew in my gut she wasn't that woman. Because once I did find that woman, I was lost forever. It was merely a matter of time before I came to my senses."

He reached into his pocket and pulled out a jeweler's box. "I know I'm supposed to wait until the fifth day of Christmas for this gift, but I'm too impatient for that." He opened the box to reveal four thin gold rings and in the center of them a wider ring with a beautiful ruby set into it. "On this first day of Christmas, dearling, will you do me the honor of agreeing to become my wife?"

"Yes," she said, tears welling in her eyes as he slid the five golden rings onto her finger. "Oh, yes, my true love."

She leaned up to kiss him, and he caught her to him for a much more thorough kiss, so thorough that it was some time later before they broke apart.

She glanced back at the hall and sighed. "I suppose we should go in and look at the tree we all worked on so laboriously."

"Or," he said, "we could take a sleigh ride over to Hawkcrest and see if a couple of blankets on the floor and a fire in the hearth might make it more suitable for that private demonstration you were craving the first time we went there."

"We don't have a sleigh," she reminded him.

"Ah, right. So we'll simply have to sneak upstairs to your bedchamber. Or mine."

She began to grin. "And then?"

"We'll have ourselves a merry little Christmas."

"Now?" she asked.

"Now."

Epilogue

March 1809

Their wedding day was exactly six months after Heywood's father had died. Heywood's mother had requested the date, since by then she would at least be in half mourning and the rest of the family no longer in mourning. She'd been forced to miss the wedding of Grey and Beatrice because of society's rules, and she said she didn't intend to miss Heywood's.

Now he was here at his wedding breakfast, with his new wife at his side. He smiled down at her. Cass's lovely face was awash with wonder at the magic his mother and the rest of the family had wrought at Hawkcrest, just for their celebration. The dining room had been repainted and the wood floors repaired. They'd even replaced the chandelier with a much finer one, fitted with costly beeswax candles.

"It's magnificent, don't you think?" Cass said.

"Yes." He gazed at her beautiful features. "Magnificent."

She caught him staring at her and blushed. "I missed you. I thought you might not make it home."

After Christmas, he'd returned to his regiment to arrange for some-one to take his place so he could retire from the Hussars. Then he'd had a devil of a time trying to get back, with the war raging on the Continent.

"Ah, dearling," he said, with his heart in his throat, "I would have been here if I'd had to *row* across the English Channel."

Kitty approached, her face wreathed in smiles. "Who's rowing across the channel?"

"No one, I hope." Heywood thrust his hand out to the fellow accompanying Kitty. "You must be the lauded Mr. Adams."

"I don't know how lauded I am," the man said as he shook Heywood's hand, "but yes, I'm that gentleman."

Kitty tucked her hand in the crook of his elbow. "My husband's being modest. He's opening a new concern in London and has already attracted twenty clients."

"It's a fine start," Heywood said. "I'll introduce you to Grey. He always has need of a good solicitor."

"I'm more interested in your other talents," Cass said, her eyes gleaming. "The ones that enabled you to whisk Kitty away to Gretna Green before we even realized you were here. And how *did* you find us, anyway?"

He flushed a bright red. "I confess I had to be duplicitous."

"That means he had to lie," Kitty said, clearly delighted that she knew the word. "He had to be duplicitous to see me at the ball, too, on account of Mama telling him all about how she just *knew* Captain Malet would offer for me that night."

"Knowing Aunt Virginia," Cass said, "that was her way of warning Mr. Adams off."

"Precisely," Adams said. "So I slipped into the ball to warn Kitty about Malet since I didn't trust him, and she told me that as long as I refused to offer for her, she would do as she pleased."

"*That* was the friend you'd been talking to who upset you so?" Cass asked.

"Yes. And he *still* didn't offer for me. He thought I could do better." Kitty laughed. "Can you imagine?"

"You deserved better," Adams said indulgently, his eyes shining with love as he gazed down at her.

Heywood knew the feeling only too well. He still couldn't believe he'd found a wife as special as Cass. He covered her hand with his.

She smiled up at him before looking back at Adams. "That doesn't explain how you found us in Lincolnshire, sir."

"Ah, yes, I'm getting to that. You see, as Kitty stormed off, I noticed Malet slip from the room. He'd apparently heard us talking. And when Kitty disappeared, I assumed he'd taken her. So I made sure to go to your aunt's house, and when Malet showed up there with your aunt, and they'd already learned from Malet's coachman that you and Kitty had been carried off by Lord Heywood . . . well, imagine my relief to learn that it was His Lordship. I knew Lord Heywood was a gentleman, and besides, he'd taken you, too, and you would watch over her."

"I tried," Cass said. "But how—"

"Lord Heywood had left his card at your home with his address, but Malet was convinced that you three had gone to Gretna Green, so he wanted to go there. I hoped that His Lordship was merely looking out for Kitty, so I took the chance that you might have come here. I was slowed down by the snow, unfortunately, but—"

"He asked to see me, said he was my solicitor," Kitty put in, clearly too impatient to let him finish, "and the servant went to fetch me. But then my dear love spotted me in the drawing room, and the sleigh was unattended outside and—"

"We took it and ran," Mr. Adams finished.

Heywood blinked. "That is quite a tale."

"It is, isn't it?" Kitty said, then glanced across the room and froze. "Oh, no, Mama has spotted us, and I can't abide another lecture. Come, my dear, let's go have some champagne."

Adams happily let himself be pulled away.

"It's like that 'babes in the wood' tale," Cass said with a laugh. "Kitty always manages to land on her feet."

"Not quite," Heywood said. "She had you and your mother, and now she has Adams. We can only hope she appreciates him."

"I'm sure she does. The same way I appreciate you." Cass beamed at him, and his heart skipped a beat.

"And I appreciate you. Because I would never have had the humility to tell you I wasn't good enough for you. Even though it's true."

"It is indeed," she said lightly. When he blinked at her, she burst into laughter. "I'm teasing you. You should know me better by now."

"Trust me, it will take me years to know you well enough." He bent to whisper, "And I should really like to start now, upstairs in our newly refurbished bedchamber."

"No, indeed, sir. There will be no sneaking around for us. Once I have you to myself, I mean to enjoy it and not have to worry about getting caught by your mother or sister or brothers." When he groaned, she added, "But trust me, once everyone is gone, I will make it well worth your while."

As his blood rose, along with another part of his body, he realized she was never going to be wide-eyed and demure like her cousin.

Thank God.

Don't miss Sabrina Jeffries' sensational new romance . . .

THE BACHELOR
on sale in Summer 2020

Read on for a preview . . .

Chapter 1

Armitage Hall, Lincolnshire
April 1809

Lady Gwyn Drake paced the ornamental bridge like a tigress in a crate. What did it mean when one's blackmailer was late? It certainly didn't bode well for the negotiations she hoped to initiate.

Perhaps she was at the wrong spot.

She drew the man's note out of her pocket and read it again:

> *To Lady Gwyn,*
>
> *Tomorrow at 4 PM, bring fifty guineas to me on the Armitage estate near the bridge that crosses the river if you wish to guarantee my silence. Otherwise, I will feel free to tell such Secrets about you and me as will ruin your good name. You know that I can.*
>
> *Captain L. Malet*

Not the wrong spot then. This was the only bridge over a river on the estate. Did he realize that the house occupied by the estate's handsome gamekeeper, Major Joshua Wolfe, was a short distance away? Or did he just not care?

She scowled. When she'd last seen "L." Malet, ten years ago, he'd been only an ensign in the army and she'd been only twenty. But if he was expecting to meet that same wide-eyed, foolish girl, he was in for a surprise.

Balling up the note, she tossed it into the river. Then she slid her hand into her muff to touch the pocket pistol she'd lifted from the bedside table of her twin brother, Thorn, otherwise known as the Duke of Thornstock. Though the pistol wasn't loaded—she had no clue how to fire a gun, much less load one—the feel of the carved ivory stock beneath her fingers was reassuring. It should look impressive enough to hold off the likes of a coward like Lionel Malet.

She heard the crunch of wheels on gravel just in time to see him descend from a phaeton. He probably owed money on it, but you wouldn't know it to look at him, sauntering down the hill to the bridge without a care in the world.

Hard to believe that she'd risked everything years ago for a pair of blue eyes, a smug smile, and a head of raven curls. Even in a mere ensign's uniform, Lionel had looked incredibly appealing to a woman surrounded by her stepfather's aging friends—or her teasing brother and half brothers.

Today, dressed even more impressively in gentleman's attire, he lacked the power to move her. How could she not have seen the truth back then, that he was debonair and slick, the kind of man who slithered his way into a naïve woman's life, then poisoned her and her future with one bite? If she'd just recognized . . .

It didn't matter. She recognized his true character now. So as he approached, looking utterly sure of himself, she drew out Thorn's pistol and aimed it at him. "That's close enough, sir."

He laughed at her, blast him. "You mean to shoot me, do you?"

"If I have to."

"But you don't." He cocked his head rakishly. "You merely need to pay my price. Fifty guineas is a reasonable amount for my silence, wouldn't you say?"

Her hands shook. She hoped he couldn't see that. "I'm surprised you ask so little, considering what you'd get if you married me."

"Are you still interested in that?" When she merely glared at him, he shrugged. "I didn't think so. What a pity. A marriage would suit both of us."

"I'm sure it would help your finances, but in what possible way could it benefit *me*?" she asked coldly.

He let his insolent gaze trail down her. "You're by no means as youthful as you were at twenty. It won't be long before you're considered an out-and-out spinster, and then no one will marry you."

"Good. That suits me perfectly." Oddly enough, it was the truth. "I'm afraid you have soured me on men, sir." That, too, was the truth. Or part of it, anyway. "Nor am I some green girl to fall for your machinations anymore."

"So why do you need the pistol?"

"My brother fears you might try to abduct me as you tried to do with Kitty Nickman at Christmastide on this very estate."

Mention of his failed plan seemed to spark his temper. "I considered it. But I know Thornstock. If I kidnapped you, he would cut you off, and then we'd both be poor. Indeed, he threatened as much years ago."

The memory of that betrayal settled into her chest like a bad cold. That it still had the power to wound infuriated her. "He was trying to protect me, as any good brother would." Still, it rankled that her twin had read Lionel's character so well when she'd been oblivious to it. "And judging from your attempt to blackmail me, he was wise to do so."

"This is not an attempt." He took a step forward. "I mean to get my money."

She steadied the pistol on him. "I don't have it."

He crossed his arms over his chest. "Then I suppose I'll be telling the world about us, starting with your brother."

A sick fear gripped her at the thought of Thorn—or anyone at all—hearing the truth. "I promise I'll get you your funds once the family goes to London for the season. That's only a few days away. Surely you can wait *that* long."

"Ah, but why should I?"

"Because if I ask Thorn for fifty guineas here in the country, he'll find the request suspicious and demand to know why I want it. There's no plausible lie I can give him. And if I answer him truthfully, he might just murder you."

Lionel chuckled. "You mean you haven't told your arse of a brother what we did?"

"Of course not. And I know you didn't tell him, either. Because you wouldn't be here trying to blackmail me if you had. Thorn would have killed you years ago."

"True." The amusement faded from his cruelly handsome face, leaving only the cold glitter in his eyes. Now *that* was the Lionel Malet she knew and hated. "Fortunately," he went on, "I am better prepared to fight your brother these days. Not for nothing have I trained as a soldier. And Thornstock has undoubtedly grown soft with age."

"If you believe that, then you haven't had much dealings with him recently."

"In any case," he said, brushing off her comment, "I have no intention of waiting for my money. If you can't pay me today, I'll just have to take something else by way of payment."

He stalked across the bridge toward her, and though she backed up swiftly, he was on her before she could get very far. Only when he snatched the gun from her did she realize it wasn't her he was after.

"You can't have that!" she cried, her heart sinking. "That's Thorn's! It's not mine to give!" It was Thorn's most recent purchase, and he was inordinately fond of it. Her brother would never forgive her if she let it be taken.

"I don't care." Lionel examined the pistol, then snorted as he realized that it wasn't loaded. "This will fetch a pretty penny in London while I wait for the rest of my money." He shoved the gun in his greatcoat pocket. "Oh, and the price for my silence has just gone up. It's a hundred guineas now."

When he turned to walk away, she grabbed his arm, trying to prevent him from escaping with Thorn's gun. "I'll get you your dratted money, but you can't have the pistol!"

She'd managed to wrestle it halfway out of his pocket before he gripped her upper arms and shook her. "I will have whatever I want of you, make no mistake. So if you wish me to keep your secrets—"

A shot sounded over their heads. Startled, she and Lionel both looked toward where it had come from, up on the rise behind her where the dower house sat.

Its tenant, Major Wolfe, now swiftly reloaded his own gun, then aimed it at Lionel's heart. Honestly, she'd never been happier to see the gruff former soldier in all her life.

"Step away from her ladyship," Major Wolfe called out as he made his way down to the bridge, somehow keeping his weapon trained on Lionel while maneuvering the uneven surfaces of the riverbank path with his cane.

Lionel sneered at him. "Or what? A mere gamekeeper wouldn't dare to shoot a viscount's son."

Gwyn frowned. "How did you know he's a game— Oh. Right." She'd forgotten that Major Wolfe had helped thwart Lionel during that abduction at Christmas. Not that it mattered. "The major is a duke's grandson and a crack shot, besides. Not only would he dare to shoot you, but he wouldn't miss."

Major Wolfe's gaze flicked to her. He seemed surprised by the remark, though she couldn't imagine why. She'd flirted often enough to make it clear what she thought of him. Then again, she'd ended that after getting a surly response time and again.

The major steadied his aim on Lionel. "Besides, you're standing on *my* land, trying to assault a member of the family *I* work for. So you'd best release the lady, or I swear I'll make you regret it. Not a magistrate in the county would blame me for shooting an armed man on my own property."

Lionel started. "I'm not armed." When Major Wolfe nodded to Lionel's coat pocket, where the ivory handle of Thorn's pistol still hung out, Lionel paled. "The pistol isn't loaded," he said, though he had the good sense to release her.

"Not to mention that it doesn't belong to you." She met Major Wolfe's gaze. "It's Thorn's. Mr. Malet took it from me."

Major Wolfe arched one dark eyebrow at her. "And what were *you* proposing to do with an unloaded pistol?"

"Never mind that. I'm merely saying I want it back."

"Ah." Major Wolfe gestured to Lionel with his firearm. "You heard the lady. Give it to her."

Lionel's eyes narrowed, and Gwyn's heart nearly failed her.

What if he chose to reveal her secret to Major Wolfe? It would be just the sort of thing he'd do to revenge himself on her. And she would die of mortification, which was saying something, since there was little that mortified her these days.

She edged closer to Lionel. "Hand it over." She lowered her voice to a whisper. "I promise you'll have your money once I reach London. But not if you say one word to *him* about our past together."

Lionel glanced from Major Wolfe's weapon to her ashen face. "I'll hold you to your promise," he murmured, then gave her Thorn's pistol and backed to the end of the bridge and then onto the path that led to where his phaeton was waiting.

Major Wolfe, who'd been watching their exchange intently, thankfully didn't ask what they'd talked about. She was fairly certain he couldn't have heard them over the roar of the river below, but she still shook from the knowledge of how narrow an escape she'd made.

And would continue to make as long as Lionel was about.

"I wish you'd killed him," she muttered as Major Wolfe approached her, keeping his eye on the retreating Lionel.

Once Lionel climbed into his phaeton and drove away, Major Wolfe relaxed his stance and unloaded his firearm. Then he shoved his large pistol into the capacious pocket of the ragged greatcoat she'd always seen him wear when working on the estate.

"I'll accompany you back to the hall." When she opened her mouth to protest, he added, "Just in case Malet is lurking nearby, waiting to get a chance at you again."

Oh. That was certainly a good point. "Thank you for coming to my rescue."

He nodded, taciturn as always, and gestured for her to go ahead of him. They crossed the bridge and climbed the hill some time in silence, with her casting him furtive glances every few steps. Lord, but the man was handsome—unfashionably so, with his long black hair tied in a queue by a simple leather string—but handsome nonetheless.

Some would say his jaw was too square and his mouth too thin to be called attractive, and that might be true. But it was his hazel eyes that distinguished him from every other man she'd met, even

Heywood, whose eyes were also hazel. The major's were actually brown in the middle with green ringing the outer edges. In some lights, the green predominated, in others the brown.

Those eyes were endlessly changing—she could stare at them all day. Not that she'd had many chances. When his sister Bea had been on the estate, Gwyn had seen him more often, but once Bea had married, he'd seemed determined not to associate with anyone who lived in Armitage Hall.

That didn't keep the maids from whispering about him—how he looked, what he said, what he did. One had even stated that she would marry Major Wolfe in a heartbeat, lame leg or no. Yet he seemed to have no idea of his appeal to the female sex, or surely he'd have taken a wife by now. Why, he was already thirty-one!

"What did Malet want?" Major Wolfe finally asked.

Thankfully, she had a plausible explanation ready for him. "To make me go with him. That's why I brandished the pistol."

Major Wolfe searched her face. "Since when do you carry a pistol with you on Armitage land?"

"Since Mr. Malet told Heywood that he meant to kidnap me in revenge for something Heywood and his friend did abroad," she snapped.

"Malet made that threat four months ago," Major Wolfe pointed out. "It's odd that he waited until now to attempt it."

"Perhaps he was waiting until our guard was down," she said dryly. "Or perhaps he had tried courting an heiress who wouldn't know all about his wicked intent, and she didn't prove viable, so he fell back on his old ways."

"And you just happened to be roaming the estate with your brother's unloaded pistol when Malet came looking to kidnap you."

She knew perfectly well that Major Wolfe wasn't credulous enough to believe *that*. Then an idea struck her. "Thorn heard that Mr. Malet was nosing around in Sanforth, so he warned me to keep an eye out."

"Your brother is presently in residence at the hall?"

"Yes. And he gave me his pocket pistol for protection."

"A valuable, unloaded pistol that he didn't teach you how to load or shoot? That seems reckless of him, and your twin has never struck me as the reckless sort."

"You'd be surprised," she muttered. A pox on Major Wolfe and his military mind. This was not going well.

"What's more, you and Malet seemed to know each other, at least well enough to be exchanging confidences."

"Confidences! Don't be silly. Whatever you think you saw isn't what you're implying."

"Hmm. If you say so." Major Wolfe moved along the path through the woods at a surprisingly good pace. "Why is your brother here anyway? Doesn't he have an estate of his own to run?"

"Of course, but he decided to accompany me and Mama to London for the season. I am to be presented at court and have my debut in society, you know."

"I'm well aware," he said tensely.

What was *that* supposed to mean?

Oh, he must be thinking of his sister Bea and the fact that she was being presented as well, but as Grey's new wife, the Duchess of Greycourt.

"Thankfully," he went on, "today's incident will impress upon Thornstock the need to keep a closer eye on you and your suitors in London."

The statement was so typically male and arrogant that she was about to blister his ears over his presumption when the greater implications of his words hit her. "Surely you don't mean to tell Thorn about this."

Major Wolfe lifted an eyebrow. "Of course I mean to tell him. He needs to know so he can make arrangements to accompany you everywhere."

She hurried her steps so she could stand in front of him, blocking the path. "But you can't! I don't want Thorn mucking about in my personal affairs. I had enough of that growing up with him in Berlin."

In the darkness of the forest, the major's eyes looked as brown as oak and just as hard. "You cannot expect me to keep silent on this matter."

"Why not? It's none of your concern. I'm a grown woman. I can handle the likes of Mr. Malet in good society, where I will never be alone."

"*Never?* Even in the Armitage town house? Or going out onto a balcony at a ball for a breath of air? Or—"

"I will be careful everywhere, I assure you. And anyway, there won't be nearly as many situations in which he could effect a kidnapping without drawing attention to himself."

And there'd be even less of them if the major told Thorn about Lionel, and her twin decided to dog her heels wherever she went. Then she'd never get the chance to meet with Lionel privately and give him his money.

Nor could she tell *Thorn* about the blackmail. He would either kill Lionel outright and end up in gaol or challenge Lionel to a duel and end up in gaol. No, Thorn could never know what Lionel was up to.

"Please, Major Wolfe, you must not tell my brother—"

"Your brother may heed your pleas, Lady Gwyn, but I know better than to do so. Either you tell him in my presence, or I will tell him myself. But one way or the other, he is going to hear what Malet attempted. That's the end of it."

Good Lord, he was like a dog with a bone. And now, thanks to him, her ability to pay Lionel his money and put an end to this madness had just become ten times harder.

One Wicked Winter Night

Mary Jo Putney

Chapter 1

Bombay, India
Summer 1816

Dawn was the best time of day here. Night had cooled the air and the savage heat of high noon was still hours away. The air was fragrant with scents unknown in England, and in the trees bright birds were busy about their early morning business.

Lady Diana Lawrence, the blackest sheep of her generation of the noble Lawrence family, curled up on the teak bench of her bedroom's balcony and admired the morning mists floating over the field that lay beyond the house. Dim shapes resolved into an elephant. An oxcart. A graceful woman in a sari carrying a bundle of sticks. The timeless rhythms of India.

She felt a sudden sharp longing for the mists of home drifting over the still surface of the Broads. Water birds and reeds and fishermen in low boats gliding across the silvery waters.

She'd left England over seven years before. The general reason was her craving to see the world; the specific one had been the shattering pain of a doomed love affair. In the years since, she'd traveled widely and seen many strange and wondrous sights.

After several years of traveling ever eastward, she'd come to rest in India, but she'd never felt that she would stay here forever. Perhaps it was time to go home, because England was home and always would be.

She took a sip of her cardamom-flavored tea. That tea would be something she would take home with her. She asked her companion, "Do you think you'd like England? It's not as warm, but I guarantee you'll continue to eat regularly."

He yawned, showing sharp feline teeth, then tucked his white nose under his long black tail. The Panda was a pragmatist. As long as there was food, he would be content.

Now the sky had lightened enough to read the letter that had arrived the evening before from her favorite niece, Lady Aurora Lawrence Vance. She was known as "Roaring Rory" in some circles, just as Diana had been proclaimed "the Dashing Diana." Or even "the Devilish Diana." More proof of how alarmingly alike she and Rory were.

But Rory's life had taken a surprising turn toward love, marriage, and stability. Though not, Diana was sure, tedium.

Having savored the anticipation long enough, she opened the oilcloth packet that had protected the letter on its journey halfway around the world.

> *My darling Aunt Diana!*
> *So much news to share! (Oh, I must be careful or I will run out of exclamation points before the end of this missive!)*
> *For someone who always found the prospect of marriage deeply alarming, I'm finding the reality quite deeply wonderful.*

Diana laughed, feeling Rory's bubbling personality as strongly as if she were in the room. She returned to the letter.

> *Once more I give thanks to my wonderful visit with you in India because that led to being captured by corsairs on the way home, which was not wonderful but did lead*

me to meeting Gabriel, which never would have happened if I'd been more sensible and less captured.

When I wrote my last letter, I believe that I said we were leasing a rather absurdly large house in London because it was the best available. I also mentioned that we were looking for a modest estate near London.

However, instead of buying an estate of our own, we decided to make Gabriel's grandfather's estate, Langbridge, our country home. It's very sensible because Gabriel will eventually inherit the property and he wants to become acquainted with the land and people. Having spent so many years at sea, he says, it will take time to learn farming and estate management.

Of course he's learning quickly and enjoying the challenge. Most of all, he loves having a stable full of horses and being able to ride whenever he wishes, which wasn't possible in his sea captain life. Now we ride together, which is a high point of our days. Or was—I'm not riding as often now for reasons I'll get to soon.

But the real issue is not learning the land, but the fact that his grandparents are getting old and they need us. His grandmother is a darling and we plotted together to persuade the men that the move was a good idea.

The negotiations made the Congress of Vienna look straightforward! The years of estrangement after Admiral Vance disowned Gabriel made matters awkward, but Gabriel wants to make up for those years, and his grandfather, once England's most rigid retired admiral, now yearns for Gabriel's company and decided he was willing to accept my unruly self as part of the package.

I miss Cousin Constance dreadfully, but we exchange letters often, the United States being much closer than India, though not precisely close. We're collaborating on new stories.

She sends her love to you, along with the happy news that she and Jason now have a baby boy! Named Richard Gabriel Landers in honor of Jason's father and my

Gabriel. She assures me that he is the best and most beau-
tiful baby in North America.

Diana thought nostalgically of the fun the three of them had had when Rory and Constance had come for a long visit, the only members of the Lawrence family to make it all the way to India. Those months were the most enjoyable Diana had experienced here. Constance was illegitimate, the daughter of Diana's least reliable brother, but she had grown up sweet and kind and wise. She was Diana's second-favorite niece, though really she shouldn't make comparisons. Rory and Constance were both wonderful.

Constance and I also have another book baby! (Oh,
dear, the exclamation points are breaking out again!) The
Shining Blade, *our corsair book, has now been published*
and is quite the rage! Have I thanked you lately for send-
ing our first books to your publisher friend in London? He
has done well by us, under the stern eye of my father, who
handles all our contracts and makes sure we aren't swin-
dled.

Have you ever thought of publishing your own work?
Not novels, as I'm the one with the lurid Gothic imagina-
tion, but your travel journals. They're quite wonderful—
you have such a keen eye and a sense of humor about the
travails of travel, and warmth for the people you meet and
the differences and the similarities among us.

Diana's brows arched as she considered. She'd never really thought about that. Her journals were her private thoughts and sketches and reflections, but travel memoirs were popular and few were written by independent, not to mention scandalous, ladies. This was definitely worth considering. She returned to reading.

I probably shouldn't ask this, my favorite aunt, but
have you considered returning to England? You are missed
here by everyone, most of all by me. You could stay with
us in London—the house is so large you'd never have to
see us if you didn't want to!

Plus—I'm also increasing, slightly behind Constance,
who is ever more efficient than I am. It won't be long
now! (Clearly I haven't written in far too long! Blast,
more exclamation points have escaped!)

Gabriel is delighted but also rather anxious, despite my
assurances that Lawrence women are famously fertile and
never, ever die in childbirth. As you know, I put the
"rude" in "rude good health."

I'd like you to be godmother to this new little person,
as you were for me. You were the best godmother! The
globe of the world you gave me was the most marvelous
present I ever received and inspired my own adventures. It
has a place of honor in our library.

And—if you don't mind and I have a girl, I want to
name her Diana.

Diana swallowed hard when she read that, sharply aware of how much she missed her family. Most of them were quite enjoyable people, and now that she was thirty and officially a spinster, they wouldn't be trying to marry her off to some boring, bossy gentleman. They wouldn't *dare!*

She reread the last lines of the letter, unable to suppress the ache of lost possibilities in her own life. For better and worse, the past had made her what she was.

Setting regret aside, she folded the paper, thinking that there was no good reason not to return. She'd had more than her share of grand sights and adventures, and the doomed love affair was no more than a faint, bittersweet memory. He'd likely forgotten her—and if he did remember, it would be with anger.

For a brief, painful moment she remembered his agonized expression when she'd left him. Young, honest, both vulnerable and strong, and hauntingly handsome. Though she knew she'd been right to leave, she hated herself for what she'd done.

She hoped he'd recovered quickly. He'd surely married by now, perhaps had a child or two. Sadly she recognized that she what she really wanted was for him to have forgotten her. That would mitigate her lingering guilt.

Her thoughts were interrupted by the arrival of Jane Evans, a round, dark-haired woman who owned the house where Diana had her rooms. The widow of a British sergeant, Jane had been struggling to support her children when Diana had arrived in India. They'd become first friends, then partners in their export business.

Jane sat on the other end of the bench and scratched the head of the Panda, who lay between them. He began purring but didn't bother opening his eyes.

Seeing the letter Diana held, Jane asked, "News from home?"

"Yes, from my niece Rory. She has much to say. She's expecting a baby. In fact, it's probably arrived by now."

"Good for her!" Jane gave her partner a shrewd glance. "Is she trying to persuade you to return to England?"

"How did you guess?" Diana asked, surprised.

"It's been obvious that you're missing England and your family, Lady Aurora most of all. I saw how close you were when she visited here. With matching figures and golden blond hair, you look more like sisters than aunt and niece." Jane chuckled. "Now that Rory has married and become respectable, perhaps you're thinking you might do the same?"

"No!" Diana said, scandalized. "For any number of reasons, just *no!* But going back to England and seeing my family again is very tempting. It's time for me to leave India. If I sail soon, I should be home before Christmas."

"Christmas. Snow. Ice. Freezing rain." Jane shuddered elaborately. "No, thank you! India is my home now. My children were born here. But your roots haven't sunken into Indian soil as deeply as mine have."

"Perhaps I'm too much an observer." Diana slanted a glance at her friend. "Rory suggests I should publish my travel writings."

"I think that's an excellent idea!" Jane bit her lip, looking worried. "But what about our export business? I don't have the money to buy you out now. It would take several years."

"I assumed we'd continue," Diana replied. "I funded the business at the beginning, but you've always been best at finding silks and perfumes and carvings that will sell well in England. When I'm back there, I can find new markets for our wares. The business should prosper even more than it already has."

Jane gave a sigh of relief. "I like this idea. But I shall miss you, Diana!" Her expression turned crafty. "I assume you'll leave the Panda here with us rather than subject the poor fellow to such a long voyage."

Diana laughed. "Keep your greedy hands off my cat! You and the children will just have to find another one. Or two or three. But where I go the Panda goes!"

"I was afraid of that." Jane reached out and caught Diana's hand. "Godspeed, my dear. I look forward to hearing of your new adventures."

Diana squeezed her friend's hand. "I don't imagine I'll have grand adventures in the future. I look forward to a peaceful life becoming an extremely eccentric old lady."

"You might believe that." Jane smiled mischievously. "But I know better!"

Chapter 2

London
December 1816

Abandoning ladylike decorum, Diana leaned forward in the carriage so she could stare out the window at the streets of London, still familiar after all these years. "We'll be at Rory's house soon, Panda. I can't wait to see her and meet her intrepid sea captain. I do hope they're in town. If not, on to Lawrence House in hopes that my brother and his wife are there, not yet gone to the country. And if family fails, it will be a hotel."

"Mrowp?"

"Of course a hotel will allow you to stay with me, Panda. I am the eccentric Lady Diana Lawrence, daughter and sister of earls." Her gaze moved to the spacious and well-padded carrying cage where Panda's annoyed black and white face could be seen behind a latticed window. "And you will be free to roam again. You're a very good traveler, but the less time you spend in your carrier, the happier you are."

"Mroof!" he replied emphatically.

The carriage rumbled to a stop in front of a grand town house. Diana guessed that it was double width, twice the size of the usual

London home. As Rory said, there would be space for her and the Panda, and the knocker was up, so the family was in town—yes!

Too excited to wait, she tumbled out of the carriage and followed the guard to the front door. The crisp December air was exhilarating. The guard solemnly knocked, the boom of the knocker echoing faintly inside.

Diana had to control herself so she wouldn't be jumping up and down. Even though Rory was in town, she could easily be out and about.

But no, a dignified butler opened the door and Diana could see over his shoulder that a familiar golden blonde was racing toward the door. "Aunt Diana! I had a feeling!" She hurled herself into her aunt's arms.

Laughing and crying, Diana hugged her back. "I'm so glad to see you!"

"It's been far too long," Rory agreed. "Egan, please have Her Ladyship's baggage brought in."

"A moment, Rory, I'll bring the Panda in myself."

"Oh, splendid! I'm so glad you brought him. You can take him into the small drawing room over there while I order refreshments." Rory enveloped her in another swift hug before turning to give more orders.

The drawing room was warmed by a cozy fire. As soon as Diana was inside, she released the cat from his cage. The Panda marched out like a king returning from exile and gave her a reproachful look from his huge green eyes.

She scratched his head, thinking what a handsome cat he was. Mostly black, he had a white muzzle, chest, and paws, like a gentleman dressed for a formal occasion. "I'm sorry for the discomfort, my darling puss, but now we're home."

Rory entered the drawing room followed by a footman pushing a well-stocked tea cart. Seeing the cat, she bent over and rubbed her fingers together enticingly. "Panda, do you remember me? You were only half-grown when I met you in India, but look at you now! What a fine, substantial cat you've become. In fact, you might have a touch of elephant in your ancestry."

He loftily turned his back on her, so she took a cheese puff from a platter on the tea cart and offered it. He immediately came to her and took the morsel daintily from her fingers. It disappeared instantly, after which the Panda politely indicated that another cheese puff would be welcomed by a cat who had just traveled halfway around the world. Rory obliged and rubbed his head affectionately as she set a second puff on the floor. "That's my Panda! Always willing to be bribed."

As Diana laughed, the Panda set off to explore the room and the women settled onto the wing chairs by the fire. As she poured tea, Rory asked, "I hope you're home for good?"

"I think so. We'll see." Diana sipped her tea and ate little sandwiches and cheese puffs as they caught up on each other's news. After finishing her repast with two deliciously spicy apple tarts, Diana leaned back in her chair with a happy smile. "But let me look at you!"

Her niece was glowing; there was no other word for it. Clearly no longer pregnant, she was a little rounder, a little softer, and had an expression of serene happiness. "I'm guessing motherhood suits you?"

"Marriage and motherhood both." Rory agreed. "Who would have believed it? Gabriel is out now, but he should be home soon. I can't wait for you to meet him. Or to meet the newest Diana."

Suppressing her pang of envy, Diana exclaimed, "A girl! Oh, I do hope she's a madcap like you and me!"

"Gabriel took one look at her after she was born and declared that she would be." Rory grinned. "He claims another dashing Lawrence female is exactly what he wanted. She's sleeping now, so I'll wait to introduce you to each other."

"I shall give her a globe of her own when she's old enough," Diana promised.

"Now that you're home we can have the christening, and then the holiday celebrations."

"A proper Christmas with cold weather," Diana said nostalgically. "Gathering greens and roasting chestnuts and, with luck, being snowed in with my favorite people."

"Don't forget icy winds, rutted roads, and being trapped inside for days until you want to scream with restlessness," her niece said wryly. "Especially if you're snowed in with people who drive you mad!"

"I'd like to be snowed in with you so we could practice our Hindu dancing. I missed that when you and Constance left. I wonder how much I remember?" Diana rose and began humming Indian dance music to accompany herself as she cupped her hands in front of her and bent her knees, sinking into the first steps.

Rory rose to her feet and began mirroring Diana's movements. "I've missed the dancing, too. It's easier when wearing Hindu clothing rather than European, though."

"Luckily we both had *salwar kameezes* made," Diana said, referring to the loose trouser-like garments and tunics that made movement easy. She increased the tempo of her humming and tried to remember the intricate footwork. "Next time we can wear them."

They fell into a simple routine as they moved across the drawing room, remembering the sensual rhythms. After they'd crossed and recrossed the room several times, Diana said rather breathlessly, "I doubt our dance would be approved by many Indians, but it's such fun! Remember the time when we were performing in front of the British Resident and I tripped over the Panda?"

"The Panda does like getting underfoot." Rory laughed. "And the Resident didn't mind your ending up in his lap!"

Her laughter was contagious and Diana joined in, bending sideways from the waist as her raised hands stroked the air like delicate birds. Rory did the same and added a slow, provocative swing of the hips.

As Diana echoed the movements, the drawing room door opened and a tall brown-haired man entered the room. So this was Rory's captain! Still dancing, Diana studied him with interest. Quietly handsome, quietly well dressed in blue coat and tan trousers, and with gray eyes that showed strength, intelligence, and humor.

Rory bounced over to him. "Look who has arrived!"

Gabriel put an arm around her and brushed a kiss on her forehead. "Clearly she's a Lawrence, and since she's not one of your sisters, she must be the Aunt Diana you've been longing for?"

"In person, Captain!" Diana swept into a graceful curtsy. "Rory has invited me to stay here for a while. If you don't object?"

"Of course not." With Rory still under his arm, Gabriel approached and offered his hand. "I didn't realize you were so young, Lady Diana. Nor that you and Rory look so much alike. Because you have the same coloring, you look even more like her than her cousin Constance."

"Call me Diana. I was the youngest of my family, one of those late mistakes," Diana explained as she took his hand. His clasp was warm and strong. "I'm only five years older than Rory, and we were always natural allies."

"Until you left England," Rory said sadly. "No one else tolerated me half so well. But I did understand your desire to escape the gilded cage."

"I'm glad you did, since we wouldn't have met if you'd behaved as a proper, boring young lady." Gabriel's eyes turned thoughtful. "Rory, you've been thinking about taking advantage of this house's grand ballroom. What about an end of the season masquerade ball to gather our friends before they travel to the country for the Christmas holidays? You and your aunt could dance together before the midnight unmasking."

"What a splendid idea!" Diana exclaimed. "But I'm amazed you suggested it. So many men dislike dressing up for masquerades."

Gabriel chuckled. "I thought I'd come as a sea captain. That would be easy."

"You must at least be a blockade-runner, my dear!" Rory said.

"When I was a blockade-runner, I dressed the same way as when I was a legitimate sea captain," he pointed out apologetically.

"We'll figure something out," Rory said. "Perhaps a tricorn hat and an eye patch like a pirate? I do like the idea of wearing Indian clothing and dancing with my aunt. It will be a way to introduce you to society again, Diana."

Diana thought of the man she didn't want to meet, but he preferred the country, so it wasn't likely their paths would cross any time soon. Still . . . "I'd prefer to quietly sneak back so no one will notice," Diana said. "The advantage of being veiled."

A long-legged feline stealthily entered the door Gabriel had left open. Diana blinked. "Is that the Spook, the ship's cat you wrote about? You're right; he is rather oddly proportioned." She grinned. "I do believe that he is a Norwegian Ice Cat."

It was Rory's turn to blink. "A what?"

"A Norwegian Ice Cat. Those long legs, the pale Viking coloring of white and soft gray, the crossed blue eyes. Clearly a Scandinavian breed."

Gabriel laughed. "I assume you just made that up, but I like it. It's a much more impressive designation than being a crossbreed wharf cat."

"His pedigree doesn't matter," Rory said as she bent and beckoned to the new arrival. The cat approached and offered his head for scratching. "His origins are mysterious and he's very shy, but he's also very sweet. A most superior cat."

Gabriel said, "Whether wharf cat or Norwegian Ice Cat, he was the best ratter I've ever had on a ship." He put a small cheese puff on a tea plate and set it on the floor. The Spook abandoned head scratching in favor of food. "His life is easier now, but he does ensure that our kitchen is vermin-free."

The Panda emerged from behind the sofa and paused, his gaze intent on the other feline. "Your cat?" Gabriel remarked. "He's a very substantial fellow. Solid, not as rangy as the Spook."

Ears flattening, the Panda moved forward with stiff legs, his gaze locked on the alleged ice cat, who began to look anxious. The three humans held their breath, hoping there wouldn't be an explosion of fur.

The Panda reached his rival and there was a long, fraught pause before he gently touched his nose to that of the other cat. The Spook relaxed and began licking the Panda's ears. There was a general sigh of relief. "That went well," Diana observed. "If they hated each other, I would have had to move to a hotel."

"Luckily that's not necessary." Rory split the rest of the small cheese puffs between two plates, then set them down a yard apart. Both cats began eating peacefully.

Diana hoped that was a good omen for her return home.

Chapter 3

Anthony Raines was serving himself breakfast eggs and ham from the sideboard when his sister Athena said, "The Vances are giving a ball that you should attend. You'll be getting a card."

"It will be the last large event of the Little Season," his other sister, Julia, added. "You really should put in an appearance to show the world you're still alive."

"No!" He drew himself up to his full, impressive height and said sternly, "I don't want to hear either of you use the world 'should' to me! I am the fifth Duke of Castleton and the head of the family and I will not be dictated to by a pair of unruly females!"

His sisters smiled at him, completely unintimidated. "But you are the youngest," his petite, dark-haired sister Julia pointed out with misleading innocence. "Since I was gone for so long, I have many years' worth of 'shoulds' to deliver."

Athena grinned. "Given that I'm illegitimate and didn't meet you until I was a grown woman, I have trouble seeing you as head of my family. In fact, after Will and I married, we agreed that our household would have no head, only a partnership of equals."

Anthony smiled ruefully as he sat at the table with his plate of food and accepted a cup of steaming tea from Julia. Though the three of them shared similar features and dark hair with a hint of auburn, they hadn't known one another well, which was why he'd suggested these fortnightly sibling breakfasts when they were all in town. He was very fond of both his brothers-in-law, but these gatherings were just for the three children of the rather dreadful fourth Duke of Castleton. It hadn't taken long for the bond of blood to lead to relaxed, teasing relationships.

But Anthony's delightful big sisters did have a lamentable tendency to tell him what to do. "We've reached an impasse. You won't become meek and obedient at my request and neither will I, which means I won't go to another annoying ball."

Both women laughed and Athena said, "Meekness seems to have been left out of the Raines family bloodline."

"True, but you really should get out more, Anthony," Julia said more seriously. "You're turning into a hermit."

"And you two seem to be turning into matchmakers who want me to find a wife and secure the succession and all that nonsense," he said dryly.

"I have no interest in whether you'll produce an heir to the noble Castleton title," Julia said. "But marriage to the right person is a very fine thing, and you seem to enjoy my two children a great deal. You won't ever meet that right person if you avoid all social occasions."

Having seen the bond between his sisters and their mates, he understood their desire to proselytize, but their situations were very different. "Neither of you had a London season. You were both fortunate enough to meet the right mate far from all that nonsense under circumstances that allowed you to discover each other in a down-to-earth way."

"I'm not sure that is how I would describe Will's courtship of me," Athena said with amusement. "But we did come to know each other quickly and well. Explain to me what a London season is like."

He grimaced. "To be an eligible duke is like being a fox surrounded by a pack of slavering hounds anxious to rip you to shreds. Only in my case, it's gimlet-eyed mothers presenting their daughters like choice riding hacks. Insipid maidens trying desperately to prove that they are perfectly suited to become my duchess. They giggle and bat their eyelashes a lot. The bolder ones might turn up in my bed at a house party, so I always take my valet as a witness when I retire in a strange house. When I'm sure there are no lurking females, I lock my door before I go to sleep."

"Really?" Julia asked in horrified fascination.

"Really," he confirmed. "The boldest are the widows who try to lure me into a dark alcove so they can . . ." He paused to find words that weren't too indelicate. "So they can grope my body. As if I will find a stranger's hand down my breeches alluring!"

Both his sisters winced. "I thought only women had to endure being mauled by arrogant brutes," Athena said.

"Usually, but being a duke pins a target on my back." He frowned. "Society needs better manners for both men and women."

Julia said, "To make it worse, you're presentable looking and generally quite affable. No wonder you're stalked by avaricious females and their mothers."

"And no wonder you've been put off of love and marriage." Athena cocked her head curiously. "Have you ever fallen in love?"

He hesitated, unsure of how much to say. "Infatuation once. I even asked her to marry me, but she turned me down, thereby proving that not all women are avaricious."

"Perhaps not, but she must have been a fool," Julia said loyally.

He shrugged, wishing he hadn't raised the subject. "She said I was too young, and she was right." A pity he'd never met a woman to compare with her since. . . .

"I understand that you don't want to be hunted, but this is a good argument for going to the Vances' ball," Athena said seriously. "It's a masquerade, so you can enjoy yourself in safety because you won't be recognized as prey. You can leave before the unmasking, but who knows? You might meet someone whose company you enjoy and you can meet face-to-face later."

"I do like dancing," Anthony admitted. And life had been rather dull of late. "Very well, you've convinced me. I'll attend in peaceful anonymity."

"What costume will you wear?" Julia asked.

"A mask and domino will do. I have a couple of them around somewhere."

"That's not good enough if anyone is stalking you." Julia considered. "What about dressing as a monk swathed in miles of robe?"

He chuckled. "I don't think of myself as arrogant, but I doubt I could carry off humility convincingly."

"And sandals would be cold at this season," Julia said. "What about going as Byron's Corsair? A 'man of loneliness and mystery.' Utterly thrilling!"

"Really, Julia! There's no mystery about me; I'm a rather dull and dutiful duke," he protested. "Nor am I particularly lonely. I have friends and rather too much work keeping me busy."

"True, but you'll look very fine and dangerous if you dress all in black," Athena said with a gleam in her eyes. "With a sweeping black cape and a black mask, then tie a long scarf around your head. That should disguise you well."

"You'll certainly attract females." Athena looked thoughtful. "If anyone asks whether I know the identity of the mysterious man in black, I'll say you're a disowned younger son on the verge of being sent to debtor's prison. That should keep you safe."

"You could add a sheathed sword to beat off encroaching maidens," Julia suggested.

"No sword, sheathed or otherwise," he said. "Swords make it very difficult to dance. But otherwise, the costume doesn't sound too uncomfortable. Very well. 'Tis a corsair I shall be!"

When his sisters applauded, he rose and bowed dramatically. Finding Athena and Julia was the best thing that had happened to him in years.

It would be unseemly to think that his father's death was the best thing.

Chapter 4

Anthony gave a quiet sigh of pleasure as they approached the ball-room and heard the dance music reach out to embrace the guests. He was glad Julia and Athena had persuaded him to come. He looked forward to dancing, good food and drink, and blessed anonymity.

Rather than arriving conspicuously alone, he'd come with Athena and her husband, Will. They were dressed as dashing Spanish gueril-las. Will was extremely easygoing, but seeing him in the costume of a mountain warrior, Anthony wouldn't want to meet him in a dark alley. Athena looked gloriously dangerous in a split-skirted female version of the costume, and as Anthony had learned from her, she'd earned her right to dress that way. He assumed the holstered pistols at their hips were not loaded.

Their host, Captain Vance, was welcoming guests at the en-trance to the ballroom. He wore a sea captain's gold-braided navy coat and white breeches, and apart from a narrow mask, he made no attempt to disguise himself.

He greeted them with a warm smile. "Will, Athena, I'm glad you could come!"

"So much for the anonymity of a masquerade," Will said with mock regret.

"You and Athena are both too magnificently tall to be easily disguised," Vance pointed out.

"I asked the modiste if she could come up with a costume that would make me look six inches shorter, but she merely shrugged with despair," Athena said mournfully. "It's hard to disguise a beanpole."

"But a magnificent beanpole," Will assured her as he patted her hand where it curled around his arm. "Is Lady Aurora lurking about somewhere?"

"Indeed she is. She wants to surprise everyone later." Vance turned to Anthony. "Welcome, man in black. I hope you'll enjoy yourself this evening."

Vance could probably make a good guess at Anthony's identity since he'd come with Athena and Will, but Anthony made a sweeping bow, his black cape swirling around him. "I am a man of loneliness and mystery," he intoned in a deep accented voice. "Though I hope to alleviate the former for a few short hours this evening."

Vance laughed. "Alleviate away, Sir Corsair. Though the mystery won't outlast the unmasking."

He turned to the next guests, who by chance were Julia and her husband, Major Alex Randall. They were dressed in rich medieval Italian garments. Recognizing her siblings, Julia explained, "Romeo and Juliet."

Since Anthony knew Randall as a serious, reserved army veteran, he said, "You're a lovely demure Juliet, but Romeo is a surprisingly romantic choice for a battle-hardened warrior."

A smile appeared below Randall's mask as he put his arm around his wife, "The costume suits because Romeo fell in love with Juliet at first glance, just as I fell in love with Julia."

Julia ducked her head with a shy smile as Anthony said, "I'm very glad that you rewrote the play with a happy ending!"

As the five of them moved into the ballroom, he realized that both his sisters had married soldiers who had turned out to be admirable husbands. Maybe that meant he ought to listen to their matchmaking advice, but little brothers weren't supposed to be obedient.

Smiling to himself, he surveyed the ballroom, which was comfortably full, but had enough room for dancing. There was sufficient light from the chandeliers to admire the costumes of other guests, but not so much light as to ruin the romantic mood. The wide space was festively decorated with sweeping lengths of sumptuously colored fabric and bundles of evergreens and berries, and like all good ballrooms, there were several alcoves where couples could retreat for a bit of privacy.

Musicians played from the gallery that ran diagonally above a far corner of the ballroom. Interestingly, curtains draped from the bottom of the gallery to the floor, perhaps concealing a surprise for later.

As he began circling the room, he realized that there was an intriguing, exotic scent in the air. Incense? But not one he was familiar with. He followed the scent and discovered a brazier in a corner tended by a masked servant who dropped a couple of pellets on the coals, intensifying the scent. A very clever idea by the Vances.

Having familiarized himself with his surroundings, Anthony looked around for a partner as the musicians struck the first notes of a popular longways dance called Apley House. Ah, that robust woman dressed as Queen Elizabeth was tapping her foot to the music, her posture that of someone yearning to dance.

He approached her and bowed, sweeping his cape before her. "Alas, I am not Sir Walter Raleigh, but would Your Royal Highness condescend to dance with a lowly corsair like me?"

Smiling mischievously, she offered her hand. "That would be a great, wicked delight, Sir Corsair!"

From her voice, he guessed that she was of mature years, but she danced well and they both enjoyed the set.

For his next dance, he found a shy female dressed as a shepherdess lurking in a corner, the very image of a wallflower even when in costume. He coaxed her into a dance. She wasn't as skilled a partner as Good Queen Bess had been, but she gained in confidence and by the end they were laughing together.

The beau monde needed more occasions like this, where people could simply enjoy each other oblivious of rank. It was a fine thing not to be a duke.

Diana had brought her champagne glass upstairs with her, and she emptied it as she and Rory entered Diana's bedroom. "Given the amount of champagne your guests are consuming, our dancing is bound to be well received!"

"This far from India, no one will know if we're any good or not," Rory said cheerfully as she removed her voluminous green domino, then her mask. Underneath she wore her dance costume. The gold-and-burgundy-patterned *salwar* were like very full trousers but narrow at the ankles. The *kameez* tunic was burgundy with gold-embroidered inserts and sleeves that ended midway between shoulder and elbow.

Diana's costume was the same, and they both wore golden slippers. With her mask gone, Diana wrapped a long gold-patterned shawl called a dopatta around her head, face, and shoulders so only her eyes were visible. Then she donned her dark blue domino again to cover her costume. "Are you ready to dazzle or at least surprise those members of the beau monde who are still in London?"

"Indeed I am, though I so wish Constance was here! The opening movements are best with three dancers."

"We'll still dazzle them," Diana promised. "This is not English country dancing!"

"And if we do badly, we disappear back upstairs and change our clothing so no one will know who the incompetent exotic dancers were," Rory said mischievously.

Diana laughed. "It's always good to have a line of retreat!"

Dominos billowing around them, they descended the back stairs to the ballroom, took their places, and waited for the music.

Midnight was nearing when Captain Vance signaled for the musicians to stop playing, then stepped in front of the curtained area beneath the small gallery. In a voice that could carry across a deck in an Atlantic hurricane, he announced, "We have something special for you tonight. A pair of dancers such as few of you have ever seen. Draw around and prepare to be enthralled!"

Curious, the guests gathered in a semicircle around the curtained area, shorter guests in front, taller ones behind. Anthony stood in back opposite the middle of the impromptu stage. Delicate flute music that sounded strange to the British ear rose from the gallery, soft at first but growing louder. A small drum began to beat, soon joined by a larger drum with a deeper tone.

The curtain drew apart to reveal a low stage with a motionless figure standing in the center. Good God, it was a colorfully garbed female with four arms! Two hands were pressed together in front of the female's heart and the other pair of arms were lifted high, the fingertips touching over her head.

This was the image of a Hindu goddess, Anthony realized. He'd seen figurines of such entities, usually with six arms if he recalled correctly.

For long moments while the music intensified, the figure was motionless. Then the audience gasped as the pairs of arms began to move with stylized precision. The tempo of the music sped up and the figure separated into two identical females. They'd been lined up so perfectly that only when they moved apart that it was clear the goddess's image had been formed from two women.

The dancers wore numerous gold and silver bangles on their wrists and the chiming of the bracelets joined flute and drum to invoke a sense of distant, fascinating lands. The dance that followed was enchanting as the veiled dancers spun and dipped and performed slow, erotic hip movements seldom seen in this part of the world.

Sometimes the dancers took identical steps, other times they mirrored each other in perfect harmony as the flowing fabric of their full trousers emphasized each movement. They were lithe, mesmerizing, and deeply sensual.

Anthony loved dancing himself and felt it was the only good reason to attend balls and assemblies. He also loved watching talented dancers, and these two women were creating magic.

After several enchanting minutes, the music slowed and the dancers moved back into their original positions, the woman in front casting her eyes downward as she pressed her palms together in front of her breasts, the woman behind visible only as a pair of arms raised heavenward with palms pressed together over her head.

The music faded to nothing and the dance was done.

There was a long, awed silence before the audience broke into enthusiastic applause. Laughing, the dancers separated and bowed together, their hands clasped. Anthony was wondering where the devil Vance had found these wonderful creatures when the musicians in the gallery struck up a waltz, the latest fashion in wicked dances.

Grinning, Vance moved forward and reached out to the left-hand dancer to help her down from the low stage. When she was on the dance floor, he tugged down her veil to reveal the laughing face of Lady Aurora Vance. "Wonderful, my lady bright!"

He brushed a kiss on his wife's hair before they swung into the waltz with hands clasped as they gazed into each other's eyes.

But there was still a woman unclaimed. Anthony cut through the crowd toward the low stage, hoping the dancer was as magical as her dance.

Chapter 5

Laughing and heated from dancing, Diana smiled under her veil as Gabriel swept Rory away. It was time now for Diana to withdraw and vanish before midnight.

Then a tall man dressed all in black as a corsair approached the stage and lifted a beckoning hand, his cape swirling around him as if he were the devil coming to tempt a maiden to sweet damnation. The eyes framed by the black mask were a piercing blue.

In a deep, lightly accented voice he asked, "Dance with me, mysterious exotic lady?"

She had noticed him earlier because he was such a fine figure of a man and he danced very well. She'd also noticed that he chose a variety of partners, some of whom she suspected were shy young girls who blossomed under his attention. He might be a nice man under his menacing masquerade costume, but that didn't matter. What interested her was that he could dance.

"Gladly, Sir Corsair," she purred as she took his hand and skipped lightly to the dance floor, her bangles chiming on her wrists. Since she intended to stay anonymous, she didn't lower the veil wrapped over her forehead and lower face.

Now that she was on the dance floor, she realized he was even taller and broader than she'd thought, which had the happy effect of making her feel delicately female. She rather enjoyed the feeling after so many years of taking care of herself under sometimes-challenging circumstances.

He clasped her hands and drew her into waltz position. Then they spun across the ballroom. Diana always felt sensual awareness when she danced with a man, and never more so than tonight. She guessed that was because dancing with Rory had already heated her blood and made her feel a little reckless. The champagne earlier hadn't hurt, either. She asked, "Did you enjoy our little performance?"

"You and your partner were superb," he said seriously. "I'm glad you chose to honor us with your skill. It was like traveling to another land."

She smiled, glad they'd invoked such feelings. "The dancing was our pleasure, though not something we'll make a habit of. Lady Aurora thought it would make her ball memorable."

"It is a night I shall remember," he said softly.

She realized that sensual awareness was moving into intense attraction and the feelings were mutual. And wasn't that an outrageous thought? He was a stranger and his easy confidence suggested that he was a married man. Even if he wasn't, she was not about to give up her independent life, and she was not a woman to take casual lovers.

Though there was nothing casual about how she felt tonight. As they waltzed, their bodies drew closer than was respectable. He was all male heat and strength, a wordless invitation to sin.

She felt reckless and a little wild, and she made no protest when he swept them into one of the ballroom's shadowed alcoves. "You are enchanting, my exotic lady," he breathed. "Will you join me for the supper dance?"

He wanted more than that, and so did she. "Perhaps I will. But first . . ." She tugged her veil from her lower face in a not very subtle invitation for a kiss.

An invitation he accepted. Their lips met in a warm, sweet thank-you for the pleasure of their dancing. Then his arms closed around her, and lightness dissolved into a desire that scorched her to her marrow. She leaned into him, their bodies molding together as the kiss deepened. He kissed like a god, she thought hazily. She'd never before experienced such a fierce response—

No, she *had* felt this scorching sensuality before! She jerked away until her back was pressed against the wall. "Anthony?" she gasped as she reached up to yank off his mask, revealing the face and deep blue eyes that were burned on her heart by the flames of first love.

Anthony Raines was perhaps taller and certainly broader than when they'd known each other. He'd been barely nineteen then, a beautiful, charming, and lonely boy. Now he was a beautiful man in his prime, commanding, confident, and profoundly male.

His expression stunned, he unwound the dopatta from her head, revealing her face and hair. "Merciful heaven," he said in a choked voice. "Diana!"

She couldn't speak as they stared at each other. She shouldn't have been surprised. Now that she was back in London, it was only a matter of time until their paths crossed, but she wasn't *ready!* She certainly hadn't expected this flood of the heedless desire that nearly destroyed them before.

He recovered first, stepping back from her with his handsome face settling into an expression of cool courtesy, though she had the impression that his control masked intense and possibly dangerous emotions. "I hadn't heard that you'd returned to London, Lady Diana. Are you one of Lady Aurora's sisters? I must admit I'm not familiar with all the Lovely Lawrences."

The beau monde had bestowed the nickname on the blond and good-looking women of her family, but tonight it failed to amuse her. "I'm only been back for a week or two," she said, pleased that her voice was steady. "I've been staying here with Rory and Gabriel. I'm only five years older than she is, but her aunt, one of those late accidental children."

"A very lucky accident." He offered his arm. "From all the noise behind me, the unmasking is going on and guests are moving into the supper room. Will you join me? I'd like to learn about your travels." There was a distinct edge to his polite invitation.

Warily she took his arm because fleeing would be undignified and he certainly would not create a hellacious scene in a public place like this. Perhaps a mundane chat about the intervening years would dissipate the fierce energies surging between them. Their past relationship was just that: *past.* "I should like that, Lord Stoneleigh. Dancing always gives me an appetite."

His arm tensed under hers as they moved into the ballroom and crossed to the supper room, which was rapidly filling up with chattering people. "Not Stoneleigh. I'm the Duke of Castleton now."

She hesitated, remembering how beastly his father had been. "I'm not sure what to say. Condolences may not be in order."

His mouth twisted. "Very true, though most people didn't have the honesty to say so. It's three years since he died of apoplexy in a fit of rage." He'd been screaming at Anthony when it happened, a fact he preferred not to think about.

"How do you like being the duke?"

His brow furrowed. "No one has asked me that. It's assumed that becoming a duke is always welcome. I will say that it's better than being the old duke's heir."

"Is it not welcome to you?"

"It increased the number of ambitious would-be duchesses by two- or threefold," he said dryly.

She winced. The Anthony she'd known was a deeply private young man and she didn't think that had changed. "Being stalked by ambitious harpies must be very unpleasant."

"You have no idea."

They entered the supper room and saw that most of the small tables were occupied, but to the left an arm waved at them. Diana said, "My oldest brother and his wife are beckoning, I believe. Shall we join them?"

He nodded assent and they made their way through the maze of tables to her brother and his wife, who were garbed in eighteenth-century splendor with garments that might have come from trunks in the Lawrence attic.

Geoffrey, Earl Lawrence and head of the family, was old enough to be her father, with silver showing in his blond hair, but he'd doted on his baby sister, and vice versa. He rose and gave her a hug. "We haven't seen enough of you since your return, Diana!"

Releasing her, he turned and offered his hand to Anthony. "Good to see you, Castleton. Did you know that in some circles you're known as the Disappearing Duke because of your reluctance to attend social events?"

Anthony laughed, no sign of his earlier tension visible. This could be just another evening, except that it wasn't. "I was lured by the anonymity of a masquerade, then enchanted by the dancing of the two Lovely Lawrences. Shall we forage food for Lady Lawrence and Lady Diana?"

"Didn't the girls do a splendid job with that dance? My Rory knows how to throw a memorable ball!" Geoffrey said proudly.

As the men headed toward the buffet tables, Diana's sister-in-law Sylvia rose to give another hug, somewhat constrained by the size of her hoop skirt. "You and Rory were marvelous! I am beginning to see the value of travel to distant places."

Diana laughed as she seated herself by Sylvia. "Advantages and discomforts twined together. The dance would have been even better if our niece Constance was here. Then we'd have had all six arms for our goddess."

"I should like to see that someday." Sylvia signaled to a passing footman who carried a tray of champagne flutes, and secured four glasses for their table.

When they both had champagne, Sylvia clinked her glass against Diana's. "To happy reunions!"

Diana clinked back, wondering if the toast would bring about future meetings with Anthony. Not likely. "It's been so wonderful to see family and old friends. Perhaps I should have come back sooner!"

Sylvia's voice lowered mischievously. "You work quickly. Congratulations on securing the attention of Castleton, the most eligible and elusive bachelor in the British empire."

Diana's throat seemed to close. After a swallow of champagne, she was able to say lightly, "He was just intrigued by our dancing. After the unmasking, we realized we'd met in passing before I went on my travels, when he was the Marquess of Stoneleigh. He's a pleasant young man, isn't he?"

"Yes, he's more relaxed since his father died." Sylvia's voice lowered. "One shouldn't speak ill of the dead, but the old duke was one of the meanest men in England. He loathed Geoffrey for some reason, possibly because Geoffrey is well liked while the late

Castleton was generally despised. And they never agreed on anything political."

Diana grimaced. "I met the old duke once. He radiated malice. I could barely stand to be in the same room with him. Stoneleigh seems very different."

"Luckily he takes after his mother. The late duchess was a lovely woman who died too young. We made our come-out the same year," Sylvia said nostalgically. "I don't know young Castleton well because he seldom comes to social events. He's said to have an aversion to fortune hunters, and one can hardly blame him." Sylvia gave her sister-in-law a curious glance. "He seemed interested in you."

"No matchmaking!" Diana ordered. "If he shows interest in me, it's thanks to my Hindu dancing and perhaps the fact that I'm an older woman and he's safe from my wiles. If he's interested in securing a wife, he could be quietly courting a suitable one out of sight of the *ton*."

"That does sound like what he'd do," Sylvia admitted. "But if so, I've not heard any rumors."

"He's young yet. I suspect he isn't ready to find a wife and contents himself with ravishing mistresses."

"I suppose you're right, but it seems such a waste." Sylvia's gaze went to the men, who were returning with plates laden with delicacies. "I wouldn't have minded having him for one of my girls, but Rory was the only one the right age and they had no interest in each other. No doubt that's for the best. Gabriel seems to have settled her nicely."

"That's because he and Rory are perfect for each other," Diana said. "And why matchmaking is such a frustrating business. A mother concerned to settle her daughter well will say, 'Let me introduce you to that duke, who is a perfect gentleman and known for his admirable character.' Meanwhile, her daughter is looking out the window and saying, 'Mama, there's the most delicious blockade-runner outside. I must have him!'"

Sylvia was laughing as the two men set plates heaping with delicious food on the table. Lobster patties, delicate pastries with sweet or savory fillings, small meatballs made of lamb, and a dozen other things.

Geoffrey asked, "Is the joke worth sharing, my dear?"

"We were just talking about the frustration of matchmaking," his wife explained. "Which is why I've given it up."

"You gave up serious matchmaking because all of our children have married," her husband said as he sampled a meatball. "But you still get a gleam in your eyes when you see someone who is single and in need of a mate."

Anthony said dourly, "May we have a change of topic? I feel like a goose in the kitchen having to listen to various recipes for cooking geese."

The others laughed and the conversation moved to less personal topics. Food was eaten, wine was consumed, opinions were offered, gossip was exchanged, and it was altogether an enjoyable supper. Hard to believe what fierce emotions had flared when Diana and Anthony had first unmasked each other.

Diana was relieved when Anthony stood and excused himself early, saying he must leave. He gave the same pleasant smile to everyone at their table with no special attention to her. Obviously he'd recovered from the shock of seeing her unexpectedly and had no interest in renewing their acquaintance. That was a relief. Really, it was.

Yet her gaze followed him to the door of the supper room, where he met a tall, striking woman dressed as a Spanish bandit queen. She linked her arm with his in easy intimacy. He smiled at her warmly as they left the room. Perhaps he really was quietly courting someone. The tall woman looked like the right kind of female for him.

Not that it was any of Diana's business. . . .

Chapter 6

Anthony had known they'd leave early because Athena was increasing. It was early days and she didn't show yet, but she tired more easily than usual. Will was inclined to hover over her, and Anthony wasn't much better. Athena, the Warrior Queen of San Gabriel, laughed at their solicitude, though she rather enjoyed the pampering.

It had been a relief when she signaled across the supper room that she was ready to leave. Anthony excused himself from his supper companions, forcing himself not to stare at Diana. After thanking his hostess, he left, hoping he didn't look as if he were fleeing the scene of the crime.

When he climbed into the Masterson carriage, he took the backward-facing seat opposite Athena and Will. It was a relief to sink into the darkness and let go of his control before it snapped.

After they'd settled in and the carriage started toward home, his sister said cheerfully, "That was thoroughly enjoyable. I've decided that I like masquerades and dressing up as someone else."

Her husband said with amusement, "But you were wearing the same Spanish clothing you wore when fighting the French. You were going as yourself tonight, not as someone else."

"But my pistol wasn't loaded," she explained. "So it was a costume, not reality."

Laughing, Will put an arm around her shoulders. "One masquerade a year sounds about right. Any more and I'd rapidly run out of ideas for costumes, and I don't fancy myself in a toga."

"I think you would be *very* fanciable!" Athena said provocatively.

"Togas would be cold at this season," Anthony murmured.

"Very true," Athena said. "Please excuse our silliness, Anthony. Given that Julia and I almost forced you to come to the ball, I hope you enjoyed yourself. I didn't know you were such a good dancer. I think you danced every dance, and your corsair cape swirled magnificently."

"I enjoy dancing almost too much for a duke. If I hadn't been heir to Castleton, I think I would have made a tolerably good dancing master."

Athena chuckled. "Another role in which you'd have had to endure females hurling themselves at you."

"Perhaps, but as least they wouldn't have wanted marriage," he said dryly.

Will and Athena laughed. Hoping he wouldn't have to talk any more, Anthony rubbed his temple, trying to forestall a headache. He'd had them regularly until his father died and almost never since.

Will said, "I saw that you went into supper with Lady Diana Lawrence, the second Hindu dancer. Is she as charming as she is talented?"

Anthony tried for a light answer, but he couldn't. He couldn't even speak. He buried his face in his hands and began to shake.

Athena leaned forward and asked with concern, "Anthony, are you ill?"

He choked out, "Nothing physical."

His sister rested a hand on his knee. "What's wrong?" she asked quietly.

He might have managed to regain his control if the carriage weren't dark. If he hadn't had so much champagne. If it weren't his sister who asked. But he had to talk to someone, and who better than his sister and her husband? "Remember I told you and Julia I'd once become infatuated and proposed marriage and the lady turned me down?"

"Yes," she said with soft encouragement.

"I saw her tonight for the first time in years."

"Lady Diana Lawrence?" Will asked quietly.

Will's wits were much quicker than his appearance suggested. Anthony lowered his hands. "Yes. If the ball wasn't a masquerade, I would have recognized her sooner and been able to escape. As it was, I danced with her, not knowing who she was. When we unmasked, it was . . . .a considerable shock. Rather like being kicked in the gut by an angry horse. For both of us, I think."

"She was equally shocked?" Athena asked.

"I believe so. She's only just back in England. In the nature of things, we were bound to run into each other eventually, but she probably didn't expect it so soon, or in such circumstances."

"I think surprises are greatly overrated," Will said. "Did you part in anger all those years ago?"

"More in sorrow than in anger," Anthony said slowly. "We fell in love so quickly and it ended so quickly when I asked her to marry me. She was horrified and bolted, leaving England almost immediately. I heard that she'd become a dashing lady traveler and ended up in India. I thought she'd never return. Which made seeing her tonight all the more shocking."

"Did she explain why she turned you down? Did she think it was a mere flirtation and she was shocked when you proposed?"

"I think her feelings were much like mine. She is not the sort to play games. But I don't think she expected a proposal. She explained why marriage was impossible, and then she was gone."

"At least you've had one female in your life who wasn't trying to trap a future duke into marriage," Will said thoughtfully. "Why did she think marriage was impossible?"

"For one thing, I was not of legal age. For another, she's five years older than I."

"Not an outrageous difference," Athena said. "Surely there was more."

"Castleton," Anthony said bitterly. "Our thrice-damned sire.

He would never have given permission for any number of reasons, starting with the fact that he certainly did not want me to choose my own bride. He had someone else in mind for me."

"Granted you were young, but as the daughter of an earl, Lady Diana is sufficiently wellborn and the age difference was not insurmountable. What more did the old duke want for you?" Athena asked, puzzled.

"You only met him once in your life," Anthony said wearily. "For which you can be thankful. He had anger in his veins instead of blood. Railing against others was his greatest pleasure, and he *loathed* all Lawrences. That was Diana's main reason for refusing, I think. She believed I would be put in an intolerable position."

He sighed. "She may well have been right. And the reverse is true. If we had run off to Scotland to get married, the consequences for her might have been disastrous."

"Are you still in love with her?" Athena asked softly.

"I don't know. It's been seven years and we're both vastly different." He smiled without humor. "Was I ever in love with her, or is infatuation something different? I do know it was a mutual madness that was the most important thing in my world for a time. Now . . ." He spread his hands helplessly. "Just seeing her almost paralyzed me. I have no idea what to do about her. Or me."

"I'm not sure there is a difference between love and infatuation. Perhaps infatuation is the first stage of a great and lasting love," Will mused. "But I do know that losing a great love can paralyze one's heart for a very long time. I married young and when my wife died in childbirth I joined the army and hoped the French would give me an honorable death. They didn't, thank God. I survived long enough for my heart to heal, and to meet Athena."

Anthony hadn't known that Will had been married before, and the revelation gave him a new appreciation for his brother-in-law. "I don't think that joining the army is the answer for me, but I'm not sure what is."

"You need to spend some time with Lady Diana," Athena said seriously. "Just now you're stuck in the shock of a lost love who has reappeared. Put on your best cool but courteous ducal face and call on her. Take her for a drive in the park and buy her an ice at Gunter's. Though it may be too cold for that. Just be very casual as if you had never been more than mere acquaintances. As you come to know her better now, the magic of the past may fade away, leaving only a few fond memories. Or perhaps you will become friends, or you may find that you don't like the woman she is now."

Anthony doubted that. "Your advice is good, but what if I find I'm still mad about her?"

"Then you can court her again, this time being of legal age and without the dark cloud of the duke hanging over you," Will said promptly. "And if she accepts you, you'll know that she is the one woman in London who isn't after your title and wealth."

Anthony had to laugh. "There is that. Very well, I shall pay a courtesy call on her and Lady Aurora tomorrow in thanks for the masquerade. I shall be pleasant, friendly, and casual. And we shall see what happens."

Chapter 7

The ball had gone on to the wee hours and Diana hadn't slept well after, so she came down late and found the breakfast room filling with flowers. Rory had arrived earlier and was yawning delicately over a cup of tea. "The number of flowers delivered this late in the year is a tribute to the success of the ball."

She waved at the long serving table set against a wall that was now almost completely covered with bouquets. "The servants are bringing them here so we can enjoy the wonderful colors while we eat. Your duke sent two floral offerings, one to me as hostess and one for you as performer. They're on the left end of the serving table."

"He's not my duke," Diana said a bit tartly. "Merely an acquaintance." She surveyed the flowers. Between a vase of chrysanthemums and another of lilies, she saw a long gray and white face with crossed blue eyes. She scratched between his pointed ears. "Your Norwegian Ice Cat is lurking amidst the blossoms."

"He likes the illusion of forest," Rory explained.

Diana's gaze moved on. "Let me guess. This largest bouquet with wildly expensive out of season roses is from Castleton? Yes, I see that it is. Courteous of him, but since he could afford to buy Denmark, I'm not overly impressed by the cost."

"True," Rory said, her eyes dancing. "But I find it interesting that he sent you the nosegay next to it. Small and not at all expensive, but very pretty. Is there any significance to that?"

"He probably only sends extravagant bouquets to hostesses." Diana found the nosegay, which was an exquisite arrangement of daisies and tiny ferns tied with a gold ribbon. Damn the man! He was reminding her of an afternoon walk through the forest they'd made one early summer day not long after they met. They'd settled on a log by a stream and he'd assembled a similar nosegay for her and presented it with a kiss. Their first kiss . . .

She swallowed hard and opened the small note attached to the nosegay. "It's a thank-you for the dancing, which was kind of him."

"I met him a time or two during my first London season, when he was still Stoneleigh. I found him rather boring, but he has beautiful manners." Rory poured a cup of tea for Diana. "Tell me, what were your favorite parts of the ball?"

Diana seated herself and complied. Soon they were laughing over coddled eggs and toast. As she finished her second cup of tea, she said, "You may want to start a tradition of late season masquerade balls. All the guests seemed to have a fine time."

"Our dance helped make it special. Maybe the tradition should include us always performing a Hindu dance?"

"Sorry, I can make no promises. If we never perform again, the dance last night can become a legend." Diana lowered her voice soulfully. "People will boast they were here the night it was performed!"

Always willing to play along, Rory said breathlessly, "It will become such a remarkable occurrence that members of the *ton* will lie about having seen us! Soon the number of people claiming they were guests last night shall exceed the capacity of the house!"

Diana laughed. They'd always loved batting comments and jokes back and forth. She'd missed this banter. Oddly, she and Anthony had bantered rather like this. He was not boring when he was alone with her. He'd been quietly witty, with an inquiring mind and a deliciously dry sense of humor. Did he still have those traits, or had they been crushed by the responsibilities of the dukedom?

Smiling, Rory rose from the table. "It's my nursery time now.

Every day little Diana does something new, and I must be there to witness it."

"You are the very model of a modern mother." Diana also stood, knowing that her niece wouldn't want company during this private time with her baby. "I imagine there will be a number of courtesy calls this afternoon, so I'll work on my travel memoirs this morning. I thought I'd be done by the time I returned to London, but I kept thinking of new things to add that hadn't made it into the original journals. This is turning into a series. I'm not sure the results will be worth the effort!"

Rory shook her head emphatically. "You're wrong! Your travel memoirs are going to be bestsellers, and I speak as someone who knows something of publishing. The original journals were wonderful, and the expanded, polished versions will be even better. I can't wait to read the first one."

"You'll be my first reader," Diana promised. "But I have trouble believing that my tales of misadventures will be of general interest.

"You're suffering from writer's anxiety," Rory said firmly before she left the breakfast room. "Keep working and eventually it will pass. I promise!"

Diana headed to the small drawing room, the coziest of the public rooms. It was her usual work area and she'd taken over the desk, which was perhaps less neat than the rest of the household.

The Panda was already there, curled up on a folded blanket that Diana had placed on the sofa to protect the upholstery. He raised his head at her entrance, offering the perfect angle for her to scratch his throat. She complied before settling down to work.

She was copying the next to the last chapter of her volume of Greek experiences when a footman entered to announce, "The Duke of Castleton is calling. Will you receive him?"

Her heart gave an odd little lurch. "Of course. Show him in."

"Shall I summon Lady Aurora?" the footman asked doubtfully.

"Nonsense, I don't need a chaperone. I'm no schoolroom girl and I've known Castleton for donkey's years," she said briskly, while wondering if her hair needed attention.

Reminding herself that this was merely a courtesy call, she straightened her papers so they wouldn't look untidy. By the time she finished that, Castleton was entering the room. Her heart did that strange lurch again.

The night before in his corsair garb, he'd been a perfect fantasy. Now superb tailoring in a quiet style made him a perfect gentleman. With sudden insight, she realized that his present appearance was as much a costume as his corsair clothing the night before. Both appearances were meant to conceal his true self behind the polished façade. He inclined his head courteously. "Thank you for receiving me, Lady Diana."

She rose and offered her hand. His gloved clasp was warm and firm, exerting just the right amount of pressure. What to say? She must mention the daisies but not single them out. "Good morning, Your Grace. Lady Aurora and I thank you for the flowers. Roses and daisies at this time of year! You have a conservatory?"

"Yes, it was one of the first improvements I made to Castleton House after I inherited. I enjoy flowers."

So did Diana. It was one of many simple pleasures they shared. "Please have a seat, Your Grace. But have I been away from England so long that I missed the fact that morning calls are now actually made in the morning instead of the afternoon?"

He smiled as he took a chair opposite her. "An advantage to being a duke is that if I break a social rule it's considered charmingly eccentric rather than rude. I was hoping that by my coming early we'd have a chance to talk. Last night I never did get the opportunity to ask you about your travels."

She gestured to her desk. "It would be easiest to wait until I publish my journals. Lady Aurora convinced me to work on them on the voyage back from India, so I've been copying and polishing my traveler's impressions. I have grave doubts that a publisher will be interested, but I might do a private publication for friends and family. It will save me answering a lot of the same questions over and over."

"Please put me down for a copy," he said a little wistfully. "I should love to visit faraway places, but I have too many responsibilities here to take such a long journey. I'll likely never travel farther from home than Paris."

"I have known people who yearned for a duke's wealth and

power," she said with a wry smile. "But I've never heard a man yearn for the endless responsibilities and documents and toadies seeking to curry a duke's favor."

"And you never will," he said dryly.

The Panda suddenly jumped from the sofa and marched majestically to greet the visitor, looking up with his huge green eyes. Anthony regarded him with interest. "Is this fellow a kitchen cat who has decided he likes upstairs more than downstairs?"

"Mrrrp!"

Recognizing a request for attention, Anthony bent to scratch the cat's head. "Given his size, I'm guessing he spends much of his time in the kitchen, coaxing the cook to give him extra food."

Diana laughed. "The Panda isn't a kitchen cat. He's mine. I brought him back from India."

The Panda suddenly gathered himself and leaped onto the visitor's lap, an action that could not be ignored, not least because the cat was shedding black and white hair over the duke's well-tailored clothing. "He really is huge!" Anthony exclaimed as he scratched the cat's neck. "He must weigh a stone and a half at least."

"It's because he is an Imperial Chinese Throne Cat," Diana explained mischievously. "Very rare. They are bred to protect members of the imperial court."

Anthony's expression was amused. "You're sure he's not an overfed alley cat who landed in clover when you brought him inside?"

"Sir, you insult his heritage!" But Anthony's comment reminded her of his tendency to rescue stray animals. His father would have disapproved violently, so Anthony had secretly made arrangements with tenants and estate workers to take the animals in, with Anthony subsidizing the costs.

"My apologies, Sir Cat," Anthony said solemnly. "What does 'Panda' mean?"

"A panda is a kind of Chinese bear, black and white like my Panda. The name 'panda' means something like 'giant bear cat.' The local maharajah had a pair of them in his private menagerie. I was very lucky to see them. I was told pandas are completely unknown in Europe. They're gentle beasts who eat only bamboo."

"Whereas your Panda will apparently eat anything." Anthony had definitely not lost his sense of humor in recent years.

"You're not wrong," she admitted. "But Imperial Chinese Throne Cats need to keep up their energy in case they must fight to defend their masters."

Panda rolled over in Anthony's lap. The four white paws in the air indicated a willingness to have his equally white tummy scratched. Anthony obliged. "Your Panda has energy? He seems like a cat who has settled into a life of total sybaritic pleasure."

She had to laugh. "Again, you're not wrong. But he's a wonderful friendly companion, except when he decides to flop in the middle of my journal writing."

"He likes being the center of attention," Anthony said. The Panda was purring so loudly under the ducal ministrations that Diana could hear him from across the room.

"Imperial Chinese Throne Cats are known for being sociable. Unlike Norwegian Ice Cats, such as that one behind the draperies." She gestured toward the long velvet draperies where she'd spotted the Spook peeking out at them.

Anthony glanced over and his brows rose. "Pale fur, long face and gangling legs, and crossed blue eyes. Yes, definitely a Norwegian Ice Cat. I saw a picture of one once, but rare, very rare. Is he also yours?"

Smiling, Diana said, "No, the Spook belongs to Lady Aurora and Captain Vance. He was the captain's ship cat. He's a mighty hunter, but shy." Her comment was accompanied by the Spook's darting out of sight behind the folds of velvet. "Is there a rare cat breed you'd like to acquire?"

He considered, a gleam in his eyes. "My sister Lady Masterson has one of the Fabulous Fabled Fishing Cats of Sumatra. Did you meet any in your travels in the East? They lurk on giant lily pads and the banks of ponds to hook unwary fish from the water."

Enchanted, Diana asked, "What do they look like?"

"They're very large striped cats with tufted ears and side whiskers," he said with complete seriousness. "My sister's cat looks quite fearsome, but he's a fine companion. I have often envied her for having persuaded Khan to live with her."

"They sound rather like the cats who are fathered by Scottish wildcats, but Scotland is a long way from Sumatra," she replied with equal seriousness. "If I discover a Fabulous Fabled Fishing Cat of Sumatra, I shall attempt to secure it for you."

Their gazes met, and they both burst into laughter. She was briefly transported seven years into the past, when she'd met Anthony while she was visiting a pair of aged aunts whose property adjoined the Castleton estate. The aunts napped a lot, leaving Diana free to ride and walk through summer fields and the ancient woods that lay between the two properties.

She'd met Anthony one day while riding in the woods. They introduced themselves, began to talk, began riding side by side, and both were late for dinner because they lost track of time.

For the next two months, they'd met in secret whenever possible. It was the best summer of her life, until their relationship came crashing down.

On impulse, she said, "Is this merely a courtesy visit, Anthony?," deliberately using his personal name. "Or is there more to it?"

He became very still, his gaze direct. "There was once a great deal between us, Diana. I can't help but wonder what is there now. Seeing you last night was quite a shock."

"The shock was entirely mutual!" she said fervently.

He smiled wryly. "Now that that has worn off, I'd like to learn what, if anything, is left between us. So much time has passed. You said I was too young, and you were right. We're different people now, long past youthful infatuation. But I think perhaps we could be friends. Would you like to see if that's possible?"

His honesty shattered the control she'd been attempting to maintain. Certainly there was still attraction between them; that had been proved by their kiss the night before. But so much time had passed, and they'd lived very different lives. She was now an aging spinster used to always having her own way. That moment of mutual love, when there had been at least a chance to build something lasting, was long gone.

Yet they had a bond of shared memories, and so far she liked what she'd seen of the man he'd become. He'd make a loyal friend, and she needed more friends.

Glad he'd reached out to her, she replied, "I'd like very much to build a friendship. I've left too many friends behind in my travels. If I'm here in England to stay, and I think I am, I need to cultivate friendships."

"We might find each other annoying now," he warned. "You brighten any room you enter, while I'm a rather dull and dutiful fellow."

"I never found you dull," she said honestly. "I always found you fascinatingly complicated, with a core of steel."

He blinked. "That's a flattering assessment, I think, but I'm not sure what it's based on. You were older than I, but still young."

She realized that they hadn't discussed such things in the old days. She must match his honesty. "I admired your strength tremendously. You father was the greatest bully in England, and as his only son, you were the target of much of his anger. Yet you never ran away. You could have taken your inheritance from your grandparents and lived a riotous life in London.

"Instead you went to university and graduated with double firsts at a ridiculously young age, then quietly went to work mitigating your father's destructive actions. I was amazed by that then, and am even more amazed as I look back. How did you survive his abuse with your sanity intact?"

Anthony's face tightened. "It was . . . difficult. Yet how could I leave the servants and tenants and other dependents to suffer my father's volatile rages? Running away to live a life of self-indulgence would have been cowardice. I learned early to develop an emotional shield that his words couldn't penetrate. I let them roll off like rain and reminded myself that I had a duty to protect those more vulnerable than I."

"Leaving would have made you sensible, not a coward," she said with quiet intensity. "Staying made you a hero."

Anthony looked uncomfortable at her praise. "You never met my mother, but she was warm and wise and good, and she taught us never to take the easy way out at someone else's cost."

"I wish I'd known her. She must have been a remarkable woman."

"She was. My sister Lady Julia is very like her." His voice changed. "Would you like to go for a drive? The day is mild and the sun occasionally deigns to shine."

There was no courtship in his eyes, but friendship was perhaps even more precious. "I'd love some fresh air. Give me a moment to put my work away so it doesn't become scattered all over the drawing room."

Anthony lifted the Panda from his lap and politely set him on the floor, receiving an annoyed look despite his care. "The Panda has been deprived of his pampering."

"He'll be asleep on the sofa again before we leave the room," she predicted accurately as she put away her manuscript.

Diana collected her cloak and left a message for Rory, then set out to enjoy a day that was pleasantly mild for December. Anthony's curricle was fashionable, naturally, and his horses superb. After he settled her and swung up on the seat next to her, he asked, "Is there any particular place you'd like to visit, or would you prefer a relaxed drive in the park?"

"The park, please. But there is something I'd like to ask you about," she said. "I am completely a fallen woman, for I am now engaged in trade. Shocking, isn't it?"

He laughed as he deftly set the horses in motion. "Trade may be officially scorned in some circles, but a large proportion of the aristocracy stay afloat financially by investing in some form of it. Agriculture alone isn't always enough to maintain large estates. Most of the great lords own or invest in mines, mills, canal building, shipping companies and other enterprises."

"Does that include you?" Diana asked with interest.

"Yes, I own large parts of some mills, which gives me the chance to demonstrate that a mill can be profitable without putting young children to work under dangerous conditions. What form of trade are you engaged in?"

"The import business. India produces wonderful textiles and jewelry and carvings and other such things. My partner in the business is an Englishwoman who has put down her roots in India, and I promised her I'd find new markets for our imports now that I'm back in Britain. You're a fashionable fellow. Can you think of shops I should visit to try to sell my wares?"

He considered. "I could probably come up with some suggestions, but the person you need to talk to is Lady Kiri Mackenzie, who has an amazing sense of style. She's in trade in a small way herself, selling the wonderful perfumes she creates. She is also half-

Hindu, the sister of the Duke of Ashton. I'm sure she'd be happy to make suggestions."

"I'd love to meet her!"

Anthony glanced down at her, his intense blue eyes warm. "The knocker is down on their house so I imagine they've gone to the country for the holidays, but I shall arrange a meeting as soon as is feasible."

Friendship was going to work, she realized with pleasure. Which was good, because she wanted Anthony in her life.

Chapter 8

Anthony was impressed at how well he could lie; he hadn't realized he had such talent. Rationally, he knew that Athena and Will and his own common sense were correct: For all practical purposes, he and Diana were strangers to each other. Even when they'd first met, their differences were obvious. Yet so was the intense attraction.

Life under the heavy hand of the old duke was an endless struggle to stay sane and civil. Then Anthony had met Diana, who was filled with joyous light. Her appetite for life was infectious, and she brought out a lighter side of him that had been buried years before. He had needed her like the air in his lungs.

But his proposal had appalled her, and then she was gone. Within days, she sailed from England, and once more his life became a matter of endurance. His father's death had been a great release, but joy had been only a memory. Until last night.

Yes, it was wise to be wary. He should carefully explore the possibilities. Become better acquainted slowly, making no promises.

But dammit! He didn't want her for a friend, or, at least, only a friend. He wanted her to be his playmate, his partner, his lover. His *wife*. He wanted to hold her in his arms until he felt joy again.

But he daren't frighten her off by wanting too much too soon.

This was a casual drive with a friend. Conversation should be casual. Where to begin?

They'd never talked much about their families, except for occasional oblique references to his father. He remarked, "You and Lady Aurora seem very close, more like sisters than aunt and niece."

"You're exactly right," Diana said. "My mother was never very fond of children. She felt ill-used at having me when she thought that she was long past babies, so I was sent to the nursery of my oldest brother, Geoffrey. He and his wife like children and ended up with eight of their own, so adding another little girl to the household was not a problem. Geoffrey and Sylvia were more my parents than my actual parents."

"You were fortunate to have a good alternative family," he said, wishing he'd had that.

"Very fortunate! I had three much older brothers and no sisters. Moving in with Geoffrey gave me four sisters and four brothers, all of them quite lovely in different ways. But Rory and I were close in age, and the most alike."

"Sisters are indeed great fun, though occasionally a trial." He chuckled. "Mine decided to turn a small family dinner party into a reading of Byron's *Corsair* with each of us having to read selections. All three males present groaned at the prospect, but I admit it was rather amusing, though we wondered why the poem was so popular."

"At the least, it provided the inspiration for your costume last night." She frowned. "But I thought your only sister, Lady Julia, died when you were still at school?"

His hands tightened on the reins as he was reminded of his father's worst behavior in a lifetime of bad behavior. "Because you were traveling, you missed the resurrection."

Diana turned to stare at him. "The *what*?"

How much to say? "When Julia was only sixteen, my father forced her into a marriage that turned into a nightmare," he said tersely. "Her husband died of an accident when he was drunk, and both my father and her father-in-law blamed her for the death. My father disowned her and refused to let her come home. The situation was so dreadful that she faked her own death and hid in the far north for years."

"At the time, I heard a rumor that she'd killed herself and the family hushed it up. To think that she was driven to such despair! What strength she must have." Diana glanced up at him, her gaze sympathetic. "And how dreadful for you. I had the impression that you'd been very close and mourned her greatly."

He drew a slow breath as he halted the carriage to allow several children and an elderly woman to cross the street. This wasn't turning out to be as casual a conversation as he'd intended. "It was . . . devastating. As hard as losing my mother."

Why had he said something so personal? Because it had always been so easy to talk to Diana. He'd told her things he'd told no one else.

In silent commiseration, she laid her hand on his where he held the reins, not removing it until he signaled his horses to start moving again. After a silence, she asked hesitantly, "Were you angry with your sister when she returned, for leaving you alone with your father and not letting you know she was alive?"

Diana had always been unnervingly perceptive. "Briefly." More hurt really. "That didn't last long, not when I saw her again and learned the full story."

"What persuaded her to return?"

"She married a rather formidable army major who could stand up to my father, even at the old duke's worst," Anthony explained. "Randall is a very decent fellow, but as an experienced soldier, he said that Conrad, the hero of *The Corsair*, was an idiot."

"A lot of women love the poem, but really! All that romantic doom and melodramatic extravagance!" Diana shook her head. "Conrad had no common sense whatsoever."

Anthony had to laugh. "Says the woman who has lived a wildly romantic life of adventure!"

She gave an unladylike snort. "One must have a great deal of common sense to travel as I did. Luck, too. I'm certainly not sorry I did it, but I would not say my travels have been wildly romantic."

"How would you describe your adventures?"

She thought about that. "Interesting. Surprising. Life changing. Occasionally dangerous. But only rarely romantic."

He wondered what she considered romantic, but perhaps he was better off not knowing. "I'm really looking forward to those memoirs. Do you have a title for the book?"

"My memoirs are becoming a series! I'm thinking something like *Travels of an Independent Lady, Volume 1, Greece*, but that might well change." She cocked her head quizzically. "But you said 'sisters,' plural? Did your father remarry?"

"No, Athena is an illegitimate half sister. Her mother was a scandalous wellborn lady who was so irresistible that even the old duke succumbed to her charms. He acknowledged Athena as his daughter and paid for her schooling after her mother died. He did give her a very modest allowance on the condition that she never, ever, reveal her identity to anyone."

"I knew your father was dreadful, but he was even worse than I thought!" Diana said, appalled. "To treat all his children so abominably!"

"He didn't much like people, and in particular he didn't like women," Anthony said dryly. "After my father had his heir, he and my mother lived separate lives. She was very happy with that arrangement." And she'd quietly found love with a kind, quiet gentleman. Anthony was grateful that she'd had that.

"How did you discover your unknown sister? Did she come forward after your father's death?"

"No, she was living on the Peninsula and didn't know he'd died." Didn't know and would not have cared. "After I succeeded to the title and was working night and day with the family lawyer to sort it all out, I discovered regular payments to a mysterious female for decades. The lawyer enlightened me."

"Were you shocked? Horrified?" Diana asked with interest.

"Shocked that my father had done something so passionate as have an affair with a beautiful wicked woman," he said, his voice dry again. "Horrified because of the way Athena had been treated."

Diana sighed. "I've never understood why so many people blame a child for the sins of their fathers and mothers. My mother was like that. I have a niece around my age whom I knew nothing about until a couple of years ago. She's delightful, but my mother was not the most tolerant woman. She loathed scandal, so she sent the poor infant out to be fostered and ordered her son not to tell anyone of the girl's existence."

Startled, Anthony said, "Was she your brother Geoffrey's daughter? Surely he would never have treated a child of his like that!"

"No, she was the daughter of the youngest of my three brothers. He was what I believe was called 'a loose fish.' Rather charming and never meant harm, but quite unreliable."

"How did Lord and Lady Lawrence react when they discovered her existence?"

"They welcomed her into the family and Geoffrey immediately arranged a dowry for her. She was recently married and kept saying she didn't need that, but Geoffrey, bless him, said it was hers by right."

"Well done." Anthony had done the same thing for Athena when he discovered her existence even though she hadn't needn't the money, either. It was hers by right. "Julia and I were both keen to meet our unknown half sister, so when she returned to England we swooped in and claimed her for our own. There are family resemblances among the three of us, but she didn't inherit my father's temperament, for which we're all grateful."

"I love a story with a happy ending," Diana said seriously. "She was lucky you and Julia accepted her so warmly."

"Athena is a remarkable woman and very likable. Julia and I agree that we are the ones who are lucky to have a new relative that we like." After a moment he continued thoughtfully, "Though I think it's interesting that my sisters both married distinguished soldiers, as if they needed defense against my father."

Diana shook her head, smiling. "I hope they married for love. As I said, I like stories with happy endings."

"Both my sisters found love matches." He couldn't stop himself from looking at Diana, with her lovely face and warm understanding. "They give me hope that such things are possible."

He caught Diana's gaze as he said those words. He'd felt very close to her during their ride, but even the hint of marriage caused a flash of panic in her eyes and he sensed her drawing away.

Yet her voice was steady when she said, "I've seen happy marriages and I applaud them. But some people simply aren't suited to marriage. Women in particular tend to marry because they have so few choices. It's better for everyone if persons unsuited to marriage realize that before they make a devastating mistake."

The message was clear. "Quite right, though I've known people who thought themselves confirmed bachelors or spinsters who changed their minds when they met the right person." It was time for a strategic retreat. "Would you like to drive to Gunter's for an ice? Granted it's a cold day, but they are always delicious."

"That would be lovely!" she said with relief, obviously glad to change the topic. "What are your plans for Christmas?"

"Athena and her husband have a place in Oxfordshire where the family is gathering for Christmas. Julia and her husband and their children will be there, too. We did the same thing last year and it was very enjoyable." It had been the best Christmas of his life. "What will you be doing? Staying in town with Lady Aurora and her husband?"

"No, tomorrow they're heading to Gabriel's grandparents for the holidays, then they'll join the Lawrence celebration. I'm staying in London for a few days because I'm expecting a shipment from my partner in India." She wrinkled her nose. "Then I'll travel to the Lawrence family seat, where I will be surrounded by countless relatives who will hug me and ask impertinent questions."

"It sounds quite lovely," Anthony said.

"It will be," she said with a smile. "Geoffrey and Sylvia are wonderful hosts. Luckily I'm good at deflecting impertinent questions!"

Yes, she was, but he was good at persistence. The irresistible force and the immovable object? They'd see.

The ices were indeed delicious even on a cold December day. After, Anthony returned Diana to the Vance home, where she left him with a charming, unreadable smile and best wishes for the holidays.

It had become blindingly clear that she didn't want to talk about the past, still less any possible future. Perhaps she really was unsuited to marriage. Some people were. But with that mysterious mutual connection that refused to go away, he was sure there was more than she was telling him.

He might never persuade Diana to marry him, but he couldn't move forward without fully understanding why she'd left. Even more important, he needed to know why she was keeping him at a distance now when the obvious barriers were gone.

She was not unaffected by him; that he was sure of. He needed to understand her reasoning, and the only way to discover that was by full frontal assault.

Chapter 9

Anthony waited three days to be sure the Vances had left for the country and that Diana would be alone in the house. Then he called on her. He hoped it wasn't a bad omen that a bone-chilling rain was falling.

Despite his dripping multi-caped coachman's coat, the footman gave him a knowing smile when he arrived. The servants were probably placing bets belowstairs on what was going on between Lady Diana and her distinguished visitor.

Since Anthony might be thrown out very quickly, he kept his coat on when he was escorted to the small drawing room. Diana was writing at her desk, the Panda at her feet. She looked up with an expression of dismay, quickly concealed.

Rising, she said, "How nice to see you again, Castleton. Are you coming to say farewell before leaving for Christmas in the country?"

Her use of his title was not a good sign. "No."

The Panda ambled over to greet the visitor, rubbing against Anthony's wet boots and accepting head scratches. Then water dripped from the coat and drove the cat from the room with whiskers twitching indignantly.

Anthony deliberately closed the door. "I'm here for some answers, Diana. The full story of why you left me, and your reasons for skittering away when I try to talk to you now. You owe me that. I understand it will be painful for both of us, but I have to know before I can move on with my life."

He hoped with her, but if not, so be it. Meeting Diana again had made him realize how emotionally paralyzed he'd been these last years. If he couldn't persuade her to be his wife, it was time to put that past behind him.

"Yes, I do owe you that," Diana said quietly. "It won't surprise you to know that the main reason was your father." She leaned against the desk, her fingers curling around the edge as she bit her lip and considered what to say.

"We knew he'd be difficult," Anthony said. "But I had an independent income, and so did you. We could have managed."

"He was even worse than you know," she said bleakly. "You and I were living in an enchanted bubble that summer. Anything seemed possible. I was even dreaming that someday we might marry, though I thought we should wait until you were of age. That would make everything easier."

She had really been willing to consider marriage then? "Simpler, yes, though it would have been a very long wait when we wanted so much to be together," he pointed out. He'd calculated how long it would take to reach Gretna Green, where they could marry legally even though he was a minor under English law. They would have made it easily even if his father had sent pursuers. "Did you decide you didn't want to wait for two years?"

"I would have waited," she said with a wistful smile. "But I was worried about your father. You didn't complain about him directly, but it was clear that he made your life impossibly difficult. I didn't want your relationship with him to get even worse."

"I was prepared for him to behave badly." Anthony smiled humorlessly. "I'd been quietly enduring him for years. Yes, he would have raged if we'd married, but I assumed we'd move away from Raines Abbey, so my life would become much easier." Easier and infinitely happier.

Her face tightened. "What I didn't tell you was that he called on me at my aunts' house. He bellowed that he'd heard I was sniffing around his son. I gathered that someone on your estate saw us together and reported it."

Anthony swore. "What an outrageously vulgar thing to say! And quite wrong." Their attraction had been completely and dizzyingly mutual.

"I could have survived his vulgar insinuations, but not the threats that came next." She stopped, pain on her face. "He swore that if I didn't leave you alone, he'd make your life a living hell. When his heir married, it would be to a bride of his own choosing, and it would *certainly* not be a Lawrence. He despised my whole family, root and branch."

Anthony stared at her. "You should have told me!"

"Anthony, hatred *poured* from him!" she cried. "Not just hatred. I felt that he wanted me *annihilated*. He wanted to drink my blood and steal my soul! I spent the rest of the day in my room crying and shaking. I couldn't imagine what it was like to be his child."

Anthony winced at her vivid imagery, because he'd experienced that himself. "All the more reason to marry and get away from him."

"We could have escaped, but you have a profound love for your land and your people, and you'd taken it on yourself to protect them from your father's fury as much as possible," she said flatly. "Would you have been able to live with yourself if you walked away? He might not have been able to avenge himself on you or me but swore that he'd punish all his tenants and estate workers if you defied him. That he'd burn the fields and slaughter the livestock and even torch the abbey!"

Anthony gasped, shocked beyond imagining. "Surely he wouldn't have destroyed the source of his wealth, even to avenge himself on me!"

"Perhaps not. But he sounded more than half-mad and utterly convincing." She shuddered. "He terrified me."

"Dammit, Diana, you should have *told* me!"

She shook her head, her face profoundly sad. "I couldn't put you in the position of having to choose between me and your home and people. A broken heart is agonizing, but not as bad as what your father was threatening. You were strong, so strong, but I feared that he might break you." Tears glinted in her eyes. "I couldn't bear to be the cause of such disaster."

He was shaken by a tumult of emotions. Shock, anger, understanding, and, beneath it all, agonizing grief for what they had both suffered. "I understand much better now. But you said my father was the main reason, implying that there were others?"

She shrugged. "Remember how we talked of traveling? Getting away from England then seemed wise, so I did."

"We had talked of traveling together."

She sighed. "Even then I knew that our traveling to far places was only a dream for you because your responsibilities tethered you to England."

"But it was a good dream," he said softly. A dream of romance and freedom.

She gave a tired smile. "The reality I found was also good, though very different."

"Were there other reasons that contributed to your leaving?"

She looked away from him. "Not really."

She was lying; he was sure of it. Given her general honesty, there would have to be a good reason for that, but it seemed a very large leap to go from "I wanted to marry you" to "too late, sorry" at a time when there were no more worldly barriers in their way.

Whatever she was concealing, he doubted he'd be able to coax it out of her today, when they were both shaken by the discussion they'd just had. He drew a steadying breath. "Thank you for telling me that so I could understand the past. Next I'd like to discuss the future, though probably not today."

Diana shook her head. "We have no future, Anthony. That moment in time when we were young and innocent and uncomplicated is long past. There is nothing more to discuss. Please don't call on me again. It's too difficult."

"It wouldn't be difficult if you didn't care about me still," he said quietly.

"Of course I care about you!" she said almost angrily. "I always will. But that is not a sound basis for the future. *Don't call on me again!* I don't want to see you. Ever. Is that clear enough?"

He was having trouble breathing. "Crystal clear." Unable to say more and fearing that he might fall apart in front of her, he turned on his heel and left the room.

His coat had almost stopped dripping, but it was still raining outside. Gray futility in all directions.

The Panda trotted toward him and looked up inquiringly. He really was a fine and memorable cat. No wonder Diana loved him so much.

She *doted* on the furry cannonball. What would she do if . . . ?

Driven by a mad impulse, Anthony bent to scoop up the Panda. Many cats didn't like being picked up, but the Panda settled onto Anthony's arm as if being carried around was his due. Anthony petted him and received a rumbling purr in return.

"Panda," he said softly. "You're about to go on another journey. Don't worry, your meals will still be regular. And God willing, your lady will come after you." He pulled one of the capes of the voluminous coat over the cat and walked out into the weeping rain.

Diana was too disturbed to concentrate on her editing, so she switched to writing letters. When even that pastime proved hopeless, she took refuge in the arrival of Jane's shipment of Indian wares. She spent a delightful afternoon inventorying jewelry, carvings, shawls, scarves, and more. Jane had a wonderful eye for what was special and beautiful.

Diana chose some of the very best pieces to use as samples when she looked for new outlets for their goods after the holidays. Then she picked out presents for her family and friends. She'd made substantial inroads on the shipment by the time she finished, but she kept track of it all, and having people wear the presents would be good for business later.

Only then did she wonder where the Panda was. Ordinarily he would have joined her and she'd have had to protect the delicate silks and shawls from his claws, but he hadn't shown up. He was probably indulging himself in an all-day nap, or he'd been accidentally shut into a room, though she'd often suspected that he had the magical ability to pass through solid doors.

She didn't start to worry until he failed to show up for dinner. He *never* missed meals! The Spook had gone with Rory and Gabriel to his grandparents' estate. Could the Panda be mourning because his friend was gone? *Where could he be?*

She moved through the house asking all the servants if they'd seen him. No one had. What if he'd slipped out when Anthony left? What if he'd been run down by a carriage or attacked by a dog or was shivering helplessly in the cold rain?

She was almost frantic when the footman delivered a note sealed with the Castleton arms. Anthony had not been happy when he'd left, so she broke the seal warily. Though he was entitled to hurl invective at her, she hoped he was too much a gentleman for that.

The message was short and to the point:

If you ever want to see the Panda again, come to the lodge.

She read it again, then again, her eyes wide with astonishment. The lodge had to be the one on the Castleton estate. A good distance from the main house, it had once been the home of a forester and his family. Quiet and cozy, it was a favorite retreat of Anthony's. It had also been their meeting place in that golden summer.

She read the note again, then balled it up in her fist and snarled, "I'm going to kill him. *I'm bloody going to kill him!*"

Since he couldn't leave Diana to worry about her cat for very long, Anthony had to work fast. He sent a note to Athena and Will at their Oxfordshire home to say he'd been delayed and wasn't sure he'd be able to make it for the family Christmas.

He was interrupted by the Panda politely reminding him that food would be welcome. The cat found poached salmon very agreeable. He was a highly adaptable feline.

It wasn't unusual for Anthony to retreat to the lodge when he wanted peace and quiet, so it was well stocked with fuel, staple foods, and high-quality drink. It also had painfully pleasant memories of the times he'd spent there with Diana.

Any new memories of her at the lodge would be explosive, because she was going to show up blazing like a cavalry charge. Understandably so; abducting a lady's beloved cat was very low, but it was the only thing he could imagine that was guaranteed to bring

Diana after him. Once she arrived, well, he couldn't predict what would happen, but he thought he would achieve certainty at last.

With hampers full of delicacies and a hastily improvised cat carrier that was comfortably padded for the Panda, he set off for Raines Abbey and the isolated lodge where he'd known both heaven and hell.

Chapter 10

Hoping to catch Anthony before he left London, Diana ordered the Vance carriage that had been left for her convenience to take her to Castleton House. Icy winter rain saturated her cloak in the short dash from her coach to the duke's front door.

The knocker was up, so she hoped the scoundrel was still there. The Castleton knocker was a massive ram's head, a creature that figured prominently in the Raines family coat of arms. She wielded it ferociously, the boom echoing through the house.

When a footman opened the huge door, she swept into the atrium entry hall, not caring that she was dripping all over the mosaic floor. An earlier duke had probably stolen it from a Roman temple. She snapped at the footman, "Tell your disgraceful master that Lady Diana Lawrence demands to see him *right now!*"

Nervously the footman said, "I'm sorry, my lady, but His Grace just left for his country estate."

"How long since he left?"

"Perhaps an hour?" The footman looked as if he couldn't wait for this madwoman to depart.

She swore and swirled to go, managing to bang the heavy door as she left. It was late and the weather was wretched. The roads would be in dreadful shape.

No matter. She knew where he was going, and Raines Abbey wasn't far, less than a day's journey away in Berkshire, not very distant from the Lawrence family estate. She'd go and collect the Panda and continue on to her family gathering.

After she wrung that traitorous duke's neck.

By the time Anthony reached the lodge, it was near dark and the rain was turning into snow. He had his coachman deposit him, cat, and hampers there, assuring his servants he just wanted some peace and quiet for a few days and he'd be fine.

Which was true; his servants had standing orders to keep the lodge and the small stable fully stocked with anything that Anthony might need if he decided to retreat here. Used to his eccentric ways, the coachman and guard headed off to the abbey, where they would find a warm fire, a hot meal, and an audience to discuss the mad behavior of their master.

Naturally the first thing he did was feed the Panda, who then settled down to watch as Anthony built a fire, warmed a couple of Cornish pasties he'd brought with him, and opened a bottle of excellent Bordeaux from the locked cabinet that held wine and spirits.

The simple rituals of life were soothing. Ever since he was a boy, he'd liked coming here to be free of servants and his father's thunderous presence. The lodge was comfortably furnished with plain cottage tables and chairs that time and long use had burnished to reveal the rich patterns of the natural wood. Worn Oriental rugs scavenged from the abbey attics added a note of faded grandeur.

The sizable front room had a cooking corner and the large double-sided fireplace warmed the bedroom behind the sitting area. In front of the fire were a battered but very comfortable sofa and a pair of equally battered wing chairs, also items that had been banished from the abbey as being too old and worn.

Over the years, Anthony had added books and extra lamps and objects that amused him, like a slightly lopsided wooden owl that he'd carved as a boy and a shimmering, mysterious conch shell Julia had given him. Next to that was a very old Portuguese statuette of the Madonna that had been a gift from Athena. Far more than the grand abbey, this was his home. He'd even learned to cook a bit.

While he ate, the Panda leaped onto the table and settled at the other end, paws tucked under him and his reproachful green gaze on Anthony. "Are you missing her, Panda, my lad? So am I."

Anthony broke a piece from the savory pasty and set it in front of the cat's nose. A pink tongue licked out and the morsel disappeared. "Don't worry, you'll see her soon. Despite your lady's generally sunny disposition, she has a temper. I'm sure she's never exercised it on you because you're a gentleman and her chief courtier, but she's going to want to skin me alive."

After eating, he brought out some proposed legislation that Parliament would consider in the upcoming session. His usual habit was to read through and make notes in the margins, but he found that Diana had spoken true when she said the Panda liked to sit right on top of paperwork. Though he didn't mind having the cat on the table, he did mind when the Panda deliberately stretched out one snow white paw and knocked over the ink bottle, sending a jet-black pool spreading in all directions.

"Dammit, Panda, have you no respect for the rule of law?" Anthony swore as he shoved back his chair and leaped to his feet so the ink wouldn't drip on his clothing. The handkerchief he used to blot the ink was ruined and so were several pages of legislation, all while the Panda watched with an expression of angelic innocence.

"I think you're telling me it's time to go to bed," Anthony said dryly. "You're probably right. But first I want to see what the weather is doing."

He opened the front door and was blasted by snow and a freezing wind. The cat flattened his whiskers in distaste and made a quick trip out and an even quicker return. Several inches of snow had fallen and more was on the way. The storm wasn't quite a blizzard, but it had aspirations.

Diana would be slowed down, maybe even forced to stay at an inn for a night or two. Angry though she would be, she wasn't foolish enough to force her way through weather like this.

Was she?

Anthony hung lanterns in both the front windows. Surely Diana wouldn't arrive tonight, but anyone who might be caught out here in the woods would need shelter from the storm.

As he closed the door, he uttered a silent prayer that all his people were safe and warm on this wicked winter night.

Diana's coach made good time, considering the weather. She'd hoped to reach the lodge by nightfall, but they were forced to stop at the end of the day when the coachman told her the snow and darkness were making it impossible to see the road.

No one's life should be risked on this endeavor, so she gave orders to stop at the next inn. The Vance servants were grateful for the warmth and hot food, and so was she, briefly. Too restless to settle down for the night, she sought out the landlord. "Mr. Mullins, do you have a good strong horse that I could hire to ride for a few miles?"

"You want to go out in this?" he asked incredulously.

"My destination isn't far and I know the way well." She made her eyes huge and tragic. "It's an urgent family matter. I assure you, I'm an excellent rider and have traveled in conditions like this." Not enthusiastically, but she'd managed.

"I've got no sidesaddle," the landlord said, clearly hoping that would discourage her.

"No matter, I can ride astride." Seeing that he was wavering, she said intensely, "I'm an experienced traveler who has gone safely all the way to India and back. *Please,* Mr. Mullins! I swear I'll be all right, but I *must* go as soon as possible or it may be too late." She let tears show in her eyes. "It may already be too late," she whispered.

Though it was too late for her and Anthony, she damn well intended to get her cat back.

Diana wrapped her scarf more tightly around her numb face in a futile attempt to protect it from the icy wind. She'd made a grave mistake by attempting to complete her mission tonight. Now that she was thinking rationally, she realized that even if she reached the lodge, she'd be insane to leave again in this storm, and she didn't even have a good way to carry the Panda.

The Panda would *not* like being out in this weather! He was a cat who loved his comforts.

The horse was a stalwart gelding, but his pace slowed to a shambling as he forced his way through the deepening snow. Though she knew the way well under normal conditions, the snow and wind changed the look of everything.

She thought she couldn't be far from the lodge, but she might be wrong and hopelessly lost. Grimly she recognized that her life was at risk. It was mildly interesting to imagine Anthony's horror when her frozen body was found in his woods come spring, but she'd never had an ambition to end up like one of Gunter's ices.

Was that a glint of light in the distance? She squinted against the wind, unsure of what she was seeing. If there was a light, it was a long way off. She urged the horse in that direction. Even if the light was in the devil's own sitting room, she wouldn't care as long as it was warm. Hellfires were her likely destination and at least she wouldn't be cold there.

Chapter 11

The Panda was adept at finding warmth, which meant that after Anthony lay down under the sumptuous down quilt the cat had leaped onto the bed and marched over to settle heavily on Anthony's chest. That meant the cat could touch his nose to his host's chin, which seemed to be an invitation to pet his regal feline self.

"Imperial Chinese Throne Cat, ha! I think you're a simple street thug and you're in danger of crushing my lungs so I can't breathe," Anthony muttered when he pulled his right arm out from under the quilt and began scratching the Panda's neck.

The purring that rumbled through Anthony's chest was some consolation for the fact that he couldn't move without dislodging the cat. There was also a certain odd intimacy in knowing that the Panda must sleep on top of Diana like this.

His hand stilled and he dozed off—until the Panda gave an ear-piercing wail and kicked off with clawed back feet that would have eviscerated Anthony if not for the protection of the quilt.

What the devil? Anthony shoved himself upright and realized that the Panda had bolted to the front door in the living room and was howling loud enough to raise the dead.

Something was wrong! Heart pounding, Anthony shoved his feet into his boots, grabbed his hat and scarf, and pulled his coachman's coat over the drawers and loose shirt he'd worn to bed. Something or someone was out in the storm, and Panda's behavior suggested that it might be Diana.

Anthony yanked open the door. The whirling snowflakes caught glimmers of light that enabled him to see a dark form barely visible down the lane that led to the lodge. A man? No, too large. It moved like a horse, and there might have been a crumpled figure on its back.

Would anyone other than Diana be mad enough to be heading toward the lodge on a night like this? Forcing down his fear, he plunged into the knee-deep snow and floundered along the lane. Yes, a horse wearily tromped toward him, and on his back a small figure slumped over the reins. "Diana? *Diana!*"

He reached the horse and the gelding stopped, head drooping. Anthony reached up to the rider, who tumbled into his arms in a solid frozen shape. Yes, it was Diana, her delicate features still as sculpted marble. For an agonized moment he feared she was dead.

Then she said in a raw whisper, "The horse. Take care of the horse."

Almost dizzy with relief that she was alive and sensible, he promised, "I will."

He shifted Diana so he was supporting her with one arm and her head rested against his neck. With his left hand, he caught the reins and headed back along the trail he'd broken through the snow. The tired horse was content to stumble along behind.

The lanterns hung in the windows were a beacon that took far too long to reach. Anthony was near collapse himself by the time he reached the lodge.

He dropped the reins, sure the horse wouldn't go anywhere on his own, and dragged the door open against the wind. When he carried Diana inside, she was moving feebly. "Anthony?"

"Yes, my dear. You are mad but safe now." He set her on her feet and stripped off hat, scarf, and cloak. He was bemused to see that underneath she wore her comfortable Indian dancing costume. Very practical for riding astride.

Then he set her on the sofa and dragged off her riding boots. She moved obediently like a jointed doll. A large, warm blanket was folded over the back of the sofa and he used that to wrap around her before settling her on the sofa.

Knowing she'd be furious if he didn't take care of her mount, he said, "I'll be back as soon as I've tended your horse."

Her head was drooping, but she managed to mumble, "Good. He's a good horse."

Anthony carried a lantern outside, caught the horse's reins, and led him into the small stable on the right side of the yard. Like the main lodge, the stable was well stocked and had hay, straw, grain, and horse blankets. There was water in a bucket—Anthony's people took very good care of his retreat—though he had to break the ice on top before the gelding could drink.

The horse wasn't groomed for as long as he deserved, but the beast was fed, watered, and content under a blanket when Anthony returned to the lodge with Diana's saddlebags. He dumped them on the floor and hung his dripping greatcoat on a peg by the door as he studied Diana. She was huddled in a ball in her blanket in front of the fire, shivering, but she was being aided by the Panda, who was a large bundle of furry warmth on her lap. She'd tucked both hands under him.

Among the specialty items Anthony had brought from London was a creamy potato and leek soup that he'd hung on the hob to warm earlier. He scooped soup into two mugs, then poured two glasses of brandy with a little water and set them on the sofa's end table by the soup.

Finally he sank into the sofa and transferred the blanket-wrapped Diana to his lap, Panda and all. Even inside the blanket, she was shivering. If they'd been at the abbey he could have had a hot bath drawn for her, but here sharing body warmth would have to do.

He placed one glass of brandy in her hand and wrapped her chilled fingers around it. "Drink," he ordered.

Obediently she took a small sip, then a larger one while he swallowed half of his own brandy in one long gulp. The burn was welcome as it made its way down. When his brandy was gone along with most of hers, he set the glasses aside and started them on the nicely warmed soup.

She drank that with more enthusiasm than she'd shown for the brandy. It was a very fine soup, smooth and rich and warming. When he set his empty mug aside, he said conversationally, "You're insane, you know. Surely wringing my worthless neck could have waited a day."

She gave a little hiccup of laughter. "I had my rage to keep me warm." The hand that wasn't holding the brandy glass moved to scratch the Panda's neck. "Stealing my cat was a rotten thing to do!"

"Yes, though it wasn't theft but abduction. Surely you didn't think I'd hurt him!"

"No, but you might keep him! He likes you."

"He likes anyone who will pet and feed him," Anthony said dryly.

"But he has his favorites." The Panda underlined her point by raising his head to nuzzle against Diana's neck. "What's the difference between theft and abduction?"

"Theft is stealing goods for profit. Abduction is taking a person for more complicated reasons, and Panda is very much a person." Anthony smiled a little. "Though a furry one. In this case, I didn't mean to keep him. He's a hostage."

Diana frowned. "What kind of ransom do you want? You don't need money."

"His ransom is for you to talk to me," Anthony said crisply. "I know now why you left me so abruptly, and while I think it might have been possible to deal with my father's threats in a different way, I do understand why you did what you did. Perhaps your abandoning me was the best of a bad lot of choices."

"I thought so then." She sighed. "I still think so. But what's done is done, Anthony. The past can't be changed."

"But the future can be." He drew a deep breath, unable to forget the pain he'd felt when she said she never wanted to see him again. "Desperate times call for desperate measures. Abducting the Panda was the one thing I could think of that would bring you to me, since I was banned from your presence."

"I'm sorry," she said in a voice fading to a whisper. "I didn't want to hurt you, but I can't see a future with you. I just *can't*." The soup mug sagged from her fingers.

Anthony gently removed the mug and set it aside before it could fall. She must be exhausted after her dangerous struggle through the storm—though he wasn't entirely sure that she wasn't feigning sleep to avoid talking to him. He'd grant her this night, but tomorrow would be a different matter.

This time the Panda jumped away when Anthony stood with Diana in his arms. He carried her into the bedroom and tucked her under the down quilt, folding the blanket and spreading it over her for additional warmth.

He was still wearing his boots, so he tugged them off and climbed into the other side of the bed. The situation was ruinous for any number of reasons, but he was too tired to care. He rolled over and drew Diana into his arms. She'd warmed up some but was still chilled. No matter. He had enough heat for both of them.

It was sweet, so sweet, to hold her like this. . . .

Before drifting off to sleep, he felt the bed shake as the Panda landed and found a comfortable spot on top of their feet. What a good Panda he was, to bring Diana into Anthony's arms, even if only for a single night.

Diana gradually emerged from sleep, wondering why she'd dreamed of icy cold and bitter winds when she was so warm and secure.

Warm, secure, and enfolded in a male embrace. Her eyes shot open, but she remained very still as she assessed her situation.

She could see the window, and the outside sky was no longer dark, but it looked gray and heavy. She guessed that it was still snowing. The deadly storm had been real, and Anthony had rescued her and brought her into the safety of the lodge.

She'd been cold, so cold, with the kind of deep chill that went to the marrow and seemed as if it would never go away. But the warm bed and Anthony's warm body had melted the chill away. They were lying face-to-face, his arm around her waist as they shared a pillow. She was still in her *salwar* and *kameez* while he wore drawers and a shirt, so they were both minimally respectable.

He still slept, so she was free to study his face close up. Handsome, always, with a faint shadowing of dark whiskers on his chin and lower cheeks. In the last seven years there had been a firming of the softer lines of youth.

She'd always known he was younger than she, and it hadn't mattered because of the swift bond that had formed between them.

Now she realized that he no longer seemed younger. He was fully mature, a man in the prime of life who had endured a brutal upbringing to become wise and compassionate.

Though he no longer seemed young, now she felt old. Worn out and useless.

His intense blue eyes opened and they stared at each other with mere inches between them. She felt as if she was looking into his soul, and merciful heaven, what was he seeing in her?

The heat and tension between them swiftly turned combustible and she rolled away from him and out of bed before there was an explosion. He'd lured her here for answers, and he would not be satisfied without the truth. She painfully recognized that she must provide that. As he said, she owed him that much.

The Panda rose from the foot of the bed and arched into a stretch. "Mroowp!"

"He's hungry," she said.

"He's always hungry as near as I can tell," Anthony said dryly as he rolled from the other side of the bed. He stretched, not unlike the Panda, all lithe male grace. The illicit intimacy of sharing a bed with him was equally irresistible and alarming. "Would you like tea and toast?"

Hot tea! "Yes, please." She moved closer to the window. "It's still snowing, but less than last night, I think."

"You're right, but we won't be getting out of here today and probably not tomorrow. I brought your saddlebags in last night. Do you have a change of clothing inside?"

She nodded. "Fresh clothes would be welcome."

He brought her saddlebags and moved into the front room. From the sounds, he was putting coal on the fire and setting a kettle to boil for the tea. Diana splashed cold water from the basin on her face and changed into a plain but warm blue gown, wrapping a patterned Indian shawl around her shoulders.

They changed places and she moved into the kitchen while he retreated to the bedroom to dress. The Panda was polishing off the breakfast Anthony had set out for him. She surveyed the food supplies and saw that none of them were in danger of starving.

She found the bread and cheese and began toasting it, then

made a pot of tea when water came to the boil. Excellent oolong tea it was, with honey to sweeten it.

She looked up warily when he entered the room, dressed in casual country buckskin breeches and a blue coat cut more loosely than formal wear. As always, he had the innate elegance that had captivated her the first time they met.

"Don't look as if I'm a lion about to pounce," he said with amusement. "I won't start the interrogation until we've eaten."

It didn't take long to consume their simple breakfast. Anthony swallowed the last of his tea and set aside the cup. "Are you ready for the lion to pounce?"

The last bite of her cheese toast turned to sawdust in her mouth. She washed it down with a swig of tea. "As ready as I'll ever be."

"Good, but first a prologue." He stood and closed the space between them with two long steps so he could pull her to her feet and kiss her.

Her shock instantly dissolved. She gripped his arms, dizzily aware that this was a kiss designed to burn away all rational thought and it was succeeding. His mouth was hot and demanding and called forth an intoxicated response from her. Her body molded into his like heated wax. *This* was why they'd been so insane seven years ago—this passionate need to become one heart, one flesh, that had seared away all doubts and common sense.

Too much time passed before she managed to summon the will to wrench herself away. "You cheat, Castleton!" she gasped.

"If the prize seems worth it," he said, not pursuing her. "Words aren't enough, my lady fair. Passion is so much a part of this particular relationship that it can't be left out of the calculation."

He'd called her his lady fair in that early, more innocent time. She swallowed hard. "What exactly do you want to know?"

He leaned back on the fieldstone surround of the fireplace, crossing his arms on his chest as he watched her. "Your explanation of why you left made sense and I understand now why you behaved as you did. But why are you trying to run away from me now? Yes, seven years have passed, but I still feel the same connection with you that I felt before. Am I imaging that you feel it, too?"

She turned and began pacing the wide room, unable to meet his gaze. "There is still connection," she admitted, "but it's not enough.

The reasons why I feel we have no future are less clear than the vicious threats your father made."

"Start with unclear reasons and perhaps we may work our way to clarity," he said.

"It's not really that complicated, Anthony. Then you were too young. Now I'm too old." She stopped pacing and turned to face him. "You're one of the most powerful men in Britain, and it's a blessing and a tribute to your mother that you want to use that power wisely. You need to marry a wellborn young virgin who is wise in the ways of politics and society, not a jaded, scandalous older woman like me."

"I know you're not a virgin," he said, his gaze piercing. "Remember? I was *there*."

Hot blood flooded her face and her gaze dropped. She would never forget the sweet miracle of that afternoon when they had given their virginity to each other in this very place. Their mutual wonder and sense of discovery had seemed like a forever pledge of love and trust.

Three days later his father had called on her and destroyed it all. In a whisper, she replied, "How could I forget? But seven long years have passed since then. I have not always slept alone."

"Nor have I," he said easily. "Shall we compare lists? Did you bed the nearest regiment? That would be exhausting."

"Of course not!" she snapped.

"In case you're wondering, I didn't use my wealth to purchase the favors of every expensive beauty in the muslin company," he said in a conversational tone. "Nor have I caught any vile diseases. Have you?"

She shook her head. "No regiment, but there were a few times when I was lonely enough to seek comfort in another man's arms. Any comfort was brief, so I decided to devote myself to needlepoint and good works."

He broke into laughter. "Good works, perhaps, but surely not needlepoint. Are you saying you're not worthy of my magnificent ducal consequence? I'm having trouble understanding this."

She looked away. "Something like that."

"I'm disappointed in you, Diana."

Her gaze snapped back to him. He continued, "Once upon a time you thought that women should have the same freedom to experiment with passion as men did. It was a dazzling point of view, one that I decided I shared. If you're saying that you're too experienced for me, I'm not convinced."

She gazed at him as he watched her, passionate and formidable, and realized that she would have to reveal the devastating reality she'd concealed from everyone. "You want the whole truth?" she asked in a raw whisper. "Very well, you shall have it! After I left you, I found that I was with child."

Chapter 12

That was a truth so shocking that it cracked his control. He tensed, no longer lounging against the fieldstone wall. "And?"

"I'd already set sail for Greece when I realized. I was . . . horrified but also jubilant that I would have something of you." She closed her eyes as the tormented emotions of that time flared to scalding new life. "I had it all worked out. I would arrive in Greece as a widow and have my child there. After the child was born, perhaps I'd travel on to India. I would decide what was best when the time came."

"But that didn't happen?" he asked, his voice still quiet.

"There was a storm that tossed the ship around like a cockleshell. I thought I was going to die. I survived . . . but our child didn't. I miscarried. No one knew but me. But I can never forget." Tears were streaming down her face, driven by the harrowing grief she'd hidden for so many years. "I failed you; I failed myself; I failed the child we made together! How can there be a future for us after that?"

"My darling girl!" He crossed the room and enfolded her in his arms, surrounding her with compassion and comfort. "I'm so sorry you had to bear all that alone! What happened was our tragedy, not your sin."

She shook her head, her face pressed into his shoulder. "I wish I could believe that," she said in a thin whisper.

"Well, you should." He sat on the sofa and pulled her down into his lap again. She shouldn't allow this closeness, but she couldn't bear to move away, not yet.

He continued, "A high percentage of early pregnancies end in miscarriage, perhaps as many as one in four. It's not the fault of the mother. It's God saying 'not yet.'"

She tilted her head back to look at him with a frown. "Are you making this up? I can't imagine a man knowing such things."

He grinned at her. "Did I mention that my sister Julia earned her living as a midwife during her years in the wilderness? She's a very good one, too, and showed a certain ruthlessness in explaining the facts of life to her younger brother."

"How did the topic even come up?" she asked, as curious as she was surprised.

His expression sobered. "She had a miscarriage a year after the birth of her first child. She and Randall were very saddened, of course, but under the influence of laudanum she told me much more than I wanted to know about the mysteries of childbirth. It was hair-raising but enlightening."

His broad hand stroked soothingly down her back. "She has since had a fine and healthy second child, a budding young hellion whose middle name is Anthony. I was honored."

"This is all true?" Diana asked doubtfully. "You aren't making things up to help me feel better?"

Anthony nodded. "As Julia told me then, sometimes things happen that we don't understand. We are allowed to mourn, but it is wisdom to then move on. Your miscarriage is one of those things we can't understand. Yes, it was a great grief to you, but it's not an event that you should allow to ruin your life. And mine, too."

She rested her head on his chest and thought about that. A tragedy, not a sin? She hadn't failed Anthony or failed as a woman? It was an amazingly liberating thought. She had felt guilty and unworthy ever since the miscarriage.

"Your words are like a key that has unlocked a whole cabinetful of guilt I could never bear to look at," she said haltingly. "When we met I couldn't resist you, but I felt that I was taking advantage of you. You were younger and more vulnerable because of your age and your dreadful father. Every problem that followed from our coming together was my fault."

"If you felt you were taking advantage of me, your memory is faulty," he said seriously. "Our falling in love was as mutual as falling in love can be, I think. The only regret I had was when you left. I felt that a limb had been torn off and I was no longer whole."

She began weeping for his pain and her own. "Wouldn't we have been better off if we'd never known each other? I was trespassing on Castleton land the day we met."

"No!" he said sharply. "I know that I would not be better off and I don't think you would have been, either. We grow through living our lives and that means pain as well as joy. From you I learned what I wanted from life." His voice softened. "And it seems that what I want is you. No one else will do."

She lay back in his arms so she could see his face. "How did you become so wise and kind?"

"I've been fortunate in the females in my life," he said seriously. "My mother, my grandmother, my sisters. Most of all, you, because you taught me the most about giving and receiving love."

She swallowed hard, almost unbearably moved. "If what you're saying is true, it certainly undercuts my conviction that I am unworthy of you."

"Good! For a generally sensible woman, you weren't being sensible at all." He tilted her face upward so they were gazing into each other's eyes. "Do you still feel too old to be my wife?" He bent into a kiss of tenderness and promise of what might be.

She summoned all her memories of sunshine and joy to dissolve the pain and guilt that had clouded her spirit for so many years. It was time to open herself to him as fully and honestly as in the summer of their first love.

Golden light began filling her as she accepted that this strong, compassionate man could see her in all her weaknesses and love her still. She kissed him back, offering everything she had. The embrace intensified and they almost fell off the sofa as he responded.

He caught her before they landed on the floor. Laughing, she lay back in his arms and said, "I feel amazingly younger than I did before we had this little discussion!"

He grinned back at her. "Does this mean you'll marry me?"

She turned serious. "Yes, my one and only love. And the sooner the better!"

"Then I suggest we celebrate our betrothal in the most scandalous possible way." He rose from the sofa while holding her in his arms, a tribute to his strength. "Unless you object?"

"No." She wrapped her arms around his neck and kissed him again. "I do not object at all. I want to see if my memory of lying with you was exaggerated."

He set her on her feet and led her into the bedroom. They disrobed each other garment by garment, murmuring words of love and appreciation.

And when they lay down together, skin to skin and heart to heart, she found that memory had not exaggerated. Indeed, the tenderness and fire exceeded her imagination.

After, she fell asleep in his arms, knowing she had truly come home.

When Anthony woke, he quietly rose to replenish the fire and feed the appreciative cat. Then he slid back into the bed beside Diana's delicious warmth. He loved studying her face in the pearly light, seeing the faint lines of maturity, lessons learned, wisdom acquired the hard way.

Beautiful. Beloved. She would always be beautiful, no matter how many years passed, and he prayed they'd have decades together.

Her eyes opened sleepily when he brushed a kiss on her forehead. "You haven't changed your mind about marrying me, have you?" he murmured. "If so, I'll have to demonstrate again the advantages of marriage."

She smiled with sweet mischief. "I've wanted to marry you since we first met, my one and only love, so I won't be changing my mind. Though I wouldn't mind another demonstration of why we should wed as soon as possible!"

"I shall be happy to provide that." He combed his fingertips through her silky golden hair, loving the texture and the intimacy of how it cascaded freely. "The storm is diminishing, but we're snowed in for today and travel will be difficult tomorrow. The next day will be Christmas Eve. In the morning I can run up the flag and we can reenter the world. Where would you like to spend Christmas?"

Diverted, she asked, "Run up the flag?"

"There's a flagpole behind the stables," he explained. "When I'm ready to emerge from my retreat, I run up a signal flag. Someone in the household will notice, and since I'm here without transportation, a carriage will soon appear." Seeing her expression, he said with amusement, "There are some advantages to being a duke, you know."

"Indeed!" she said with a peal of laughter. "But how very strange that I'm going to be a duchess! I never really thought about that until now."

"Is it easier to imagine being my wife?" he asked softly.

"Until now, that was only a dream." She laid a warm palm against his cheek. "Shall we spend Christmas with your family? You were planning on that, and the Masterson estate isn't far, is it?"

He nodded. "Even with bad roads, we should reach Hayden Hall before dark. I want to show you off to my sisters, who bullied me into going to the masquerade. I owe them a considerable debt."

"So do I." She snuggled even closer. "I want to meet them and their husbands, but I'm glad we'll have these days to ourselves. It's such wicked bliss to just lie here in bed with you, skin to skin. No other people, no obligations. Just us."

He couldn't agree more. His hand began wandering over smooth, warm curves. "Then onward to the Lawrence family gathering to celebrate the New Year?"

"I'd like that, but I warn you, there are a lot more Lawrences than members of your family!" she said. "Expect a great deal of squealing, hugs, and some smug satisfaction."

"Where would the smugness come from?" he asked, puzzled.

"On the night of the ball, my sister-in-law Sylvia said she'd have liked you for one of her girls," Diana explained. "But you and Rory weren't interested in each other so she assumed you were lost to the Lawrence clan. She'll be pleased to learn that the Lawrence family spinster has won the greatest prize in the marriage mart."

He made a face. "I've always loathed that phrase!"

"Then it's good that you are now safely off the marriage mart." She patted his chest, then began stroking downward. "Mine. *Mine!*"

He sucked in his breath sharply. "I believe it's time for that demonstration I mentioned earlier."

She made a purring sound as her hand inched ever lower. He kissed her then, knowing that she was right. The wedding would be soon, but this was their honeymoon. Sweet days of tenderness and fire and discovery. *You are mine and I am yours . . .*

Chapter 13

Christmas Eve morning dawned with brilliant sunshine and a sky as intensely blue as Anthony's eyes. Diana left the lodge with some reluctance, but one couldn't live in a bubble of enchanted solitude forever. They'd be back. Oh, yes, they'd be back. She envisioned many years of their regularly retreating here to rejoice in each other's company in peaceful solitude.

As Anthony had promised, not long after he hoisted his flag a Castleton travel coach rumbled up the forest lane and collected man, woman, and cat. Their first stop was at the inn where Diana had left her entourage. There, they returned her hired horse and she sent her carriage and servants on to the Lawrence family estate with the message that she'd join the house party before the New Year.

She retrieved her baggage and gratefully packed away the *salwar kameez* and riding boots that had proved so useful when she rode out to the lodge. Since she was about to meet her future in-laws, she changed into a demure gown of a soft dark green and covered that with her fur-trimmed burgundy velvet cloak. She didn't think the Raines sisters would actually believe she was demure, not when she was emerging with their brother after several scandalous days and nights, but Diana wanted to show willing.

The roads were predictably dreadful, but the coach was comfortable and the snow-covered countryside shimmered gloriously in the sunshine. She and Anthony spent the hours holding hands and talking endlessly about their lives and hopes for the future.

The short winter day passed swiftly and it was dusk when they pulled up in front of Hayden House. The windows of the rambling Tudor manor glowed with welcoming candlelight.

Anthony alighted and gave orders to take the coach around to the stables. A light snow was falling and flakes drifted over his dark cloak and hat in a drift of white stars. She would never get tired of admiring him.

He lifted the Panda's carrier from the coach, then offered his other hand to Diana. She stepped out feeling tight with nerves.

"Don't worry," he said perceptively. "They'll love you."

"You don't know sisters," she said darkly. "The lovely Lawrence sisters still haven't forgiven the young lady who treated the second oldest brother badly."

He patted her hand where it curled tightly around his arm. "Commendable loyalty, but the Raines family has a different dynamic since we didn't grow up together in the same way the Lawrences did. We have fewer expectations of how people should behave."

She prayed he was right.

Anthony wielded the heavy door knocker with vigor, and they were admitted almost immediately into a front hall decorated with greens and scarlet ribbons and rife with the tantalizing scents of roast meats and spice and holiday baking.

Diana inhaled with deep pleasure. The British in Bombay had Christmas feasts, but greens and the scents just didn't have the same effect in blazing tropical heat.

The butler who opened the door smiled broadly. "Your Grace! The family had given up hope that you would arrive in time for Christmas."

The door to a reception room on the right opened and a woman's voice called, "Is Anthony here?"

Two couples emerged from the reception room, where Diana guessed they'd been sharing a pre-dinner drink. In the lead were two women, their husbands following. The tall lady was the one who had shared those intimate moments with Anthony as he was leaving the supper room at the ball. Ah, one of his sisters! No wonder they had seemed close.

At her elbow was a petite dark-haired woman. Both shared family coloring and a similar cast of features with Anthony. They paused, eyes widening at the sight of Diana.

Anthony set the cat carrier down and placed a warm, reassuring hand on the small of Diana's back. "Julia, Athena, remember I told you I once offered for a young lady who turned me down? To my great delight, she has finally agreed to become my wife."

After a stunned moment, the broader of the two military gentlemen said warmly, "Lady Diana Lawrence! Welcome to Hayden Hall." So he would be Lord Masterson, her host. The blond man would be Major Randall, husband to Lady Julia.

Diana said shyly, "Lady Julia, Lady Masterson, I'm so pleased to meet you. Anthony has told me much about his wonderful sisters."

The taller woman laughed and offered Diana her hand. "He exaggerates, which I'm grateful for. Please, call me Athena, and this is Julia. The pleasure is ours."

Diana took the other woman's hand with relief, giving thanks that Anthony's sisters were willing to forgive her breaking their brother's heart seven years earlier. They were as warm and accepting as he'd said they would be.

Lady Julia also offered her hand. "Any woman who can make my brother look so happy makes me happy as well!"

Anthony accepted congratulatory handshakes from his beaming brothers-in-law, and it was clear that the three men were great friends. She was so glad that Anthony had the family he deserved.

Then the air was shattered by a piercing feline cry of annoyance. "*MROOOOOOOOOOWP!*"

Diana jumped, guilty for having forgotten to release the Panda. "Sorry!"

Anthony bent hastily and unlatched the door of the carrier. The Panda stomped out, looking ill-used, though he began to preen when he realized that all eyes were on him. "My cat," Diana said rather unnecessarily.

"There is a potential for trouble here," Athena said, her brow furrowing.

As if by magic, a massive striped cat with tufted ears appeared, stalking toward the intruder. Diana bit her lip, knowing that the new cat must be Khan, and he didn't appear to be as timid as the Spook. She prepared to move quickly in case she had to break up a cat fight.

The Panda straightened, his fur rising a little. Khan stopped a yard away and sized up the new arrival. Then he inclined his massive head politely, a gesture echoed by the Panda. Diana was reminded of Eastern fighters offering formal recognition of each other.

Luckily the salute wasn't the prelude to a battle for dominance. Khan turned and sauntered off, his plumy tail waving elegantly behind him. Diana guessed that he was heading into the reception room, where there might be food. "What a splendid fellow, Athena! Anthony told me that you have one of the Famous Fabulous Fishing Cats of Sumatra, but I've never seen one before."

Athena shot an incredulous glance at her brother before saying with a straight face, "Yes, they're very rare. Khan is a particularly fine example of the breed. But come, join us for some mulled wine while your rooms are prepared. Then you can freshen up before we dine."

Rooms, plural, Diana noticed with regret. It was only to be expected. There were months of cold weather ahead, so she and Anthony needed to marry as soon as possible!

Before her cup of hot spiced wine was finished, any unease she'd felt had dissipated. Everyone was making an effort to make her feel welcome, and she was finding connections between her family and Anthony's.

Will admired Lord Lawrence's leadership in the House of Lords, and he and Alex Randall both knew her military brother Arthur from serving together on the Peninsula. Lady Julia had worked with Lady Lawrence on a charity to benefit military widows and orphans. And both her new sisters wanted a private showing of her Indian imports when they returned to London.

Bemused, Diana realized that although she'd feared she wouldn't belong when she returned to London, she'd been wrong. She was fitting seamlessly back into the life she'd been born to, and she liked the feeling.

Athena personally escorted her up to her room. "Since you're traveling without a maid, I sent one up here earlier to start a fire and unpack your belongings. We dine in about an hour. A bell will ring five minutes before."

Diana glanced around and saw that the two women were alone. "Athena, Anthony told me he'd like a cat like your Khan. Where might I find one for him? I'm sure there is one closer than Sumatra."

Athena grinned. "Which of you came up with the Fishing Cats of Sumatra name?"

"Anthony, after I claimed that the Panda was an Imperial Chinese Throne Cat," Diana explained. "He likes my silliness, I think."

"I like seeing him silly," Athena said with a chuckle. "He's too often serious. I've never seen him so happy as he is with you."

"I'm glad to hear that," Diana said seriously. "Being with him makes me so happy also."

"Kittens increase happiness, " Athena said, "and you're in luck. Khan has fathered a litter of kittens in Will's barn and one of them looks very like him. She's sweet and friendly and I think Anthony will love her."

"Is she old enough to leave her mother?"

Athena nodded. "Do you have a plan in mind?"

"Indeed, I do," Diana said, her eyes gleaming. This was going to be the best Christmas ever.

Anthony came to collect her when the dinner bell sounded. "You look much more relaxed," he observed.

"I am." She gave him a swift kiss because he looked so utterly delectable. "I love your sisters and their husbands. This is a marvelous place to celebrate Christmas."

The dining room sparkled with crystal and candles and shining silverware. The Mastersons and Randalls gave a formal toast of congratulation on the betrothal, so Diana returned a toast of gratitude for their welcome.

Conversation flowed easily as they laughed and ate delicious food. The two couples made Diana feel deeply and completely at home.

As she studied Anthony's sisters, she realized perhaps because of their horrid father, they needed their brother to find the happiness they'd found. Now the trauma of the past no longer held sway and their family circle was complete. So she toasted the three Raines offspring as well, joined warmly by Will and Alex.

Family.

After dinner, Anthony escorted Diana to her room, giving her a chaste kiss outside the door. "Sleep well, my lady fair. You've had a long day."

She nodded, regret in her eyes at the separate rooms. "So have you." She kissed him back, her hands curling into his waist before he broke away.

He was whistling softly as he withdrew to his own room. He had a surprise for Diana, who hadn't realized that their rooms had a connecting door. After he changed into nightwear and a robe, he quietly knocked on the door to her room, then let himself in. "Are you willing to have company tonight?"

Diana was brushing out her hair, and she almost dropped her hairbrush when she saw him. "Anthony! I thought that door led to a closet. Your sister won't mind if we . . . we anticipate our vows?"

He grinned and closed the door behind him. "She must have noticed how we look at each other and decided it's none of her business how we arrange matters. I certainly wouldn't ask her about her courtship with Will! But it's not an accident that she put us in these rooms."

"So we can enjoy another wicked winter night!" Eyes glowing, Diana set down the hairbrush and went into his arms, warm and soft and utterly desirable.

He closed his eyes, still awed by the miracle of finding each other. "You're the best Christmas present ever."

"No, you are, my love." She smiled at him playfully. "Now about that wicked winter night . . . !"

Laughing, he swept her up in his arms. The bed had been turned down so he laid her in the center. She was all gold and ivory welcome. "I love you, Diana, even more than I could have imagined that summer we met," he said huskily as he peeled off his robe.

"I feel the same, my beloved," she whispered. "You have become so much more than I had ever imagined."

As he slid into the bed beside her, the Panda leaped up and

found a spot at the lower corner of the counterpane. Anthony smiled as he leaned into a kiss. There was room enough, and love enough, for all.

The windows were pinkening with dawn when Diana heard a faint sound at the door. A tiny meow, she thought. Moving silently so as not to disturb Anthony, she slipped from the bed and padded to the door. She opened it to find a basket with a small kitten inside, as she and Athena had arranged.

She brought the basket into her room and lifted out the kitten. Fluff, stripes, tufted ears, and totally adorable.

Anthony said sleepily, "Come back to bed, my lady fair. We don't have to get up for breakfast and church for hours."

"I have a present for you." She placed the kitten on the pillow.

"You gave me an amazing one last night," he murmured, not opening his eyes. "I'd like to return it with interest."

She climbed back into the bed, watching the kitten make its wobbly way across the pillow.

Anthony was reaching for her when a small, raspy pink tongue licked his nose. His eyes shot open and he came instantly awake. "What the . . . ?"

He saw the kitten and began to laugh as he sat up and enfolded the small creature in his hands. "I presume that this is a Famous Fabulous Fishing Kitten of Sumatra?"

She nodded. "Compliments of Athena and Will. I plotted with her and she sent Will out to the barn to collect your gift."

The kitten jumped from Anthony's hands and began to lurch toward the Panda, her tiny legs finding the deep quilt heavy going. The older cat rose and approached the kitten. They met and touched noses. Then the Panda put a large paw on the kitten's back and began to wash her.

They both laughed as Diana cuddled under Anthony's arm. She had never felt happier or more content in her life. "I think I'll have a diamond-studded collar made for the Panda."

"He's a very fine fellow," Anthony agreed. "But diamonds? He'd rather have potted shrimp, I'm sure."

Diana chuckled and kissed Anthony's ear. "Diamonds because he's the *cat*alyst who brought us together!"

Read on for an excerpt from Mary Jo Putney's newest Rogues Redeemed novel, *Once a Spy*, available now.

LOVE AND SURVIVAL IN THE SHADOW
OF WATERLOO . . .

Wearied by his years as a British intelligence officer, Simon Duval resigns his commission after Napoleon's abdication. Hoping to find new meaning in his life, he returns to England, where he discovers his cousin's widow, Suzanne Duval, the Comtesse de Chambron. Working as a seamstress, living in reduced circumstances, Suzanne has had a life as complicated as Simon's. While both believe they are beyond love, their sympathetic bond leads him to propose a marriage of companionship, and Suzanne accepts.

She didn't want or expect a true marriage, but as Suzanne joins Simon in a search for his long-missing foster brother, warmth and caring begin to heal both their scars—and a powerful passion sparks between them. Then news from France threatens to disrupt their happiness. Napoleon has escaped from Elba and Wellington personally asks Simon to help prevent another devastating war. Only this time, Simon does not go into danger alone. He and Suzanne will face deadly peril together and pray that love will carry them through. . . .

Chapter 1

London
February 1815

Even though Suzanne was working under the small window in her room to get the best light, it was now too dark to continue sewing. England was much farther north than where she'd been living, and in midwinter the days were short and often rainy or overcast. She might have to buy candles to finish these alterations by the end of the week.

She set aside the gown and stood to stretch. Perhaps she should go for a short walk. The day was raw and her old cloak barely adequate, but she loved having the freedom to go outside whenever she wished.

Solid steps sounded on the stairs outside her room and she recognized the dignified approach of her landlord, Mr. Potter. He knocked on the door and announced, "Madame Duval, there's a fellow here who says he's your cousin, Colonel Duval. He's down in the sitting room. Do you have a cousin who is a colonel?"

Suzanne opened her door, surprised. After the last tumultuous years, she had no idea what relatives might still be alive, or what they had been doing. "I might, but I'll have to see him to be sure. I assume he looks respectable or you wouldn't have allowed him in."

"He has the look of a soldier, not that being one would make him a saint," her landlord said dourly. "I'll go down with you in case you want me to send him away."

She nodded her thanks. Mr. Potter was very protective of the female tenants in his boardinghouse. It was one of the reasons she'd chosen to live here.

She peeled off the fingerless gloves she wore to keep her hands warm while sewing, brushed a casual hand over her dark hair, and straightened her knit shawl over her shoulders, glad that her appearance was no longer a matter of life and death. Then she followed her landlord down the narrow stairs.

When she opened the door to the small sitting room, the dim light revealed a man gazing out the window, his hands clasped behind his back as he studied the shabby neighborhood. Lean and powerful, he did indeed have the bearing of a soldier. His wavy dark hair was in need of cutting and he had a familiar grace as he turned at her entrance. His searching gaze met hers and he became very still.

She froze, paralyzed with shock. *Jean-Louis!*

But her husband was dead—she'd seen him murdered with her own eyes. Also, Jean-Louis had been twice her age when they married. This man was younger.

When she saw his cool, light gray eyes, she remembered a young second cousin of her husband. Simon Duval had been a boy, only a couple of years older than she'd been as a very young bride, but he'd shared a strong family resemblance to her husband. The years had emphasized subtle differences in his features and she guessed that he was a shade taller and more broad-shouldered than Jean-Louis had been.

Realizing she wasn't breathing, she inhaled slowly. "Well met, Simon. Or should I call you Monsieur le Comte?"

"So it really is you, my cousin Suzanne," her visitor said with soft amazement. "The name is not uncommon and Hawkins didn't say you were the Comtesse de Chambron. But though you are a countess, I am no count. Merely a distant cousin by marriage who is very glad to see that you are alive."

He spoke English with no hint of a French accent and she remembered that his mother had been English. "Though I no longer think myself a countess, you might be the Comte de Chambron if enough members of my husband's family have died." Which was true, but even more true was that the world where French courtly titles mattered seemed very far away. She extended her hand. "Mr. Potter announced you as a colonel. Which army? British, French royalist, or French imperial?"

"So many possibilities! The British army, though I'm going to sell out now that the emperor has abdicated." He smiled a little as he took her hand and bent over it, a gesture wholly French. "I'm glad to see you well and more beautiful than ever. I'd heard you were dead."

His hand was warm and strong and competent. She released it with reluctance. "You flatter like a Frenchman, Simon," she replied, returning his smile. "I am no longer a dewy young bride and I was very nearly dead several times over. But yes, I have survived."

Her landlord cleared his throat and she realized that he'd been monitoring this meeting from the doorway. "Madame Duval, I imagine you and the colonel have much to discuss, so I'll bring you some tea."

"That would be lovely, Mr. Potter." After he left, she knelt on the hearth and added a small scoop of coals to the embers of the fire. "Indeed, we have much to catch up on, cousin. It's been a dozen years or more."

Simon had been one of many guests at her wedding to the Comte de Chambron. She'd been only fifteen, dazzled by suave Jean-Louis and thrilled to be making such a grand marriage. Since Simon had been near her age, they'd developed a teasing friendship in the days before the wedding, but that had been a lifetime ago.

She settled in the chair to the right of the fireplace. "How did you find me?"

"Captain Gabriel Hawkins." Simon took the seat opposite her. "He and I shared an alarming adventure in Portugal some years back. By chance we ran into each other and, as we exchanged news, I learned that he's just returned from a voyage to Constantinople and you were a passenger."

She stiffened. "Did he tell you my circumstances?"

Voice gentle, Simon said, "He said you were in the harem of a powerful and deeply corrupt Turkish official, and that your aid was invaluable in rescuing two Englishwomen, including the young lady who is now his wife."

Those were the bare facts. She hoped that Hawkins had said no more than that. "And in return, he rescued me and brought me here."

"Hawkins said he offered to take you to France, but that you chose to join émigré relatives who were in the French community in Soho." His perceptive gaze was evaluating her and the clean but worn sitting room. She could guess his thoughts. In London, Soho was the French quarter where the wealthy émigrés lived. The poor ones struggled to make a living in this rundown neighborhood in the St. Pancras parish.

Answering his unasked question, she said, "After Napoleon abdicated, those cousins returned to France to reclaim their property. I was not surprised to find them gone. But no matter. I prefer to make my own way in England rather than return to France. There is nothing for me there."

His gaze flicked around the worn sitting room again. "Forgive me for asking, but how are you managing?"

"I sew well and I've been doing piecework. Soon I should be able to find a permanent position." She smiled wryly. "But I do wish I'd been able to bring the jewels I had when I was a favorite in the harem! I'd have been able to buy my own shop."

"Money makes everything easier," he agreed, his brow furrowed. "I'm fortunate that my mother came from a successful English merchant family and her fortune remained on this side of the channel."

"Very prudent of your mother and her family." She cocked her head to one side. "Are you here only to look up a distant family connection? Perhaps you are bored now that you've sold out of the army?"

"Not bored, though I am rather at loose ends," he admitted. "But as soon as Hawkins mentioned you, I wanted to see if you were the right Suzanne Duval, and if so, to learn how you are faring."

Mr. Potter returned, a tea tray in hand. The tray was dented pewter and there was a chip in the spout of the teapot, but her landlord presented the refreshments with the air of a duke's butler. There was also a dish of shortbread.

"Thank you, Mr. Potter!" Suzanne said warmly. "You and your wife have outdone yourselves."

"The pleasure is ours, my lady." He inclined his head and withdrew from the room.

"My lady?" Simon asked as she poured tea for them. "He knows that you're an aristocrat?"

"He was just being polite, though you might have changed that." She sipped her tea, then offered him the shortbread. "Have a piece. Mrs. Potter is a wonderful baker."

He followed her advice and murmured appreciatively after he bit into it. "She is, and she doesn't stint on the butter." He finished his tea in a long swallow and set the cup down with a clink. "I wonder if I might find old friends or relations in the émigré community. Have you found your compatriots welcoming, even though your relatives have returned to France?"

Her mouth twisted. "The grand émigrés in Soho will have nothing to do with a woman who was a whore in Turkey."

He winced. "Surely no one said such an appalling thing!"

"The aristocratic ladies did. Their husbands tried to corner me in empty rooms," she said tartly. "I decided I would be safer among my more humble countrymen here in St. Pancras."

He bit off a curse. "You deserve so much better than this, Suzanne!"

She sighed. "If there is one thing I have learned, it's that no one 'deserves' anything more than the right to struggle for survival. I'd rather be here altering gowns in a cold room than living in luxury in a Turkish harem and wondering which night might be my last, so I think I am doing well." She raised her teacup in a mock toast. "Will you drink to my survival, Simon?"

"I can do more than that," he said, his gaze intense. "Marry me, Suzanne."

Chapter 2

Suzanne set down her teacup so quickly that the tea sloshed out. "Good heavens, Simon! You look so sane, but clearly I misjudged."

He smiled, enjoying the musical lilt of her French accent, the grace of her petite, perfectly proportioned figure, the shine of her rich, tobacco brown hair. "I am as astonished by my proposal as you are. Yet it feels right."

"Why?" She tilted her head, her startling green eyes curious and amused. "Why ask, and why does it feel right?"

This was a question he needed to answer for himself as well as her. "I have spent years of my life working for the demise of Napoleon," he said slowly. "He and his regime cost me much of my family and the girl I loved. Now he is gone, for good, I hope. What does a soldier do when the wars are over?"

"What do any of us who survived do?" she asked softly.

It was the question that had haunted him for months, and gradually he was finding answers. "Cultivate the ways of peace. I'll open my long-neglected house. Put away my uniform. Plant a garden. Take a wife." He studied Suzanne's lovely face. In many ways she was a stranger but, on some deep level, familiar. "You have survived great losses and tumult in your life, so perhaps you want the same things?"

She set her teacup down and rose to drift across the room. Ending at the window, she gazed absently at the street outside. "You and I met a dozen years ago during the Peace of Amiens. The naive and optimistic girl that I was then thought the wars were over and we could look forward to bright futures. Then the world dissolved once more into violence and chaos. Perhaps your proposal stems from a desire to recapture those days of peace and optimism? But they are gone forever."

"That time has passed," he admitted, "but weren't we friends, even though we didn't know each other for long? I enjoyed your intelligence and warmth and envied my cousin his choice of bride. You seemed to enjoy my company as well. Isn't that worth building on?"

"That is a frail, distant connection," she said as she turned from the window to look at him. "We are strangers to each other now."

"Are we?" He caught her gaze. "Much has happened to us both, but do you feel as if you are a different person from that young bride? I may be battered and weary, but I feel that at heart, I'm the same man I was when we met."

"I suppose I am also the same deep down." Her expression tightened and he saw pain in her eyes. "But I don't know if I'll ever be suited to marriage again."

When she fell silent, he asked tentatively, "Are you willing to say why?"

At first he thought she'd refuse, but then she sighed. "Years in a harem where my survival depended on being a whore and pretending to enjoy it have damaged me, perhaps beyond repair. I'm not sure if I'll ever know desire again. The way I feel now, the answer is probably no."

He winced internally as he recognized how much pain lay under her flat, honest words. Yet he felt a surprising kinship with her. "My circumstances were nothing like yours, but I do understand the death of desire." For a brief, piercing moment he remembered the intoxicating mutual madness he'd known with his fiancée, Alette. "For me, desire is not much more than a memory, buried with all the other bright memories. Yet I can imagine a satisfactory marriage without physical intimacy. Can you?"

She looked startled, then thoughtful. "For myself, yes, I can imagine it. But you're a man in the prime of life, and in my experience, men are more physically passionate. What if desire returns for you and not for me? I should be a great inconvenience to you then."

It was an important question. He thought before replying, "You would still be my wife and my friend. I would do nothing to humiliate you. What if the reverse is true, and you recover desire and I don't?"

"Like you, I would be discreet and do nothing to bring shame on your name." She laughed suddenly, her face alive with amusement. "This is a very French conversation!"

He laughed with her. "So it is. Perhaps we would be very sophisticated and both quietly keep lovers on the side. But this is mere speculation. All we can know is this moment, how we feel now. And what I feel is that I would be profoundly grateful if you agreed to share my life."

"But why?" she asked a little helplessly.

If there was to be any chance she would accept his proposal, he must be honest and vulnerable. "I have felt lonely for many years, Suzanne," he said quietly. "When I walked into this room, my first emotion was great happiness to see that you are alive. And in the next moment, I realized I didn't feel lonely anymore."

Her gaze was searching. "I also feel less alone, but what if we don't suit?"

"We courteously go our separate ways within the marriage and treat each other with respect and kindness. That shouldn't be too difficult. It's great passion that creates anger. If we are both beyond passion, surely we can be friends."

"The idea sounds simple, but human beings are seldom simple," she said skeptically.

Just talking to Suzanne made him feel more alive even when they disagreed. "You're right, of course. But let us not overlook the shockingly practical side of my proposal," Simon said. "As my wife you could live quite comfortably. Not with the luxury of a countess, but you will not have to work long hours in order to eat."

"I can't deny that has appeal," Suzanne said. "But marriage is a great leap of faith at the best of the times, and I scarcely know you. The same difficult years that are something of a bond between us might also have produced deep scars that could prove hard to live with."

"Those are all good points, but we need not decide today. Let us spend some time together. Become reacquainted."

"That is *essential*! At the moment, sir, you are a pig in a poke."

He laughed outright. "I have been called many unflattering things, but never that." He gestured at the lightening sky outside. "The sun is attempting to shine. After calling here, I planned to visit my London house. I've been staying in a hotel since returning to the city, but it's time to move into my own home."

She glanced out the window at the brightening day. "I should finish my sewing commission while there is light."

After a moment's thought, he said, "If you join me for this small excursion, I will supply candles so you can work into the night."

"You are courting me with candles?" she asked with interest.

"If you find that appealing, they can be courtship candles. Or you can think of them as merely helpful."

She studied him thoughtfully, then nodded. "Candles will indeed be helpful, and I should like some fresh air. Let me get my cloak."

He watched her depart, and wondered if he was mad to offer marriage. But he felt no inclination to withdraw his offer.

Suzanne felt a little reckless as Simon handed her into his curricle, then swung up beside her and took the reins from his groom. Reaching under the seat, he pulled out a dark blue carriage robe. "You might find this useful. There's a hint of spring in the air, but warmth is still some distance off."

"But this is very pleasant after days of rain." She adjusted the robe around her. It was woven from some marvelously soft wool and she enjoyed the touch of luxury. Even more she enjoyed his consideration.

As Simon deftly turned the carriage in the narrow street and headed west, she studied his profile. Now that the initial shock of his resemblance to her late husband had passed, she was seeing the differences. Jean-Louis had had the air of a jaded sophisticate while Simon was contained and . . . enigmatic? She thought of still waters running deep. He surely had interesting tales to tell. As did she.

She enjoyed studying the streets and buildings and energetic inhabitants they passed. "It's pleasant to finally see something of London."

"You're not familiar with the city?"

She shook her head. "I'd never been here before I arrived from Constantinople."

"You were willing to risk your future in an unknown place?"

She shrugged. "It's easier to become a new woman here. By the time I sailed the length of the Mediterranean on an English ship, I was reasonably fluent in the language and I knew I could manage."

He nodded, understanding the desire to start a new life.

"You've seen more of Europe's great cities. Which is your favorite?" she asked. "Paris? So many people love Paris."

"But you are not one of them," he said in what wasn't a question. "All the great cities have their own souls, their beauties and blemishes. Paris, Rome, Vienna, Lisbon. I'm particularly fond of Lisbon, a lovely city of light and wide vistas. But my favorite is London because this is most my home."

"Did you live here when you were a child?"

"Yes, my mother's father gave her this Mayfair house when she married to make it easy for her to visit her family, so when we fled the Reign of Terror, the house was waiting to receive us. I've spent more time in England than in France."

The neighborhoods became grander until Simon drew up in front of a substantial town house in a square with a small green park in the center. Turning the curricle over to the young groom who'd ridden on the back of the vehicle, he helped Suzanne from the carriage and up the few steps to a dark green painted door. The door knocker was a polished brass lion that glinted confidently in the afternoon light.

Simon hesitated for a long moment, visibly steeling himself as he produced a heavy key from his pocket. "The old knocker was an eagle that looked too much like Napoleon's imperial eagle standard, which French troops carried into battle. I had it changed to a British lion."

"Symbols matter." After a long silence, she asked quietly, "Are you reluctant to return because the house holds too many bad memories?"

"Too many good ones. This is part of the golden past that is forever gone." Face set, he unlocked the door and ushered her into the small vestibule.

A gilt-framed mirror hung above a polished mahogany table opposite the door. Suzanne and Simon were reflected there and she felt a jolt of surprise, as if he were a stranger. When he'd first greeted her, for a stunned moment she'd thought he was her late husband. Then she remembered him as Simon, a charming young man she'd liked very much in the golden days before her marriage.

But the image in the mirror reflected the man he was now. Austerely handsome. Quietly masterful. A man at ease in any situation, as dangerous as he needed to be—and carrying a bone-deep weariness that was eating away at his soul.

She drew a shaky breath as she absorbed this fuller understanding of the man who wanted her for his wife. Oddly, in that mirror they seemed well matched: She looked attractive and had the cool elegance of the countess she'd once been, even though she wore an altered, secondhand gown.

But the strongest resemblance was that she shared his weariness. Was soul-deep fatigue a foundation strong enough to support a marriage, or reason for her to run in the opposite direction?

Her thoughts were interrupted when Simon opened a door on the right and revealed a drawing room. The draperies were drawn so the light was dim, but she could see the elegant lines of the furniture and appreciate the softness of the Turkish carpet beneath her feet.

As she entered, she brushed her fingertips across the gleaming surface of a satinwood table. "It's a handsome house. Has it been empty for years?"

"No, a French couple who served my father's family for many years live here." Simon moved to a window and drew the draperies back, allowing the pale winter sunshine into the room. "When war erupted after the Peace of Amiens, I helped the Merciers out of France. They needed a new home and the house needed caretakers. A fortnight ago I sent a message that I'd be returning soon, and asked that they take the Holland covers off the furniture and prepare the house for me to take up residence."

He crossed the room and pulled the bell rope by the fireplace.

A distant ringing sounded on the floor below in the servants' quarters. "I haven't been here in years. It's rather eerie to see how nothing has changed."

Well-proportioned tables, chairs, and sofas were clustered into conversational groupings, the upholstery only a little faded with time. Her gaze was drawn to the portrait that hung above the fireplace. A dark-haired woman with a warm smile sat in a chair in this very room, an older man standing behind her with his hand on her shoulder.

"Your parents," she said. "I met them briefly before my wedding, but I met so many of Jean-Louis's relatives then that I did no more than exchange a few words." There was a strong resemblance between Simon and his father, a resemblance shared by her husband. The Duval family blood ran strong.

Simon joined her, his gaze on the portrait. "This was painted at a happy time. My father was French to the bone, but he was philosophical and made the best of his exile to England. The world would be changing, he said, so he made sure I was equally fluent in French and English. The plan was that I would attend school here and university in Paris if the wars were over by then, but that wasn't possible."

"What school?" She searched her memory for the names of the most famous British schools and came up with only one. "Eton?"

"Harrow. Like Eton, it's close to London." He smiled a little. "As an old Harrovian, I am honor bound to say that my school was superior to Eton, but in truth they are much the same."

Her brow furrowed as new memories surfaced. "Do you have a brother? I remember you talking warmly about a Lucas."

"He was my cousin, but yes, as close as a brother. Our mothers were sisters. He was orphaned young and came to live with my family." He gestured to a smaller portrait that hung over a sofa. It showed two young boys, perhaps ten years old. One was clearly Simon, and the other a boy with fair coloring and mischief in his eyes. "We attended Harrow together and looked out for each other."

"Is he . . . gone?" she asked softly. "Another victim of the wars?"

"Yes," Simon said bleakly. "Lucas was in the Royal Navy. His ship was sunk with no known survivors, though I've never quite given up hope that he might be a prisoner of war somewhere in France."

She frowned. "Weren't all prisoners released after the emperor abdicated?"

"Yes. But hope is a difficult habit to give up."

Their conversation was interrupted by the arrival of a middle-aged couple who were clearly the French caretakers. The broad, capable-looking man bowed deeply. "Milord, how good to see you home and well!"

Madame Mercier, round and sharp-eyed, bobbed a curtsy. "All is in readiness, milord. Will you be moving in today?" Her curious gaze slid to Suzanne.

"Perhaps tomorrow," Simon replied. "I've brought my cousin, the Comtesse de Chambron, to see the house. I'd thought her dead, so it was a great pleasure to find her alive and recently arrived in London."

Suzanne smiled at the Merciers and said in French, "The house is lovely and you've kept it well."

Looking pleased, Madame Mercier replied in the same language, "Thank you, Madame la Comtesse." After a moment's hesitation, she added, "Would monsieur and madam like to have a light luncheon here? There isn't time to prepare a proper meal, but I can offer simple bistro fare, beef bourguignon and good French bread."

The thought made Suzanne's mouth water. She had too little money to eat well. "I should like that above all things! It's been years since I've had decent French cooking."

The couple gave approving smiles. Mercier suggested, "Would monsieur and madam like a glass of wine while the meal is prepared?"

Good French wine, Suzanne hoped, but she said, "I'd like to see the rest of the house, Simon, if that's not too impolite of me."

"I'd like to show it to you. I'll ring when we're done, Mercier. We'll eat in the breakfast room."

The Merciers inclined their heads and withdrew, probably to speculate on the meaning of Suzanne's presence at their master's

side. She wished them luck with their speculations since she herself
had no idea what the future held.

Simon offered his arm. "Shall we explore, milady?"

She took his arm with a smile. Even if she decided marriage
would be unwise, at the least she'd get a good French meal out of
this expedition.